The Betrayal of the Blood Lily

The Betrayal of the Blood Lily

Lauren Willig

DUTTON

DUTTON
Published by Penguin Group (USA) Inc.
375 Hudson Street, New York, New York 10014, U.S.A.
Penguin Group (Canada), 90 Eglinton Avenue East, Suite 700, Toronto, Ontario M4P 2Y3,
Canada (a division of Pearson Penguin Canada Inc.); Penguin Books Ltd, 80 Strand, London
WC2R 0RL, England; Penguin Ireland, 25 St Stephen's Green, Dublin 2, Ireland (a division of
Penguin Books Ltd); Penguin Group (Australia), 250 Camberwell Road, Camberwell, Victoria
3124, Australia (a division of Pearson Australia Group Pty Ltd); Penguin Books India Pvt Ltd,
11 Community Centre, Panchsheel Park, New Delhi—110 017, India; Penguin Group (NZ), 67
Apollo Drive, Rosedale, North Shore 0632, New Zealand (a division of Pearson New Zealand
Ltd); Penguin Books (South Africa) (Pty) Ltd, 24 Sturdee Avenue, Rosebank, Johannesburg
2196, South Africa

Penguin Books Ltd, Registered Offices: 80 Strand, London WC2R 0RL, England

Published by Dutton, a member of Penguin Group (USA) Inc.

First printing, January 2010
1   3   5   7   9   10   8   6   4   2

REGISTERED TRADEMARK — MARCA REGISTRADA

Library of Congress Cataloging-in-Publication Data

Willig, Lauren.
Betrayal of the blood lily / by Lauren Willig.
p.   cm.
ISBN 978-0-525-95150-6
1. Aristocracy (Social class)—England—Fiction. 2. British—India—
Fiction. 3. Hyderabad (India: State)—Fiction. I. Title.
PS3623.I575B47   2010
813'.6—dc22   2009036179

Printed in the United States of America
Set in Granjon
Designed by Alissa Amell

PUBLISHER'S NOTE

To Claudia Brittenham,
the best of all possible roommates
at the best of all possible Yales

Acknowledgments

Six years ago, two unsuspecting professors hired me as their teaching assistant for a class on the second British Empire. Little did they realize what they were starting. Huge thanks go to Professors Susan Pedersen and Robert Travers for introducing me to early-nineteenth-century India, providing the backbone for this book.

Oodles of thanks go to my editor, for hopping on board with taking the series to a whole new continent; to my agent, for making this book and all the others possible; and to all the folks at Dutton and NAL, for doing the magical things they do, especially with the covers. Have I mentioned recently that I love these covers?

As always, much love to my family, for putting up with incoherent babble about character, plot, and cobras; to Nancy, Abby, Claudia, Liz, Jenny, Weatherly, and Emily, for making time for dramas both fictional and personal; and to my Tweedos (you know who you are), for cocktails and an ever more absurd collection of running jokes (no one expects Gold Ascot Man!), many of which will one day undoubtedly make their way between the pages of these books. A good running joke is a terrible thing to waste.

Thanks also go to my summerhouse girls (and guy), Abby, Lara, Sarah, Stephanie, and Matt, for providing me with a writer's retreat during the week and plenty of new material on the weekends. The first hundred pages of this book belong to you.

The biggest *thank-you* of all goes out to my readers. Without you, this book wouldn't even have a title (or at least not the title it does). Thanks go to everyone who suggested flowers and titles during the duration of Pink VI Flower Idol, with special thanks due to Brie Porter and Jennifer Klouse for coming up with the Blood Lily, a flower that suits Penelope to a tee, and to Pamela for the euphonious noun "betrayal." This title was an ensemble effort and all the better for it.

Thank you for making the time to chime in on my Web site, pop by a reading, or drop me an e-mail. Most of all, thank you for bringing my characters to life by believing in them. Keep all that good energy coming!

The Betrayal of the Blood Lily

Prologue

The food of love isn't music. It's grilled cheese and tomato sandwiches.

As the waiter set the plate down in front of me, I could see that the tomato had sunk down into the cheese, creating an edible sculpture in the shape of a heart. It seemed appropriate for the occasion.

Outside, it was the sort of crispy, clear winter day that you get occasionally even in England, beautiful and sunny, without a hint of a cloud. It was the season of white lace doilies and heart-shaped boxes of chocolates and teddy bears that squawked mawkish sentiments when you pressed their distended tummies. In other words, it was almost Valentine's Day, and I had decided to do a little matchmaking of my own. Why should Cupid have all the fun? My boyfriend's sister was desperately in need of a romantic intervention.

Boyfriend. It still boggled my mind that I had one. I was very aware of Colin's arm draped casually over the back of my chair, as though it had always belonged there. It gave me a weird little thrill to realize that we were the established couple here, beaming benevolently upon the singles.

It was hard to remember that a mere three months ago both my personal and professional life had been scraping rock bottom. Like many a historian before me, I had come to England on academic pilgrimage, worshipping at that altar of scholarship, the British Library, with its multitudinous manuscript collections, in the hopes that the great god of the archives would prove merciful and shower footnotes down upon me. Surely, I had thought with all the boundless optimism of the fourth-year graduate student, the mere fact that scholars had been through those documents time and again didn't necessarily mean that I wouldn't find anything new. Those scholars hadn't been *me*.

Which, in retrospect, probably meant that they were better qualified, but that only occurred to me once it was already too late to turn back.

I should have known something was wrong when my advisor's parting words were *Good luck*. To his credit, he had—very gently—suggested that I might want to consider a different sort of topic. But I didn't want to consider another topic. I was madly in love with my topic: "Aristocratic Espionage during the Wars with France, 1789–1815." It had dash, it had swash, it had buckle.

It also had no primary sources. My life would have been much easier had I followed my advisor's suggestion and looked more closely into the careers of those men who spied for England under government auspices, and thus might reasonably be expected to show up in government dispatches and payrolls. That was far too easy. What I intended to unravel were the networks of independent adventurers, those daring souls who had struck out on their own for King and country, using their family connections and the benefit of independent income to create elaborate bouquets of flower-named spies: the League of the Scarlet Pimpernel, the League of the Purple Gentian, and finally, the most intriguing of the them all, the League of the Pink Carnation.

You can see where this is going, can't you? I had arrived in London in September. By November, my fingernails were all gone, chewed to the quick. I had no footnotes; I had no dissertation. I was stranded in a country where the sun sets at four and I was never ever going to get an academic job, much less a tenure-track one.

They always say execution clarifies the mind wonderfully. So does the prospect of law school. I made one last desperate attempt. I sent out letters to all the known descendants of the Purple Gentian and the Scarlet Pimpernel, politely asking if I might please, pretty, pretty please, have access to any family papers they didn't mind showing to a humble little Harvard student.

Have I mentioned that Colin is a direct descendant of Lord Richard Selwick, also known as the Purple Gentian?

Three months later, I was still reeling over my good fortune. I had enough footnotes to make my advisor's eyes go pop; I had been given access to archival material the likes of which I had never dared to dream existed; and I was dating someone who could make my heart do a little tap dance simply by showing up in the room. I was so happy, it was scary.

Oh, I still suffered from the usual slings and arrows to which flesh is heir, like the Tube breaking down on me every other morning and the British Library cafeteria serving potato soup three days in a row. There were also the looming clouds of larger worries, like the fact that, although Colin claimed to be writing a spy novel, I still wasn't convinced that his so-called research on the subject was entirely fictional in nature.

Colin's great-great-great-grandparents had founded a school for spies; from what little he had let slip, his father had carried on in the family tradition, under the auspices of the army. Not to mention that Colin had been more than usually resistant to my poking around in his family's past. Nothing more than that fabled British reticence? Perhaps. But I couldn't quite exorcise the nagging feeling that there might be something more to it. The spy novel story was just a little too pat. If you were a spy looking for a cover story, wouldn't the best cover be just that, a story? On the other hand, maybe I was just out-clevering myself, building up complications where there were none. Not like I'd ever done that to myself before.

When Colin hit the *Times* bestseller list, I'd be the first in line applauding.

Even leaving aside all the cloak-and-dagger stuff, there were practical problems on the horizon. Colin's life was based three quarters in Sussex and one quarter in London, while I was due to return to Cambridge—the American one—in May.

But it was only February now. May felt a very long time away. I could deal with May when I got there. And in the meantime, I had extended visits with Colin both in London and Sussex, a grilled cheese and tomato sandwich on my plate, and a full cup of coffee in front of me, with free refills to come. Life was good. Life was very, very good.

It only seemed fair to pass some of the happiness along.

I beamed across the table at Colin's sister, Serena, who was doing a very good job of toying with her salad without actually eating any of it. Next to her, Colin's friend Martin was devouring his pasta Bolognese as though personally determined to eat enough for both of them.

That wasn't exactly how I had planned for lunch to go when I decided to take Serena up as my personal project.

It wasn't that Serena was frumpy or dowdy or any of the usual devices of those teen movies where the more popular girl takes on the plainer one and makes her into prom queen. When it came to sartorial sense, Serena was several steps ahead of me. She had that fragile thinness so beloved of fashion magazines and whoever those cruel people are who create designer jeans: long, elegant bones with only the bare rudiments of skin over them. Her hair was long and soft and shiny and naturally straight and her face had the sorts of interesting hollows one gets from weighing about twenty percent below one's recommended body weight. She was the sort of girl whose hair never frizzes and whose skirt never gets rumpled.

She was also painfully shy, borderline anorexic, potentially bulimic, and a disaster when it came to dealing with men.

Not to put too fine a point on it, Serena was an emotional train wreck. She might be an aesthetically pleasing and sweet-natured train wreck, but those are the most dangerous kind. Their looks attract all sorts of bottom-feeding predators, while their innate gentleness of spirit makes it impossible for them to stand up for themselves (see *bottom-feeding predators*, above). Her last boyfriend, whom I had had the misfortune to meet, had been a classic example of the type. He had used her and dumped her, but not before taking the opportunity to deliver a few more completely gratuitous blows to Serena's already tottering self-esteem.

Serena needed a massive ego boost. And I, in my infinite matchmaking wisdom, had decided that boost was Martin.

If you're wondering why I was taking such a touching concern in my very recent boyfriend's sister, I'd like to claim it's because I'm such a nice person. And I usually do like to think of myself as at least a reasonably nice person—I don't kick puppies or cut the tails off kittens, and when I remember to, I generally slip some spare change into the Salvation Army collection box. But in this case, my interest was less altruism than self-defense. There's nothing like competing for your boyfriend's attention with an emotionally needy sibling to make you feel like the worst sort of evil psycho-bitch.

I know, I know. We're supposed to be glad when the men we're dating show a proper sense of concern for their fellow family members. It shows a heartwarming sense of responsibility and says good things about their potential husbanding skills. In the short term, however, it's a pain in the ass. It was not that I wished Serena ill. Quite the contrary. I wanted her to be as happy as I was, so that when Colin and I went to parties, I wouldn't have to worry whether she was going to have a meltdown in the middle of it.

Easier said than done.

I looked across the table, where Serena and Martin were doing a pretty good impression of two strangers at a Tube station, shoulders a safe twelve inches apart, profiles carefully averted. God forbid any spontaneous eye contact might occur. From there it was just a slippery slope to conversation. And heaven only knew what *that* might lead to. Nothing less than the fall of the British Empire, I was sure. Oh, wait, that had already happened.

It had seemed like such a good idea at the time. Colin's friend Martin was another of your common garden-variety emotional disaster areas. Just this past November, he had been dumped by the girlfriend he had met during his first week at University lo these many years ago. Martin was a broken man. From what Colin had said, I gathered that he was brilliant at accountancy, but after seven years of cohabitation, things like picking his own socks sent him into a full-blown panic attack.

Serena would choose lovely socks for him. After all, she worked in a gallery. After dealing with Degas and Renoir, the question of argyle or solid would be like a walk in the park. And it might, I had thought, be rather pleasant for each to have someone else to look after for a change. Serena could fuss over Martin and Colin wouldn't have to keep fussing over her. It would be perfect.

Ha. It could have been perfect. I had forgotten that I was setting up two finalists in Britain's Most Reserved Person contest. I bet they didn't even talk to themselves in the mirror at home, much less to other people. At the moment, each was doing a fairly good job of pretending the other didn't exist. My brilliant idea was tanking faster than the Hindenburg.

I didn't even need to look over at Colin to read the I-told-you-so there. When I had broached the plan, his reply had been, manlike, "If anything were to happen between them, wouldn't it just happen?"

Sometimes, guys just have no clue at all.

It was rather sweet, really. Adorably naïve, even. Our relationship had "just happened" in much the same way as the Treaty of Versailles had just happened, after months of plotting, scheming, maneuvering, and significant reversals.

Like I said, rather sweet really.

"So, Martin," I asked, in the overly loud voice you use when asking friends' children about school, "how is work going?"

"Not bad," he said. It might have been the most positive statement I had ever heard him make.

"What is it exactly that you do?" I urged, leaning slightly forward in my chair and trying to feign an expression of interest in the hopes that it would inspire Serena to do the same. It inspired Serena to undertake a careful inspection of her arugula. "I'm not sure Colin's ever told me."

He told me. As my eyes glazed over, I wondered if that had really been quite the right technique. Asking an accountant to explain—in depth—what he does for a living isn't the sort of move calculated to cause the impressionable to swoon. Not the right kind of swoon, at any rate. The arugula was far more interesting.

But perhaps Serena didn't think so. As I snuck a peek at her averted face, her eyes suddenly lit up like the Fourth of July. A becoming hint of color bloomed in her cheeks and the hollows under her eyes didn't seem quite so pronounced as usual.

I'd never seen anyone react that way to accounting principles before, but, hey, if it worked for Serena . . .

It wasn't the accounting. Half-rising from her chair, Serena angled her wrist in a tentative wave. Martin petered to a belated stop. Scraping my chair around, I saw Colin's friend Nick loping his way towards us.

"Hello, all," said Nick, dragging up a chair from another table and plunking himself unceremoniously down into it. "How goes it?"

Our table was quite definitely meant for four—a cozy four—but that didn't bother Nick. He cheerfully tilted backwards in his purloined chair, blocking the aisle.

An outraged waiter made a noise that wanted to be a growl when it grew up. Hearing it, Nick glanced up and raised a casual hand. "I'll have a coffee. And can you toss me a menu? Cheers."

Frigidly, the waiter handed over a menu with only a little less ceremony than Lord Lytton presiding at the official durbar proclaiming Queen Victoria Empress of India.

Letting his chair rock forward with a clunk, Nick flicked open the menu, leaving the waiter with no choice but to retreat, speechless, to the nether regions of the kitchen to procure the desired caffeinated beverage. I presume he spat in it a few times in the privacy of the kitchen.

I felt like spitting myself. Serena wasn't supposed to be twinkling for Nick; she was supposed to be twinkling for Martin.

Aside from the fact that she and Martin were Just Perfect for Each Other (if only they would wake up and realize it), I was pretty sure our mutual friend Pammy had designs on Nick. That was all I needed, for Serena to get herself mashed flat in Pammy's wake. And we all knew what that meant: Colin having to swoop in to pick up the pieces again, while I gritted my teeth and did my best to be patient and understanding. Even though she might be technically the prettier of the two, Serena didn't stand a chance against Pammy. No one did. Pammy was the romantic equivalent of an artillery barrage. There was nothing to do but dive for cover as soon as you saw it—I mean, her—coming. Resistance was futile.

Pammy had tried to impress the wisdom of this approach upon me, but I had proved a poor student in that. I was more of the princess-in-tower school of dating, where you drop your hair out the tower window and desperately hope your chosen prince will take the hint and choose to climb up. If he doesn't, you hastily coil your hair back up, retreat into the tower, and pretend you never meant it in the first place. Hair, what hair? Never seen that hair in my life.

I leaned more comfortably into the crook of Colin's arm, marveling at the wonder of having an arm to lean into. Under those circumstances, it was hard to get too worked up about Nick's gate-crashing.

Letting the menu drop to the table, Nick grinned at me. "Eloise, right?"

We'd only met two times before. They do say third time is the charm. Maybe it takes three times for boys to assume that you're there to stay and it's worth their while to remember your name. Not exactly a pleasant thought. I bitterly disliked the thought of any other girl sitting there beneath Colin's arm.

"That it is," I said cheerfully. "Nigel?"

"Nick," he corrected, without rancor. Okay, fine, so it had been petty of me. He was so good-natured, it was hard to be annoyed, even if Serena's chair was now angled a good forty-five degrees away from Martin, towards Nick. Martin had a resigned expression on his face, as though he was used to this happening. Since they had all gone to University together, he probably was.

"And what do you do, again?" Nick asked, keeping the charm on high.

"I'm a grad student. I'm working on my dissertation."

"About spies during the Napoleonic Wars," Colin contributed for me, squeezing my shoulder affectionately.

Awwwww.

Martin looked away. It must be hard for him, I thought, when he had been used to being the one in the couple, now suddenly being on his own, forced to watch other people being all couple-y. I knew how that felt.

"Napoleonic spies? That sounds right up your alley," said Nick to Colin. Turning back to me, he added, "Did you know that Colin's family—"

"Ah, your coffee," said Colin rather gratuitously. It was hard to avoid noticing Nick's coffee, as the waiter set it down in front of him with an audible clunk that sent coffee swimming over the rim and into the saucer. "Nick works at the BBC," he informed me, as the waiter retreated in a glow of petty triumph.

"Can you make them put *Monarch of the Glen* back on?" I suggested, pouring more cream into my own coffee. "I'm sick of *Emmerdale.*"

"That's ITV," said Nick unapologetically, "not us. So I'm afraid you're stuck with it." He threw a wink at Serena, who actually produced a small giggle.

Hmmm.

"We should have a show about your spies," suggested Nick, raising his coffee cup. "What have they been up to?"

"Oh, all sorts of skullduggery," I replied, in the same bantering tone. "Kidnapping King George, blowing up theatres, plotting mayhem in India . . . You're right. It would make a brilliant series. Much more fun than a dissertation."

"India?" asked Colin curiously, leaning sideways to look at me.

"Oh." What with one thing and another, I hadn't quite gotten around to mentioning that to him yet. There had been other things to do last night. Flushing, I admitted, "It's sort of a tangent. You see," I explained to the others, "my dissertation mostly focuses on the behavior of spy networks in England and France during the Napoleonic Wars. But, recently, I came across a reference to a French spy network deployed in India during the period. It might make an interesting chapter. History departments are big on the non-Western these days."

At least, that's what I had been telling myself. You can always find an excuse for doing what you feel like doing if you try hard enough. And it was true that having a non-Western angle played well in the academic job market. Mostly, though, my curiosity had been piqued.

"What were the Frogs doing in India?" asked Nick idly, rocking his chair back and forth.

"They'd always been there," I said, with a confidence that came of having spent the last week reading up on the topic. "Well, since the 1660s, at any rate. They had trading posts there, just as the British did. When

Bonaparte rose to power, in the 1790s, they still had strongholds in Mauritius and Pondicherry and a lot of the local rulers had French officers in charge of their armed forces. It's kind of neat, actually," I added, twisting my head to look back at Colin. "In Hyderabad, the Nizam—that's the ruler—employed both an English force and a French force, with their own separate camps on different sides of the river. I guess he thought the competition would keep them on their toes."

"Did it?"

I shrugged. "It kept a lot of spies in business. The French had people in the English camp and the English had people in the French camp and the Nizam had people in both camps."

"It sounds like fashion designers," suggested Serena tentatively.

"Or celebrity chefs," contributed Nick, grinning at her, "guarding their top-secret recipes."

"The English Resident—that's a sort of ambassador—persuaded the Nizam to get rid of the French camp eventually, but it was all very touch and go. In fact, Lord Wellesley made it a condition of a bunch of peace treaties with local rulers in 1803 that anyone who had hired French officers had to ship them back to France."

"Wellesley as in Wellington?" asked Colin.

"Right family, wrong brother. This Wellesley was the older brother. He was the Governor General of India right around the turn of the nineteenth century. Little Wellesley—the one who became Wellington—got his start soldiering under him in India."

I considered trying to explain about the Mahratta Wars, but thought better of it. People's eyes were beginning to glaze over the same way mine had when Martin was talking about accounting. I would bore Colin with it later.

"I'm sorry," I said, grimacing apologetically around the table. "I've been doing background reading on this all week, so I'm a little obsessed right now. I've sort of hit a dead end, though."

Having exhausted the Institute of Historical Research's collection of monographs on late-eighteenth-century India, I wasn't quite sure where to go for the primary sources. It was my time period, but quite definitely not my field.

"I wonder what happened to all the old East India Company documents," mused Colin, his fingers tapping against the back of my chair. "They had to go somewhere after they tore the East India House down."

"I don't know. I've never done any work with Indian documents." There was a very nice new professor in the history department back at Harvard whose specialty was eighteenth-century India, but I had only met him very briefly at a department cocktail party the previous spring, hardly enough of an acquaintance to feel comfortable e-mailing and nagging him for advice. I was sure he would have no idea who I was. After the first thirty or so introductions, one grad student begins to look much like another.

"You could ask Aunt Arabella," suggested Serena. "She spent a good deal of time in that part of the world."

"Really?" I remembered Mrs. Selwick-Alderly's flat, with its chintz and white moldings and unexpectedly exotic accoutrements, relics of the last gasp of Empire. There had been a tufted Zulu spear and many-legged Indian gods sitting side by side with the usual Dresden shepherdesses and Minton candy dishes.

Because it had been Mrs. Selwick-Alderly who had introduced me to Colin—so to speak—I had warm and fuzzy feelings for her, even if we weren't quite on "Aunt Arabella" terms yet.

"Her husband was stationed out there during World War Two," said Colin. "And they stayed on until the transfer of power in 1947. If nothing else, she should at least have some idea of where you can start to look."

"Thanks," I said. "I'll do that."

Feeling like I had hogged the conversation long enough, I quickly turned to Serena and asked her a question about the party her gallery was throwing for Valentine's Day. Nick and Martin both pledged their attendance. I knew Serena had invited Pammy, too. This was going to get very interesting very quickly. I wondered, distractedly, whether Pammy might be rerouted to Martin. But he wasn't really her type. It wasn't that he wasn't good-looking; he was pleasant enough with his close-cropped, curly dark hair and broad-shouldered build.

But Pammy tended to go more for Masters of the Universe types, not Eeyore. As she was fond of saying, she didn't take on reclamation projects.

I decided to table the whole question for later. It was still a good week till Valentine's Day. I had time to sound out Pammy and lay my plans. In the meantime, I was just happy. Happy to be out on a sunny Sunday, happy to be with Colin, happy, happy, happy. It helped that I had had about seven cups of coffee at lunch. I was flying high on caffeine and contentment.

I hugged Colin's arm close to my side as we strolled away from the restaurant. "That was fun."

It was frigid cold out, but without having to arrange it between us, we set out to walk back to my flat. That was another thing we had in common, I thought happily; we both liked walking places. It would have been a shame to waste all that lovely sunshine by going down into the dark depths of the Tube. With Colin going back to Sussex tomorrow morning, I didn't want to waste a single, golden moment.

"I hadn't realized you were researching India," he said, as we walked down a street lined with stucco town houses.

"I wasn't," I admitted. "But the last time I was up at Selwick Hall with you, I found a couple of letters from Penelope Deveraux."

"From who?"

I wasn't surprised by the blank look. Colin had mentioned that as a young man he had read through some of the family papers related to the Pink Carnation, but there was no reason for him to remember Penelope. She had been only peripherally involved in the Pink Carnation's activities. "She was a friend of the Purple Gentian's younger sister."

"And that makes her—?" prompted Colin.

"Absolutely nothing," I replied, quoting *Spaceballs*. "Actually, what it makes her is Henrietta's correspondent. She got herself into a bit of trouble and was married off in a hurry and sent to India until the scandal could die down at home. When I was rooting around in your archives, I found a couple of letters from her to Henrietta."

There had been two letters, both from the autumn of 1804, one marked Calcutta, the second, written a month later, from Hyderabad. It was the second letter that had mentioned a spy called the Marigold.

I had come across a previous reference to the Marigold in a different set of papers, connected to the same group who had tried to kidnap King George and replace him with an imposter under the guise of a recurrence of his old madness. The connection had piqued my interest. Plus, I kind of wanted to know what happened to Penelope. It is amazing how attached one can get to the historical subjects in the course of research. It becomes a bit like gossiping about old friends. You want to know how things turned out for them.

Boy that he was, Colin wasn't interested in the personal bits, like just how Penelope had gotten herself into trouble and with whom. He cut straight to the chase. "Where do the spies come in?"

"Well," I said, taking a deep breath. "Here's what I have so far. . . ."

Chapter One

There were times when Lady Frederick Staines, nee Miss Penelope Deveraux, deeply regretted her lack of a portable rack and thumbscrews.

Now was one of them. Rain drummed against the roof of the carriage like a set of impatient fingers. Penelope knew just how it felt.

"You spoke to Lord Wellesley, didn't you?" she asked her husband, as though her husband's interview with the Governor General of India were one of complete indifference to her and nothing at all to do with the way she was expected to spend the next year of her life.

Freddy shrugged.

Penelope was learning to hate that shrug. It was a shrug amply indicative of her place in the world, somewhere just about on a level with a sofa cushion, convenient to lean against but unworthy of conversational effort.

That hadn't been the case eight months ago.

Eight months ago they hadn't been married. Eight months ago Freddy had still been trying to get her out of the ballroom into an alcove, a balcony, a bedroom, whichever enclosed space could best suit the purpose of seduction. It was a fitting enough commentary on the rake's progress, from silver-tongued seducer to indifferent spouse in the space of less than a year.

Not that Freddy had ever been all that silver-tongued. Nor, to be fair, had he done all the seducing.

How was she to have known that a bit of canoodling would land them both in India?

Outside, rain pounded against the roof of the carriage, not the gentle *tippety tap* of an English drizzle, but the full-out deluge of an Oriental monsoon. They had sailed up the Hooghly into Calcutta that morning after five endless months on a creaking, pitching vessel, replacing water beneath them with water all around them, rain crashing against the esplanade, grinding the carefully planted English flowers that lined the sides into the muck, all but obscuring the conveyance that had been sent for them by the Governor General himself, with its attendant clutter of soaked and chattering servants, proffering umbrellas, squabbling over luggage, pulling and propelling them into a very large, very heavy carriage.

If she had thought about it at all, Penelope would have expected Calcutta to be sunny.

But then, she hadn't given it much thought, not any of it. It had all happened too quickly for thought, ruined in January, married in February, on a boat to the tropics by March. The future had seemed unimportant compared to the exigencies of the present. Penelope had been too busy brazening it out to wonder about little things like where they were to go and how they were to live. India was away and that was enough. Away from her mother's shrill reproaches (*If you had to get yourself compromised, couldn't you at least have picked an older son?*); Charlotte's wide-eyed concern; Henrietta's clumsy attempts to get her to *talk about it*, as though talking would make the least bit of difference to the reality of it all. Ruined was ruined was ruined, so what was the point of compounding it by discussing it?

There was even, if she was being honest, a certain grim pleasure to it, to having put paid to her mother's matrimonial scheming and poked a finger in the eye of every carping old matron who had ever called her fast. Ha! Let them see how fast she could be. All things considered, she had got out of it rather lightly. Freddy might be selfish, but he was seldom cruel. He didn't have crossed eyes or a hunchback (unlike that earl her mother had been throwing at her). He wasn't violent in his cups, he might be a dreadful card player but he had more than enough blunt to cover his losses, and he possessed a reasonable proficiency in those amorous activities that had propelled them into matrimony.

Freddy was, however, still sulky about having been roped into wedlock. It wasn't the being married he seemed to mind—as he had said, with a shrug, when he tossed her a betrothal ring, one had to get married sooner or later and it might as well be to a stunner—as the loss of face among his cronies at being forced into it. He tended to forget his displeasure in the bedroom, but it surfaced in a dozen other minor ways.

Including deliberately failing to tell her anything at all about his interview with Lord Wellesley.

"Well?" demanded Penelope. "Where are we to go?"

Freddy engaged in a lengthy readjustment of his neck cloth. Even with his high shirt points beginning to droop in the heat and his face flushed with the Governor General's best Madeira, he was still a strapping specimen of aristocratic pulchritude, the product of generations of breeding, polishing, and grooming from the burnished dark blond of his hair to the perfectly honed contours of his face. Penelope could picture him pinned up in a naturalist's cupboard, a perfect example of *Homo aristocraticus*.

"Hyderabad," he said at last.

"Hyderawhere?" It sounded like a sneeze.

"Hyderabad," repeated Freddy, in that upper-class drawl that turned boredom into a form of art. "It's in the Deccan."

That might have helped had she had the slightest notion of where—or what—the Deccan was.

In retrospect, it might have been wiser to have spent some time aboard ship learning about the country that was to be her home for the next year, rather than poking about in the rigging and flirting with the decidedly middle-aged Mr. Buntington in the hope of readjusting Freddy's attention from the card table. The upshot of it all was that she had learned more than she ever wanted to know about the indigo trade and Freddy had lost five hundred pounds by the time they reached the Cape of Good Hope.

"And what are we to do there?" she asked, in tones of exaggerated patience.

"I," said Freddy, idly stretching his shoulders within the confines of the tight cut of his coat, "am to be Special Envoy to the Court of Hyderabad."

And what of me? Penelope wanted to ask. But she already knew the answer to that. She was to be toted along like so much unwanted baggage, expected to bow to his every whim in atonement for an act that was as much his doing as hers. An ungrateful baggage, her mother had called her, tossing up to her all the benefits that had been showered upon her, the lessons, the dresses, the multitude of golden guineas that had been expended upon her launch into Society.

It didn't matter that Penelope would have preferred to have run tame in Norfolk, riding the wildest of her father's horses and terrifying the local foxes. She was, she had been told, to be grateful for the lessons, the dresses, the Season, just as she was to be grateful that Freddy had condescended to marry her, even if she knew that his acquiescence had been bought and bullied out of him by the considerable wealth and influence of the Dowager Duchess of Dovedale.

The thought of the Dowager brought a pinched feeling to Penelope's chest, as though her corset strings were tied too tight. Penelope elbowed it aside. There was no point in being homesick for the Dowager or Lady Uppington or Henrietta or Charlotte. They would all have forgotten about her within the month. Oh, they would write, letters that would be six months out of date by the time they arrived, but they had their own families, their own concerns, of which Penelope was, at best, on the very periphery.

That left only Freddy.

"What, no residency of your own?" goaded Penelope. "Only a little envoy-ship?"

That got his attention. Freddy's ego, Penelope had learned after their abrupt engagement, was a remarkably tender thing, sublimely susceptible to poking.

Freddy looked down his nose at her. It might not be quite a Norman nose, but Penelope was sure it was at least Plantagenet. "Welles-ley had a special assignment for me, one only I could accomplish."

"Bon vivant?" suggested Penelope sweetly. "Or official loser at cards?"

Freddy scrubbed a hand through his guinea gold hair. "I had a run of bad luck," he said irritably. "It happens to everyone."

"Mmm-hmm," purred Penelope. "To some more frequently than others."

"Wellesley needs me in Hyderabad," Freddy said stiffly. "I'm to be his eyes and ears."

Penelope made a show of playing with the edge of her fan. "Hasn't he a set of his own?"

"Intelligence," Freddy corrected. "I'm to gather intelligence for him."

Penelope broke into laughter at the absurdity of Freddy playing spy in a native palace. He would stand out like a Norman knight in Saladin's court. "A fine pair of ears you'll make when you can't even speak the language. Unless the inhabitants choose to express them-selves in mime."

"The inhabitants?" Freddy wrinkled his brow. "Oh, you mean the *natives*. Wouldn't bother with them. It's James Kirkpatrick the Gov-ernor General wants me to keep an eye on. The Resident. Wellesley thinks he's gone soft. Too much time in India, you know."

"I should think that would be an asset in governing the place."

Freddy regarded her with all the superiority of his nine months' stint in a cavalry unit in Seringapatam. From what she had heard, he had spent far more time in the officer's mess than the countryside. "Hardly. They go batty with the heat and start reading Persian po-etry and wearing native dress. Wellesley says there's even a chance that Kirkpatrick's turned Mohammedan. It's a disgrace."

"I think I should enjoy native dress," said Penelope, lounging side-ways against the carriage seat, like a perpendicular Mme. Recamier. The thin muslin of her dress shifted with her as she moved, molded to her limbs by the damp. "It should allow one more . . . freedom."

"Well, I'll be damned before I go about in a dress," declared Freddy, but he was looking at her, genuinely looking at her for the first time since he had rolled out of bed that morning.

Letting her eyelids drop provocatively, Penelope delicately ran her tongue around her lips, reveling in the way his gaze sharpened on her.

"You'll probably be damned anyway," murmured Penelope, allowing the motion of the carriage to carry her towards him, "so why fuss about the wardrobe?"

With an inarticulate murmur, Freddy caught her hard around the waist. Penelope twined her arms around his neck, pressing closer, despite the wide silver buttons that bored through the muslin of her dress, branding his crest into the flesh above her ribs.

At least they had this, if nothing else. She knew his smell, his taste, the curve of his cheek against the palm of her hand as one knew the gaits of a favorite horse, with a comfort grown of eight months' constant use. Penelope wiggled closer, running her hands against the by-now-familiar muscles of arm and shoulder, giving herself up to the fleeting counterfeit of intimacy offered by his hand pressed against her back, his lips moving along the curve of her neck.

Until the carriage rocked to a stop and Freddy set her aside with no more concern than if she had been a carriage rug provided for his convenience on the journey. Lust might work to get his attention, but it was remarkably ineffectual at keeping it.

Penelope quickly straightened her bodice as the inevitable crowd of servants descended upon the carriage, yanking open the door, carrying over a portable flight of steps, running forward with blazing torches that too clearly illuminated Penelope's disarray.

By the time Penelope reached up to fix her hair, Freddy had already swung out of the carriage. He had been trained to do the gentlemanly thing, so he held out a hand in her general direction, but he was already angled towards the portico, the party, the inevitable card room.

"Pen . . . ," he said impatiently, waggling his hand.

Penelope paused as she was, arms curved above her head, pressing her breasts into prominence. She leaned forward just that extra inch.

"If you *will* muss my hair . . . ," she said provocatively.

Freddy was no longer in the mood to play. "If you will behave like a wanton," he countered, hauling her down from the carriage.

Penelope narrowed her amber eyes. "I'm not a wanton. I'm your wife. *Darling.*"

Freddy might be lazy, but he had a marksman's eye. "And who's responsible for that? Ah, Cleave!" Donning charm like a second skin, he waved to an acquaintance and carried on without pausing to introduce Penelope.

"Whose party is this?" hissed Penelope as she trotted along beside him.

"Begum Johnson—Lord Liverpool's grandmother," Freddy tossed in, as though that explained it all. "She's a Calcutta institution, been here longer than anyone. It's the first place one comes on arrival."

"Begum?"

"I think it means 'lady' in the local lingo," Freddy said vaguely. "Some sort of form of honorific. It's what they call her, is all."

With that elucidating explanation, Penelope found herself swept along in his wake into a vast white-walled mansion decorated with English furniture and English guests as Freddy scattered greetings here and there to acquaintances. The rooms were a colorful blur of brass-buttoned uniforms from every conceivable regiment, embroidered waistcoats straining across the bellies of prosperous merchant traders, large jewels decking the hands and headdresses of the middle-aged ladies in their rich silks. In one room, a set of couples formed rows while a sallow young lady in sweat-damped muslin and a cavalry officer cinched into a woolen jacket danced down the aisle, the familiar tune and figures of the country dance contrasting oddly with the fan sweeping slowly overhead. It did more to displace than dispel the muggy air. Through one archway, Penelope could see bowls of cool beverages sweating beads of water down the sides and iced cakes on porcelain platters. Through another, a room had been set out for cards, in small clusters of four to a table.

Freddy's eyes lit up at the sight of that last. "You'll excuse me, won't you, old thing?" he said, without looking properly at her. "I have a few old scores to settle."

Without waiting for a response, without introducing her to their hostess or fetching her a beverage or even making sure she had a chair to sit in, he was off. Penelope found herself standing alone in a drawing room that smelled faintly of foreign spices as a tropical monsoon battered against the windows and the chatter of the other guests shrilled against her ears like so many brightly colored parrots. Penelope gathered her pride around her like a mantle, trying to look as though she had always meant to be standing there on her own, as though she weren't entirely without acquaintance or purpose in a strange drawing room in a strange city, abandoned by her husband in a lamentable breach of manners that he would no doubt justify to himself by the fact that he had never intended to shackle himself to her in the first place.

Unfortunately, the little scene had not gone unobserved. Penelope found herself facing the regard of a man in the bright red uniform of one of the native regiments, spangled with enough gold braid to suggest that he had attained a suitably impressive form of command. He was no longer in the first, or even the second, flush of youth. His hair must once have been as red as her own, but age had speckled it with white, making his face seem even ruddier in contrast. His face was seared by sunshine and laugh lines and liberally spattered with a lifetime of freckles. Beneath wrinkled lids, his pale blue eyes were kindly.

Too kindly. It made Penelope want to shake him.

He strolled forward in an unhurried fashion. Just as Penelope was prepared to stare him down with her best Dowager Duchess of Dovedale glare, he said, "That's always the way of it with these young men, isn't it?"

He gave a sympathetic wag of his head, his matter-of-fact tone making it sound as though abandonment by one's spouse was commonplace, and nothing to be bothered about at all.

"No sooner do they arrive at a party than they're straight off to the card tables. A blight on society, it is, and a lamentable offense to all the fairer sex."

Penelope's stiff posture relaxed. It wasn't that she cared what people thought—but it was very unpleasant to be left standing by oneself.

"I imagine you are a notable card player yourself, sir," she riposted.

"Not I," he averred, pressing one hand to the general vicinity of his heart, but there was a twinkle in his sun-bleached blue eyes that told Penelope he must have been quite a rogue in his youth. It took one to know one, after all. "I have my share of vices, to be sure, but the cards are not among them. At least, not when there's a lovely lady present." He swept into a bow that would have done credit to the court of St. James. "Colonel William Reid, at your service, fair lady."

"I am—," Penelope began, and stuck. She had been about to say Penelope Deveraux, only she wasn't anymore. She was Lady Frederick Staines now, her identity subsumed within her husband's. She wasn't quite sure who Lady Frederick was, only that it wasn't really her. "Pleased to make your acquaintance," she substituted.

Mistaking her hesitation, the Colonel leaned away, holding up both hands in a gesture of contrition. "But not without a proper introduction, I wager. I should beg your pardon for being so bold as to impose myself upon you. After years in a mess, one forgets how to go about."

"Nothing of the sort," Penelope hastened to correct him. "It's just that I'm recently married and I still forget which name I'm meant to call myself. My husband's name doesn't feel quite my own."

A sentiment with which Freddy would heartily agree.

"Married?" The Colonel rearranged his features in a comical look of dismay. "That's a pity. I meant to introduce you to my Alex."

"Your Alex?"

"My boy," the Colonel said proudly. Before Penelope could stop him, he raised his arm to hail a man who stood in conversation with an elderly lady in an exuberant silk turban, his back to them. "Alex! Alex, lad."

Hearing his father's exuberant hail, the man turned in a fluid movement that bespoke a swordsman's grace. "Boy" was the last word

Penelope would have used to refer to him; he was tall and lean, with the muscles of a man used to spending long hours in the saddle. Unlike his father, he wore civilian dress, but the indifferently tailored breeches and blue frock coat looked wrong on him, like a costume that didn't quite fit. His face was as tan as the Colonel's was ruddy. Had she not been told otherwise, Penelope would have taken him for an Indian, so dark were his hair and eyes. A thin scar showed white against the dark skin of his face, starting just to the left of one eyebrow and disappearing into his hair. He was a handsome man, but not in the way the Colonel must have been handsome once. Where one could picture the Colonel in a kilt and claymore, standing by a distant loch, his son looked as though he belonged in a white robe and Persian trousers with a falcon perched upon his wrist.

Tact had never been Penelope's strong suit. "Are you quite sure you're related?"

Far from being offended, the Colonel chuckled comfortably. "It takes many people that way on first meeting—sometimes after, too! My Maria, the boy's mother, was of Welsh extraction. He gets his coloring from her. It's been a mixed blessing for him out here," said the Colonel.

Penelope looked at him quizzically.

"Life is seldom kind to the half-caste," explained the Colonel, and some of the twinkle seemed to go out of him. "Or those perceived to be so. And especially not in India."

"I'm half Irish," Penelope volunteered, by way of solidarity.

She could picture her mother cringing as she said it. Respectably brunette herself, her mother had spent most of her life trying to pretend that she was as English as Wedgwood pottery. Penelope's hair had been a sore point with her mother, who saw her secret shame revealed every time her daughter's flaming head hove into view.

"A fine people, the Irish, and bonny fighters," said the Colonel politely. From his name and his diction, he was Scots, although his accent veered off in odd ways on vowels in a way that was no longer quite any one particular accent at all. "Ah," he said with pleasure, looking over her shoulder. "Here comes my Alex. He'll be far more entertaining for you than an old man like me."

"Nonsense," said Penelope, smiling up at the darling old colonel. "I couldn't have been better entertained."

His Alex appeared just as the Colonel was tapping a finger against Penelope's cheek. He looked from his father to her with a resigned expression that suggested that this was not the first time he had come upon his father chatting up an attractive young woman.

But all he said was, "Forgive me. I didn't like to rush away from the Begum." Unlike his father's, his accent was unimpeachably English.

The Colonel laughed his rolling laugh. "She's in her usual form, is she?"

"Invariably," he said fondly, with a glance over his shoulder to where the Begum held court in her chair. Recalling himself to his social duties, he looked quizzically at his father.

His father knew exactly what was required. With all the bombast of a born raconteur, he began, "Alex, this charming young lady has been kind enough to sacrifice her own amusement to enliven an old man's dull existence—"

"Scarcely old," interjected Penelope, "and never dull."

The Colonel beamed approval at her, clearly delighted to have found someone who played the game as he did. "See what I mean, Alex? An angel of goodness, she is. Now, my dear, you must allow me to introduce to you my son, Captain Alex Reid."

"Captain Reid." Penelope nodded to him, her eyes alight with laughter.

Captain Reid smiled ruefully in response, complicit in the joke on his father.

The Colonel waved a hand at Penelope. "And this is—"

"Lady Frederick Staines," supplied Penelope.

The unaccustomed name felt clumsy on her tongue, but certainly not clumsy enough to warrant the reaction it garnered from the two Reids. Any glimmer of warmth disappeared from the Captain's eyes, while the Colonel looked perturbed, as though he knew there were some bad odor about the name, but he couldn't remember quite what.

There was only one conclusion to be drawn. The news had spread.

She ought to have expected it would. Just because Calcutta was half a world away didn't mean that it took no interest in London gossip.

"What brings you to India, Lady Frederick?" the Captain asked. His studiedly casual tone brought a flush to Penelope's cheeks.

"My husband is undertaking a commission from the government," she said sharply. "He is to be envoy to the Court of Hyderabad."

"And you, Lady Frederick?" he asked, in an uncomfortable echo of her own thoughts earlier that evening. Those dark eyes of his were too piercing by half. It was as though he were rooting about in her mind. Penelope didn't like it one bit.

"Wither he goest, I goest," said Penelope flippantly.

"I see," said Captain Reid, but whatever he saw appeared to bring him no pleasure. After a brooding moment, he said abruptly, "Lady Frederick, do you know anything of Hyderabad?"

Penelope eyed him suspiciously, but before she could reply, a hand settled itself familiarly on her bare shoulder.

"There you are, old thing," Freddy said, as though it was she who had walked away from him, rather than the other way around. "I wondered where you had got to."

He had brought two friends with him, one in regimentals, the other in evening clothes. Penelope wondered which one of them carried Freddy's vowels this time. From the smug expression on the face of the army man, Penelope suspected it was he. On the other hand, smugness might very well be his habitual expression. Penelope would expect nothing less of a man who wore three rings on one hand.

Penelope stepped out from under Freddy's questing hand. "I've been very gallantly entertained by Colonel Reid," she said, batting her lashes at the Colonel and achieving a very petty satisfaction at completely ignoring his son.

Freddy nodded lazily to the Colonel, the gesture amply conveying his complete lack of interest in any man who had served in the East

India Company's army rather than a proper royal regiment. Having dispatched the Colonel, Freddy took inventory of the Captain's tanned face, his uninspired tailoring.

"And you are?" he demanded.

For a moment, Captain Reid forbore to answer. He simply stood there, studying Freddy with an expression of such clinical detachment that Penelope could feel Freddy beginning to shift from one foot to the other beside her.

After a very long moment, a grim smile sifted across Captain Reid's face.

"I," said Captain Reid, "am the man who has the honor of escorting you to Hyderabad."

Chapter Two

"Right," said Lord Frederick, with an obvious lack of interest. "Wellesley mentioned he would be sending someone."

From the moment Captain Alex Reid set eyes on the new Special Envoy to the Court of Hyderabad, he had that sinking sensation in his gut that attends a slow tumble off a steep cliff.

He had been, to put it mildly, less than pleased when Wellesley had summarily summoned him to Calcutta, expecting him to drop all his duties in Hyderabad and spend more than a week in travel for an hour's interview. He had been even less pleased when the Governor General had informed him that he was to play nursemaid to the new envoy, a special envoy the Resident had never requested and certainly didn't need. Wellesley had not been amused when he pointed that out.

But all that was as nothing compared to the reality of Lord Frederick and his wife. Maybe, if he were very, very lucky, he would wake up in his own bed and find that this had all been a bad dream. One could always hope.

The bad dream, alarmingly corporeal in his London-tailored evening clothes, waved a languid hand at the two men standing beside him. "Do you know . . . ?"

Alex did know them. Daniel Cleave had been in school with him in England. Like him, Cleave had been the son of an officer in the Madras Native Cavalry, sent back to Britain for schooling. Unlike him, Cleave's father had died in action, and he remained for some years in Tunbridge Wells with his widowed mother before returning to take up a post on the political side of the service. He was, as he had been in school, thorough, conscientious, and entirely incapable of seeing the larger picture. It was that very myopia that had elevated him to the post of Wellesley's private secretary; the Governor General, thought Alex bitterly, being afflicted with exactly that same shortness of sight.

The other man he knew largely by reputation. Lieutenant Sir Leamington Fiske had been up to his obviously plucked eyebrows in a sordid secret society run by one Arthur Wrothan, pandering to the perversions and prejudices of recent English expatriates. There had been one incident that had trickled even to Alex's ears, one involving the Anglo-Indian daughter of an officer in the Bengal Light Cavalry. Fiske and his cronies had gotten off with a rap on the knuckles. The girl had died.

Had Lord Frederick Staines been one of that crew?

Alex rather thought he might. It was not a cheering thought. If Lord Frederick pulled a trick like that in Hyderabad, he might well find himself missing key parts of his anatomy. Wellesley, who had caused this whole mess by dumping Lord Frederick on them, would find himself missing a key ally. That was all it would take to make the Nizam of Hyderabad drop what his ministers were already vociferously telling him was an increasingly unattractive association.

Disaster didn't cover the half of it.

"Cleave." Alex nodded to his old schoolfellow. His voice hardened as he turned to the other man. "Fiske."

Fiske blinked at him in a manner meant to convey that he had no interest in ascertaining Alex's identity. Fiske fixed his gaze on Lady Frederick, conducting a leisurely examination of her physical attributes. His insolent inspection had no effect at all upon the lady's husband, but prompted Alex's father to take a protective step forward, an attenuated Don Quixote bustling to the defense of his Dulcinea.

"You must be Freddy's wife," declared Fiske. There was an arch lilt to his voice that was just short of being effeminate. The man looked like an elongated codfish in uniform, thought Alex dispassionately. His mouth opened and closed like the fish's as he spoke. "I heard about your marriage."

For a perfectly conventional remark, it had a rather odd effect. Lord Frederick looked as though he had just swallowed something rotten.

Lady Frederick maintained her expression of fashionable boredom, but her shoulder blades were as taut as bowstrings as she said, "I imagine you did. We had a notice put in the *Morning Post*. I assume you do get that here?"

"Eventually," said Fiske, looking like the guppy that got the seaweed. "All the news from home arrives in Calcutta eventually."

"How very unfortunate for you," shot back Lady Frederick, "to be always so far behind."

Alex rocked impatiently back on his heels. Whatever was going on, it was none of his business, and he wished they would deal with it on their own time. Preferably after he had left Calcutta. Alone.

He was just about to excuse himself and leave them to their aristocratic sniping, when Lord Frederick turned abruptly to Alex. "When do we leave for Hyderabad?"

Never, if Alex had his way about it.

"That is, of course, up to you." Doing his best to sound more diplomatic than he felt, Alex said, "It might, however, be prudent to take some time in Calcutta to consult with the Governor General's staff about conditions in Hyderabad before proceeding to the territory itself. And," he added, with a bow in Lady Frederick's direction, "I am sure your wife would enjoy the entertainments afforded by the capital."

If he could just have some time, a few months—a few weeks, even—for Kirkpatrick to get the situation under control, then, he told himself, he could endure Lord Frederick with equanimity. As for Lady Frederick, she scarcely figured into it, he told himself. Except as a potential hostage for the anti-English faction should events take an unfortunate turn. That would certainly do wonders for Alex's career.

Lord Frederick was unimpressed. "I don't see why I should waste time with Wellesley's subordinates when I've already seen the man himself. A bit backwards, don't you think?"

Lord Frederick's expression was a study in arrogance. Alex knew what he was about to say was probably the equivalent of howling into a gorge, but duty was duty. He had to try.

"As I was about to explain to your wife"—Alex bared his teeth at Lady Frederick in a simulacrum of a smile—"the situation in Hyderabad is not all that could be desired. The province is, at present, somewhat unsettled."

"Wellesley never mentioned anything of the kind," said Lord Frederick carelessly, as though that were the last word in the matter.

Alex glanced sideways at Cleave, choosing his words as though he were walking a rope bridge across a gorge. "Lord Wellesley has other concerns on his mind. The war with Holcar, for one." At least, he ought to have. The latest reports from the north had been distinctly sobering.

"Holcar?" asked Lady Frederick.

"Nothing for you to worry about, Lady Frederick," Cleave hastened to assure her, like the good little lackey he was. To be fair, he did have a widowed mother to support. But even so. "A local warlord got a bit out of hand, but Lord Lake is dealing with him. We had a similar unpleasantness with some of the other Mahratta chieftains last year, but it's all been dealt with now."

That wasn't quite the way Alex would have explained it. It was true that the crushing victory at Assaye, followed by a series of similar successes, had forced the leaders of the Mahratta Confederacy into signing a series of treaties with the English. But with Holcar making a fool of Lord Lake in the north, Alex had no illusions as to how long those treaties would hold. It was only the myth of British military invincibility that kept the defeated Mahratta leaders in line. Explode that legend, as Holcar was rather effectively managing to do, and they were all in very hot water indeed.

"This Holcar, I take it, is not actually in Hyderabad?" Lady Frederick was asking Cleave.

Good God. At least it wasn't her husband asking the question, though from the studiedly blank expression on his face, Alex suspected he didn't know either. A monkey, thought Alex. A monkey would be a better choice as envoy to the Nizam. What in the hell was Wellesley thinking?

Unfortunately, he knew what Wellesley was thinking. The same thing he had been thinking three years ago when he set up a special commission to investigate Kirkpatrick, with special attention to the Resident's marriage to a Hyderabadi lady of quality. The Governor General had a bee in his bonnet about Kirkpatrick's chosen way of life, as though a man's loyalties could be measured by the clothes he chose to wear or the woman with whom he chose to share his bed. The Governor General's probing had been irksome enough three years ago. But three years ago, the old Nizam had still been alive. Three years ago, there had been a pro-British First Minister. Three years ago, the whole province hadn't been in danger of going up like a powder keg in dry weather.

"No," said Alex shortly. "Holcar is based in the north. Hyderabad is more southerly."

Lady Frederick smiled beatifically up at him, but her amber eyes glinted with a hint of hellfire. "If the war is in the north and Hyderabad is in the south . . ."

"I'm afraid it's not so simple as that," Alex said stiffly.

"No, nothing ever is, is it," agreed Lady Frederick. "I generally prefer to see for myself."

"You might," said Alex, striving for cordiality, "prefer to see for yourself after the monsoon. The trip is not a pleasant one during the rains."

He looked pointedly at his father.

With an abrupt cough, his father belatedly picked up his cue. The Colonel beamed at Lady Frederick with all the force of his considerable charm. "You wouldn't want to be missing the Calcutta season, Lady Frederick. We have routs and balls and theatrical entertainments. You couldn't be so cruel as to deprive us of your company, could you, now?"

"Yes, do stay," contributed Fiske, his guppy mouth conducting its own fishy orgy of innuendo. "I promise to personally see to your entertainment. I'm sure Freddy won't mind, will you, old bean?"

"You needn't trouble yourself," said Lady Frederick, with an inscrutable look in the direction of her husband. "I had enough of society in London."

She might think so now, but Alex doubted she would be of that opinion three months from now. He had never known a less appealing cluster of people than the handful of English ladies washed up with their husbands in Hyderabad, bitter with boredom and universally discontented with their lots. Of all the Residency ladies, only Mrs. Ure, the physician's wife, appeared content, and that was because her one passion was food, a passion that she satisfied daily to the extreme detriment of both the Residency larder and her figure.

It was true that Begum Johnson had lived for some time away from English society, but she was different; she had been born in India, grown up in India, knew it and loved it as he did. They didn't make women like her anymore.

Alex's thoughts turned to his two sisters, Kat and Lizzy, sent home to Kat's maternal grandmother in England to learn to become proper English gentlewomen. He knew it was necessary; he knew that Lizzy, born of his father's extended liaison with a Rajput lady, would have a better life in England, where prejudice towards half-castes was less pronounced than among the increasingly insular British community in India; but he still hated to think of them turning their backs on their early upbringing, taking on the senseless airs and graces so prized by lady visitors to Calcutta, becoming foreign to him. Becoming, in fact, like Lady Frederick.

It only took one look at her to know that Lady Frederick Staines was entirely unfit to undertake the trip to Hyderabad. Her muslin dress looked as if it might rip if anyone so much breathed on it. There were pearls twined in her flaming red hair along with white flowers fresh from the Governor General's own gardens. They were fragile blossoms, English flowers of the sort that flourished in India only in the English areas, with fussing and watering and careful handling. In the candlelight, her skin, liberally displayed by the scooped neck and short sleeves of her gown, appeared to be nearly the same color as the petals and possessed of the same haunting scent.

And would, Alex reminded himself, bruise just as quickly as those petals. That skin of hers wouldn't last two minutes in the sun. The first part of the journey could be accomplished by boat, but how would she fare on the grueling seven-day trek from the coast to the British Residency in Hyderabad? Once there—if Mrs. Dalrymple and her cronies complained of boredom, it could be worse for a London lady. On top of the boredom, there would be the hundred small irritations born of an unfamiliar climate, the intestinal disorders, the sunstroke, the prickly heat, and boils that would mar that impossible skin. Lady Frederick was a thing of mother-of-pearl and moonlight, designed for costly drawing rooms in a cold climate. Not for India and certainly not for Hyderabad.

She might, thought Alex callously, do well enough in Calcutta. The cold season was almost upon them and there would be balls and entertainments enough even for a spoiled daughter of the aristocracy. There would be plenty to fawn over her for the sake of her husband's title.

"I don't think you realize quite how dull a provincial residency can be," Alex warned. "We have none of the amenities to which you are accustomed. There are no concerts, no balls, no—" He struggled to recall the complaints he had heard from the Englishwomen resident in Hyderabad.

"No milliners," finished the Colonel for him. "Nor dressmakers, either."

Lord Frederick appeared entirely unconcerned about his wife's haberdashery. "As long as the shooting is good, I'm sure we'll jog along all right. Right, old thing?" Without waiting for his wife's response, he looked to Alex. "We leave tomorrow."

Alex wondered just why he was so anxious to go. Was it Wellesley prodding him? Or something else?

"With all due respect, there are arrangements to be made. It's not exactly the same as traveling from London to Surrey." Alex couldn't quite manage to keep the asperity out of his voice.

"I don't see why not," said Lord Frederick. "It's always bally raining there, too."

Fiske hee-hawed and Cleave contrived a restrained chuckle. Alex managed not to bang his head against the wall. "Yes," he said mildly, "but there are fewer elephants in Surrey."

"What the lad means," intervened his father, with the glibness for which he was known throughout the cantonments of India, "is that it takes time to arrange a fitting entourage for a personage of your stature. You wouldn't want the Hyderabadis to think you were a person of no account, now, would you?"

That appeared to resonate with their young lordling. He nodded in a thoughtful way, his lips pursing. "A week Tuesday, then." Reaching into his waistcoat pocket, he flipped a gold coin in Alex's direction. "See that you hire a few extra elephants."

Well, they already had an ass.

Alex's father slipped the guinea from Alex's nerveless fingers and handed it back to Lord Frederick. "You can settle accounts with the Governor General," he said.

Alex didn't need his father's warning look to tell him that departure was the better part of valor. "If you'll excuse me," he said in a voice like granite, "I'll go see to those arrangements. Lord Frederick, Lady Frederick. Cleave. Fiske."

"Good man." Lord Frederick favored him with a perfunctory nod before turning back to Fiske. "Now about that filly . . ." Alex heard him saying as he walked away.

Alex concentrated on putting one foot in front of another and breathing deeply through his nose. The Begum's house was as familiar to Alex as his own quarters. He turned to the left, pushing open the door to the deserted book room. Behind him, he could hear the slap and shuffle of his father's boots against the marble floor.

"Easy, my lad, easy," warned his father, peering down the corridor and pushing the door shut behind them. "Keep a rein on that temper of yours."

Alex regarded his father sourly. His father had many virtues, but restraint of any kind was not known to be one of them. Otherwise, Alex would never have had quite so many half-siblings.

Besides, he had no temper. He was a remarkably even-tempered man. Except in the face of sheer stupidity. Unfortunately, there seemed to be a good deal of that going around Calcutta.

"That," Alex said pointedly, jerking his head towards the room they had just vacated, "is a disaster waiting to happen."

"Just so long as you don't allow it to happen to you," returned his father equably. Beneath their wrinkled lids, his faded blue eyes were surprisingly shrewd. Self-indulgent he might be, but no one had ever called him stupid. "I'm within an ace of wrangling that district commissionership for you. So don't go fouling it up out of some high-minded notion."

At the moment, Alex was feeling more bloody-minded than high-minded. It was all very well for his father to counsel prudence, but as far as Alex could see, he was damned either way.

"Fine," said Alex. "Let's say I hold my tongue and cart Lord and Lady Freddy meekly off to Hyderabad a week Tuesday. What happens when that idiot sparks off a civil war? I doubt I'll receive commendations when Mir Alam's lads kick us out of Hyderabad, lock, stock, and barrel. With matters the way they stand, Wellesley's new pet could undo in a moment what Kirkpatrick took six years to accomplish."

His father regarded him patiently. "It's not all on your shoulders, Alex."

"Then whose?" Alex demanded, frustration ringing through his voice. "Wellesley doesn't trust Kirkpatrick to piss without someone writing a secret report on it; Russell isn't a bad sort, but he's untried—"

"—and a bit too much in love with himself," the Colonel humored him by adding.

Alex glowered at his father. Just because he had said it before didn't make it any less true or any less problematic. "Precisely. The new Nizam is a tin-pot Nero who gets his amusement using silk handkerchiefs to throttle his concubines. He'll go wherever Mir Alam tells him to, just so long as Alam doesn't cut off his supply of expensive hankies and cheap women. And Mir Alam is half rotted with leprosy and demented with the desire to be revenged upon the British, because he blames us for his bloody exile four years ago."

"It is unfortunate, that," admitted his father.

"'Unfortunate' doesn't even begin to cover it. It's a bloody fiasco. And do you know what makes it even worse?"

"No, but I'm sure you'll tell me, lad," said his father, patting him fondly on the shoulder.

Alex ought to have resented the pat, but he was too busy with his main rant to waste time on peripheral grievances. "It was Wellesley that bloody saddled us with Mir Alam! He met him years ago in Mysore and decided he was a good chap. But, no, he couldn't be bothered to look into what might have happened in the interim! He's too busy poking into Kirkpatrick's bedchamber, like a bloody peeping Tom!"

"Whoa, there." The Colonel's hand tightened on his arm. "Keep your voice down. You don't want to be losing your post for a moment's ill-humor."

"It's more than a moment," said Alex tiredly, feeling the rage wash out of him, leaving him feeling like a fish washed up on the beach. "It's been months, ever since Wellesley pushed Mir Alam's appointment as First Minister. And what's the point of hanging on to my post if there's nothing I can do with it? Except play lackey to a walking disaster," he added bitterly. "It's like being asked to play host to one's own executioner."

"Patience," advised the Colonel.

"For what?" demanded Alex. "More of the same?"

Looking to the left and right, the Colonel tapped a finger against the side of his nose. "Word to the wise, my boy," he said sotto voce. "It isn't generally known yet, but the word is that Wellesley is on his way out. Apparently the folks back home on the Board of Control are none too happy with the Governor General's expenditures."

Alex looked at his father closely. "How 'none too happy'?"

His father regarded him shrewdly. "Between the cost of the war with the Mahrattas and that grand Government House the Governor General has been building, they're feeling the pinch in their purses, lad. You can guess how unhappy that makes them."

Alex absorbed the information. "Is there any word on whom they might send to replace him?"

The Colonel shook his head. "It's all just rumor, as yet. But if you get yourself disciplined before Wellesley goes, it won't matter who the new man is."

He would have to be right, wouldn't he? Feeling like a small boy caught out in some petty carelessness, Alex inclined his head in the briefest of acknowledgments. "Point taken."

His father clapped him on the shoulder, the reward after the scolding. "It will be all right, my boy, just you wait and see."

"When do you sail?" Alex asked, deeming it wise to change the subject while he was still ahead.

Having served for four decades in the Madras Native Cavalry, his father had finally deemed it time to retire from active service. After a childhood in Charleston, a lifetime soldiering in India, and amours of various extractions, the Laughing Colonel, scourge of Madras, was retiring to Bath to be closer to his daughters. Alex's Jacobite grandparents must be turning in their graves.

"That depends in part on you." The Colonel paused to allow the impact of his words to sink in. Alex folded his arms across his chest, signaling to his father that he knew exactly what he was up to. Feigning obliviousness, the Colonel carried on innocently, "I shouldn't like to go until I see you settled. Although it will be that glad I am to see Kat and Lizzy again."

"Give them my love when you see them," said Alex. It seemed a more manly way of saying good-bye than *I'll miss you.*

As much as he hated to admit it, he would miss the old reprobate. His father might have had eccentric notions of family life, but they had been affectionate ones, for all that. The Colonel had never repudiated any of his offspring, no matter how irregular the circumstances. Of five living siblings, only Alex and his sister Kat were technically legitimate, but the Colonel had always treated all of his children with exactly the same rambunctious affection, no matter which side of the blanket they had tumbled out of. He had seen to their schooling and found placement for Alex in his own cavalry unit. For George, who was barred from the East India Company's army by virtue of being the offspring of an Indian woman, he had wrangled a command in the service of a native ruler, the Begum Sumroo.

As a young man eager to make his own mark on the world, Alex had often found his father's constant oversight irksome. He had left the cavalry for the political service, left Madras for Hyderabad, done everything he could to make his own way in his own way, gritting his teeth at the invariable "Oh, Reid's boy, are you? Splendid chap!" that greased his way even as it did damage to his molars. But over the years, he and his father had come to a comfortable sort of understanding.

There was a curious emptiness that came with the thought that henceforth the old rascal would be a full five months away. He would miss him.

"You'll keep an eye on George for me, won't you?" said the Colonel.

Alex raised both eyebrows. "You've asked George the same about me, haven't you?"

The Colonel stretched his arms comfortably in front him. "I like to see you all looking out for one another," he said placidly. "It's what a family is for."

"Except Jack," said Alex.

His father didn't like to talk about Jack.

The Colonel's bland smile didn't wobble, but there was nothing he could do to hide the slight trembling of his hands. "That Lord Frederick Staines is a piece of work and no mistaking," he said, changing the subject as though that was what they had been talking about all along, "but his wife seems to have a head on her shoulders."

"I hadn't realized it was her head that interested you," said Alex, letting the subject of Jack drop. It wasn't particularly pleasant for any of them.

"Now, now. I appreciate a witty woman as well as the next man. She seems like a feisty lass, with no nonsense about her," announced the Colonel. "I like her."

This did not exactly come as a surprise. "Have you ever met a woman you haven't liked?"

After giving the matter deep consideration, the Colonel said triumphantly, "There was your sister's governess ... Miss Furnival, as she was."

"She didn't like you," corrected Alex. "That's not the same thing."

"Poor girl," said the Colonel generously. "She had that unfortunate problem with spots. It would be enough to sour anybody. But your Lady Frederick is a different matter."

"I should say she is," said Alex. She was an irritant. A very attractive irritant, but an irritant nonetheless. A very attractive, very married irritant. "She's Lord Frederick's matter. And even if she weren't," he added, before the gleam in his father's eye could translate into advice of which the resident religious authorities—of any denomination—would not approve, "I don't have time to dabble in dalliance."

The Colonel laughed that rolling laugh that had earned him the sobriquet the "Laughing Colonel." "Nonsense!" he declared. "All it will take is the right woman to make you change your mind."

"Or women?" Alex shot back. It was a cheap blow and he knew it.

Alex would have taken it back if he could, but it had already hit its mark. His father's face seemed to sag around the edges.

"We can never undo what we've done," said the Colonel, with none of his usual bluster. He looked his full age and more. "But I never meant ill by any of you. You know that."

"I know," said Alex roughly. "It doesn't matter."

"Until it does," said the Colonel, looking at Alex far too acutely for Alex's comfort. Alex hated when his father looked at him like that. If his father wanted to be philosophical in his old age, well and good, just so long as his father didn't philosophize about him. "Don't shut yourself off from all the pleasant things in life, lad."

"Trust me," said Alex dryly, "I enjoy a good day's hunting as much as the next man."

The Colonel looked at him closely, realized he wasn't going to get anywhere, and gave up, with a philosophical shrug of his shoulders.

"Humor an old man's fancy and write me a letter to let me know how you get on once you get that lot to Hyderabad."

There was a glint in the old rogue's eyes that made Alex feel decidedly twitchy. "With any luck, there won't be anything to tell."

His father grinned at him, displaying a full set of yellowing teeth. "That depends on your definition of luck."

Chapter Three

O n the bank, a crocodile yawned in the heat, its jaws stretching
open until Penelope thought its head must surely snap in two.

The air was thick with moisture and mosquitoes as the pilot's schooner plowed slowly down the Hooghly River. They had left the boats and villages nearer Calcutta behind them. They had left behind the women carrying their washing down to the banks, the houses and temples visible through the trees. Instead, the jungle grew close by the banks of the river, like something out of a lyric poet's tortured dreams, and crocodiles waddled to the edge of the waters to yawn their contempt to potential trespassers.

Penelope bared her teeth right back, even if the dental display wasn't quite as impressive. It wouldn't do to let an amphibian stare her down. Although it did rather help that she was on a boat and the crocodile wasn't.

The water churned muddy and dark behind them, thick with silt, but Penelope could already see the breakers ahead of them that signaled the mouth of the Hooghly and the place where they were to change to a proper sailing ship to bring them all the way down the coast.

She yawned again, this time in earnest. In London, she had grown accustomed to sleeping well past noon. The schedule of the London Season was a nocturnal one, lighting the night with the artificial glow of candles and drawing the drapes against the intrusive light of day. Her father's mother, who preferred the saddle to the ballroom, had always been frankly contemptuous of the whole process, wondering loudly why anyone would be fool enough to waste the day God gave them (this usually said with a pointed look at her daughter-in-law). Her grandmother, Penelope thought, leaning her arms on the rail, would have enjoyed India.

Breakers lay to one side, but on the other squatted a dense mass of thickly matted vegetation. Penelope thought she could see a tiger through the trees, its striped pelt a vivid amber against the hanging fronds of the trees.

"What is that?" she asked Captain Reid as he passed behind her.

"The island of Sangor," he said briefly. After a moment, he added, "The island is sacred to Kali. Sangor has long been used as a ritual center for human sacrifice."

Penelope could feel the Captain's eyes on her, gauging the impact of his comment. He no doubt expected her to be spooked, to express womanly alarm, to demand his protection against the big, bad beasties who ate pretty little Englishwomen—or, even better, to demand that he turn around and take her back to the metropolitan protection of Calcutta posthaste, tide or no.

There was only one thing to be done.

"What kind of human sacrifices?" Penelope demanded, twisting around to look up at him.

It was marvelous watching Captain Reid's discomfiture.

Blinking rapidly, he managed to effect a quick recovery. "In human sacrifices one generally sacrifices humans. I understand that that is the usual practice."

Penelope rolled her eyes. "Yes, but how do they go about it? Do they burn them? Cut them up into little bits? Flay them alive?"

Captain Reid backed up a step. "I believe they generally fling them into the river."

Penelope made a moue of disappointment. "That is fairly tame, I must say. If one is to have a blood sacrifice, I would hope there would at least be a bit more drama about it. Otherwise, it strikes me as a waste of a perfectly good human."

A tiny glint of humor showed in Captain Reid's steely eyes, clearly much against his own inclination. "If it makes you feel better, they do have a fair amount of ceremonial around the event. The devotees are robed in scarlet and draped in flowers. There are hymns and all that sort of thing."

"Rather like Evensong," commented Penelope, with an arch glance at Captain Reid.

"Only rather more fatal." He had given up the battle against his better self; the glint expanded into a bona fide grin. It was a quirky sort of grin, pulling up one side of his mouth more than the other, but it was oddly engaging for all that.

He was really rather attractive when he wasn't scowling at her.

"Why do they do it?" she asked.

"Why? For the same reason one petitions any deity; for riches, for health, for advancement. It is," he added wryly, "rather amazing what a man will do for the hope of advancement."

There was a self-mockery in his tone that suggested there was more than abstract philosophy at play.

Penelope wondered just what dubious measures Captain Reid might have been driven to in the interests of advancement. Human sacrifice didn't seem likely to be on the list, but it wasn't beyond the realm of possibility that he might have joined with the Resident in selling out British interests for Hyderabadi gold. Or, perhaps, as the Resident was rumored to have done, even converted to Islam for the purposes of currying local favor. That would explain why Reid was so dead opposed to Freddy's fulfilling Wellesley's commission in Hyderabad, why he was so transparently eager to see them both back to Calcutta, even if he had to make up tall tales about ritual sacrifice to accomplish it.

Oh, he thought he had been so subtle about it at Begum Johnson's soiree, making those stilted comments about the wonders of the Calcutta Season, the rigors of the road, the unalleviated monotony of life in the provinces, but the pretense had been so laughable that a child of five could have seen through it. Captain Reid obviously didn't give a damn about balls or routs or the wonders of the Calcutta Season; what he did give a damn about was detaining her and Freddy in Calcutta as long as possible. He appeared to be under the misguided impression that she had any influence at all over her husband, and that if she teased and wheedled, Freddy would dawdle away the cold months in Calcutta with her, leaving Captain Reid a free hand to do whatever it was he intended to do in Hyderabad unsupervised.

Penelope could have told Captain Reid that there were two fallacies at play in that approach. The first mistake was assuming that she had any interest at all in the social life of Calcutta.

The second was presuming that she had any influence over Freddy.

It would, Penelope thought, be rather a nice shot in the eye to her spouse if she was to uncover what was rotten in the state of Hyderabad before he did. Freddy wouldn't recognize treason at work unless it happened to get between him and a hand of cards. Add in a spot of hunting, and Wellesley's suspicions could go hang.

Lord Wellesley had sent Freddy to investigate James Kirkpatrick, but what if he was misinformed? What if the source of the unrest in Hyderabad wasn't Kirkpatrick at all, but his subordinate, Captain Reid?

"How long have you been in Hyderabad, Captain Reid?" Penelope asked cunningly.

"Long enough to know the route," he said with polite finality. "We're almost to Point Palmyras. If you'll excuse me, I really should see about the baggage before we change ships."

"I doubt it's going anywhere on its own," pointed out Penelope.

Captain Reid inclined his head. "My point precisely, Lady Frederick."

Penelope watched with narrowed eyes as Captain Reid exchanged a few words with the pilot of the schooner. Tugging at the brim of her hat to deflect the sun, which was full in her eyes, she saw the passage of a pale packet being passed from Captain Reid to the pilot. Letters? Penelope squinted against the sun, but it was no use. Whatever it was had already disappeared from Captain Reid's hand into the pilot's pocket. That is, if there had been anything there at all. The glare of the sun seemed to bleach the insides of her eyes, creating inverted shadows that slithered upon the scene like ornamental goldfish in a fountain. Penelope blinked hard, trying to clear her vision, but the spots wouldn't seem to go away.

"You need to get out of the sun for a bit," said Captain Reid, assessing her condition with a professional air, as he handed her across the deck, Freddy having blithely traipsed along ahead. "Or get a wider hat."

"Nonsense!" Penelope snapped, sounding more like the Dowager Duchess of Dovedale than the Dowager Duchess, but she was forced to cling to his arm as she navigated her way into the dinghy that was to row them to the *Intractable*, the sailing ship contracted to convey them down the coast.

Penelope added that into the account against him and resolved to buy a broader hat.

It must have been the sun, because she found herself doing the unthinkable and taking an afternoon nap, curled into the cool of her berth in the ship's very best cabin, from which she was shaken awake by an impatient Freddy, who wanted his dinner and informed her they were keeping everyone waiting.

"Everyone" turned out to be no one more than their small party and the captain of the ship, who was incoherent in his excitement at having such exalted passengers. Freddy seemed to grow even more burnished in the candlelight as he preened at the praise, like a medieval saint's painting limned in gold leaf. Captain Reid held his tongue, but there was something sarcastic about his shadow as it fell against the wall, as though made darker by Freddy's luster.

"And how have you been occupying yourself, Captain Reid?" she asked, as they sat down to dinner in a narrow chamber where the roof sloped down sharply on one side, and navigational maps had been thrust hastily out of the way to make room for the soup tureen on the sideboard. "More human sacrifices?"

The young ship captain's fork rattled against his plate as he looked from her to Captain Reid with palpable alarm, as though expecting to see severed limbs sticking out of the Captain's waistcoat pockets. Penelope smiled reassuringly at the young man. He smiled uneasily back, but Penelope noticed him sneaking another nervous glance at Captain Reid.

"Nothing so interesting as that," Captain Reid said equably, helping himself to fish from a dish that swayed with the movement of the ship. His fingers bore the slight traces of ink, testament to his afternoon's activities. Penelope wondered just what it was that he had been writing. "I've had a tedious afternoon of facts and figures. An overland journey for a large party always requires a certain amount of advance preparation."

"But we aren't a large party," Penelope protested. Even if one counted the servants the Governor General had been kind enough to have engaged for them in Calcutta, they were no more than ten at most.

Captain Reid regarded her with a jaded eye. "We will be."

"Where are you bound?" asked the ship captain, a young man with a faint fuzz on his cheeks that gave the impression he hadn't quite graduated to shaving yet. He had a pink-cheeked look about him that marked him as not long out of England. "After Masulipatam, I mean," he added, with an embarrassed duck of his head. "I know you're going there, of course. Since I'm bringing you."

"Hyderabad," said Freddy, dealing with the problem of wine splashing over the rim of his glass by the simple expedient of draining it in one long swallow. "I'm to be joining the Residency there."

He chose his phrasing carefully to avoid any mention of his subordinate role. It was such a silly sort of snobbery, thought Penelope impatiently. What did he care what a ship captain he was never going to see again thought of his role in the Residency? The man was clearly flustered enough at having a titled gentleman on his ship, even if it was only a courtesy title.

"Lord Frederick is to be a sort of messenger to the Court at Hyderabad," Penelope specified helpfully. "Aren't you, darling?"

"I am a Special Envoy." Freddy gave her a look over his wineglass that promised retribution later. It was an empty promise. By bedtime, he would be far enough in his cups—or deep enough into a game of cards—that he would have entirely forgotten.

"Who is the current Resident at Hyderabad?" asked young Wheeley or Weatherly or whatever his name was. Something beginning with *W*, at any event. His fair face flushed as he admitted, "I'm new to this part of the world, you see, so I don't know as much as I ought yet."

"Kirk-something," said Freddy offhandedly, toying with his turbot.

"Kirkpatrick," supplied Captain Reid, the hard consonants sounding like gunshots. "James Kirkpatrick. He has devoted a decade of his life to serving British interests in Hyderabad."

"You admire him, then?" asked Penelope, watching Reid closely.

"I think he has done admirable work," said Reid simply. "But for Kirkpatrick, Hyderabad might well have gone over to the French in 1798. There were more than fourteen thousand soldiers under French command in Hyderabad. Kirkpatrick got the Nizam on his side and engineered a bloodless coup. It was a brilliant piece of maneuvering, and one that saved our government in Calcutta a great deal of bother."

He might not have come right out and charged the Governor General with ingratitude, but the meaning was clear.

Freddy looked down his nose at Reid, exuding aristocratic hauteur. "What about the rumors of a native wife?" challenged Freddy. "From what I've heard, Kirkpatrick has conducted himself most irregularly."

Captain Reid smiled a tight social smile. "I believe a man's private life is his own."

Freddy crossed his arms over his chest and kicked back in his chair, nearly oversetting Wheeley's glass in the process. The young captain made a hasty grab for his wine before it could land in his lap. "Even when he's meant to be serving the Crown?"

Captain Reid raised one brow. "I fail to see how the two are connected. Would you contract your marriage to suit the wishes of your superiors?"

The words acted on Freddy like a match to tinder. Penelope could practically hear the flames crackling in the suddenly too-still air. Mandated marriages were a sensitive topic for Freddy at the moment.

Penelope broke the tension by saying languidly, "Lord Frederick doesn't believe he has superiors."

It came out somewhat more acidly than she had intended it, but it served the desired cause.

"Oh, but everyone has superiors," broke in Captain Wheeley earnestly, delighted at having something to add and entirely immune to atmosphere. "There's the King—and we shouldn't forget the Lord Almighty, King of us all."

"Unless you're Hindu," put in Captain Reid blandly. Under his blank façade, Penelope had the impression that he was still seething, although over what she wasn't quite sure. Kirkpatrick's native wife? Perhaps he had a local amour of his own, and resented the slur on such alliances. "They have gods and kings of their own."

"But you can't count them, surely?" said the young captain uncertainly. "Since they're heathens."

"From their viewpoint, we're probably the heathens," pointed out Penelope frivolously. "With our silly ceremonies and one measly divinity. It's positively parsimonious of us. And not a human sacrifice to be had in all of the Anglican communion."

Over the rim of his glass, Captain Reid eyed her assessingly. Unlike Freddy's, his glass was still three quarters full. Candlelight reflected off the wine, casting a warm glow on his cheeks, like sunlight through a stained-glass window.

"That might depend on how one interpreted sacrifice," he suggested, like a boy dangling a stick in front of a dog to see if he would jump.

"Being forced to sit in a drafty church on cold Sundays, you mean?" said Penelope. "Quite. Especially when the sermon is a long one."

"Lady Frederick is joking," interjected Freddy repressively. "She frequently does."

"I believe that life is one large jest," agreed Penelope, baring her teeth at her spouse. "Usually on us."

In that, at least, she and Freddy were perfectly in accord. Their marriage was little more than a massive joke. On them.

Young Wheeley looked uneasily from Penelope to Freddy and back again, as though he feared that sentiment might be theologically unsound, but didn't dare to contradict a lady, especially not a lady who had already expressed an interest in taking up human sacrifice as a hobby.

Penelope tossed down her napkin and pushed her seat back from the table. The men rose as well, the unfortunate young captain cracking his head on the sloping ceiling in the process.

Penelope favored them with a sultry glance all around. "Enjoy your port, gentlemen."

She processed to the door in queenly fashion, head held high, well aware of the way that candlelight played against the fine muslin of her dress, offering the illusion of transparency that had entrapped more than one male fancy in the past. She held the pose until the door had closed behind her, giving the gentlemen time to recover from her presence and get back to suffering one another's company. Then, with a quick look to either side, she slipped light-footed down the passage.

It wasn't merely tact that had prompted her to withdraw. She had another mission in mind, one best accomplished while Captain Reid was fully occupied. It would be rude for him to excuse himself without the ritual glass of port. There would be toasts to be drunk, rude stories to be told, all the usual sort of things men did once the women had demurely retreated to the drawing room.

Penelope had a different room in mind, and there was nothing demure about it.

Instead of stopping at the cabin she shared with Freddy, she fumbled her way to the next door down, pushing the portal open with one swift, decisive movement. A movement on the far wall caused her a moment's alarm, but it was only the shadow cast by the lantern swaying on its hook. Cast in relief on the opposite wall, it looked like a condemned man swaying in a gibbet. Ugh. Penelope pushed the macabre thought aside. After all, it wasn't thievery she was engaged in, just a spot of . . . inspection. That was it. A nice clean word for a somewhat dubious activity.

Slipping into the room, Penelope eased the door shut behind her and took stock of her surroundings. Captain Reid's quarters were smaller than the cabin she shared with Freddy, a narrow rectangle with space for little more than the basic amenities. The room already displayed all the obvious signs of masculine occupation. A shirt was tossed carelessly across the narrow berth and the Captain's shaving kit jostled for space with a set of battered, wood-backed brushes on the narrow washstand. There was a book left open on the bed, something to do with irrigation and agricultural improvements. After shaking it vigorously to check for hidden letters, Penelope left it alone.

There were more books in a narrow bookcase, which had been bolted to the floor, a motley collection of works, apparently abandoned by a series of occupants over time, unless they were overflow from young Captain Wheeley's own library. He did seem the sort to wallow in *Lyrical Ballads* in his spare time. Penelope didn't waste any time on them. She had found what she was looking for.

On the warped table by the bookshelf, a portable writing desk lay open, several pages distributed across its surface, as though the writer had left them to dry before going off to dinner. They were closely written, in a tidy hand.

They were also completely illegible.

The hand might be tidy, but it was a script that Penelope had never seen before, all dots and curlicues like eyelashes scattered across the page. It was a letter to be sure—there was something that looked like a salutation at the top—but about what? And to whom? It felt like a cruel joke. On her.

There were other pages beneath, though, pages that looked as though they might be written in English. Penelope had only managed to wiggle the first one free, one that began with the salutation, "Dear Lizzy"—a woman's name, but not exactly a loverly beginning—when a horrible sound made her freeze like a rabbit in a hedgerow.

Someone was turning the doorknob.

His servant, Penelope prayed, shoving the page back beneath the others and springing away from the desk. *Please let it be his servant.* It would still be embarrassing, but she could make up a silly excuse about having lost her way or felt faint or some other nonsense.

It wasn't a servant.

Captain Reid stood in the doorway, regarding her with an expression that could only have been described as nonplussed. Penelope would have enjoyed seeing him so had she not been showing to even worse advantage. It sapped all the pleasure from it.

"Lady Frederick?"

The very title came out as a question. Well, Penelope couldn't begrudge him that. One did tend to question the status of women who showed up unannounced in one's bedchamber.

Penelope would have given anything to flee. Unfortunately, Captain Reid stood between her and the door, and there was nothing outside the window but water. Water and crocodiles. Penelope couldn't see the crocodiles, but she deemed it safer to presume their existence.

There was nothing to do but brazen it out. Fortunately, she had had a good deal of experience at being brazen.

Tossing Captain Reid an arch look, Penelope fluttered her fingers at the closely written pages on the writing desk. "Love letters, Captain Reid?" she said. "The lady is fortunate, indeed."

If he was perturbed at finding her pawing through his belongings, he hid it well. "Did you want something, Lady Frederick?"

"Yes." It was the curved script on the letter that gave her the idea. Penelope shook back her hair and smiled up at him with the assurance of one well practiced in wiggling out of sticky situations. "I was looking for an Indian grammar. I had thought you might have one."

"An Indian grammar," Captain Reid repeated.

"Yes," repeated Penelope, daring him to challenge her. "Is it really so odd that one would wish to learn the language of the place one intends to occupy? One wouldn't live in England without learning English." Of course, one was born in England, so one never had to bother with learning it, but that was quite another matter. "If I were to live in Italy, I would learn Italian. If I were to live in France—"

"I believe I have the general idea," said Captain Reid, cutting Penelope off in the midst of her continental tour. Had he believed her excuse? She couldn't tell. The angle of the light was in his favor, falling from behind him so that his face remained in shadow, while hers was lit like a sinner's conscience at the call of the last trump. "You may find it more difficult than you anticipated."

"I've always been rather quick at learning a language." It was true enough. It had driven Henrietta mad that Penelope had managed to master the rudiments of Italian while Henrietta was still struggling with basic pronunciation. Penelope was lazy, but she was quick—at least, that was what her sorely tried governesses had reported to her mother.

"Languages," Captain Reid corrected. "I'm afraid you'll find not one Indian language but many. Hindustani is the most common, but by no means universal."

"What do they speak in Hyderabad?"

"Deccani. It's an offshoot of Urdu." That might have helped had she had any idea what Urdu was. One thing was clear, it wasn't Italian, French, or German. "My advice is to hire a *munshi* once we arrive. A tutor," he translated. "Although I doubt you'll have much use for it."

"Why?" Penelope took a step towards him, bringing them only a hand's breadth apart in the tiny cabin. The lantern on its peg in the corner swayed with the movement of the ship, creating a ripping river of gold on the scarred wood floor between them. "Because you think I'll leave?"

With a wry smile, Captain Reid shook his head. "No. Because the English community tends to keep to itself. And I imagine your husband will follow them in that."

"There's nothing to say that I need to follow my husband."

"You said it yourself. Whither he goest . . ."

"That was purely a matter of geography, not the mind."

"Freethinking, Lady Frederick?"

She hated that name. It was like a shackle around her neck, engraved with the name of her master. She took a step back, her face openly mutinous in the light of the single lamp. "I don't like being told what to do."

Captain Reid quirked an eyebrow. "I shall remember that."

Unexpectedly, Penelope grinned. "No, I don't expect you will. But I shall keep reminding you." Turning her back on him quite deliberately, she scanned the books scattered across the shelves. "Do you have that Hindustani grammar for me?"

"This one." He reached from behind her to tip a book out of the row. His sleeve brushed her shoulder in passing. It was a coarser weave than Freddy favored, which must have been why it seemed to leave such a trail across her bare skin. She could smell the clean scent of shaving soap on his jaw and port on his breath, almost overwhelming the small space, as though not being able to see him somehow made him larger than he was, blowing his presence out of proportion in the brush of fabric against her back, the whisper of breath against her hair.

Penelope twisted around, so that the bookshelf pressed into her back, pinning her between the writing desk on one side and Captain Reid's extended arm on the other. She tipped her head back to look him in the eye, the ribbons in her hair snagging against the shelf.

Captain Reid made no move to remove his arm. They were face-to-face, chest-to-chest, close enough to kiss. But for the fact that they weren't on a balcony, and there was no champagne in evidence, it might have been a dozen other encounters in Penelope's existence, a dozen dangerous preludes to a kiss. But this wasn't a ballroom, and this man wasn't any of the spoiled society boys she had known in London. He studied her face in the strange, shifting light, as the ship rocked back and forth and they rocked with it, pinned in place, frozen in tableau, his own face dark and unreadable in the half-light.

One might, thought Penelope hazily, her eyes dropping to his lips, attempt to seduce information out of him. From what she had heard, it was a far-from-uncommon technique. One needn't go too far, after all. A sultry glance, a subtle caress . . . a kiss. It was all for a good cause— and it could be so easy.

Or maybe not.

Captain Reid was no Freddy. Stepping abruptly back, he favored her with a stiff, social smile, the sort one would give a maiden aunt who was being tedious at a party, but to whom one was bound to be polite.

With a brusque motion, he thrust the red-bound book into her hands, gesturing her, with unmistakable finality, towards the door. "Here is your grammar, Lady Frederick. I wish you . . . an instructive time with it."

"Oh, yes," said Penelope, with more bravado than she felt. "It has certainly been most instructive."

Chapter Four

The scent of Lady Frederick's perfume lingered behind her, as pungent as crushed frangipani petals, in the confined cabin.

Shaking his head to clear it, like a sleepwalker slapping himself into wakefulness, Alex forced his attention to his writing desk, where the letter he had been writing to George appeared to have dried. It was, he thought, rather a good thing he had written in Urdu. The description he had provided of Lord and Lady Frederick had not been a flattering one.

Why in the devil had she suddenly felt the burning need for a Hindi grammar? And why come to his room to find it? It would have been just as easy to have made the request at dinner.

Shuffling the pages together, Alex snaked a glance over at the bookshelf. She hadn't been trying to . . . No. Too absurd. Alex shook his head and went on shuffling. He rooted about with one hand, feeling for the sealing wax. And yet. There had been that odd moment, by the bookshelf, where a letter opener could scarcely have sliced through the space between them. Admittedly, there wasn't that much space in the cabin to begin with, but . . . Opening the glass door of the lantern, Alex abstractedly thrust the wick of the wax at the small flame.

She hadn't been trying to seduce him, had she?

Crimson dots spattered across the worn wood floor like freshly shed blood.

Alex flapped his hand up and down, cursing vehemently in three languages. He had just dripped hot wax all down his hand and it bloody well stung.

Served him right.

Scowling, Alex picked up the fallen wafer and finished the job with brutal efficiency, stamping the wax with far more force than the act required. A burnt hand was no more than he deserved. Lady Frederick wasn't trying to seduce him; she simply flirted as naturally as she breathed. Like his father. They were two of a kind, masters of the meaningless flirtation. Look at the state to which she had reduced that poor, calf-eyed dolt of a captain.

Even if she did have a bit of dalliance in mind—and it was purely a hypothetical situation, Alex assured himself, slamming the lid of his writing case—there wasn't anything the least bit flattering about it. It didn't take more than ordinary intelligence to notice that something wasn't quite right between her and her titled goop of a husband. Alex had no desire to play the pawn in a civil war between husband and wife. Being assaulted by a jealous husband—or doing the assaulting oneself—would do little to enhance his bid for a district commissionership. Even his father would have to agree with that.

Alex didn't like to think what else his father would have to say about the affair. Not that there was an affair. English could be a bloody infuriating language at times, with its denotations and connotations and multiple meanings running rampant around perfectly innocent words. It had been no more than an encounter, a chance brush in a too-small room.

Flopping backwards onto his berth, Alex took up the book he had been reading before dinner but the words refused to behave in a proper manner, all running together into a gray blur. It was no use. He couldn't make himself concentrate on the wonders of irrigation. It had all been a bit premature, to be sure, educating himself on improved agricultural methods. There was no guarantee that the district commissionership would be his, or that he would ever have the chance to put any of his plans into practice. No guarantee, but a good shot. With the efficiency of born bureaucrats, the Governor General's office was parceling out the land extracted by treaty from the Nizam of Hyderabad into new districts, districts to be run by appointees of the British government. This would be no diplomatic mission, no perpetual practice of persuasion on a vacillating ruler, but the chance to govern oneself, to govern justly and directly, with minimal interference from either Calcutta or Bombay. It was the chance of a lifetime.

But first, he had to get Lord and Lady Frederick to Hyderabad. It was, thought Alex bitterly, as he tried to make his eyes focus on canals and waterways, rather like one of those fairy tales in which the hero was put to absurd tests before he could win the hand of his lady fair and half the kingdom.

For ten days, Alex stayed mostly to his cabin, making interminable lists of supplies needed and dodging Lord Frederick's increasingly frequent inquiries about the nightlife of Hyderabad, the quality of the available women, and the hunting around the Residency (animals, women, or both). Alex experienced a very un-Christian sense of relief when Lord Frederick succumbed to a stomach ailment midway through the voyage.

Of Lady Frederick, Alex saw little, although there was once or twice a lingering scent of frangipani when he returned to his cabin after the nightly ritual of port with the captain. Alex put that down to an overactive imagination and prescribed himself a course of reading about irrigation. The books didn't extinguish inappropriate musings but they did at least bore him to sleep and that was close enough.

When they finally docked in the decaying port city of Masulipatam, there were letters waiting for him, responses to the communications he had sent out from Calcutta. Nothing from George, but Kirkpatrick had taken Alex's message under advisement and replied that someone would be there to meet him once he had crossed the Krishna. That was all, but it was enough. Alex went about the task of assembling the necessaries for an overland journey in much-improved spirits, despite the vile stench of fish that hung over the city, clinging to its human inhabitants and making everything smell like yesterday's rotting catch.

It took five days to assemble the army of beasts and attendants necessary for their journey. After five days of the stench of fish, Alex had assumed that his charges would be delighted at anything designed to convey them hence. But when she saw the conveyance in which she was to travel, Lady Frederick balked.

"No," said Lady Frederick.

Alex lifted an eyebrow. "No?"

Admittedly, the palanquin was a little old-fashioned. Many of the newer ones were fitted with sliding doors and glass windows in imitation of a carriage, but the curtains were lighter for the bearers to carry over such an extended trip as theirs was to be. Otherwise, it was a perfectly good palanquin, hung with silk, lined with cushions, supported with sturdy bamboo poles.

Having been up since before dawn, organizing a battalion of servants and pack animals, Alex was in no mood to pander to the petty pretensions of the peerage. He had already been spat at by a camel; ladylike tantrums were superfluous. This was precisely the sort of nonsense he had expected from her, pointless and time-consuming carping about an insufficiently fashionable equipage. And yet, he was oddly disappointed.

He was disappointed at the delay, that was all. Nothing more.

"This is, I assure you," Alex said, with a tinge of asperity in his voice, "the best that could be had. If it displeases you, you are certainly welcome to return to Calcutta to commission a more appropriate one."

"You'd like that, wouldn't you?" said Lady Frederick. She made a show of looking around. "And where is your palanquin? I only see the one."

"I don't have one. I ride."

"My point precisely."

"Your— What?" Alex's jaw dropped in genuine shock as the import of what she was saying hit home. Realigning his facial muscles to their usual position, he managed to get out, "You can't expect to ride."

"Why not? You are."

"This is not a pleasure jaunt, Lady Frederick. We won't be galloping around Hyde Park three times then coming home for tea."

"Of course not. Tea would be absurd in this heat. And one seldom gallops in Hyde Park. There are usually people in the way. Now," she said, looking around as though that had settled everything, "do you have a mount for me?"

In fact, they had sixty-two horses, forty ponies, eleven camels, and ten bullocks. Whether any of the riding animals were suited for a lady's mount was another question entirely. He was also fairly sure that he had neglected to procure a sidesaddle, having assumed that the lady would prefer to travel by palanquin.

Alex sighed, envisioning further delays and complications, while the whole caravan sweated and scratched and wilted in the growing heat. "I'll see what I can arrange," he lied. "If you would consent to ride in the palanquin just for today, until we can find something more fitting . . ."

Hopefully, by then, she would be fast asleep in the palanquin with the curtains drawn against the heat, having entirely forgotten that she had ever desired otherwise.

"Never mind," said Lady Frederick airily, and Alex felt his shoulders relax. "I'll find my own. Ah! Perfect."

It wasn't perfect. It was Alex's horse. And Lady Frederick was maneuvering herself up into the saddle—with a leg up from a too-helpful groom, who grinned at Alex as though to say, *What was one to do?*—as though she had every right to be there.

"Oh no," began Alex, but it was too late. With a valedictory wave of her hat, Lady Frederick was off down the road like a shot.

"That's torn it," muttered Lord Frederick, and settled back against the side of the palanquin with his hat tipped over his eyes, as though the very high likelihood of his wife's breaking her neck were a matter of complete indifference to him.

Perhaps it was.

"Bloody—!" There was no time to curse. Alex snatched the reins of Lord Frederick's horse, Aurangzeb, away from the syce, swinging hastily up into the saddle.

Applying his heels to its sides, he set off in pursuit of Lady Frederick. Lord Frederick's was an excellent mount. It should be; Alex had picked it himself. Unfortunately, his own horse was even better, and it appeared to have run away with its current rider, galloping flat out along the road as though a pack of devils were in pursuit.

Astonishingly, Lady Frederick had managed to keep her seat. Her skirts were kilted nearly to her knees as she leaned low over the horse's neck. The stirrups were too long for her, so she had abandoned them altogether, staying in the saddle by the pressure of her knees alone. Her hair had come uncoiled, flapping behind her like a triumphal pennant in the breeze of her passage.

As he drew closer, riding for all he was worth, he realized that the sound she was making wasn't screaming; it was laughter. She was laughing, laughing with the sheer exhilaration of movement and the joy of the ride.

Bathsheba, that traitor, flung back her head and whinnied in equine response, as happy to be ridden as Lady Frederick was to ride.

Women!

Taking pity on him, Lady Frederick reined up, drawing Bathsheba around in a graceful circle to face him. Both women, female and horse, grinned at him for all they were worth.

"No oats for you," said Alex to Bathsheba.

Unrepentant, Bathsheba swiped a hoof through the mud.

"Well?" Lady Frederick demanded, swinging herself lightly to the ground. "What do you say, Captain Reid? Am I to have my oats taken away, too?"

She stumbled slightly as she landed, but that was the only sign of weakness she betrayed. Her cheeks were flushed with the exercise, her amber eyes glinted with mischief, and her red hair stood out all around her like a river of flame. There were streaks on the skirt of her serge dress from the saddle leather, where she had pressed too hard and her bonnet was nothing but a straw-colored splotch half a mile down the road. As Alex watched, she began prospecting for pins in her hair, smoothing the heavy mass away from her face and twisting it into a careless coil.

"That was a damn fool stunt," Alex said shortly, doing his best to disguise the raggedness of his breathing.

Hers appeared entirely unaltered. But, then, she had known she wasn't being run away with, while Alex had been riding hell-for-leather to an entirely unnecessary rescue. So much for dealing with damsels in distress. What about his distress, damn it? What about the food rotting in the heat, the animals getting restless, the—well, something else had to be going wrong. He was sure he would find out as soon as he got Lady Frederick back down the road and into the palanquin where she belonged.

Lady Frederick looked at him from under her lashes. "Only because it was your horse."

There was something infectious about the glint of mischief in her eyes. Alex refused to give way to it.

"On anyone's horse," Alex said sternly, feeling like someone's governess. It wasn't a pleasant sensation. "You don't know the terrain. The road could have been pitted with potholes or studded with nails—"

"Are the roads in India generally studded with nails?"

Alex gave her a look. "You know very well what I meant." What was the use? He had had enough of diplomacy—and governessing. "You can break your own neck if you like," he said bluntly, "but leave my horse out of it."

Lady Frederick wasn't the least bit offended. Patting Bathsheba's neck, she said, "I would sooner break my own neck than harm such a beauty. Admit it. I ride beautifully."

"That little exhibition just cost us a good half hour."

"We'll move much faster if you don't cart me around in a palanquin like a parcel. You'll make up your half hour and more."

"Not when you get sunstroke. You may ride beautifully, Lady Frederick—"

"Ha!" said she triumphantly.

"—but you have no experience with the climate. Or with spending twelve hours a day in the saddle."

Lady Frederick shrugged. "I can manage. And if I don't, on my own head be it."

"Your head isn't the one Wellesley will come after if anything happens to you," said Alex, with some asperity. He turned to look back down the road, where the members of the camp were, according to their temperaments, either craning their necks to enjoy the free show or seizing the opportunity for a last-minute nap. "We should be getting back. We've delayed our start long enough."

"And our five days with Mr. Alexander didn't?" The face she made spoke eloquently of Lady Frederick's opinion of the East India Company's agent in Masulipatam. There was a reason young Henry Russell had nicknamed the agent Old Mother Alexander. The man was as fussy as an old woman and twice as proper. "Were you waiting for more love letters, Captain Reid?"

"Buying tents," he corrected succinctly, snagging Bathsheba's reins and pointedly handing her those of her husband's mount. "And cooking pots and blankets. I doubt you would enjoy sleeping directly on the ground. It tends to be prickly."

Lady Frederick fluttered her lashes at him. "Rather like some individuals of my acquaintance."

Alex had had enough of playing games. "If you're looking for someone to flirt with, Lady Frederick, my father is back in Calcutta."

"I rather thought you might need the practice more than he."

"How very public-spirited of you." Going down on one knee in the dust, Alex cupped his hands for her to mount.

"Oh, that's me, all right," said Lady Frederick airily, swinging up onto Aurangzeb with only the lightest pressure against Alex's hands. It was a fluid, practiced movement, accomplished without any indication of effort whatsoever. "A regular one-woman philanthropic society."

Dusting his hands on his breeches, Alex couldn't resist asking, "Where did you learn to ride like that?"

He doubted it was standard practice for London debutantes.

"I've always ridden," said Lady Frederick, setting her mount in motion with an ease that bore out her words. She looked at him challengingly as he brought his mount into pace with hers. "My grandfather bred horses."

"And he let you ride them?" Bathsheba moved forward easily

enough, but she seemed to cast a wistful look across at Lady Frederick. Brilliant. His horse and his charge were in cabal.

Lady Frederick grinned at a memory only she could see. "There was no 'let' about it."

Alex imagined it would be rather hard to stop Lady Frederick doing anything Lady Frederick wanted to do. His sympathies were with her grandfather.

"I suppose," said Alex resignedly, "that that is your way of telling me you shall be riding whether I like it or not."

"We can bring the palanquin along if you like," said Lady Frederick, generous in victory. "In case you want to use it."

Over the next few days, they made better time than Alex had imagined they would. If Lady Frederick was feeling the strain of the unaccustomed activity, she hid it well, although he saw her wince once or twice when she thought herself unobserved, as she lowered herself into a sitting position in the dining tent.

The dwindling rains of the monsoon fell mostly at night, leaving the roads muddy but the skies clear during the day, casting an eerie mist over the early morning hours through which the cackling calls of monkeys swinging between the palms echoed oddly around them. Lady Frederick did a fair job of maintaining her veneer of bored sophistication, but from time to time Alex would see the façade slip as they passed roadside temples tenanted with many-legged gods and strewn with the remains of recent offerings, or crumbling suttee monuments onto which the images of long-dead warriors and their loyal ladies had been painstakingly carved in rounded relief. She held colloquy with the chattering monkeys from beneath the broad straw hat that had replaced her London bonnet, nearly unseated herself from her horse reaching for a palm gourd, and tucked a blue lotus flower in her hair in the style of the native women they had seen along the route.

Five days into the journey, Alex caught her attempting to make conversation in stilted Hindi with a group of short-skirted villagers, who clearly wanted nothing more than to be allowed to till their cotton fields in peace.

"They don't speak Hindi," Alex said, unsuccessfully trying to hide his grin.

He didn't add that even if they did, they would have had a very hard time trying to make sense of her pronunciation. The grammar that she had been given, produced for the use of British soldiers recently come to India, was not known for its accuracy.

Lady Frederick turned her flushed face to his. Her skin had acquired a golden sheen from the sun, like sunlight on wheat, doubtless from her habit of impatiently shoving her hat back, as she was doing now.

"Then what do they speak?" she demanded, snatching off her hat and fanning her face with it. Crumpled strands of red hair stood out around her face like weeds. She looked a world removed from the creature of moonlight and muslin in Begum Johnson's drawing room.

"Telagu. Besides," he added, the grin breaking free, "even if they did speak Hindi . . ."

Lady Frederick stopped fanning. "What?"

". . . You just told them to 'row harder.' Not exactly applicable, wouldn't you agree?" And with that, he spurred ahead, in the happy assurance of having got the last word.

Lady Frederick cantered up beside him. "How do you say 'good day' in Telagu?"

"Why do you want to know?"

"Because 'row faster' has limited utility."

"You wouldn't say that if you were on a boat," said Alex blandly. There was something oddly enjoyable about talking pure nonsense with Lady Frederick. Obviously a sign that the heat was addling his brain, rather than hers. "And you will be on one soon enough."

"Trying to send me back to Calcutta again, Captain Reid?"

"A boat going in the opposite direction. We need to cross the Krishna. It's generally not a bad crossing, but during the monsoon . . ."

"Dangerous?" asked Lady Frederick.

"Potentially." Under ordinary circumstances, the crossing was not a bad one. Swollen with monsoon waters, the normally placid expanse of river was fiendishly dangerous to cross. "The waters are too deep to be forded just now, so we'll have to ferry everyone across. The animals don't always submit well to that."

Lady Frederick considered for a moment, as though searching for a hidden sting. After a pause, she said, "Let me know what I can do."

"Don't jump in," said Alex.

"Don't be silly," said Lady Frederick, and rode on.

Chapter Five

F reddy stretched his arms out over his head until the joints cracked.
"It will be good to be back in the saddle, eh, old girl?"

"Are you talking to me, or the horse?" inquired Penelope.

Freddy slapped her hard on the rump. "Whichever you prefer."

They were crammed onto the ferry along with their mounts, their
grooms, and their personal servants, waiting to be pulled across to the
other side. They had spent the better part of the day by the banks of the
Krishna, watching as group after group was ferried across the choppy
brown waters by a ferry that was little more than a raft on a pulley.
Some of the animals had put up a bit of a fuss at being herded onto the
rickety wooden conveyance, having to be coaxed and prodded aboard.
Penelope didn't blame them. The river was running fast beneath the
warped planks of the ferry and it smelled vile in the humid heat.

From her vantage point on the ferry, Penelope could see Captain
Reid efficiently dispatching the jumbled mass of men and animals on
the opposite bank, sending groups ahead with tents and provisions to
their next camping stage. She had seen the same scene played out in
variants at every stage of their journey, the creation of order out of
chaos as tents were raised or struck, provisions loaded or unloaded,
and an unwieldy group of more than eighty souls propelled along the
road. By the time she and Freddy reached the next stage, their tent
would be up, their beds laid out, water provided warm for washing,
and their dinner ready to be served.

The prolonged wait by the bank had been too much for Freddy,
who was chafing to get back on horseback. Despite the fact that they

were only halfway across, Freddy's groom—or, if Penelope were trying to be local about it, his syce—held out two cupped hands for Freddy to mount.

"Oughtn't you to wait till we land?" suggested Penelope. The raft didn't strike her as the sturdiest construction, and Aurangzeb, Freddy's mount, stood worryingly near to the edge.

Freddy grabbed hold of the bridle, wedging one booted foot into the stirrup. "Don't be absurd. What can possibly happen?"

As he heaved himself upwards, a loud, cracking noise rent the air. Penelope grabbed on to her own horse's bridle as Buttercup shied at the noise, half-expecting to see the raft coming apart beneath them.

It wasn't the raft that had given way, but Freddy's girth. Freddy teetered for balance, one foot sticking comically up in the air, as his saddle lurched sideways. With an expression of frozen disbelief that would have been amusing under other circumstances, Freddy plummeted sideways, straight at his horrified syce. Seeing the danger too late, his syce made a belated and futile attempt to back out of the way.

It was like watching dominos, very large, very human dominos. Freddy slammed straight into the syce's shoulder, sending him toppling backwards off the edge of the raft into the churning waters of the Krishna. Freddy landed heavily on his stomach on the deck, blinking as he tried to get the air back into his lungs.

"Oh no," said Penelope involuntarily, a statement that did nothing at all to rectify the fact that the groom's head appeared to be heading below, rather than above, the muddy waters.

Still flat on the deck, Freddy winced as he gingerly flexed his back. There were cries and exclamations and whinnying of horses. Penelope didn't wait to see what they might do. Unhooking Buttercup's lead, she tied it hastily around her waist, cinching the knot into security.

"Here," she said, thrusting the other end at her bewildered spouse. "Hold this." And without stopping to think, she plunged into the turgid waters of the Krishna.

It was colder than she had thought it would be, colder and choppier. Penelope came up sputtering, spitting out foul-tasting water, flavored with silt and crocodile dung and goodness only knew what else.

The lead yanked painfully against her lower ribs. Thank God Freddy was holding firm. Either that, or he had handed it to someone else who was. Penelope didn't bother to check.

Ahead of her, she saw a flash of something pale against the dark waters, a hand briefly rising above the surface. She tried to strike out in that direction, but her sodden skirts tangled in her legs, pulling her down. It was all she could do to stay above water herself. Bloody clothes. Whatever would Freddy tell them back home when he tried to explain how he had so quickly become a widower?

The lead jerked her upright again as she started to go under. Penelope flailed with both her arms against the water for traction as she scanned for that disappearing burst of human flesh.

There it was, a hank of sodden white cloth beginning to turn as brown as the water. Penelope grabbed blindly at the struggling figure in front of her, grasping at cloth and missing.

"Grab on to me!" she shouted, but the water was loud in her ears and her own voice sounded dim to her, choked with water and interrupted by a fit of coughing.

Striking out again, she got cloth, a good handful of cloth, and held on for all she was worth, hoping she wasn't accidentally choking the man in the process. That would be a fine kettle of fish, to save him from drowning only to strangle him with the collar of his own robe.

Raising her other arm, Penelope signaled wildly in the direction of the boat. At least, she hoped she was signaling at the boat. Stinging sprays of water clouded her vision, reducing the whole of her world to the buffeting of the waves and the dead weight yanking against the cloth in her hands.

The rope jerked hard against her ribs, knocking the wind out of her, but at least she was moving, propelled back against the current of the water. Fumbling with the floating folds of his robe, Penelope managed to grab the drowning man beneath the armpits, yanking him up against her chest as she let herself be hauled back, making sure his head stayed above water.

Penelope thought vaguely that now she knew how a fish on a line must feel, as the rope jerked her backwards in unsteady strokes. The man in her arms was completely inert, his head lolling back against her chest, his beard like a trickle of ink along his robe. Penelope couldn't tell whether he was still breathing. The slap of the water, buoying them up and down, made it hard to gauge.

Someone reached down and heaved her burden away from her, while a pair of ungentle hands grasped her under the armpits and hauled her up over the edge. Penelope lay gasping for air like a fish in a net. For the moment, nothing mattered but the glorious working of her lungs, in and out. No one had bothered to untie the lead, and she could feel it seizing against her ribs as her lungs expanded with air. Such a lovely thing, breathing. Somewhere nearby, she could hear choking and sputtering going on as someone worked over the syce, pumping the water out of his lungs.

A large face hove into view over her. Funny, how bizarre a man's features could look turned upside down. But there was no mistaking him. Penelope wondered vaguely if it was he who had reeled her in and, even more vaguely, when it was that the boat had docked.

"When I said I wouldn't jump in the water," Penelope managed to get out, with a shadow of her usual bravado, "I hadn't thought that someone else might do it first."

Bravado wasn't quite so easy when one was flat on one's back.

But Captain Reid didn't tax her with it. Instead, he held out a hand, helping her to a sitting position.

"Are you all right?" he asked, squatting down beside her.

"A little damp"—Penelope experimentally shook her wrists, splattering the deck with fat drops of water—"but otherwise tip-top."

Her voice was hoarse, but still recognizably her own. Penelope luxuriated in the sensation of good, hard wooden planks beneath her backside, splinters and all, sun-warmed and solid. A sudden thought struck her.

"Are the horses all right?" she asked anxiously.

Captain Reid choked on a laugh. "Perfectly," he said. "Far better than you. Do you think you can stand?"

"Of course," said Penelope, with more confidence than she felt.

Her legs felt about as stable as undercooked soufflé, but she took the hand he offered her, making a show of shaking out her soaking skirts as a pretense to hide the fact that she wasn't quite as steady on her legs as she ought to be. Water dripped down the folds of her skirt and pooled around her legs, leaving puddles on the planks. Her hair dripped in sodden clumps down her back, the majority of her hairpins being currently engaged in bobbing their way down the river. Penelope thought inconsequentially that she did seem to lose a great many hairpins where Captain Reid was involved.

Blinking against the water trickling down from her hairline, Penelope dashed the back of her hand against her eyes.

Without comment, Captain Reid handed her a very large, very white handkerchief.

Penelope applied it to her face. "I would have used my own," she explained rather indistinctly, "but . . ."

"No need," said Captain Reid, as Penelope finished mopping her face with his handkerchief, which was no longer so white nor so tidy as it had been a moment before. "I understand perfectly."

The handkerchief had been marked in one corner with his initials. Instead of thread, the monogram had been lovingly stitched with strands of reddish brown hair, threaded again and again to satiny thickness against the white cambric. It was a terribly intimate sort of thing, hair, the sort of present one made only to a family member or a lover.

Penelope crumpled the handkerchief in one hand.

"Where is Freddy?" she asked crisply. "Lord Frederick, I mean."

"Safely on shore. Mehdi Yar broke his fall," Captain Reid added dryly.

"Who? Oh—Freddy's groom." It had never occurred to her to ask his name before she jumped into the water after him. He had been just a body in the water to be hauled in again. At home, the coachman was always called John, regardless of his real name, just as Cook was always Cook, whatever Cook might have been before she became Cook.

It was, thought Penelope, rather impressive that Captain Reid should know the groom's name, out of a camp so large as theirs. He had engaged most of the servants and handlers who were to see to their comfort on the voyage, but the syce, along with Freddy's valet, his cook, and Penelope's ayah, had come with them from Calcutta.

"You didn't even know who he was, but you jumped into the Krishna after him."

"You make it sound like it's strange," complained Penelope. "Someone had to do it. And I rather felt like a swim." She tried to toss her hair, but it clung damply to the back of her dress and refused to comply.

Captain Reid eyed her approvingly. "They should make you an honorary member of the Zuffir Plutun."

Penelope looked at him suspiciously. That was the problem with foreign terms; it was so hard to tell if one had just been insulted. "The what?"

"The . . ." Captain Reid cast about for a translation. "I suppose you would call it the Victorious Battalion. They're the Nizam's women's regiment, brilliant in battle and completely fearless. A sort of latter-day Amazon."

An Amazon. Penelope rather liked the sound of that. It sounded so much better than "impossible hoyden," "unnatural girl," or any other of her mother's preferred terms for describing her sporting proclivities.

Penelope hid her pleasure behind an arched brow. "Was that a compliment, Captain Reid?"

"It was intended as one. Whether you choose to take it as such is entirely up to you. Ah," Captain Reid stepped aside, making way for a bedraggled figure in a silt-striped white muslin robe. "I believe someone else desires a moment of your company."

Mehdi Yar had lost his turban, and his hair stood up damply around his head. On the other hand, he was breathing, which Penelope took as a personal accomplishment.

Apparently, so did he.

"Sahiba," he said, bowing low before her, "I owe you a great debt."

"Nonsense," said Penelope bracingly, acutely conscious of her straggling hair and sodden dress and Captain Reid's watching over her shoulder. "Anyone would have done the same."

"Would they?" murmured Captain Reid. Penelope frowned at him over her shoulder. It was like having a fly in one's ear. A fly too large to swat properly.

"But you did," said the syce, who appeared to incline to Captain Reid's view of the world. Matter-of-factly, as though he were offering her a cup of tea at a church bazaar, he said, "My life and my honor are yours."

With one last inclination of his head over his joined hands, he melted away to his place among the horses.

"Well," said Penelope brightly to Captain Reid, trying to make light of it, "I can't imagine where I'll put them. Do you think they'll show to good advantage on my mantelpiece?"

"He means it, you know. You saved his life."

"I only speeded the process. We weren't that far from shore. He might have made it there on his own."

"'Might.' It's not the same as 'would.' A man prefers not to deal in maybes when his existence is on the line."

Penelope made a slight snorting sound.

Calmly appropriating her arm, Captain Reid led her off the ferry and onto the bank, where her own syce waited with her mare. "I wouldn't brush it off so lightly if I were you. You might want to call in that debt someday."

There was water still jiggling around between her ears. Angling her head to one side, Penelope banged at one ear with the flat of her hand. "Whatever for?"

"It never hurts to have friends, Lady Frederick."

It might have just been the echo of the water in her ears, but there was something very odd in Captain Reid's voice.

Stumbling against her sodden skirt, Penelope frowned up at him. "Are you telling me that I have something to fear?"

He considered the question for a moment too long.

Penelope wished she could crack that impassive façade like an egg-shell, to see what was going on beneath.

"Not from me," he said at last.

Penelope made a face at him. "I didn't think I had."

But that wasn't entirely true, was it? With some difficulty, she managed to get her soggy self onto Buttercup, refusing Captain Reid's suggestion of the palanquin. Freddy, of course, had already gone on ahead, too flown at the delight of being on horseback again to wait for his sopping wet wife.

For all that she enjoyed Captain Reid's deadpan way with an insult, she hadn't allowed herself to forget that he, as well as his employer, was under investigation by the Governor General's office. A man could quip and quip and quip and still remain a villain.

Freddy had only fallen ill once they had embarked from Calcutta with Captain Reid. It was also rather curious that Captain Reid had known the name of Freddy's syce, in a camp of quite so many people. Nearly as curious as Freddy's syce urging Freddy to mount while on a crowded ferry in the middle of a river, a course of action that spoke, at best, of an extreme lack of common sense, or, at worst, of malicious intent. The Captain had received letters in Masulipatam; Penelope had seen him thrust them into his waistcoat pocket. Could they have been orders from the Resident of Hyderabad, instructing him to dispatch Wellesley's spy en route?

On the other hand, girths had been known to fray and snap of their own accord, and Freddy's saddle had taken its fair share of abuse over the past week. One would expect his groom to notice any significant wear and tear while saddling the beast, but Freddy, as was his way, had been decidedly importunate about having his horse saddled quickly, damn it, and no dawdling about it. And Penelope had had a good deal of opportunity to observe the Captain over the past few days. She rather doubted that a man of Captain Reid's efficiency would go about trying to dispatch someone in such a bungling way.

A stomach ailment and a broken girth. Neither of those in themselves was the least bit remarkable. Taken together, the whole thing smelled decidedly fishy, and it wasn't just the remnant of river water trickling down from her hair.

The object of Penelope's solicitude, however, appeared to be feeling decidedly less solicitous of her. Freddy was lying in wait for Penelope when she arrived back in camp, standing outside their tent with a cheroot that he crushed out as soon as she slid off her horse.

Penelope couldn't blame Freddy for wrinkling his nose at the sight of her. She longed for nothing more than dry linen and a hot bath, not necessarily in that order. Her damp clothes itched abominably and her hair smelled as though a crocodile had died in it.

But it wasn't the eau de crocodile clinging to her person that was driving a furrow into Freddy's brow.

"You won't be able to go on like this once we get to Hyderabad, you know," said Freddy, following her into the tent.

Plopping down onto a camp stool, Penelope vigorously wrung out her hair. "Like what?" asked Penelope, even though she knew very well what he meant.

Freddy took a hasty step back as foul-smelling droplets spattered his shiny boot tops. "Like—this." He made a quick, impatient gesture that took in her sopping hair, her rumpled, river-stained skirt. "Riding astride. Jumping into rivers after grooms. There'll be people there."

"I only jumped after him because *you* fell on him." Shifting on her seat, Penelope shot her husband an incredulous look. "There must be a hundred people in the camp. What do you call all of them? Fairies?"

Freddy was not amused. "*English* people," he specified. "People who will have certain expectations of behavior."

Penelope looked at him from under her lashes, striking where she knew it would hurt. "To bow to other people's expectations is too, too frightfully bourgeois. I'm surprised at you, Freddy."

Standing over her, his hands on his hips, Freddy regarded her with baffled irritation. "Must everything be an argument, Pen?"

Beneath the irritation, he looked tired, almost as tired as she was. All she had to do was hold out a hand, smile at him, lift up her face to be kissed, and it would all be forgotten. At least, this particular argument would be. It was, she knew, as much of an olive branch as Freddy was capable of offering.

Penelope lifted both her shoulders in a shrug. "If you insist on making it so."

Freddy folded his arms across his chest, looking down his not-quite-Norman nose at her. "You promised to obey."

"You promised to love. We both said a lot of silly things at that altar. And, no," she added, as his eyes slid down from her face in a direction she knew all too well, "making love doesn't count."

Stung, Freddy's head snapped up. "That's not what you thought last winter."

Penelope arranged her face along familiar lines of bored sophistication. "I was under the influence of mistletoe. What was your excuse?"

"Insanity," Freddy said shortly, and stalked out beneath the flap of the tent.

As the canvas flap slapped shut behind him, Penelope pressed her balled fists to her forehead. That had not been wise. She could hear Henrietta's *Oh, Pen* in a ghostly whisper across a thousand miles of ocean.

Her bruised ribs chafed against the still-damp material of her dress. Her skin was raw from where the rope had rubbed repeatedly against her. Her whole body felt battered and buffeted and drained of all energy. It had been silly to insist on riding from the river to the camp. She ought to have taken the offer of the palanquin and dozed her way to camp.

Perhaps Freddy was right and she oughtn't to have jumped into the river in the first place.

But, then, who would have? Penelope rested her elbows against her knees, propping her head in her hands, her damp hair falling straight around her face, screening the world in red. It never curled unless she curled it, stick-straight and as much of a disappointment to her mother as everything else about her.

She was tired, so tired, tired and soggy and drained, and all she wanted was someone to put a warm blanket around her shoulders and hug her close. Back in London, the last time she had careened into a large body of water, Henrietta had been there, to comb out her hair and hug and scold her and tell her she was an idiot and bring her tea and want to know what exactly the water of the Serpentine tasted like, all in the same breath. There had been a proper bed with proper blankets and a maid coming in to tend the fire and Lady Uppington bustling about with disgusting smelling possets, which Penelope had poured out into the chamber pot as soon as she wasn't looking. Lady Uppington had wanted to know what the Serpentine had tasted like, too, although only after delivering a proper maternal lecture on the follies of driving other people's curricles into large bodies of water. So much love and so much care and all of it so very far away.

With difficulty, Penelope worked free the buttons on the short jacket of her riding habit. The wet fabric clung stubbornly to her arms, tailored too close for convenience. She peeled it painfully off, sleeve by sleeve, every movement feeling like a minor battle. The blue dye had soaked through to the cambric shirt below, and the once-white fabric clung bluely to her skin, like the painted pelt of a Pictish princess.

She had gone as Boadicea to a masquerade last Season, brandishing a spear and thirsting for the opportunity to drive a chariot into battle, rather like—what was it that Captain Reid had called her?—an Amazon.

Penelope didn't feel much like a warrior maiden at the moment.

It was bloody tiring being so fractious all the time. Had Boadicea ever felt tired? Worn out? Unhooking the suspenders that held up her riding skirt, Penelope let the weight of the wet wool drag it to the floor, leaving her clammy and blue in her chemise. The hand mirror revealed that not only was she vaguely blue, but she had streaks of dirt across her face and there was mud caked in her hair. She didn't look like Lady Frederick Staines, consort of the new Envoy to the Court of Hyderabad, or even like the dashing Miss Penelope Deveraux, scourge of the London Season. Snarl-haired and hollow-eyed in her discolored chemise, she looked like the less-prosperous class of harlot.

What had possessed her to pick a fight with Freddy just now?

Penelope spat on a handkerchief, scrubbing the square of cloth against a streak of dried mud on one cheek. It was just so irresistible when he was so . . . well, Freddy. But he was all she had here, stranded in the middle of a strange land with unfamiliar birds chattering around her head and flowers to which she couldn't give names unfurling unfamiliar blossoms on curiously shaped trees.

Shrugging into a light muslin dress and flinging a shawl over it against the dropping temperatures of the evening, Penelope poked her head out of the flap of the tent. Cotton fields lay to one side, the Musi River to the other. Penelope could already see the dots of dozens of cook fires reflecting eerily off the waters of the river, like Chinese lanterns in a garden. From the bank came the muted sound of mealtime conversations, as foreign as the scent of the rice and spices steeping in the pot-bellied pots. By the makeshift paddock, the hamals had lit a great fire of cotton scrub to keep the flies from the horses. The smoke grimed the evening air, blending with the falling dusk, creating shadows against shadows.

"Freddy," she called softly, but no one answered.

It didn't take much imagination to guess where he might have gone. Either he had grabbed up his gun and tramped off into the brush to see what he could shoot as a way of soothing his wounded feelings, or he would have made for the sepoy encampment, where the guard that made up part of their escort lay. Lieutenant Breese, their commanding officer, had only an East India Company commission. Under normal circumstances, Freddy might have been inclined to snub him. But in a party in which Englishmen were scarce, he was still an officer and a gentleman—of sorts—and thus good enough to play cards with.

Unless, of course, something else had befallen Freddy. There was that broken girth. . . .

Moving with more haste than grace, Penelope threaded her way towards the sepoy encampment on the very edge of their camp. Through the canvas of the largest tent, she thought she could see the outline of two men at a table, a bottle between them. Freddy and Lieutenant Breese? Most likely.

For a moment, Penelope stood staring at their silhouettes, caught between relief and irritation. To think she had always mocked Charlotte for having too loose a grasp on reality! That was what she got for letting her imagination run away with her. Freddy in danger, indeed. Freddy getting foxed, more like. More fool she, to come running out like an avenging Amazon to defend his person against miscellaneous malefactors. He neither needed nor wanted her for that. Or for anything else, save what could be found between the sheets.

Penelope's head throbbed and the shadow images in the tent seemed to shimmer against the canvas.

Too much river water, she told herself. Too much heat and exertion. She was just plain worn out, and that was the only reason she felt a completely inexplicable impulse to sit down in the cotton scrub and cry. It was nothing more than physical weakness, and a good night's sleep would put her right as rain again, like a toddler who had spent the day too much in the sun and needed to be put to bed.

Penelope gathered her skirt to turn back, but the hanging branch of an acacia tree scratched across her arm, tangling in her shawl. Penelope yanked at the fabric, not caring what she tore, just so long as she got away before Freddy saw her standing there, like some pathetic waif in the night, or a dog left outside its master's door. Blast it! Penelope tugged, but the fabric was as stubborn as she was, clinging to its twig like an eloping heiress to her lover. Muttering nasty things under her breath, Penelope changed tactics, fumbling at the fabric with impatient fingers, trying to disengage it from whatever malevolent collection of splinters was holding it fast.

"Do you need help?" asked a now-familiar voice.

The branch sprang free, releasing the scent of fresh flowers into the damp night air.

"I'm quite all right on my own," said Penelope stiffly, grateful for the darkness that hid the damp blue chemise beneath her too-thin frock and the appalling condition of her hair. She shouldn't have been surprised at his appearance. Captain Reid had an unsettling talent for being everywhere she didn't want him to be. She yanked her shawl firmly over her shoulders, knotting it to keep it from going astray. "As you can see."

"Of course," said Captain Reid, and she hated him for it, hated him for having caught her unprepared, hated him for being kind. Such kindness wasn't a gift but a goad, scraping against one's skin like a yoke of thorns. She would have preferred him stiff, defensive, even offensive. "Shall I see you back to your tent?"

Penelope bristled at the implied criticism, all the more infuriating for being justified. It was not the brightest thing to wander about alone at night in a camp of eighty men and miscellaneous beasts. Not that she would ever admit that to Captain Reid. "In case tigers attack me over the next ten yards?" she said belligerently.

"Merely as a courtesy," he said mildly, and she felt doubly shamed. "But if you know your own way . . ."

Penelope fought back with the only weapon in her arsenal. Her voice was as cloyingly sweet as the flowering branch and just as thorny as she looked up at him from under her lashes. "Will you miss me if I get lost along the way, Captain Reid?"

Captain Reid stepped back, as clear a rejection as a slap across the face. "I'm sure your husband would," he said stiffly.

In Lieutenant Breese's tent, the shadow Freddy reached for a card, kicking back in his chair to stare at his hand with the sort of intensity he never reserved for her. Not since last December, at any rate.

Penelope's laughter etched acid across the evening air. "I wouldn't wager on that, Captain Reid. And, no," she added bitingly, "you needn't see me back."

Without waiting for his response, she made a full turn and stomped off in the direction of her own tent. She ought, she supposed, to make an effort, to sway her hips or toss her hair, but it didn't seem worth it. Captain Reid might respect her Amazonian tendencies, but he had made quite clear he had no use for her in any other way. It was a bizarre and baffling turn of events, and one that Penelope had no interest in analyzing. One could only accept so much rejection in one evening.

Even so, she was very aware of Captain Reid's shadow in the lee of the acacia tree, watching her safely back to her tent.

Chapter Six

Watching Lady Frederick pick her way back across the camp, Alex was aware of an unexpected and inconvenient emotion: pity.

It didn't do to feel sorry for Lady Frederick. It didn't take the stiff set of her back to tell him that she wouldn't be grateful to him for it. What did he have to pity her for, after all? Her earrings alone would pay his salary for a year. It was senseless to dwell on the waste of it, a clever woman married to a lout of a husband. She had chosen her lout. And Alex had other responsibilities.

Pushing away from the tree trunk, Alex headed determinedly in the other direction, away from the camp. It had been, he told himself briskly, a bit of luck that Lady Frederick had been too distracted to demand where he was going in the middle of the night. And she would have. Alex's lips curved in the ghost of a grin. Oh, that she would.

Leaving the camp behind, Alex skirted the edge of the road they had traversed earlier that day. It was a well-traveled road, and there were other parties who had made shift for themselves for the night by the water of the river Musi, eschewing the dubious comforts of the nearest *dak-gharis* or caravanserai. Across the river, a troupe of Brinjarees, the ubiquitous grain merchants of India, had camped with their herd for the night, while farther along a party of Dutch jewelers from Masulipatam had paused on their journey to the fabled diamond market of Hyderabad.

Among all these travelers, the tent of a local nobleman, however large and well-appointed, was scarcely worth noting. The others in the column had ridden past without giving it a second glance. As Alex approached, a man emerged from the tent to lounge decoratively by its side. He might have stepped out of a Persian painting, fair complexioned and dark haired, with a small, thin mustache, dressed in a richly figured robe banded with pearls at the wrist and forearms. On his head, he wore a jaunty silk cap with a single curling feather. All that was missing was a hookah in one hand.

It wasn't a costume. Tajalli Ali Khan was exactly what he purported to be, which made his choice as messenger all the more brilliant.

"How fortunate," said Tajalli cheerfully, "that our paths should cross like this just as I return from acquiring a new falcon."

"Liar," said Alex, embracing his friend in the local fashion. "Did James send you?"

"Of course," said Tajalli. Extracting something from the folds of one sleeve, he handed over a small, rolled scroll of paper. "He sent you this."

Alex didn't need to unroll it to know that it would be in code. James might trust Tajalli, but only so far. It wasn't a slight; he only trusted anyone so far. The courts of India were rife with espionage and counterespionage, with everyone from the rulers to the British residents keeping his own stables of spies. Despite all their vigilance, Alex knew that they had informers among the Residency staff, just as their own informers were sprinkled through the household of the Nizam, the First Minister, and the major players in the durbar. Ever since a disconcerting experience during which key documents had reached their enemies before reaching Calcutta, James had been very careful to put almost everything in code.

"I did get that falcon, though," Tajalli added blandly, as Alex neatly palmed the small scroll of paper. "Wait till you see her. You'll be sick with envy."

"Until I win her off you."

"I'd like to see you try."

The two friends grinned at each other in perfect harmony.

Their backgrounds could not have been more dissimilar. The son of a Hyderabadi nobleman, Tajalli could trace his lineage straight back to the Prophet. He had been raised to be exactly what he was, the consummate courtier, quick to turn a phrase, fearless at the hunt, at ease with pomp in a way Alex could never be. He had never experienced the hardscrabble life of an army camp, never had to worry about preferment or advancement, never turned his purse inside out to find it empty. It gave Tajalli no pause to spend on a single night's entertainment what Alex earned in a year. That new falcon had probably set him back a pretty penny, more than Alex could ever countenance spending on a whim.

Yet they were friends, and had been friends since the first month of Alex's appointment in Hyderabad, when they had found themselves flung together on a cheetah hunt hosted by the Resident. Alex admired his friend's insouciant ease of manner, even while he knew he could never hope to emulate it.

"I'm surprised you didn't bring a few elephants, while you were at it," said Alex, looking pointedly at the gaudy tent. "Or maybe a few dancing girls to strew roses in your path?"

"I'm being inconspicuous by being conspicuous," retorted Tajalli. They spoke court Persian, the lingua franca of the aristocratic Mughal world, which had the additional bonus of being unlikely to be understood by any of the servants, sepoys, or miscellaneous followers of either of their camps. "Can you really see me disguised as a servant?"

Alex looked at Tajalli. Even had he been wearing a plain cotton *jama* and speaking Urdu, his friend would never be able to pass as anything but what he was. The set of his shoulders and the angle of his head marked him for what he was as surely as did the pearl bracelet on his wrist.

"No," Alex said bluntly. "You'd stand out like an elephant in a herd of cattle. What made you volunteer to play messenger boy for Kirkpatrick?"

Tajalli spread both hands in a gesture that gave the appearance of responding while indicating absolutely nothing at all. It also showed the rings on his fingers to excellent advantage. "I was bored. It's been damnably tedious with you away these past few weeks."

Alex suspected there was more to it than that, but he decided to bide his time. Tajalli would tell him when he was good and ready.

"Poor you," said Alex, peeling back the tent flap and ducking under. "Nothing but hunting and nautch girls to while away the empty hours."

"It's a damnable shame," agreed Tajalli, giving him a slight push to speed him along. "Look who else I've brought to greet you."

A figure moved in the dim interior of the tent, rising off the piles of rugs and cushions that Tajalli considered essential for even the briefest of jaunts.

"George!" exclaimed Alex.

"Surprised you, didn't I?" said his brother with evident satisfaction. The elaborately pierced lamp picked out the copper tints in his hair, part of George's legacy from their father. "I knew you wouldn't expect me."

Alex hadn't, but he was damnably glad to see him. He thumped his brother on the back in greeting. "Shouldn't you be in Sardhana? How did you persuade the Begum to give you leave?"

George's eyes shifted away. "It's not 'leave' precisely. The Begum had an errand she wanted me to run in this part of the world."

"And you're not happy about it." George had always been an open book. At least, he gave the impression of being so, an impression that was frequently very useful to him, especially in his dealings with women. It was, Alex thought, as much a part of his legacy from their father as his coppery hair and Scots blue eyes.

It was a legacy that had passed Alex entirely by. He took after his mother's side, dark-complexioned Welsh preachers with stiff spines and morals to match.

George grinned at him. "Something like that," he admitted. "I'll tell you what I can of it."

"I wouldn't ask for more," said Alex, and meant it. "Don't tell me anything that might come back to bite you."

Now that the Begum Sumroo was bound by treaty to the British, their interests were theoretically in alignment, but Alex knew it would take only a moment to change that. If George were to be caught ferrying information to the British side, his life could be forfeit. Any confidence that might endanger his little brother wasn't worth knowing.

It was a damnable situation they were in. Beginning when George was just out of swaddling clothes, a series of orders had come down from the Governor General's office, disqualifying anyone with an Indian parent from serving in the East India Company's army. With his Rajput mother, George was banned by his birth from joining his father's regiment, forced to seek service instead as a mercenary in the employ of a native ruler.

It never ceased to amaze Alex that George seemed to bear no resentment at all against his father or his father's people for the restrictions they had placed upon him for no greater fault than an accident of birth. Alex resented it for him. It was one of the reasons that Alex had decided to leave the Madras Cavalry. It didn't feel right to belong to a force that wouldn't take his own flesh and blood, simply because the blood ran darker on one side. Even that was a misnomer. George was fairer than he was and always had been, from the moment he had bounced into the world. He had been a fat, fair, chuckling baby with a cap of red curls that had gradually darkened to the color of an antique shield as he grew from a toddler's dress into boots and breeches.

The situation had gone from merely offensive to actively dangerous the year before, when George's employer, the Begum Sumroo, had joined with her overlord, Scindia, against the British. Scindia had slaughtered those British-bred mercenaries still in his pay at the start of the conflict. The Begum Sumroo, loyal to her own—and with an eye for a good-looking young man—had refused to take such drastic measures, but George's position had been an uncomfortable one, exposed to suspicion and resentment from his messmates in the Begum's camp, forced to maintain a distance from his family.

Despite it all, he had maintained his sunny disposition. George was and would always be George.

Unlike Jack.

George plopped down onto a silk-covered cushion. "I got your letter from Calcutta right before I left the Begum. How *is* the new Special Envoy to the Nizam?"

"As awful as anticipated," admitted Alex. Making a comical face, he added, "Today, he fell on his groom and knocked him into the river."

"On purpose?" asked Tajalli with interest.

"No, by accident."

Tajalli made a scornful, snorting noise.

"Had he done it on purpose, it would have been rather clever," said Alex thoughtfully. "The groom is a plant from Calcutta, one of Wellesley's men. I'm sure of it."

"Sent to keep an eye on—what is his name?"

"Lord Frederick," Alex provided. "Or Freddy, as his wife calls him. No, I don't think so. Lord Frederick is exactly what he seems and not worth the watching, either by Calcutta or anyone else. I do wonder if the point of sending Lord Frederick was less about Lord Frederick, and more a means of getting Wellesley's man into the Residency to keep an eye on James. Again," he added darkly.

"So you think the groom is the real spy?" asked Tajalli.

"Maybe yes, maybe no. It might as easily be the cook, the valet, or Lady Frederick's ayah. All of them were hand-picked by Wellesley's staff."

George leaned forward on his cushion. "What do you think of Lady Frederick?" he asked.

Alex smelled a rat. "Did Father write you?"

"No," demurred George, at his most guileless. If his eyes opened any wider, they would be in danger of popping right out. "Why?"

"Never mind," said Alex. "Lady Frederick is . . . not what I expected."

That was the understatement of the century.

"Worse?" asked George with an irrepressible grin.

"Different," said Alex, with great finality. "But you didn't come to meet me just to ask me about my trip. What's going on?"

His brother and his best friend exchanged a long look. "You start," said George generously.

"No, no," demurred Tajalli. "It really begins with you."

"For the love of God," intervened Alex. "I don't care who tells it as long as someone does."

"So impatient," complained Tajalli, with a wag of his head.

"Always," agreed George. "Never takes the time to sit back and smell the frangipani."

"That's because I was too busy looking after you lot," said Alex with some asperity. "What is it?"

Leaning back against his cushions, George steepled his hands together at the fingertips in the classic pose of the storyteller.

"You've heard of the Rajah of Berar's treasure, of course," he began importantly.

"You mean the hoard he claims disappeared at the siege of Gawilighur last December? Everyone's heard that tale." Heard it, looked for it, failed to find it. Wellesley had had teams of soldiers combing the fort, and Alex suspected more than one soldier had done a little unauthorized treasure hunting of his own. Not a rupee had been found. "It's a classic fairy story. All it wants is a dragon."

There it was again, that look, a look from his brother to his friend, the sort of look that said they knew something he didn't know.

Alex folded his arms across his chest. "What?" he demanded.

"It's not a fairy story," said Tajalli. "At least, someone claims it's not."

George leaned forward, so that the light of the lantern fell across his face, illuminating the bone structure that was so uncannily like their father's. "Someone sent a message to the Begum Sumroo offering her a tenth part of the Rajah of Berar's treasure if she would break her treaty with the British and join in a new alliance against the British."

"A new alliance with whom? Holcar?" To be fair, the northern Mahratta leader appeared to being doing pretty well against the British all on his own.

"Not just Holcar," said George seriously. "The entire Mahratta Confederacy. And Hyderabad."

"That's nonsense," said Alex reflexively. "The Nizam would never—"

He broke off, suddenly unsure of the truth of what he had been about to say. The Hindu Mahrattas had always been to the Islamic state of Hyderabad what the French were to the English, a constant threat upon their borders, to be neutralized with defensive diplomacy when not being pushed off by force of arms. It was largely due to the Mahratta threat that the British even had a military foothold in Hyderabad; the old Nizam having treated with the British for a military force to protect his domains against his Marathi neighbors.

But the recent war had changed all that. The Maratha Confederacy was—at least momentarily—broken. The new threat to Hyderabad's sovereignty was no longer the Marathi. It was the British.

"Exactly," said Tajalli, watching as Alex's mouth clamped shut. "The new Nizam isn't the old one."

"And Mir Alam isn't Aristu Jah," Alex agreed. The new First Minister might once have been a friend of the British, but a combination of exile and leprosy had twisted his mind and his allegiances. "Fine. I see your point. For the sake of argument, let's say that someone is trying to broker an alliance between the Marathi and Hyderabad against the British. Who's at the heart of it? Holcar? Scindia?"

George shifted on his cushion, looking uncomfortable. "It's unclear who he represents," he admitted reluctantly. "Whoever it is calls himself the Marigold."

"The *Marigold*?" repeated Alex.

"As in the flower," provided George helpfully. "He signs his notes with a rather attractive little orange flower. It's actually quite well drawn. Very detailed."

"You must be joking."

"It isn't a joke," protested George, with all a little brother's indignation at not being taken seriously. "It's a conspiracy."

"Of flowers."

"No, just run by a flower," said Tajalli, with his usual irrepressible good humor. "It is rather amusing, isn't it? But perhaps that's what this Marigold wants, to amuse us into a false sense of security. Who would be afraid of a gentle blossom?"

"It's not even poisonous," agreed Alex in disgust. "What sort of alias is that?"

"The alias of a clever man who wants us to think he's not," suggested Tajalli.

"Or a clever woman," pointed out George, who worked for one. "Don't underestimate the zenana."

Alex felt that they were rather straying from the point. "Or someone who just likes to draw flowers. If this . . . *Marigold* approached the Begum Sumroo, I imagine he must also have made contact with someone in Hyderabad." The pieces clicked neatly into place. He looked hard at Tajalli. "That's where you come into it, isn't it? That's why you volunteered to play messenger."

Tajalli made a resigned face. "Naturally. The Marigold sent my father a very nice ring as a token of his esteem."

"In exchange for—?"

"My father's influence with the other members of the durbar. At least, so far as I know. I am not," he said, and Alex glimpsed a hint of something steely behind his friend's pleasant mask, "exactly in my father's confidence."

"If you were," said Alex, with an equal measure of steel, "you would not be here."

Tajalli inclined his head in acknowledgment of the point. His father, Ahmed Ali Khan, had been one of the most vociferous supporters of the French faction at the Nizam's court during those tense days not so long ago when both the French and the English maintained corps of troops outside the city of Hyderabad, each vying for the Nizam's favor. But Ahmed Ali's political opposition had only reached the level of personal vendetta when news came out of the English Resident's secret marriage to a Hyderabadi lady of quality, Khair-un-Nissa. Apart from his revulsion at a descendant of the Prophet marrying an infidel, Ahmed Ali had a more personal reason to be affronted. Khair-un-Nissa had been promised in marriage to Tajalli's older brother. The girl's marriage to the Resident was an insult that made the Montagues and Capulets look like good neighbors.

Alex sometimes wondered how much his own friendship with Ahmed's son owed to the son's desire to flout his father. He liked to think there was more to it than that, but there were times when he found Tajalli as difficult to decipher as the intricately penned verse on a Persian scroll.

"Whoever it was knew to go to your father," said Alex. "Whoever it was knew that he would be sympathetic."

"He hasn't made any secret of his sympathies." Tajalli held out both hands, palm up. "You know how word travels."

His expression very clearly indicated that further discussion about his father would be unwelcome. Tajalli might be allowed to criticize him, but for an outsider to do was to cross an unwritten line.

Fair enough. Alex felt much the same way about his own father. Turning back to George, he asked, "Did you see this man when he waited upon the Begum?"

"Man, woman, camel—no idea," said George, shaking his head. "The Begum is too canny to allow me near anything like this. Doesn't want to expose me to temptation," he added, with a grin.

"But she trusts you to relay her letters," pointed out Alex.

"All in code," countered George without rancor. "You can't expect her to trust me that far. It's rather nice of her, really, not to put me in positions in which my loyalty would be tested."

"Nice" wasn't quite how Alex would have put it, but he decided to let it go. The Begum Sumroo hadn't risen from dancing girl to ruler of her own state by being nice.

"Fortunately for you," George continued cheerfully, "Fyze doesn't feel at all the same way. She was the one who told me about the orange flowers and all that."

"I see," said Alex slowly. George had for some time had an understanding with one of the Begum's favorites, an association that had served to cement his position in the Begum's court. It helped that George appeared to be genuinely fond of the girl.

Tajalli grinned. "Nicely done."

"It's not like that," protested George, looking hurt. "I wouldn't have asked her if I hadn't thought she would volunteer." Being George, he actually believed it. "She said there was something odd about the syntax of the letters."

"Odd how?" asked Alex.

George squinted at the gaily striped canvas of the tent. "Slightly awkward. As though the writer weren't quite proficient in the language but was trying to sound as though he were. Although," he added, "that could be a result of it having all been mangled into code and back again."

"What language was it written in?"

"Persian," supplied George. It was the official language of the Mughal court, the common tongue of aristocrats and scholars across the Islamic world. It certainly wasn't definitive, but it strengthened Alex's suspicion that the source of the notes was probably Marathi. And why wouldn't it be? Holcar was currently engaged in a struggle against the British; if his resources were secretly failing, he might be looking to drum up allies.

An even more convincing case might be made for Scindia, Britain's primary adversary in the recent Anglo-Maratha war. He would still be smarting from his humiliation at the hands of the British, reluctant to allow Holcar to seize all the glory. Like Scots clans, the Marathi tended to spend their time intriguing against one another as much as their enemies. It would be very like Scindia to attempt to scrape together a new confederacy so that he might complete what Holcar had begun, seizing the leading role for himself.

"Presumably a Marathi, then," said Alex.

"Or a European," suggested Tajalli. "Imperfectly schooled in the language."

"To what end?" demanded Alex. "I don't see what a European would have to gain."

The topaz rings on Tajalli's fingers glinted in the lamplight like Lady Frederick's eyes. "Captain Raymond had grand plans for uniting the states of India against the British."

"Yes, I know. And for handing them off to Bonaparte, all tied up with a pretty bow." Alex dismissed the ambitions of the former French commander in Hyderabad with a wave of his hand. "But Raymond is dead. There's a large mausoleum to prove it. And Piron went back to France with his tail between his legs."

"As far as we know," interjected Tajalli. "He was told to do so and he promised to do so, but what a man may promise and what a man may do may be two very different things."

"Marvelous," muttered Alex. "That would be all we need. French-men lurking about in disguise, modeling themselves after marigolds."

His money was still on Scindia. Raymond and Piron might have made a nuisance of themselves conspiring with other French commanders in India, training large numbers of troops under the revolutionary *tricolore*, and flaunting their Caps of Liberty, but their dreams of conquest had died with Bonaparte's aborted mission to Egypt more than five years before. James had put paid to the French force in Hyderabad and Wellesley had dealt with the rest by treaty, making it a condition of the Marathi leaders' surrender that they dismiss from their service any Frenchman. Despite General Perron still throwing his weight about in the service of Scindia, as far as Alex was concerned, the French threat was long over.

Alex said as much.

"Of course, he might not be French," suggested Tajalli, watching Alex closely. "He might as well be one of your own."

"You mean one of our half-breeds," said Alex flatly, not looking at his brother. "Banned from any useful occupation and out for revenge."

"Do you think Jack—," George began.

"No." The negation was ingrained reflex. "No. What does James say about all this?"

Tajalli smiled at him. "Like you, he says it is a fairy story, a—what was the phrase?—a tempest in a teapot. He does not believe in the Rajah of Berar's gold and he thinks that the Marigold is merely an attempt at agitation, and not a concerted conspiracy of which one should take notice. He had other matters to concern him."

The Special Envoy among them, Alex was sure. Kirkpatrick didn't react well to Wellesley's rooting about in his private life.

For a moment, Alex found himself confronted by the image of the Special Envoy's wife, standing forlornly outside the canvas walls of a tent, while her husband drank and gamed within. Kirkpatrick's wasn't the only private life that didn't bear close examination.

How in the hell had she come to be married to him?

"Alex!"

With the patience for which he was known, his brother poked him in the arm. Hard.

Alex grimaced. "Was that entirely necessary?" he inquired, rubbing the offended appendage.

"You were a million miles away," complained George.

"Not quite that far," said Alex. Just a stretch down the road and a hundred leagues out of his depth.

Chapter Seven

I waited until Colin had gone back to Sussex before calling Mrs. Selwick-Alderly.

I told myself it was because I didn't want to waste any of our time together trawling through old archives, but it wasn't really that. Despite the fact that it was those archives that had brought us together in the first place (well, that and a fair amount of spilled champagne), I didn't want Colin to be my conduit to the Pink Carnation papers. I wanted him to be my boyfriend. The fact that the one had come through the other only made me all the more determined to keep them separate in future.

The weather had repented of its good behavior over the weekend and reverted back to form, a mizzling drizzle that stung my cheeks as it fell. It wanted to be snow when it grew up, but it wasn't quite cold enough for that, so instead it fell in small pellets of icy rain, gray and cold and miserable. I made a mad dash from the South Kensington Tube stop to Onslow Square, my frozen fingers sliding numbly off the buzzer when I tried to press it.

I was a little nervous as to what my reception would be, now that Colin and I were officially an item. Even though it was Mrs. Selwick-Alderly who had put me in his path in the first place, people are funny, especially about things like family. However much she liked me as a perky, independent researcher, she might feel otherwise about me as a girlfriend for her favorite great-nephew. That was another reason I had preferred to come alone, *sans* Colin. We had spoken very briefly on the phone when I had called to ask for advice about matters Indian, but it's always hard to read tone accurately on a telephone, and even more so on a cell phone. If she had deeply disapproved, I imagined she wouldn't have invited me over.

Then again, what if she wanted to take the opportunity to warn me away, like Lady Catherine de Bourgh inviting Lizzy Bennet for a turn in the shrubbery? She, too, had been an aunt. Although, as far as I knew, Mrs. Selwick-Alderly had no daughter she wished to marry off to Colin. I didn't even know if she had a daughter. And if she did, that daughter would be a generation too old for Colin.

Swiping my damp hair off my cheek, I realized I had reached whole new levels of paranoia.

Upstairs, a door opened and a perfectly coiffed white head peered down through the stair rails. "Come along up!" she called gaily.

Maybe Colin hadn't told her.

"Hi!" I called back up, trying to wave and push back my hair all at the same time, which I do not recommend as a technique. My slushy boots skidded on the stairs and I had to clutch at the railing to keep from pitching ignominiously upwards. There's nothing quite like falling up stairs for really embarrassing yourself.

Inside, all was accustomed and ceremonious. In honor of the hideous weather, Mrs. Selwick-Alderly had a fire crackling in the drawing room, beneath the mantel where the picture of Colin that had first caught my interest three long months ago jostled with a beautiful studio portrait of Mrs. Selwick-Alderly in her debutante year, and a cheerful array of other family photos. As always, Mrs. Selwick-Alderly was impeccably dressed, even for a day at home. Her wool blazer was a deep navy, with pretty braiding on the cuff and lapels.

There was no tea tray on the drawing room table this time.

"I had thought you would want to get stuck in right away," said Mrs. Selwick-Alderly knowingly, leading the way past the drawing room and down the long corridor that led to the back bedrooms. I knew that corridor well; I had blundered down it in the dead of night once when Mrs. Selwick-Alderly had kindly put me up.

"Thank you for helping me—again," I said incoherently, as I followed her down the hall.

"It's no bother," she said, leading me into the bedroom in which I had stayed on my first visit. The squat African statue on the dresser beamed at me like an old acquaintance.

Flipping on the light switch, she made for the closet, moving aside a tufted spear that wobbled next to the frame. "It should be in here," she murmured, as she shoved aside a molting mink coat and several dresses swathed in plastic.

I hurried to help her as she dragged out a battered cardboard box. Together, we set it down on the bed. Mrs. Selwick-Alderly tossed a faux leather-bound album onto the cream-colored counterpane. Sending a second album the way of the first, she dove down into the box, the way one does, muttering distractedly to herself.

"Not this one, then," she said firmly, frowning down at the box. "It must be the other box. Oh, bother, that's the phone. If you'll excuse me . . ."

There was no extension in the spare bedroom. I could hear the slap of her flat-heeled shoes as she hurried down the hallway to her study and the click of the study door closing behind her. For a moment, I simply stood as I was, like a schoolgirl left in the headmistress's office, hovering next to the bed, my hands clasped behind my back. The Dresden shepherdess on the dresser smirked at me scornfully.

I stuck out my tongue at her, then glanced guiltily over my shoulder at the open door. No, Mrs. Selwick-Alderly hadn't seen.

Propping myself against the edge of the bed, I reached for one of the discarded albums. They looked like the sort I had delighted in looking through at my grandparents' house, flatter and broader than the ones we use now, with the pictures held to the page by triangular stickies. The worn cover fell open easily, onto a picture of a slender woman in a full-skirted dress smiling from beneath the shade of an exotic-looking tree. It didn't take much work to identify her as a much younger version of my hostess. It helped that the legend underneath read, "Self in Pindi, Fall '45."

I remembered what Serena had said—or had it been Colin?—about Mrs. Selwick-Alderly having been in India right before Indian Independence. It was one thing to hear about it, another to see it played out in pictures, all the day-to-day matters of someone's life, mundane to them, no doubt, but terribly exotic to me. Most of the pictures were labeled with the names of British settlements I only vaguely recognized from M. M. Kaye novels. There was a picture of a very young Mrs. Selwick-Alderly, in a full-skirted frock patterned with roses, seated in front of the Taj Mahal, and another in heavy sweater and slacks, balanced on a pair of very odd-looking skis, labeled, "Self and Dodo, skiing in Kashmir, 1946." Dodo had to be the shorter woman next to her, equally bundled up in scarf and ski cap, and looking like she wasn't entirely sure she wanted to push off down the slope just yet. There were polo matches and tennis parties, tea dances and picnics, "hops" and houseboats. It was all terribly exotic and very far away, the relics of a forgotten world.

Picking up another album, I opened it at random. Okay, I'll admit it, I was looking for pictures of Colin. There was a man in the picture, a tall, broadly built man with a weather-beaten sort of face, but it was the woman you noticed first. She was dressed in clothes I wouldn't have minded owning, tall black boots with a high-necked dress that came down to just below her thighs. Her long straight hair blew back behind her in the wind, reinforcing the impression of movement caused by the lively expression on her fashion-model pretty face. She reminded me of someone, but I couldn't quite place who, unless it was the generic seventies-ness of the image I was responding to, the iconic look of dress, boots, and strong-boned face. The caption underneath read: "William and Caroline, November 1972." The woman's dark blond hair was almost the same color as Colin's.

And then it clicked. I realized who the woman reminded me of. Serena. She had the same elegant cheekbones and long-boned build, but on her, it looked more fashionable than fragile. If Serena was sepia and autumn tones, this woman was primary colors, like watching the remastered version of an old film, suddenly in glowing color.

I examined the photo with new interest. If that was Colin's mother, then the man with her had to be his father, the father who had died of cancer just a few years ago while Colin's mother, from what I gathered, had absconded to Italy with husband number two. He looked considerably older than his wife, although part of that might have been the expression on his face as he looked down at her, all kindly indulgence and not a little bit of bemusement. She wasn't looking at him at all, but at something away, beyond the edge of the photo frame.

"Eloise?"

The album slipped from my hands and I had to make a clumsy grab for it to keep it from falling.

"I'm sorry," I babbled, grappling with the album. "I didn't mean to pry. It was just that—"

"They were there?" My hostess didn't seem annoyed. Her eyes twinkled knowingly. "And I expect you were curious to see what Colin looked like as a little boy."

Tugging at the neck of my turtleneck, I blushed a deep, telling red. "Pretty much," I admitted.

So Colin *had* told her about us, then. Fortunately, she didn't seem to mind.

Taking the album from me, Mrs. Selwick-Alderly's long, elegant hands turned the pages with the ease of ownership. "Colin should be in this one somewhere. Ah, there we are."

There was a tiny, red-faced bundle of baby in the blond girl's arms, squalling at the camera. She was smiling over her shoulder at someone out of the range of the camera, as though entirely unconscious of the blue bundle in her arms, despite the fact that the baby was obviously screaming his lungs out. His face was all screwed up and his mouth wide-open.

"That's Colin's mother?" I said.

Some of what I was thinking must have leaked into my voice. Still turning the pages of the album, Mrs. Selwick-Alderly smiled wryly. "Yes," she confirmed. "That is Caroline."

There were more pictures of little Colin, almost always with his father: little Colin playing cricket; little Colin with his first pony; little Colin poking his fingers up the nose of a very unhappy statue of some Victorian dignitary (in Colin's defense, whoever the guy was, he did have unusually deep nostrils); little Colin holding on with one hand to a much younger Mrs. Selwick-Alderly while dripping ice cream all down his shirt with the other. There were pictures of Colin's mother, too, but hers were generally Colin-less, always in motion and always laughing. She looked flighty, I thought. Certainly not like the mother of a small child.

I don't want to give the wrong impression, though. The Colin pictures were scattered unevenly through, the way one would expect with so peripheral a relative as a great-nephew, no matter how beloved. The bulk of the album was devoted to pictures of a forty- or fifty-something Mrs. Selwick-Alderly, incredibly polished and elegant in the high-waisted skirts and ruffled blouses of the mid-seventies. In the earlier pictures, she was sometimes accompanied by the tall, dissipated-looking man I recognized from the other album as her husband, but he gradually faded out as the pictures went on. Death or divorce? I didn't want to ask.

Many pictures featured a handsome boy in his early teens, with the same lanky build, shiny dark hair, and fifties' movie-star features as Mrs. Selwick-Alderly's disappearing husband.

"My grandson Jeremy," she said shortly, when I asked. "His father died while serving in Northern Ireland in 1969."

So she did have children of her own. I had wondered about that. Colin's family did seem to run heavily to the service of Crown and Country. There were more than a few uniforms on prominent display in the albums, including Colin's father's. Somewhere along the line, the family had made the switch from freelance espionage to the army. And then there was Colin, who didn't fall under either. Or did he?

There were no pictures of Mrs. Selwick-Alderly's soldier son—those must have been in a previous album—but there was a dark-haired woman with an impish grin who she identified proudly as "my daughter, Amy. She and her husband live in the UAE now," she added regretfully. "David works for BP."

"Do they have children?" I asked, remembering the family pictures on the mantelpiece.

"Three," said Mrs. Selwick-Alderly promptly, flicking over another page. "Tommy started university this year, and the twins, Sally and Posy, are still at school."

"Do you see them much?" I asked tentatively.

She smiled kindly, as though understanding what I was trying to ask. It made me feel very young and very naïve. "We manage," she said gently. "And I send them sweets during term-time."

"Tommy, too?" I asked.

"Especially Tommy."

As the pages kept turning, Baby Serena showed up on the scene, but this time there were no pictures at all of baby and Mummy, not even the requisite hospital picture. I looked thoughtfully at a photo of an outing to Hyde Park—I knew it was Hyde Park because I recognized the statue of Peter Pan in the background—featuring a tiny Serena in a pram, a sturdy little five-year-old Colin standing to one side, offering the baby a grubby finger to hold, and their father behind, one hand on the handle of the pram, the other resting protectively on Colin's head, in that way fathers have.

"There aren't many pictures of the children with their mother," I ventured, shamelessly fishing.

"Caroline liked to think of herself as a free spirit." There was more than a hint of acid in Mrs. Selwick-Alderly's voice. Glancing up, I saw that her lips had compressed into a thin, tight line. "I've found that 'free spirit' is frequently nothing more than a creative synonym for 'self-indulgence.'"

"Was Colin's mother . . . ?" My voice trailed off. I was on very uncertain ground, dying to know, but afraid to ask for fear she would cease to tell me if I pushed too hard.

Fortunately, Mrs. Selwick-Alderly's eyes were on the album, pulled back by the pictures to a world thirty years away. "Caroline was spoiled first by her parents, then by her husband," Mrs. Selwick-Alderly said crisply. "What Caroline wanted, Caroline got, or life was made very unpleasant."

"What about her second husband—Colin's stepfather?"

A peculiar expression settled across Mrs. Selwick-Alderly's face. "Unfortunately, he, too, was too much indulged," she said slowly. With a quick, almost convulsive movement, she clamped the cover shut on the album, looking up at me with the bright, apologetic smile of the practiced hostess. "But I am making a terrible waste of your time, rambling on about strangers when it was the Penelope Staines papers you were wanting."

Dropping the album back into the box, she moved with long-legged grace to the closet, excavating behind the hanging clothes for the next box down.

"She was something of a free spirit, too," I volunteered, hoping I could work the conversation back around to Colin's mother and whatever it was she had done to make her aunt by marriage hate her quite so much.

"Penelope?" Straightening, Mrs. Selwick-Alderly glanced over her shoulder at me. "Do you think so? I've always thought her much more of a troubled soul, acting out not so much because she wants to, but because others expect it of her. Very sad, I've always thought."

She bent forward to tug at the box and I slid off the bed and scooted down next to her. "Please. Let me."

The box looked heavy, and for all her ramrod-straight carriage, Mrs. Selwick-Alderly must have been at least eighty, judging from the dates on the pictures in the albums. Remembering the debutante picture on the mantel in the living room, I wondered what it must have been to be a debutante on the very eve of World War II, the last gasp of extravagant parties and great estates and prolonged country house weekends. I remembered her bitter comment about Colin's mother, the free spirit. By the seventies, when Colin's mother came into the picture, the world around her must have been all but unrecognizable.

She relinquished the box with good grace, saying cheerfully, "Better you than me," as she straightened, brushing the palms of her hands against her cream wool trousers.

Clutching the box to my abdomen, I tottered with it to the bed, gratefully dropping it onto the counterpane.

"Ha!" said Mrs. Selwick-Alderly, rustling among the contents. "I knew I had it there."

Inching closer, I tried to peer over her shoulder. Inside, instead of the folios or acid-proof boxes to which a researcher becomes accustomed, was notebook after notebook after notebook, all with metal ring binding and yellowed covers. An autocratic hand, which I recognized from the captions on the photos, had scrawled numbers on the covers.

"These," said Mrs. Selwick-Alderly with great satisfaction, "should be precisely what you were looking for."

Were they? I tried not to look too dubious.

Perching on the edge of the bed next to the box, she explained, "I spent a winter at the Residency at Karnatabad—oh, years and years ago. Karnatabad was a British construct," she added briskly, "a district drawn up out of the Ceded Territories, the lands ceded by the Nizam after the second Mahratta War. Lady Frederick's papers were kept in the archives there. Such a mess they were, too! Generation after generation had simply stuffed books and papers onto shelves without making the least effort to sort them."

I nodded vigorously in sympathy. I had visited records offices like that in England, including one, which shall remain nameless, where the archivist plaintively asked me if I would mind making a record of whatever papers I came across as I sifted through them since he had never gotten around to doing it himself.

"These notebooks," said Mrs. Selwick-Alderly, peering down fondly into the box, "are my gleanings from that chaos."

I couldn't resist asking. "What made you decide to, er, glean?"

A flicker of a smile showed around Mrs. Selwick-Alderly's lips. "I used to think I wanted to write a novel," she said, as though it were a great joke. "Mollie Kaye and I both had grand ideas of writing an Indian epic. She actually did it, though."

Mollie Kaye . . . "You knew M. M. Kaye?" I yelped.

Mrs. Selwick-Alderly nodded, a gentle smile on her lips, as though she were hearing the echoes of conversations once spoken in places that no longer exist. "Yes. We all had a sense, in those days, that the world around us—British India as it had been—was vanishing, and that it was expedient to record as much as we could before it disappeared entirely. It lent a certain urgency to the exercise. And a good thing, too." Mrs. Selwick-Alderly patted the side of the box fondly. "Not long after my stay in Karnatabad, the Residency was renovated for use as a school and the archives were lost. Someone told me that much of it was simply thrown out. They hadn't the resources for keeping it," she said with a sigh, before adding briskly, "Although, of course, primary education was a far more important concern."

"Of course," I agreed. And then, because I couldn't resist, "What was your novel going to be about?"

"Dashing spies," she said lightly, getting up off the bed. "What else?"

What else, indeed? I wondered if she knew that her great-nephew was currently engaged in writing a spy novel. Or, at least, that was what he claimed. There were still times when I couldn't help but wonder whether his interest in spies was more than literary. Pretending to write a spy novel could make a very clever cover for other sorts of activities.

"I'll leave you to it, then. If you have any trouble with the handwriting, don't hesitate to find me. I have no doubt that the ink is rather faded by now."

Thanking her, I divested myself of my boots and scrambled up onto the high old bed, tucking my stockinged feet up beneath me. I tentatively lifted the first notebook out of the box. Number Fifteen. Mrs. Selwick-Alderly certainly had been methodical. On the front leaf, she had listed the date she had transcribed it, the translator she had hired to transpose the non-English documents, and the dates and authors of the historical records. If I were half that organized, I would have my dissertation long since done already.

Digging through for a notebook labeled "1," I found one without any number on it at all. Opening it at random, I saw, in Mrs. Selwick-Alderly's slanted handwriting, "She waited, breathless, in the lee of Raymond's Tomb as the dark line of conspirators rode past. To be found would be death."

Hmm. She hadn't been joking about that novel, then. I looked speculatively at the notebook. I wondered what would have happened if she had finished it. There were so many novels set around the Indian Mutiny of 1857, but it was hard to think of any set those fifty-odd years earlier, during the Mahratta Wars. It would make a good landscape for fiction.

It also made a good landscape for a dissertation chapter, I reminded myself, forcing myself to put aside the unfinished novel (working title: *Shadow of the Tomb*). Clicking on the bedside lamp, which sent a pleasant pool of light across the counterpane, I curled up against the pillows with Notebook 1, a compilation of various letters and dispatches sent by Henry Russell, the exceedingly prolific Chief Secretary to the Resident of Hyderabad.

According to Russell, the Resident had been tearing out his hair about the presentation of the new Special Envoy, Lord Frederick Staines, to the Nizam of Hyderabad at a durbar called for that purpose. No one knew quite what the unpredictable new Nizam might do. The same went for Lord Frederick, who spoke no Persian and had a worrying lack of knowledge about proper court protocol. Embassies had been banished for less.

And to make matters even worse, his wife had insisted on coming along.

Chapter Eight

"What is she doing here?" Alex demanded, as Lady Frederick climbed out of the Resident of Hyderabad's state palanquin.

The state palanquin, in which James rode with the new Special Envoy, was a testament to what raw money and talented craftsmanship could provide. The tasseled silk curtains, however, hid as much as they concealed. In this case, the presence of an extra individual in the palanquin.

For the duration of the ceremonial procession from the Residency to the Nizam's fortress, Alex had trotted blithely along beside the palanquin, entirely unaware that the tasseled curtains concealed an additional passenger. Only the Resident and the new Special Envoy had been bidden to the Nizam's durbar. It had never occurred to Alex—or, he imagined, the Nizam—that the Special Envoy's wife might take it upon herself to attend as well.

Alex gritted his teeth in a way that boded ill for his dental health. One did not just drop by on a supreme ruler unannounced. Especially not a supreme ruler with a penchant for extemporaneous executions.

All around them, armed guards in steel helmets and gauntlets stood at attention, their bearded faces impassive. There had been more guards than usual in the Nizam's palace, Alex had noticed, stationed in all of the courtyards through which they had passed on their way to the durbar at which Wellesley's new Special Envoy was to be formally presented to the Nizam.

They had guards enough of their own. The Resident and Lord

Frederick had made their way from the Residency complex on the other side of the river accompanied by no fewer than ten companies of infantry, along with five brightly bedecked elephants, a troop of cavalry, and two dozen riderless horses whose sole purpose was to show off brightly colored pennants. After a lifetime in Indian courts, James Kirkpatrick knew how to put on a show.

Would a show be enough to secure their safety in this new and dangerous political climate?

Alex had thought he had addressed his question to the Resident sotto voce. Unfortunately, the acoustics in the courtyard were excellent.

Lady Frederick swept towards him in a whisper of white satin, like moonlight on marble and just as cold. "And a good evening to you, too, Captain Reid. I had thought I might have trouble recognizing you after all this time, but your charm is unmistakable."

"I've been busy," he said stiffly. And he had been. Since returning two weeks ago, he had taken half his meals in the saddle or at his desk.

There was no reason he should feel guilty about neglecting his former charge. It wasn't as though she was likely to lack for entertainment. Since their arrival, nearly every family in the Residency had felt it incumbent on themselves to throw a dinner or a card party or a Venetian breakfast for the new arrivals. Alex had avoided all the entertainments with impartial firmness, pleading the very real pressures of work.

And since when had she become *his*, just because he had been saddled with the task of getting her husband from Calcutta to Hyderabad? His obligation to Lady Frederick Staines had ended at the Residency gates, and that was that.

Or that should have been that. Over the past two weeks, Alex had found that he couldn't quite purge Lady Frederick from his thoughts. Without seeing or consulting her, he had arranged for an Urdu tutor to be sent to her, hoping that would quell his conscience. It hadn't. He still felt, for some inexplicable reason, obscurely responsible for her, a sensation that even consistent avoidance hadn't managed to expunge entirely.

It wasn't as though that were unusual, Alex rationalized to himself. George might have carted home stray dogs, but he was the one who had been left caring for them. This was exactly the same. Lady Penelope was just another stray who had been dumped into his care, like George's pariah dogs or that one-eared kitten Lizzy had dragged home.

The analogy was an unfortunately apt one. Like Lizzy's kitten, Lady Frederick seemed determined to sharpen her claws. On him.

"I'm sure you have been," Lady Frederick agreed with deceptive complaisance. "There are so many things to keep one busy, aren't there?"

Alex had the feeling he was being accused of something more than neglect, but he couldn't imagine what. "Look," he said, with a nod towards the archway. "Someone's come to fetch us."

It should, for courtesy's sake, have been the Nizam's chief minister, Mir Alam. Instead, it was a palace functionary so minor that Alex didn't even know his name. From the expression on James's face, he didn't either. The Resident was not best pleased, but there was little he could do about. His own position was too precarious.

Fortunately, Lord Frederick didn't know enough to realize that he had just been insulted. He strutted happily along behind their escort, slowing by the instinct of long practice in the light of those candles that made his gold watch fobs glitter to their best advantage. Like a peacock, decided Alex critically, brightly plumed from a distance, but inclined to peck when one got up close.

"Keep an eye on . . . ," James murmured, tipping his head in Lady Frederick's direction, before following along behind Lord Frederick into the durbar hall.

Typical, thought Alex. Simply bloody typical. Once again, he was the one left holding the leash.

Resigning himself to the inevitable, Alex extended an arm. "Shall we?"

Lady Frederick eyed his arm as she might a dead snake. "I don't need a keeper."

"That's what you said before you jumped into the river."

"I doubt there are any bodies of water in the durbar hall," retorted Lady Frederick, marching along ahead of him. Alex was reminded more than ever of Lizzy's cat. Had Lady Frederick had a tail, it would have been sticking straight up in the air.

"That doesn't mean there aren't treacherous depths."

Lady Frederick looked up at him sideways. "Do you have treachery on the mind, Captain Reid?"

"I'm not the one I'm worried about," he said frankly.

Lady Frederick regarded him scornfully. "I shouldn't think you would be. After all, you know exactly what you're planning."

Exactly what did she think he was planning? Other than making sure she left the palace alive? Even without mysterious marigolds roaming about, there was Tajalli's father, plumping for the restoration of the French force in Hyderabad; the new Nizam, providing a target for schemers and fortune hunters across the realm; and Mir Alam, rotten with old grudges and new leprosy. Or was that old leprosy and new grudges? Either way, the combination was about as conducive to civil peace as a Montague and Capulet reunion dinner.

"What do you think I'm planning?" Alex demanded, but he had lost his opportunity. The durbar hall opened up before them and he had the rare opportunity of seeing Lady Frederick well and truly speechless.

Even Alex, who had attended the durbar time and time again, had to admit it was an impressive sight. The Nizam preferred to hold his durbars by dark. It was a practical measure, avoiding the heat of the day, but the resultant forest of candles created an artificial wonderland of the durbar hall, turning the proceedings into a page from a Deccani manuscript, too brilliant to be real. The hall was an architectural fantasy, the walls covered with trompe l'oeil scenes, so that parrots seemed suspended in flight above the heads of the courtiers and peacocks opened their mouth in eternal cry from beneath wide-leafed trees where the mango were perpetually in season.

Next to the lifelike guise of the paintings, the courtiers themselves seemed no more than an artist's illusion, a piece of Eastern decadence for a European collector to marvel at. The light of the thousand candles in their tall silver stands oscillated off their rich silks and jewels, flirting with creamy shadows along the long ropes of pearls hanging around the necks of the nobles, shimmering along priceless lengths of gold brocade, cascading off diamond-set turban ornaments, and setting ruby armbands smoldering like the acquisitive glint in a merchant's eye.

It wasn't the jewels that held Lady Frederick's attention, but the guards who stood sentry along the sides of the durbar hall, long, steel-tipped staffs propped against their soldiers. Their uniforms were similar to those worn by Madras sepoys, a long red coat over a pair of baggy trousers. They were all women.

"The Zuffir Plutun," said Alex, with a nod towards the lady guards.

"The Victorious Brigade," Lady Frederick translated, looking thoughtfully at the guards, as though she suspected them of being an optical illusion.

"Did you think I had made them up?"

Lady Frederick adopted her most inscrutable expression. Alex took that as a yes.

A cupbearer presented Alex with a small agate cup of coffee, tongue-scaldingly hot from the brazier that the Nizam kept burning in the center of the durbar. Slightly uncertainly, the cupbearer offered a twin of his cup to Lady Frederick. Looking as nonchalant as though she had been drinking at durbars all her life, Lady Frederick lifted the cup to her lips.

Alex curled his fingers around the polished surface, which was deceptively cool. "You might want to—"

Lady Frederick knocked back the contents.

"—sip that," finished Alex, as Lady Frederick's face turned an interesting color of puce.

Her throat worked convulsively as she swallowed the burning liquid, grounds and all.

"I'm fine," she said hoarsely, giving him a look that dared him to contradict her.

Alex blew lightly at the surface of his own cup before taking a very small sip. "The Nizam likes his coffee hot," he said helpfully.

Lady Frederick gave him a look of death. "I know."

"Would you like another cup?" Alex made as though to summon the cupbearer. Never let it be said that he hadn't behaved like a gentleman.

"Not to drink," said Lady Frederick, in a tone that left no doubt as to where she would have liked to pour it.

The chuckle welled up in Alex's throat before he had time to clamp it down again. He turned it into a cough, but not quite quickly enough.

A reluctant grin curled the corner of Lady Frederick's lips. She had a coffee ground stuck between her two front teeth, giving her a charmingly gapped-tooth expression.

Alex held out his cup. "You can have mine, if you like," he said. "It ought to be cool by now. At least, cooler," he amended.

Lady Frederick started to reach for it, and then drew back her hand, as thought she had thought better of it. "No. Thank you."

Alex glanced down at his cup, but he didn't see anything suspect about it. There were no drowned flies floating on the surface, or even particularly large coffee grounds impersonating dead flies. It was a perfectly potable cup of Turkish coffee. More potable, Alex suspected, than the beverages pretending to that name being served in London. On the other hand, had he just bolted a cup of boiling coffee, he wouldn't be too keen on the beverage either.

At the front of the *diwan khaneh*, the Nizam's master of ceremonies, Mama Champa, was leading Lord Frederick up to the dais, her gilt-edged white robe and pink *choli* making Lord Frederick's English evening dress seem even more drab in contrast. In addition to being the Nizam's master of ceremonies, she was also a commanding officer of the Zuffir Plutun. The little push she gave Lord Frederick had enough force behind it to send him staggering to his knees before the ruler. Which, of course, was exactly where Mama Champa had wanted him.

Tall blue poles had been placed to either side of the Nizam, the

blue lights lending an unhealthy tint to his already sallow complexion. Even the jewels and silks with which he had decked himself
couldn't hide the unhealthy hang of his jowls, the lines of dissipation
in his face that made him look old beyond his years. Alex thought
wistfully of the old Nizam, a dignified old warrior with a knack for
political maneuvering and a taste for mechanical curiosities. The old
Nizam had looked better at seventy than Sikunder Jah looked at
thirty-five.

The old Nizam also hadn't had Mir Alam hanging over his shoulder like death in a morality tale.

Mir Alam looked like hell, Alex thought dispassionately. He had
always been slightly built, but now, besieged by disease, his narrow
frame seemed to have caved in upon itself like a crone's clawed hand.
The fair complexion of which he had been so proud, token of his
Persian ancestry, was blotched with open sores that turned his once-
pleasant-featured face into something resembling a blob of raw meat,
rendered even more hideous by the cavern in the center of his face
where his nose used to be, collapsed in upon itself from the disease that
was eating him from the inside out.

But even in those days when his body had been whole, there had
been something unsettling about him, a cold-blooded lack of fellow
feeling so profound as to be somehow inhuman. *All ambition and no
heart*, James's assistant, Henry Russell, had said with a shudder, adding that he'd sooner be sewed into a sack with a cobra than rely on Mir
Alam's mercy. Jack, who had a sneaking fondness for literature, had
come up with an even more apt epitaph for Mir Alam. *The Deccani
Iago*, Jack had called him, back before—well, before.

No need to let himself be distracted by Jack. Alex forced himself to
concentrate on Mir Alam, Mir Alam who sat like a serpent poised to
strike, the pipe of a golden hookah coiling snakelike from his mouth.

Alex recognized that hookah. It had, until very recently, belonged
to the former First Minister, Aristu Jah, who seldom went anywhere
without it. It had been a source of endless speculation among the
younger wags of the court whether he brought it to bed with him, and
if so, what role it played.

The hookah ought, by rights, to have been with Aristu Jah's widow, not dangling from Mir Alam's lips.

That did not bode well.

Alex could hear Lord Frederick's startled grunt as Mama Champa shoved him down into the proper prostrate position. A few courtiers snickered behind their hands. The snickers turned to snorts as Lord Frederick bumbled his way through the elegant Persian oration James had crafted for him, blithely butchering vowels and changing minor words. Not that it mattered, reflected Alex cynically. The Nizam wasn't listening anyway. Alex saw his eyes wandering off to the cane screen that concealed his current concubines.

At James's prompting, Lord Frederick proffered the ceremonial gift that James had so carefully chosen. Passing off the present to a waiting functionary, the Nizam handed him in return a jeweled turban ornament, a cluster of emeralds and sapphires in the shape of peacock feathers. Lord Frederick promptly tried to stick it in his cravat, clearly believing it to be a sort of outré stickpin. Another friendly push from Mama Champa bowled him into the proper salaam, and then, thank the stars, the interview was over.

Only it wasn't.

At a slight gesture, Mir Alam's servant removed the point of his hookah from his mouth. Bending slightly, so that his mouth was level with the Nizam's ear, Mir Alam murmured something to his master. Whatever it was made the Nizam sit up a little straighter, scanning the room in a way that made more than one courtier take a hasty step back. Alex didn't blame them; the Nizam's tastes ran much towards Nero's. Or was it Caligula's? It was Jack who had been the bookish one.

Mir Alam whispered something else in the Nizam's ear, redirecting his attention, with the sort of veiled impatience governesses use for their charges. Alex went as cold as a dead Roman emperor as the Nizam followed the swing of Mir Alam's finger—straight to Lady Frederick, who was idly and unconcernedly running her tongue experimentally along the edge of her burned lip, as though testing the new scar tissue.

The Nizam gestured Lady Frederick forward with an imperious flick of his wrist.

Alex felt Lady Frederick stiffen beside him, looking from one side to the other as though to say, *Who me?* No fools, the courtiers on either side of them backed away, leaving Lady Frederick and Alex alone in a pool of harsh tallow light, while Mama Champa progressed purposefully in their direction.

"Just curtsy," whispered Alex out of the side of his mouth, experiencing a powerful urge to strangle Mir Alam with his ill-gotten hookah. "Curtsy and try to look humble."

Lady Frederick cast him a haughty look. "I have been to court, you know," she whispered back, rising regally to her full height. "If I can manage Queen Charlotte, I can manage him."

Alex rather doubted that, but it was too late to do anything about it. Lady Frederick was already on the move, striding to the front of the room with the careless confidence of an accomplished rider about to take a fence. Without any help from Mama Champa, she sank to the floor, prostrating herself before the Nizam's feet. She was, perhaps, a little too prostrate, but no one seemed to mind, not least the courtiers clustered around Alex, who were rating the properties of her nether regions, or at least such as could be discerned beneath the concealing fabric of her dress.

As the Nizam considered the view, Mir Alam leaned forward and murmured something in his ear. It was like watching a puppet show. All that was needed were the strings.

Instructing Mama Champa to raise Lady Frederick to her feet, the Nizam slurred out a question in an indistinct voice that suggested that he had been hitting a hookah of his own before the durbar.

"Where is my *nuzzar?*" piped up the translator, his voice reedy in the hushed silence. "Have you no gift for me?"

At the Nizam's elbow, his Prime Minister's eyes were bright sparks in the ruined mass of his face as he waited for the new English envoy's wife to stammer her way into a gaffe, a gaffe that would embarrass the English embassy, a gaffe that could be trotted out as a bargaining chip by the Nizam's chief minister on future occasions. It was like watching two baggage carts about to collide and knowing there was nothing one could do to stop it.   .

Just as Alex was on the verge of barging forward and interceding, faux pas or not, Lady Frederick took matters into her own hands.

She lifted her eyes to the Nizam in a skillful mimicry of humility. "I would not," she said, in a voice that carried to the farthest reaches of the hall, "do you the dishonor of appearing before you empty handed."

Mir Alam looked pointedly at her hands. They were, not to put too fine a point on it, empty.

Lady Frederick waited out the translator's anxious murmur before striking a pose worthy of a nautch dancer, both hands extended palm up in the classic gesture of supplication.

"But what might so insignificant a creature as myself possibly offer that would be worthy of so great a ruler?"

The courtiers on either side of Alex had their own opinions on that matter, mostly of the sort better not overheard by the lady's husband. Too skinny, opined the man on Alex's left, comparing her figure unfavorable to that of Nur Bai's, one of the city's more expensive courtesans.

Lady Frederick had to speak very loudly to be heard over the assorted whispers and murmurings. "Not riches, for those you have in plenty. Nor wisdom, of which Your Majesty has more than I by far."

The translator hurried to relay her words to the Nizam, while those courtiers who spoke some English spread their own mangled translations through the crowd.

Like an actress anticipating her cue, Lady Frederick stood poised, waiting for the din to die down.

It worked. Bit by bit, the chatter fell off, the translations ceased, and all eyes turned to the still, poised figure at the front of the room. In her unadorned white satin, she made the brocades of the courtiers look fussy and loud, turning priceless jewels into little more than trumpery bazaar ornaments. Bathed in blue light from the candles by the Nizam, she seemed to crackle with a cold energy, unearthly, uncanny, and more than a little imperious.

Alex couldn't help but receive the distinct impression that she was enjoying every moment of it.

In the hushed silence, Lady Frederick brought one hand to her breast. As one, the cream of Hyderabad stared, expectant, at Lady Frederick's chest. When her hand came away, she held a single blossom from the nosegay at her bodice. It was a white bud, half-opened. It was also beginning to wilt from the heat of the room, the one false note in an otherwise masterly tableau.

Lifting it high enough for all the curious members of the durbar to see, Lady Frederick held the blossom out to the Nizam.

She spoke very slowly and clearly, allowing the translator time to follow. "Having found nothing else worthy of you, I offer you this humble flower, which I have carried close by my heart, in token of the warm regard I feel for Your Majesty and in the hopes that our friendship shall blossom like the rose."

The only noise was the low tones of the translator behind the Nizam's chair, hastily gabbling back Lady Frederick's speech into the Nizam's ear. The courtiers ceased their chatter, all eyes on the Nizam as they waited for his reaction. Only Lady Frederick appeared unperturbed, her arm unmoving as marble as she extended the flower to the Nizam.

The seconds ticked by, marked by the guttering of the candles and the crackle of the brazier. Alex could feel the sweat beginning to trickle down his neck.

Alex looked to Mir Alam, but the minister was staying his hand, watching with the same fixed attention as the other bystanders, his assumptions betrayed only by the slight smile that played around the corners of his mouth. He had rolled the dice; now he was waiting for them to fall.

As she held her pose for one minute, then another, and another, almost imperceptibly, Lady Frederick's arm began to tremble.

What would she do if the Nizam refused her? What would they all do?

A sigh went through the room as the Nizam extended his hand to accept the token from Lady Frederick's hand. The sigh savored more of disappointment than relief. It would have been much more amusing for all concerned had the new envoy's wife been summarily savaged by lions.

Lady Frederick dropped her arm and sank into a deep European curtsy. Damp darkened the fabric beneath her sleeves in discrete circles, like shadows on the moon.

Balked of a bloodletting, the courtiers had begun to breathe again and to return to their own private intrigues when Mir Alam's voice rustled through the renewed chatter like a snake in the grass.

Speaking as though for the Nizam's ears alone, but pitching his voice high enough to carry, he said, "Does not the rose fade?"

Alex mentally damned Mir Alam and all his progeny to the tenth generation. From the look on Lady Frederick's face, she was entertaining similar fantasies, many involving exceedingly pointy pitchforks and boiling pots of Turkish coffee.

Rising from her curtsy, Lady Frederick gave a brisk shake of her skirts, the only sign of nervousness she betrayed. Her smile was very fixed and very bright as she batted her eyelashes at the Nizam's chief minister. "The petals may indeed fade, but the fragrance lingers on. Like the goodwill between our countries."

It was a well-aimed barb, designed to remind all concerned that she had the might of England behind her, backed by infantry, elephants, and an expansionist Governor General who was prone to invading first and asking questions later.

The implications weren't lost on Mir Alam, who closed his mouth tightly over whatever else he had been about to say and took a subtle step back from the Nizam's chair, like a tennis player conceding a match. A match, but not the game. Whether she knew it or not, Lady Frederick had just made a powerful enemy.

Alex suppressed a groan. Just what they needed.

The Nizam, on the other hand, had already reached the limits of his boredom. As he turned to say something to a courtier behind him, Mama Champa waved Lady Frederick away from the dais, and gestured to her counterpart, Mama Barun, to begin herding courtiers towards the gardens for the nautch that was to follow the durbar. In gaily colored groupings, chattering like the parrots painted on the walls, the courtiers began to drift towards the gardens, already intent on the next intrigue, the next scandal, whatever it might be.

Only Mir Alam continued to watch Lady Frederick, the pipe of the hookah dangling like a snake from his lips.

Taking her arm, Alex hauled her away, manhandling her into the stream of courtiers heading out of the durbar hall.

"You would have done better to have stayed in the Residency," he said softly, in English.

Neatly twisting her arm out of his grasp, Lady Frederick said flippantly, "I thought the Nizam was rather a dear, actually."

"You have an odd definition of 'dear,'" said Alex grimly. "He's as mad as a hatter and he wields the power of life and death in this part of the world."

"Our military escort—"

"Is all outside. And Calcutta is a very long way away."

Lady Frederick's lips pursed as she considered. "I'm glad he liked my flower," she said.

Chapter Nine

There was a decided edge to Captain Reid's tone. "What would you have done if you hadn't been wearing a flower?"

"Torn a ribbon off my dress, I suppose," said Penelope with a shrug. "Or offered him a kiss."

Captain Reid favored her with an exasperated look. "No, you wouldn't have."

Penelope conceded the point with an airy wave of one hand. "Probably not. He looks the sort who would slobber. But if the situation called for it, there are worse fates. Kisses are currency like anything else."

"Only in one profession." He had clearly spoken without thinking. Penelope could register the exact moment when Captain Reid realized he had just called her a whore.

Fair enough. It wasn't anything that hadn't been said before.

She could practically see the wheels turning as he tried to work out a way to apologize without putting his foot even farther down his throat. Well, no need to make it easy for him. Penelope had always believed in living down to people's expectations.

Penelope favored him with her sultriest smile. "Have you never used a judicious embrace to attain your ends, Captain Reid?"

From the appalled expression on his face, the answer to that was clearly no. "If I tried to embrace Lord Wellesley, he'd most likely have me court-martialed."

The image surprised a startled snort out of Penelope. She couldn't decide which was the more amusing, the image of the dignified, hawk-nosed Lord Wellesley suffering an embrace, or the equally taciturn Captain Reid offering one.

Naturally, Captain Reid took advantage of her momentary good humor to try to get rid of her. "Shall I escort you back to the Residency?"

"And miss the nautch? Not for the wide world. But if you're so eager to be rid of me, you can deliver me back into the care of my husband."

Some care that was. Looking around for Freddy, Penelope saw him standing with the Nizam's chief minister, the same who had caused her so much discomfort in the durbar hall. That, thought Penelope with satisfaction, would be the last time the Nizam's minister tried *that*. The Dowager Duchess of Dovedale would be so proud of her.

Of course, knowing the Dowager Duchess, she would probably have expressed her point with a good deal more force. Force applied with the pointy side of her cane, that was. When it came to moving men, the Dowager was in agreement with Signor Machiavelli that it was far better to rule by fear than love.

Penelope looked to Freddy, who seemed to be having a grand old time with the Nizam's chief minister, although Penelope noticed that Freddy avoided looking directly at the man's collapsing face, preferring instead to focus on the elaborate ruby diadem that fronted his white silk turban. Like a magpie, Freddy was invariably entranced by shiny objects, a category that included his own reflection.

"The Nizam's minister appears to have taken to Freddy," observed Penelope, as Captain Reid led her across the durbar hall.

"The Nizam's minister," replied Captain Reid spiritedly, "has all the fellow-feeling of an asp. If Mir Alam is cultivating your husband, he has a reason for it."

Mir Alam. Penelope filed away the name for future use. "Are you implying that this Mir Alam is wiggling into Freddy's bosom in order to bite?"

Captain Reid scrupulously avoided looking at her bosom. "If you choose to put it that way, yes."

"One might almost think you didn't want me to trust him. I wonder why?"

"Because he is entirely untrustworthy," said Captain Reid flatly. "Or what would you call his attempt to embarrass you just now?"

Penelope indulged in a little smirk. "I don't think he'll be trying that again, do you?"

"No." The thought didn't appear to please him as much as it did her. There was a distinctly troubled cast to Captain Reid's face as he looked down at her. "Watch your back, Lady Frederick."

"I will when you're behind it," said Penelope spiritedly.

He had said something like that to her before, on the road. It was, Penelope decided, the human sacrifice bit all over again, trying to scare her away with vague threats and hints of bloody barbarity. What made him so eager to keep her on the bad side of the Nizam's chief minister, Mir—well, whatever his name was?

Wellesley had suspected Kirkpatrick of placing Hyderabadi interests above British ones. Reid was unmistakably Kirkpatrick's man; each spoke of the other with affectionate respect. Both were the sons of East India Company army officers, both had served in East India Company regiments, both were more Indian in their habits than English, although Captain Reid, unlike the Resident, still sported English dress, at least on those occasions when Penelope had been in his presence.

What if Captain Reid and the Nizam's chief minister were in collusion? Freddy was as much Wellesley's man as Reid was Kirkpatrick's. If Freddy had been a different sort of man—or a different sort of husband—that scene before the Nizam might have had a very different sort of outcome. Penelope could imagine more than a few ways it might have played out, any of which would have resulted in Freddy's summary dismissal or departure from Hyderabad.

Penelope smiled sourly to herself. Neither of them had reckoned on Freddy's indifference.

"Pen, old thing," he said lazily, as she drew forward, dragging Captain Reid along with her. "You haven't met the Nizam's chief minister yet, have you?"

"Not as such," said Penelope smilingly. Lord, Freddy could be thick sometimes. The barb was completely wasted on him, although it was duly registered by Mir Whatever-His-Name-Was.

She kept a close eye on both the chief minister and Captain Reid as Freddy performed the obligatory introduction, but neither obliged her by exchanging so much as a conspiratorial glance. Quite to the contrary, they reminded Penelope of nothing so much as two dogs circling each other, each prepared to make a jab for the other's jugular. If they had had fur, it would have been standing on end.

If it was a performance, it was an awfully good one.

"Captain Reid. How charming to see you again," said Mir Alam. His smile bared more teeth than were strictly socially required.

Captain Reid wasn't smiling. He was a picture of military discipline, his back as straight as the proverbial ramrod and just about as friendly. "May I take that to mean that you have changed your position on the matter of the three soldiers since this morning?"

The Prime Minister carried on as though Captain Reid had never spoken. "Lord Frederick and I have been having the most delightful conversation."

"Delightful," Captain Reid said in clipped tones. "Shall we address another delightful topic? I doubt Lord Frederick will be delighted to know that three soldiers from the English cantonments were arrested last night in the name of Nizam on the charge of appearing drunk in the streets of the city."

"English soldiers?" Freddy asked.

"Sepoys," Captain Reid said shortly.

Freddy gave a slight shrug, as if to disclaim any further interest in the matter.

"They are, however, under English command," said Captain Reid, with heavy emphasis. Penelope had to admire his tactics. What Freddy wouldn't champion for justice, he would for pride.

"What is the sentence?" she asked.

Captain Reid turned to her, his expression inscrutable. "Being blown alive from the mouth of a cannon."

"Oh," said Penelope.

"The same cannon or different cannons?" Freddy asked Mir Alam.

A small smile played across the remains of Mir Alam's lips. He knew he had his man. "Three cannon to be fired in unison. It is," he added, "a spectacle to impress all would-be transgressors with the force of the law."

"All for drunkenness?" interjected Penelope. "Surely a flogging would do as well. And be far less messy," she added as an afterthought.

"Not merely for drunkenness," said the chief minister with just the right amount of sorrowful solicitude. "There have been, of late, a number of thefts committed within the city. In his infinite wisdom, the Nizam has increased the penalties for those who loiter as a means of discouraging crime."

"*His* infinite wisdom?" said Captain Reid in disgust.

"Can you doubt it?" said the chief minister smoothly, but there was something about his watchful expression that reminded Penelope of the snake Captain Reid had called him, coiling to spring.

"The Nizam is all wise and all knowing. *But*"—Captain Reid pressed forward, with dogged determination—"these three men are not residents of the city. They are soldiers in the Subsidiary Force and thus under the jurisdiction of their commanding officers. Let them discipline their own."

"When they appear drunk in the cantonments, then let your officers do their own disciplining," said Mir Alam easily, with a nod to Freddy that seemed to include him in the conference. "On the streets of the Nizam's own capital, they are subject to his justice."

"Sounds sensible enough to me," said Freddy, nodding sagely. He craned his head to see over his shoulder into the garden, where lanterns twinkled tantalizingly in the trees. "Sovereign ruler and all that. Shall we go into the entertainment?"

Captain Reid's nostrils flared slightly, but he managed to hold on to his temper. Pity, that, thought Penelope. It would have been more amusing to see what would have occurred had he lost it.

"I wonder what Lord Wellesley would say about all this." Captain

Reid's pretense of offhandedness was belied by the grim set of his jaw. He added, for the chief minister's benefit, "Lord Frederick has just come directly from Lord Wellesley in Calcutta."

The chief minister was unperturbed. "Have you? I have also had the great privilege of meeting your Lord Wellesley. A wonderful man. What is your opinion of this matter of the soldiers, Lord Frederick?"

"Taken for loitering drunkenly, you say?" said Freddy, who could have given lessons on the topic. Mir Alam inclined his head in affirmation. Lord Frederick shrugged. "Well, then. If they did the deed, no reason to let them off. Set an example for the rest of the chaps."

Mir Alam's cracked lips broke into a broad smile. The smile would have been an attractive one but for the malice that animated it and the disease that made a mockery of his once-pleasant-featured face. "My feelings precisely. I knew we should get along famously, Lord Frederick."

Freddy preened himself like one of the peacocks painted on the wall, undoubtedly picturing himself being singled out in dispatches home as a statesman of unrivaled tact and skill.

"How do you know Wellesley, then?" he asked the chief minister, cutting Captain Reid neatly out of the conversation.

Mir Alam looked modestly away. Modesty, thought Penelope, sat about as well on him as flirtation did on Captain Reid. "I worked very closely with his younger brother, Arthur Wellesley, during the siege of Seringapatam."

Penelope could see the Nizam's minister rising in Freddy's estimation by the moment. For a period of months in 1800, the vanquishing of Tipu Sultan, the Tiger Sultan of Mysore had eclipsed even Gentleman Jackson's latest prize bout in the popular imagination.

"Quite a victory, wasn't it?" Freddy said expansively. "I spent some time in Seringapatam myself. After the battle, of course," he added, managing to provide the distinct impression that he had tramped in as soon as the glacis had fallen, bayoneting the odd enemy along the way, rather than being comfortably billeted there a good three years after Mysore had fallen into British hands.

"I was better acquainted with Lord Wellesley's predecessor, Lord

Cornwallis." For a moment, the chief minister's face softened in reminiscence. What was left of his face, that was. "It was he who gave me this pretty thing," he said, indicating the diamond-encrusted walking stick on which he was leaning. "As a token of his friendship."

"Not bad," Freddy said, eyeing the stick in a way that made Penelope suspect that some jewel merchants would soon be made very happy. "Not bad at all. Cornwallis is, of course, a connection on my mother's side," he added importantly.

According to Freddy's mother, everyone was a connection on his mother's side. Everyone with a page in Debrett's peerage, that was. Penelope's mother by marriage only counted the titled relations.

"He is very much missed here. Although," Mir Alam added, with a sly sideways glance at Captain Reid, "not all of us present would agree to that."

And, just to make sure Freddy got the point, he pointed his stick in the direction of Captain Reid. Penelope was impressed; the Nizam's chief minister already had Freddy's measure. Freddy's gaze followed the diamonds like a compass seeking true north.

"I have no quarrel with the man," said Captain Reid guardedly. "Merely with some of the policies he promulgated."

"What policies might those be?" asked Penelope.

"Those that bar the children of Anglo-Indian alliances from the civil service and the military," Mir Alam answered for him. "Is that not so, Captain Reid?"

Captain Reid made no move to deny it. He looked, suddenly, far older than Freddy, although Penelope suspected he might be the younger of the two in years. It might have been the bitter twist of his lips as he acknowledged the chief minister's point with a curt nod of his head that made him look like a much older man.

Penelope heard a voice that sounded like her own saying, "You take a personal interest in Anglo-Indian alliances, Captain Reid?"

There was no reason for her to be so jarred by the prospect that he went home at night to something other than an empty camp bed in a spartan bachelor establishment. All she knew of him was what she had seen on the long trek from Calcutta to Hyderabad. She knew he was efficient at organizing, fluent in the local languages, and an excellent judge of horseflesh. But that had all been a matter of duty, snatched away from his real life, rather than the text of it.

Had he gone home and complained about the hideous people he had been forced to escort? The ridiculous woman who refused to ride in her palanquin like a proper lady and made trouble by jumping into the river after grooms? It was a surprisingly disconcerting thought.

"It is," Captain Reid said simply, "a wasteful policy, barring those who know and love the country best from serving it."

Penelope wasn't interested in abstract philosophy; she wanted to know whether he had a personal reason to take an interest in the offspring of Anglo-Indian alliances.

"Ah, but which country?" said the chief minister. "Their mother's or their father's? How can you trust the loyalty of a man divided within his own bones? Lord Cornwallis was wise to avoid the risk."

Captain Reid did not agree. "Leaving hundreds excluded through no fault of their own, with no choice but to enlist as mercenaries beneath a foreign flag."

The rubies in Mir Alam's headdress glinted like a host of red eyes. "As your brother did."

So that was it, then. Not Captain Reid's children, then, but his father's. As from far away, Penelope remembered the last time she had seen someone's face look like that. It had been Colonel Reid's, at Begum Johnson's party, talking about the stigma tainting the half-caste.

Captain Reid went very still. Penelope looked from Mir Alam to Captain Reid, watching as they locked eyes in a battle of wills, the one slight and bent, the other tall and straight, but momentarily alike in the animus that crackled between them.

It was Captain Reid who looked away first. "As both my brothers did," he said levelly.

Penelope could see Freddy assessing Captain Reid's tanned skin and dark coloring and working through his own conclusions.

"But you were in the Madras Cavalry, Reid," Freddy said abruptly. "Weren't you?"

While he must have known exactly what Freddy was getting at, Captain Reid gave him no satisfaction. He smiled tightly. "Yes."

Penelope could see Freddy working that one out. If Captain Reid had been in the East India Company's army, and the East India Company's army didn't accept half-Indians, then, ipso facto or whatever that Latin phrase was, Captain Reid couldn't be half-Indian.

Even so, Freddy took a discreet step away, as though to disassociate himself from any possible taint. It was distressing enough for him having a half-Irish wife.

It would have been one thing if her grandfather had been heir to an Irish peerage, like Lord Wellesley. Irish peers might not be quite up to the level of their English counterparts, but a peerage rendered anyone at least marginally socially acceptable. No matter how hard her mother tried to hide it, Penelope's maternal grandfather had been little more than a glorified horse trader. A successful horse trader, but a horse trader for all that.

Penelope's father, comfortable in his baronetcy, Saxon to the backbone, more at home in the saddle than the drawing room, hadn't minded in the slightest. He thought it rather a good deal, finding a chit who was easy on the eyes and came with a steady supply of good horseflesh. Penelope's mother had minded. She had worked so hard at eradicating her origins that any mention of the Irish or the equine evoked a blank stare and an increasingly agitated fluttering of her fan. Discussions of breeding were enough to send her into a swoon—provided there was a soft surface behind her, that was, as Penelope's paternal grandmother had caustically pointed out on more than one occasion.

It was all, Penelope considered, rather a good joke. Her father had married her mother for her stable; her mother had married her father to get away from it. By the time each had figured out their mistake, it had been too late to do anything about it. The "I do's" had been said.

That sort of thing was becoming rather a family tradition.

Captain Reid didn't seem to notice that he had been snubbed. He was frowning over his shoulder at a young man in an unfamiliar uniform who appeared to be trying to signal something to him in an awkward species of mime.

With a palpably false smile, Captain Reid turned back to their small group. "I have already monopolized far too much of your time. Enjoy the nautch, Lady Frederick."

There went all her theories tossed into a cocked hat. If Captain Reid was in league with Mir Alam, she would eat Freddy's best hat.

As an afterthought, Freddy offered her his arm as the chief minister led them into a vast courtyard that had been tricked out with piles of vividly woven rugs and soft cushions. The scent of attar of roses perfumed the air, mingling with the chief minister's scented tobacco and the faint, smoky smell of the hundreds of candles inside their lanterns, strung up along a carefully charted wilderness of unfamiliar trees.

"Have you ever been to a nautch before, Lady Frederick?" the chief minister was asking her.

Penelope dragged her attention away from Captain Reid's retreating back, nearly tripping over one of the tiles in the process. "No," she said brightly. "I haven't."

"Then you are in for a treat." Mir Alam smiled, baring teeth whose perfection only emphasized the ruin of his face. "Some of our foremost poets plan to recite tonight. And," he added, with a nod in Freddy's direction, "there will, of course, be dancing."

"And a cannonade?" drawled Penelope.

Mir Alam's smile curdled slightly. "Not tonight."

"Pity," replied Penelope flippantly. "I do so enjoy a good execution."

"You don't approve of my methods, Lady Frederick?" Penelope noticed that the minister had dropped the careful plural that he had employed while speaking with Captain Reid, abandoning the pretense of speaking for anyone other than himself.

"Nothing of the sort." Had she said otherwise, Penelope had no doubt she would soon find herself on a more intimate acquaintance than she would like with the inner workings of large munitions. *Watch your back*, Captain Reid had said. In that, at least, he might have had a point. "It's not my business to approve or disapprove. I am merely a visitor here."

"An extended visit, one hopes," said Mir Alam mendaciously. "Having come so far. We are a very long way from Calcutta."

The words were an uncanny echo of Captain Reid's warning earlier that evening. In this case, they were quite definitely uttered as a threat.

Freddy, being Freddy, remained completely oblivious. "It was a bally long trip," he agreed. "Worse than getting to Scotland for the shooting."

"You shoot, Lord Frederick?"

"What doesn't fly away first," interjected Penelope. Below an arch of lanterns, the performance had already begun. The plaintive tones of an instrument unfamiliar to Penelope scraped across the air. It made the skin prickle on her arms, like the passing of a banshee in her mother's native land.

"There is very good hunting at my estate in Berar," commented the minister, ignoring Penelope. "I would be delighted if you would do the honor of visiting me there."

The words "estate" and "hunting" completed the process that the diamonds and rubies had begun. As far as Freddy was concerned, Mir Alam was a thoroughly decent chap. If he played cards, preferably badly, he might even be elevated to "jolly good fellow."

Captain Reid, on the other hand, clearly fell under "not quite one of us."

Tugging on Freddy's sleeve, Penelope stood on her tiptoes to hiss in his ear, "Will you make my excuses for a moment?"

"What?" demanded Freddy under his breath, making an apologetic face at Mir Alam as he leaned over towards her.

Penelope rolled her eyes at him with the familiarity of matrimony. "You know."

"Oh, right," said Freddy. He gestured vaguely back the way they had come. "I think it's that way."

That was precisely what she wanted to hear. Penelope batted her lashes up at him. "I won't be long."

Below the arch of lanterns, the first of a string of dancers had emerged, undulating her way to the center of the courtyard.

"Don't hurry back," said Freddy jocularly.

"Beast," Penelope shot back.

Waggling her fingers at Mir Alam, she wiggled her way back among the chattering groupings of courtiers, enjoying the relative freedom that came of being entirely on her own for the first time in what seemed like weeks. It was sometimes, she had learned, easier to be entirely on one's own in a ballroom full of people than it was in one's own bedroom. Especially when one shared that bedroom with a large man with a penchant for scattering his belongings across the widest possible radius.

After that coffee, she did have a vague notion of doing what she had implied and finding the nearest necessary. On the other hand, should she happen to run across Captain Reid along the way, that wouldn't be her fault, would it? Penelope squished the voice in the back of her head that was emitting a very loud, very sorrowful *Oh Pen*. It sounded a great deal like Henrietta.

Well, really. It wasn't as though she were planning to drag him out onto a balcony.

Captain Reid hadn't gone far. She spotted him just off the main courtyard, in a covered corridor with a round fountain at the center, circled with marble pots of flowering plants. The corridor echoed the shape of the fountain, the vaulted roof held up by a series of ornately carved pillars in lieu of walls, leaving it open to the garden and the breezes.

Captain Reid stood with one elbow propped against the fountain, listening with great attention to a young man with a shock of light brown hair tied back in an old-fashioned queue. The ribbon with which he had tied it was beginning to fray around the edges.

"—not a little matter," the other man was saying in a low, worried tone. "We're talking about thirty-two hundred guns gone missing! How can you expect to conceal that?"

Chapter Ten

The two men stood by a running fountain, the sound of which blurred their voices. Inching her way around a pillar, Penelope drew closer, counting on their absorption in their own affairs to hide her from their notice.

"We haven't much time," the younger man was saying worriedly. "One can hardly fail to notice they're not there!"

"Don't worry," said Captain Reid. "I'll take care of it."

"How?" The younger man looked around wildly, causing Penelope to duck behind her pillar, missing whatever it was he had to say next. She deemed it safe to pop out again just as he was saying something that ended in "—money's already gone."

Frowning, Captain Reid stared off into space. Her space. His eyes focused on her face with an expression that Penelope would not exactly have called pleased.

"Reid?" urged the younger man. "What do you—"

Following Captain Reid's gaze, he lapsed into blushing confusion.

An expert at brazening out sticky situations, Penelope strolled out from behind her pillar as though she had intended to do so all along.

"Lady Frederick," said Captain Reid.

He sounded more resigned than alarmed, a state of affairs that pricked Penelope's pride.

"Captain Reid," she drawled, giving her hips an extra undulation as she closed the space between them. "I always do seem to run across you in the most . . . unexpected places."

"Hardly unexpected, since I came with you from the durbar

hall," observed Captain Reid. "Lady Frederick, may I present to you Lieutenant Plowden. Lieutenant Plowden is with the Subsidiary Force."

Red with more than sunburn, Plowden jackknifed into a bow so energetic Penelope could hear his teeth rattle. "Ma'am."

"Perhaps you might be able to tell me, Lieutenant Plowden. What is this Subsidiary Force? I'm rather new here."

Lieutenant Plowden looked to Captain Reid before answering. At Captain Reid's slight nod, he explained haltingly, "We have a treaty with the Nizam, you see. In exchange for a subsidy from the Nizam, we maintain a force on his behalf."

"I see," said Penelope thoughtfully. Including thirty-two hundred guns. How much money had the Nizam paid for those? And how much of it had made its way into Captain Reid's pocket? As a motive for malfeasance, money made a good deal more sense than politics.

"There used to be a French force as well," Lieutenant Plowden added in a rush, "but now there's just us. There's rather a lot of us, too. We're off across the Brinjara Hills, just ten miles north of the city." He flapped his arm in a direction that Penelope, who had an excellent sense of direction, was fairly sure was south rather than north. Well, she did have that effect on men, she thought tolerantly.

Not all of them, unfortunately.

"The cantonments have become a city all their own," Captain Reid interjected in a blatant attempt to turn the topic of conversation to more neutral channels. "You'll find it a bit of home away from home. There is even," he added, like a governess dangling a treat in front of a recalcitrant child, "a Europe Shop that sells goods from England. You might want to pay a visit one day. Properly chaperoned, of course."

"If I wanted to be at home, I would have stayed at home," said Penelope tartly. She was sick of being fobbed off with promises of shopping. She didn't even like shopping. Penelope favored Lieutenant Plowden with a melting gaze. "Do tell me if I've got this quite right, Lieutenant. The Nizam pays a certain amount of money to your commanding officers in exchange for men and arms."

The candlelight picked out the downy fuzz on Lieutenant

Plowden's cheeks. He blushed slightly as he replied. "Yes, quite. You understand the matter perfectly, Lady Frederick."

"Not quite perfectly," said Penelope, looking at Captain Reid as she said it. "But I believe I begin to."

Captain Reid's gaze met hers with a jolt like steel striking steel. "Do you?"

His eyes were as hard as agates. He might, Penelope realized for the first time, be a dangerous man to cross, more dangerous by far than the conceited dandies she had so carelessly and effortlessly manipulated on London's social stage.

Well, let him be. She could be rather dangerous herself.

Made of weaker stuff, Lieutenant Plowden prudently removed himself from the line of fire. Murmuring halting excuses, he stumbled off. Penelope scarcely noticed that he had gone.

"Thirty-two hundred guns, Captain Reid?" she said.

Penelope saw his lips press very tightly together. "You know what they say about eavesdroppers," he said, with a leaden attempt at levity.

"Nicer things than they say about embezzlers."

"Em—what?" His eyes bugged out in a highly gratifying fashion.

"It's not a complicated word, Captain Reid." Penelope was rather enjoying herself. "Embezzler. E-M-B-E—"

"I know what it means, Lady Frederick. And how to spell it." Captain Reid scraped a hand through his hair in an expression of masculine agitation. "You can't possibly think that I—"

"Are lining your own pockets?" said Penelope sweetly. "With the Nizam's money? How else would you describe it?"

No one had ever accused Captain Reid of being diplomatic. "Pure bunk," he said bluntly.

"Language, language," trilled Penelope.

He gave her an exasperated look. "Oh, but it's quite all right for you to go around flinging words like *embezzlement* at people."

Penelope shrugged, feeling the lamplight sliding over her bared décolletage like a lover's caress. "If the shoe fits . . ."

Captain Reid wasn't the least bit amused. "It doesn't. Would you like me to turn out my pockets? I assure you, they're quite empty."

"I don't know how many guineas thirty-two hundred guns will fetch out here, but I imagine it's more than will fit in your waistcoat pocket," said Penelope caustically. "Just how did you intend to *take care of it?*"

Captain Reid drew in a very deep breath through his nose. Having got himself under control, he spoke very slowly and very carefully. "You don't understand what you're talking about."

"That's what you'd like me to think, isn't it? And I suppose you don't know anything about Freddy's girth, either."

After a moment of startled silence, Captain Reid's lips twitched. "I believe I can safely say that your husband's physique is a matter of supreme indifference to me."

Oh, so he thought that was funny, did he? He wouldn't be laughing so hard in the shadow of the gallows. "Not that sort of girth. The sort that attaches to a saddle. The sort that can be cut."

Captain Reid blinked at her. "I don't follow."

Penelope drew herself up importantly. "If," she said, drawing out the word with relish, "you had a lucrative interest in the sale of purloined armaments, you might not be too interested in having a representative of Lord Wellesley's around. You might even do something to eliminate him."

For a moment, Alex thought he had misheard her. "Eliminate"? What? Lady Frederick's determined face blurred in front of him in the torchlight, reminding him that he hadn't eaten anything since seven this morning, save for several cups of very strong Turkish coffee. He had spent the morning in fruitless arguments with a series of minor ministers, fighting to have the three sepoys turned over to their commanding officer. Military discipline wasn't pretty, but it was preferable to being shot out of a cannon. And now, on top of it, this business of the missing guns. He ought, he thought tiredly, to bring it up with James immediately, passing on the information that Ollie had been too afraid to bring to the Residency. But he had Lady Frederick in front of him, her lips still moving and, from the looks of it, not saying anything he particularly wanted to hear.

Could he just go to bed, pretend none of this had ever happened, and start the day all over again?

"'Eliminate him,'" Alex echoed, liked a child repeating a lesson.

"What better way to rid yourself of an inconvenient complication than a fall from a horse in the middle of a river?"

Alex gaped at Lady Frederick. No, he hadn't misheard. She appeared to be accusing him of attempted murder. He couldn't deny that there were several times he would have liked to have murdered Lord Frederick, but dash it all, didn't he deserve credit for resisting the impulse?

He was too tired to be diplomatic, too jarred by her accusations to be patient. "It doesn't take more than rudimentary intelligence to think of several more effective methods. If I had intended to murder your miserable husband, he would be long dead by now," Alex snapped. "And far less conspicuously than that."

"How can you be so sure?" taunted Lady Frederick. "Have you done it before?"

Alex rolled his eyes up to the ceiling. "Are you trying," he demanded between clenched teeth, "to test how far I can be pushed before turning homicidal? If so, you're going about it the right way."

"If you are such a saint among men," she shot back, "why does the Governor General want your activities investigated?"

"Not my activities. James's. Kirkpatrick," he specified for her, when she looked blank. The fact that she didn't even know James's bloody name raised Alex's anger to a whole new level. Through gritted teeth he enunciated, "The Resident. The man who has been forced to waste the past fortnight squiring your idiot husband about from hunt to card game when he could have been working. And do you know why Wellesley sent your husband to spy on him?"

"Treason," shot back Lady Frederick.

"Wrong answer," Alex snapped. "Because James had the poor taste to fall in love with a Hyderabadi lady and make her his wife. Considering that Wellesley's wife is French, I call that rich on his part," he added bitterly. "He should look to his own loyalties."

Lady Frederick eyed him mistrustfully. "That can't be all."

"Can't it? No," he said, in a conversational tone that raised goose-flesh on Lady Frederick's bare arms, "I suppose it's not quite all. James also has a brother who doesn't get on with Wellesley's brother. That's another strike against him. On such great matters do careers rise and fall."

Lady Frederick tossed her head in a gesture that reminded Alex of Bathsheba swishing her tail at flies. "I'm sure you're exaggerating."

Alex dropped his hands, feeling suddenly exhausted. Turning, he said, "Am I? Do me a favor. Go ask someone else. Ask anyone. They'll tell you the same."

Lady Frederick obviously wasn't in the habit of being contradicted. Yanking at his sleeve to draw him back, she said, "I don't think—"

Shaking her off, Alex glared at her. Fine. If she wanted to have it out, they could have it out. Then he was bloody going to sleep. Alone. And if she showed up in his dreams, he would—well, something nasty. "No, you don't, do you? You don't think at all. You just act. You jump into rivers, you accuse people of murder, and you make a bally big mess for everyone else to clean up."

"I saved that man's life by jumping into the river," Lady Frederick protested, plunking her hands on her hips.

"Well, chalk one up for you," Alex said unpleasantly. "And it would have been a good deal more bother if you had gone and got yourself drowned in the process. Did you ever think about that?"

"A good deal *less* bother for you, I should think. I'm surprised you didn't push me into the river yourself."

At the moment, Alex very much wished he had. He bared his teeth at her in a simulacrum of a smile. "You said it, not I. You come flounc-ing in here, leaping to all sorts of conclusions about things about which you know nothing. *Nothing*," he repeated, as Lady Frederick opened her mouth to argue. "Did you bother to read a single book about India before you came here? Speak to a single person?" Lady Frederick's mouth snapped shut. "Christ! As for that bloody girth, you don't even know whether it was cut or not, do you?"

Lady Frederick bristled. "And how would you know it was the girth if you weren't the culprit?" she demanded.

"Because *you* just told me." They stood glaring at each other like pugilists at a pause in a prize fight. Alex couldn't resist adding, "Besides, if I were a murderer, don't you think it would be a bloody stupid thing to come out and confront me with it? Alone? In a deserted corridor? If I were you, I'd be checking my girths pretty carefully, Lady Frederick."

Lady Frederick stared at him, her expression defensive. She wasn't scared, but she was uncertain, and the sensation was one that didn't please her in the slightest. He could see her desperately searching for a rearguard action, any way to retreat with honor. He might even feel sorry for her if he wasn't so bloody furious. She had just made a cake of herself and she knew it.

Lifting her nose into the air, Lady Frederick sniffed disdainfully. "Don't be absurd, Captain Reid. I'm sure you'll find a much more *effective* way of killing me. I shall look forward to it," she tossed over her shoulder, before executing a dramatic turn and stalking around the curve of the corridor with all the outraged dignity of a scalded cat.

Cursing under his breath, Alex started into the courtyard after her, although whether to apologize or continue the argument, he wasn't quite sure.

Under the floral arch, a countertenor was enumerating the charms of his mistress in a high, pure soprano: a voice like honey, thighs like banana stems, arms like lotus stalks, and hair like the Ganges. Alex recognized it as one of Mah Laqa Bai's poems, set to music.

A delicately hennaed hand on his arm arrested his forward progress. Alex recognized it as belonging to the poetess herself, the celebrated courtesan, Mah Laqa Bai. Who was also, like everyone else, a very old friend of his father's.

Mah Laqa Bai followed his gaze to Penelope, who was swishing her way purposefully to where her husband sat, her high-piled hair like living flame in the light of the lanterns. "She hasn't a voice like honey, that one."

"More like vinegar," Alex agreed. He felt as though he had just bolted an entire glass of the substance. His lips might be permanently puckered from it.

His companion cast him a mischievous glance. "And the thighs like banana stems?"

"I wouldn't know."

A slight smile played around Mah Laqa Bai's much-lauded lips. "That looked very much like a lovers' quarrel to me."

Why did everyone keep saying things like that? "Love doesn't come into it. Or making love, at that. The lady is married. And not to me."

Across the courtyard, beneath the tent reserved for the *omrahs* and honored guests, the lady's husband was watching the progress of the dancers with more than idle speculation. One dancer in particular appeared to have caught his eye, a round-breasted, round-hipped girl with jeweled bands encircling her plump arms above the elbow and at the wrist. Pearls outlined her hairline and a long collar of pearls and semiprecious stones fell between her barely veiled breasts, swinging with the tempo of the music. Lord Frederick watched the sway of the pearls as though hypnotized.

"She's married to him," Alex said, indicating Lord Frederick.

As the courtesan danced, she twined a length of orange silk shot through with gold into an elaborate, many-petaled flower. Lifting it suggestively to her lips, she tossed it straight into Lord Frederick's lap, leaning so close that the pearls, warm with the heat of her breasts, brushed his nose.

Lady Frederick did an admirable job of seeming not to notice, but Alex didn't miss the slight narrowing of her eyes. Appropriating the flower, she placed it conspicuously in her own décolletage.

Mah Laqa Bai made a moue. "The big blond? He hasn't taken his eyes off Nur Bai all evening. A poor choice, that. She's a venal little baggage. She may have breasts like pomegranates, but that's all there is to her."

She would know. Mah Laqa Bai had risen to success in her profession by her brains as much as her beauty. Her library was unrivaled in

Hyderabad, her poetry was acclaimed as the finest in the land, and as a final tribute, she had been raised to the post of senior advisor to the Nizam, the only woman so honored.

She had also been the lover of Mir Alam, one of the few men with an intellect to match her own. Before the illness had reached his brain, that was.

"There's not much to Lord Frederick, either," Alex said caustically, before turning to Mah Laqa Bai, deliberating blocking his own view of both Lord Frederick and his lady. "I'm glad to see you here. I've been wanting to speak to you."

Mah Laqa Bai tilted her head to one side. "I, too, have been wanting to speak to you."

"I did stop by last week," pointed out Alex.

Mah Laqa Bai's eyes twinkled in a way that made her look about half her official age. "But I was otherwise occupied."

Alex didn't ask with whom. Sometimes, it was better not to know.

"Whoever he was is a lucky devil," he said politely.

Mah Laqa Bai lifted a beautifully groomed eyebrow at him. "Don't flatter me. You don't do it nearly so well as your father."

More things Alex didn't want to know.

"There have been rumors," he began, moving to the topic he had intended to address.

Mah Laqa Bai's expression was as pleasant as ever, but he could sense her sudden alertness. "There are always rumors."

"Rumors about the gold of Berar," Alex said doggedly. "I had thought you might have heard something."

It was a very long moment before Mah Laqa Bai answered. In the lantern light, Alex could discern the very faintest signs of lines beneath her carefully applied paint. "May I give you some advice? As a friend?"

Alex lowered his head in a wary nod. Anything that began that way couldn't end well. Not to mention that the way she had said it made him feel about thirteen years old, freshly arrived at boarding school.

"For your own good, do not go prospecting too deeply into matters that do not concern you. The deepest well may hide the most poisonous snakes."

"The deepest well?"

"Not the most elegant metaphor," Mah Laqa Bai agreed calmly, "but none the less true for all that. Watch yourself. This is not a good time to incur Mir Alam's anger."

"Does Mir Alam have an interest in the gold?" Alex pressed on. The chief minister had been in exile in Berar when the gold had gone missing. Mir Alam and Mah Laqa Bai were, by all accounts, no longer lovers, but Alex wouldn't have been surprised to find that the latter still played the role of confidante.

"Did you hear what he did to the widow of Aristu Jah?" Mah Laqa Bai countered. Without waiting for Alex to respond, she said, "He sent five troops of the Nizam's guards to ransack her home. They dragged her bodily from her house. And that because her dead husband had incurred his enmity. Take care."

Alex attempted to make light of it. "I have too little in the way of worldly goods for him to bother with me. I heard he made a pretty haul when he confiscated her belongings."

"It is not only Sarwar Afza Begum against whom he has moved," Mah Laqa Bai said reprovingly. "But Rajah Ragotim Rao and any other he believes has crossed him. Do not allow yourself to be added to that company."

No need to tell her that it was too late for that.

Having delivered her warning, she added, in a more conversational tone, "You might also be interested to know that Major Guignon has been seen in Hyderabad."

Brilliant. A mad ruler, a demented First Minister, a sultry Englishwoman bent on accusing him of everything short of barratry (and he had no doubt she would get around to that once it occurred to her), and now a rogue French officer.

He ought to have stayed in Calcutta.

"He's banned by treaty." Frowning, Alex remembered Tajalli's theories about French plots. If Louis Guignon really had crept back into the city, it lent considerably more credence to Tajalli's suspicions.

"By your treaty," countered Mah Laqa Bai.

"Signed by the Nizam."

"By the former Nizam." Mah Laqa Bai spoke in her capacity as *omrah*. "I fail to see why we should have to relinquish the services of a talented commander—"

"Guignon wasn't that talented," murmured Alex. "The man was a pastry chef back in France."

By all accounts, he made a tantalizing brioche, but his soldiering left something to be desired.

Mah Laqa Bai shot him a reproving glance. "I fail to see why we should relinquish the services of any commander we might choose to employ, whatever his individual merits, for the sake of people who can't be bothered to keep their treaties."

Her words bit like a steel-tipped lash. And they were fair. Alex had to acknowledge that.

Closing his eyes, he said, "The guns."

"The guns," Mah Laqa Bai agreed. "And the men. The Nizam, true to his promises, has paid the money owing on his part. Where are the men and arms your government has promised us? When the Nizam called upon them to restore order in the town during the festival of Muhurram, not half of those promised appeared, and of those who did, they had not sufficient firelocks among them."

Ollie Plowden had told him the same, adding, on top of it, that not only were munitions missing, but also tents, carriages, and artillery, all listed as purchased and accounted for on the official record, none actually in place in the storehouses. The most likely explanation was that the commanders of the Subsidiary Force were pocketing the money the Nizam had sent them. James had caught them at it before, adding to the deterioration of a relationship between Residency and cantonments that was already strained.

It wouldn't be the first time James had discovered discrepancies in the equipment and muster rolls, but never before had the graft approached anything like this scale. There was no getting around it. The commanders of the Subsidiary Force were robbing the Nizam blind.

Alex turned a troubled gaze on Mah Laqa Bai. "You do know that—"

Mah Laqa Bai's expression softened. Silencing him with a finger to his lips, she said, "I know. If it were up to you, it would not be so. But . . ."

"But it isn't up to me," Alex finished for her. "Or, in the event, to James."

Both looked to the tent where the Governor General's new emissary sat sprawled on a pile of shot-silk cushions.

"Will it help if I say I'll do what I can?" said Alex wryly.

Mah Laqa Bai laid a hand lightly on his arm. "All I can do is promise you the same."

The smoothly polished stones of her rings were cool against his palm as he squeezed her hand. "You would tell me if there was anything afoot, wouldn't you? Anything dangerous?"

"Haven't I just?" she said lightly, but Alex noticed that she didn't quite meet his eyes.

Alex's stomach sank. He hadn't realized how much he had been relying on her help until she had denied it.

Fair enough. If their positions were reversed, he would have been expected to do the same, to place his loyalty to his country before personal affection.

It sounded simple enough in theory. In practice, Alex wondered what it was like to have such marvelously unclouded loyalties. Mir Alam might talk of men torn between their mother's lands and their father's, but what of men like him? British by blood, but born in India, raised in India, more comfortable with curry than claret, more at home at a nautch than a ball. He had spent his four long years at school in England talking about India, writing to India, planning his return to India. If it came down to it, which would he choose?

He knew his father's answer: England. Having eaten the East India Company's salt for thirty long years, his father would, in the end, despite children, wives, and lovers, always be the Company's man. There were times when Alex wished it could be that simple. When it came down to it, he didn't really belong to anywhere at all—not to the East India Company, not to England, not to the town where he had grown up, or the province in which he currently served.

Christ. He didn't even have a proper mother tongue. He had spoken Tamil before English, and Telagu before Tamil, the legacy of the series of ayahs who had taken over as his mother had faded first to nothing more than a soft Welsh voice in a pile of bed linen and from there to nothing more than flat lines on a painted miniature.

"I think," said Mah Laqa Bai, lightly touching his arm and jarring him out of his reverie, "you should make it up with the lady who is not your lover."

"You merely want fodder for another poem."

Mah Laqa Bai tapped a finger against his cheek. "My dear boy, I already have more than enough of *that* on my own." Glancing sideways at the stiffened silk canopy beneath which Lady Frederick sat, she added slyly, "I believe your Lady Vinegar is jealous. Look how she scowls at me."

Despite himself, Alex looked. He shouldn't, he knew, any more than he should feel a surge of smugness at the prospect. It was simply one of Mah Laqa Bai's stratagems, an attempt to keep him safely occupied, away from Mir Alam, and out of danger. But he looked nonetheless.

"You see?" said Mah Laqa Bai, leaning mischievously into Alex's arm. Lady Frederick's lips tightened.

"It's not what you think," said Alex dourly. "She's simply sizing up my neck for a noose."

Chapter Eleven

"Brilliant news!" exclaimed Freddy, looking up from a thickly scrawled piece of paper. "Fiske is coming to visit."

"Brilliant," echoed Penelope hollowly, taking the seat at the breakfast table that a servant held out for her. Her head ached as if with the aftereffects of overindulgence, even though she had taken nothing stronger than sherbet the night before. "Who is Fiske?"

"In my regiment," pronounced Freddy around a piece of toast. "He was at Begum Johnson's party. You met him."

After a moment, Penelope's sluggish memory dredged up a picture of a willowy man with a decidedly piscine leer. Brilliant.

"He's passing through on his way to Mysore," Freddy said, paper rustling as he shifted it in one hand to read down through the scrawled lines. Jam dripped from the toast he held in his other hand onto the linen tablecloth. "Excellent chap."

There were letters sitting by Penelope's place, as well. A packet must have come through. She flipped desultorily through the lot of them, avoiding watching as Freddy decapitated a soft-boiled egg with a sporting swipe of his spoon. The runny yellow innards looked the way her head felt.

Sleep had eluded her the night before. After Freddy had claimed his husbandly duties in a discouragingly perfunctory fashion, she had been left awake, staring at the mosquito netting, brooding over the mess she had made of the evening. There was no denying that she had made a cake of herself with Captain Reid. A great, big plummy cake, served up on a sterling silver platter. With custard sauce.

Penelope sniffed. If he didn't want people thinking he was up to no good, he shouldn't skulk about so.

Freddy edged his chair away. "Catching a cold, are you, old thing?" Freddy had a horror of colds.

"I'm fine," said Penelope irritably, and reached for the pile of letters. It was a sad day when one couldn't even indulge one's feelings in an audible manner without being accused of contagion.

The letter on the top of the pile was from her mother. Penelope gave the seal a savage crack.

Her mother hoped she was behaving herself and not boring her husband with any of her silly fidgets. She was sure Penelope wouldn't mind if one of Penelope's younger brothers took over her hunter while she was gone. *Such* an inappropriate mount for a lady and she didn't know what Penelope's father had been thinking to allow it. Penelope should be sure to pay her respects to Lady Clive while she was there; it didn't concern her mother at all that Lady Clive was in Madras, clear on the other end of the country, or that Penelope had never met Lady Clive, never been introduced to Lady Clive, and had no interest in anything to do with Lady Clive. The letter ended with a lengthy disquisition on Freddy's older brother's health, in the clear hope that the heir to the earldom would have the good manners to kick up his clogs, leaving Penelope with the title her mother so ardently desired.

Crumpling up the thin sheet of paper, Penelope tossed it aside. It glanced off the marmalade pot before landing in the kedgeree.

"My mother sends her regards," she told Freddy.

"Mmmph," said Freddy. "Badger Throckhurst fell into a soup tureen."

Penelope went back to her post. There was a very thin letter in the Dowager Duchess of Dovedale's characteristic scrawl, the paper poked through in the many places where the Dowager had thought it fit to emphatically jab her quill, and a much longer one from Henrietta, who informed Penelope with great glee and an excessive use of adverbs that Charlotte and her duke had reconciled and were to be married from Dovedale as soon as enough champagne could be procured.

Charlotte's courtship had been complicated by the discovery of a nest of spies in a branch of the Hellfire Club, the same branch to which Freddy had belonged, although Henrietta skirted carefully around that bit. Too carefully. Penelope scowled at the letter. The club had originated in India, among Freddy's old regiment. Charlotte was very concerned that Penelope keep an eye out for a mysterious Marigold, although Henrietta thought it unlikely that the spy ring should still be in operation by the time her letter arrived, now that they had squished the English branch.

Penelope's lips twisted in a decidedly unbecoming expression as she paged through the letter. Evil had been vanquished, good had triumphed, and everyone was happy, happy, happy. Charlotte's duke and Henrietta's Miles got along famously, according to Henrietta. Miles had even put the duke up for his club. Charlotte sent her love and was planning to write as soon as the wedding madness was over, with some pressed flowers from her wedding bouquet so that Penelope would have been there at least in part. Or at least part of something that had been there would be with Penelope. Well, Penelope knew what she meant. They all sent lots of love and missed her to bits and hoped she was having a glorious time in India, riding elephants and draping herself in rubies as big as her thumb.

Lovely, thought Penelope sourly. Everyone was one great big happy family except her. And she had brought it all on herself. She couldn't even cry injustice. Charlotte was everything the novelists approved: meek, docile, kind to small children and smaller animals, filled with love and goodwill towards her fellow man. She had never got into a scrape that Penelope hadn't dragged her into first, and her idea of rebellion was to stir an extra spoon of sugar into her tea. And Henrietta was just Henrietta, deep down basic goodness without a mean bone in her body, wholesome and nourishing, like a well-baked loaf of bread. Whereas Penelope . . .

Penelope shoved her chair abruptly away from the table. A servant scrambled for it as the legs caught on the carpet edge, sending it rocking back and forth.

"I'm going for a ride," she said shortly.

"*Mmmph,*" said Freddy.

"Yes, I will have a nice ride," she said caustically, and was rewarded by one puzzled blue eye emerging from behind a seven-month-old *Morning Post*.

She swept out before he could answer.

The last thing she wanted was to actually talk to anyone, much less Freddy. She just wanted to *go*. It didn't matter where, just as long as she was moving. Moving, moving, moving, without having to think. She was in no mood to dwell on other people's happily-ever-afters.

But that was just what Captain Reid had taken her to task for doing last night, wasn't it? Acting without thinking. Well, with any luck, she'd unthinkingly ride her horse straight into a gully and then he'd be shot of her and she wouldn't have to think about anything ever again.

But no matter how hard she tried, she couldn't quite stop thinking. The thoughts rustled around in her brain like moths in a clothespress, eating their way through her composure and her temper. She made short work of her wardrobe, scrambling into her riding habit, blazed past the startled *munshi* who had come to work with her on her Urdu, and stood snapping her riding crop on the veranda, waiting for Buttercup to be brought around. Naturally, she hit herself in the ankle. Fortunately, she was wearing sturdy boots beneath her habit, so the only welt it left was on her temper.

She had not enjoyed her first nautch. While Freddy was ogling that creature with the overdeveloped chest and Captain Reid was being pawed by a woman old enough to be his mother—well, old enough to be his aunt, but it was still revolting—she had taken the opportunity to question the Resident's Chief Secretary, Henry Russell, about Captain Reid's claims. Russell was highly thought of by Wellesley; Penelope had heard the Governor General commend him out of his own lips. He could be trusted to give her an unbiased answer.

He had. Only it wasn't at all the answer she had wanted.

Yes, he had said, Wellesley did have a bee in his bonnet about Kirkpatrick's marriage. Didn't understand it himself; lovely lady Khair-un-Nissa, and he was sure if the Governor General ever met her . . . Reid? Honest? To a fault. Quite dull about it, actually. He hoped she hadn't been too bored on the journey down. He would have gone himself to see to her comfort on the journey, but the Resident couldn't possibly spare him—and besides, Kirkpatrick had thought it would be nice for Reid to see his father again before the old man left for England. An amusing chap, Reid's father. Oh, she had met him? Pity the son hadn't inherited any of the father's address, but there it was. No one could deny that he was a hard worker, and quite good at what he did, but he played no cards, only danced when pressed to, and hadn't a coat worth looking at.

It was only with great difficulty that Penelope had extricated herself from Russell, who misinterpreted her inquiries as being directed at securing his attentions rather than his information—almost as much difficulty as she had had extracting Freddy from the cleavage of that little nautch girl, whose breasts seemed to grow more prominent with each undulation. Penelope, whose charms lay in aspects other than that sort of endowment, had felt increasingly sour as the evening wore on. It wasn't as though she could pull up her skirt and wave a leg in front of Freddy's face, although she had been sorely tempted at various points.

Her horse duly brought round, Penelope was just arranging her leg over the pommel of her sidesaddle (Freddy had been aghast at any suggestion of her riding astride once they arrived at the Residency) when she saw another rider heading past their bungalow on his way to the main gates.

Naturally. It would be Captain Reid.

Penelope resisted the urge to drop off her horse and hide behind its flank. Squaring her shoulders, she accepted her crop from the groom, waving him aside as she spurred grimly after Captain Reid.

"Captain Reid!" Penelope urged her horse forward, intercepting him before he could reach the gate.

There was no way for him to pretend he hadn't heard her. Captain Reid reined in his horse, but he didn't pretend to be happy about it.

"Lady Frederick," he said, with a stiff nod of his head.

Bathsheba was far happier to see Penelope than was her rider; the mare nickered gently as Penelope reined up beside her.

"You needn't worry," Penelope said, reaching out to rub Bathsheba's nose. "I'm not going to start flinging accusations at you."

"Arson?" he suggested. "Barratry? I believe you missed those last night."

He sounded more wry than angry. Penelope didn't know whether to be relieved or not. Belligerence would have been easier to deal with than toleration.

"What *is* barratry?"

"I'm not quite sure," he admitted. "But you can accuse me now and then look it up later."

"I believe I can forego that pleasure. Look," she said brusquely. "I seem to have got hold of the wrong end of the stick. No. Never mind that. There never even was a stick."

"Perhaps just a very small twig," offered Captain Reid blandly.

"Not even that." If one was to go to the bother of apologizing, there was no point in doing it by half measures. "As you said, I leapt to conclusions. If I were a man, you would have been within your rights to call me out."

"Within my rights, but excessively foolhardy if I had. I imagine you're a very good shot."

"I am," Penelope agreed without false modesty, taking hold of the olive branch he offered. "I doubt you would have survived the engagement."

"Please," he protested. "At least do more the honor of assuming it would have been a close run thing."

Penelope conducted a deliberate assessment of Captain Reid's person. In the interest of determining the steadiness of his shooting arm, of course. He bore it with remarkable fortitude before quirking a brow, silently inviting her verdict.

"I believe it would have been," she acknowledged. "But I would have won."

"We can test that one of these days in the field," he offered. "Aiming at sand grouse rather than each other?"

"Can we?" Realizing she sounded overeager, Penelope hastily resumed a tone of extreme aristocratic boredom. "But I should let you be on your way. I'm sure you're off somewhere *frightfully* official."

"Nothing that admirable. I'm on my way to see a friend's new falcon." On an impulse, he offered, "Would you like to join me?"

"Yes!" Her face lit with such enthusiasm that he hadn't the heart to rescind the invitation. "That is, I haven't had much practice at hawking. I should like to see it. My father doesn't keep birds." Penelope realized she was saying too much, too fast, and abruptly occupied herself readjusting her grip on her reins. "Where is your friend?"

"In the city." From his expression, he was already questioning the wisdom of having invited her. "If you don't wish to—"

Usually, Penelope would have scorned to batten onto someone else's generosity, but she was wild to get out of the Residency. The prospect of another morning of Embroidery and Writing Letters to Home in the demure confines of one of the Residency parlors acted on her like mosquito bites. The very thought of it made her twitch.

Penelope kicked her mount into movement before he could complete the thought. "Lead the way," she said briskly.

For a moment, he looked as though he might demur, but he acquiesced with good humor. They rode through the Residency gates in a silence that, if not companionable, at least was not actively hostile. After being too long pent, to be outside the Residency walls was very heaven. As they crossed the river, Penelope tipped back her head, letting the sunshine fall full on her face and breathing deep of the wonderful, strongly scented air.

"We have the same sun above the Residency, you know," said Captain Reid, but he said it not unkindly, and the expression with which he watched her held more than a little bit of understanding.

"Yes," said Penelope, "but it always feels dimmer there. As if it's trying to be English."

Captain Reid laughed. "I think that's the architecture. All those Palladian pediments and whatnot. Those ridiculous bungalows are like a little bit of Bath moved to the Deccan. One could hardly expect that the clouds wouldn't follow."

"Have you been to Bath?" asked Penelope. "I thought you spent your life out here."

"I was sent to school in England. I spent my vacations with my grandmother in Bath."

Penelope wrinkled her nose. "You must have been frightfully bored."

He smiled, but refused to allow himself to be drawn further. Shrugging, Penelope turned her attention away from him. They had reached the markets at the center of the city, and it took all her horsemanship to keep Buttercup steady as they threaded their way through a confusing mix of pedestrian and animal traffic. It was a very different thing to be riding through the city virtually on one's own, rather than shoved inside a tightly shrouded palanquin in between two men both taller than she, with troops of English soldiers to clear the way before and behind them.

Penelope navigated around half-clothed children playing in the dust, beggars clutching at the trailing end of her riding habit as she passed, and lean dogs, tucking their tails between their legs as they skulked close to the food stalls, trying to get close to roasting meats before the proprietors spotted them and shooed them away with sharp pronouncements and wildly placed kicks. Women with their veils pulled loosely around their faces inspected trays of sweetmeats and lengths of cloths, the chime of the thin gold bangles ringing their wrists adding a high, sweet note to the general cacophony of haggling, snorting, laughing, groaning, farting, barking, and squawking going on all around them. Penelope saw Chinamen with strange round caps inspecting bulbous stems of ginger, a group of Dutchmen with ginger whiskers disputing over lengths of gold brocade, and a party of Goans leading their horses to market. The strong scent of cloves and nutmeg from the spice market battled with the more acrid stench of urine from the narrow alleys that twisted off to the side. The perfumers, with their aromatic oils, appeared to be doing a brisk business.

The smell of grilling meat made Penelope's stomach rumble, reminding her that she had been too busy flinging correspondence into the breakfast dishes to actually eat.

Riding close beside her, to protect her from the press of the crowd, Captain Reid turned his head. "Are you hungry?" he asked. He looked critically at the flies swarming around the nearest stall. "I wouldn't necessarily recommend partaking of these, but if you'd like—" He broke off abruptly, his mouth dropping in an expression that Penelope could only describe as distinctly nonplussed.

Penelope followed his gaze, expecting to see a rat, at the very least, but instead all she saw was a man, staring coolly back at Captain Reid. He had just received from the vendor a bowl filled with a stewed concoction of rice and meats whose scent made Penelope's stomach renew its grumbling with added enthusiasm.

As Penelope watched, the man raised one hand in insolent salute. With the other, he tossed the bowl to a beggar with a laughing instruction in the local tongue.

Bits of hot rice and fowl went flying as several other beggars immediately pounced on the bounty, sending food scattering in all directions. It made an excellent diversion. Through the hopping of angry pedestrians as they shook rice from between their toes, Penelope could see the man, whoever he might be, swinging himself up on horseback. He had, she noticed, a very good seat, although his horse wasn't of a breed she had encountered before. The ears were the most curious aspect; they seemed to curve inward, like a goat's horns. But she didn't have time to check its configurations. With one last, backward wave, the man speedily made his exit down a side lane, leaving a melee of angry pedestrians and hungry beggars in his wake.

And one very unhappy Captain Reid. Penelope had never seen anyone's lips go quite that white, short of frostbite. Captain Reid looked as though he had just been chewing icicles.

With one impatient movement, he gathered his reins together. Penelope suspected her presence was all that prevented him from indulging in a hearty bout of profanity.

"Stay here," he tossed over his shoulder, and spurred his horse forward.

Did he really think she was just going to sit there and wait for him?

With one last, longing look at the food stalls, Penelope set off behind him. The moving waves of traffic, complicated by the high-crowned palanquins of the highborn, blocked the fleeing man from her view, and evidently from Captain Reid's as well, based on the number of times he checked his horse, rising on his stirrups for a better view. Occasionally he would shout something in Urdu, and receive either a pointing arm or a shrug in response.

They twisted this way and that way, until even Penelope had lost all sense of her bearings winding in and out of the narrow lanes of the city. They passed through cluttered complexes of noisome hovels, in front of which sprawled beggars without even loincloths to cover their nakedness, and broad, marble-fronted palaces several times the size of St. James, from which the songs of birds could be heard from the hidden pleasure gardens within. And still they went on, past the city walls, past the ruins of a forgotten palace, up, up, and up the hillside.

As she navigated around a stubborn donkey, Penelope caught a flash of a man, much farther up the hill, bent low over the neck of his horse. He wore native dress; his white robe flapped against his calves as he urged his horse up the hill. Penelope thought she could see trousers beneath, though, and when the speed and incline served to dislodge his turban, the matted hair beneath was a reddish brown rather than black. There was a curious construction at the top of the hill, an open temple more suited to Athens than India, and an obelisk in the Egyptian manner.

As the flapping white robe disappeared behind the obelisk, Captain Reid clapped his heels against his horse's flanks, urging his tired horse forward. Following suit, Penelope squinted up into the sun, which seemed to be lodged directly at the tip of the obelisk, like a ball impaled on a needle. It clouded the fleeing man in light-borne shadow, making dark blots against her eyes so that he seemed to disappear into the obelisk in an explosion of black dust.

Captain Reid arrived at the top of the hill before her, but only just, and judging from the complex of lines around his eyes, he had been no more immune to the sun's effects than she. He swung off his horse before it had fully stopped, running behind the obelisk as though he expected to find the white-robed man crouched behind it. Penelope galloped to a stop as he stomped out from behind, a decidedly disgruntled expression of his face.

"If you wanted me to go home, you could have just said," Penelope panted, resting her cheek against her horse's neck.

"Damn," Captain Reid said under his breath.

Below them, the pony scrambled his way down the hill, riderless. Pacing back and forth in short, jerky strides, Captain Reid placed one hand to his eyes, scanning the horizon for any sign of the missing rider.

Sliding off her horse, with stern abjurations to it not to move, Penelope ambled over to the temple. It was in the Greek style—at least, it looked Greek to her. And new, very new. The stone showed none of the wear and tear one would expect in a land of heat, sun, and monsoon. There wasn't much to the structure, just a simple rectangle of pillars, with a triangular pediment in front. The whole was suspended on a thick platform of the same stone. There was no place at all for anyone to hide.

As Penelope prowled through the pillars, her attention was caught by a small scrap of pale paper on the floor of the temple. There was writing on it, and in a European hand.

Penelope scooped up the scrap and stuffed it in her pocket, shooting a quick look over her shoulder at Captain Reid. Good. He hadn't noticed. He was still standing just next to the obelisk, frowning into the sun as though it had personally offended him.

"Well?" said Penelope, strolling over to join him, the scrap of paper burning a hole in the pocket of her riding habit. "Who was that?"

"A Frenchman. Named Guignon. He was second in command of the French force out here. They used to be quartered . . . just there." He pointed at a spot on the landscape indistinguishable from any other spot on the landscape.

"Why not just call at his lodgings if you wish to see him that badly?"

"That's the thing. He doesn't have lodgings. He's meant to be banned from the province."

"Cheeky on his part to come sneaking back, then," offered Penelope.

"It might not have been him," Captain Reid added hopefully, speaking more to himself than her. "It might very well have been someone else entirely."

"How good a view did you get?"

"Before he turned and ran? Enough of one to think—" Frowning, he shook his head. "But I could have been mistaken."

"If you were, why would he have run?" said Penelope practically.

"Because I was chasing him?" replied Captain Reid. Looking at Penelope, he seemed to recall himself. With a brisk shake of his head, he said, "It's no matter. Never mind. I'm sorry to have dragged you all the way out here on . . . well, a whim."

Whim wasn't quite the word Penelope would have chosen. There were deep lines incised in Captain Reid's brow that belied the light-hearted term.

"Do you always take it upon yourself to apprehend stray Frenchmen?" asked Penelope. "Or just this Frenchman?"

The walls were back up, as immovable as the obelisk. "Forgive me," he said, with a palpably strained smile. "I'm afraid I've quite wasted your morning. We won't have time to see the falcon after this. I have an appointment back at the Residency at ten."

Penelope imagined that the apocryphal appointment could best be classified as avoiding Penelope, but decided to leave him be—for the moment.

"Where are we?" she asked instead, as he gave her a leg up onto her mount. "I don't believe I've been here before."

She hadn't been anywhere outside the Residency, except for the Nizam's citadel the night before, but there was no need to belabor that point. Freddy generally slept too late to ride with her in the cool of the morning, and she had not been invited to any of the hunting parties or evening entertainments in the town to which her husband had accompanied the Resident. When she had proposed a trip to the famed bazaars of the town, the Residency ladies had pled fatigue and heat and opined that it was much easier and more sanitary for the merchants to come to them. "*So* much more civilized," had said Mrs. Dalrymple, the leader of the pack, and that had been that.

"Raymond's Tomb," said Captain Reid, swinging up onto his mare. "Raymond was the commander of the French forces here. That's his insignia on the obelisk. The large *R*."

Penelope eyed the obelisk. The *R* was indeed there, incised upon a large square of darker stone than the rest of the edifice. "So this would be a logical place for a French fugitive to flee."

Captain Reid cast her a long, inscrutable look. "Be careful going down the hill," he said shortly. "This road can sometimes be slippery. I'll go first."

Penelope let him. As he picked his way down the hill ahead of her, his back to her, she slid one hand into the pocket of her habit, feeling the crinkle of that scrap of paper. The fact that it could still crinkle suggested that it hadn't been exposed to the elements for long. Checking to make sure Captain Reid was still busily ignoring her, she drew the paper stealthily out of her pocket, pressing it flat against the folds of her skirt.

The writing was dark and clear against the page.

I am ready to sacrifice all. Await my coming to place the next steps in motion. Then, my comrade, the strength of the machine you have put together may display itself and the tree of Liberty shall blossom again in the courtyards of the East.

Chapter Twelve

The tree of liberty shall blossom? Penelope had never heard such melodramatic babble in her life, and that included some of Charlotte's early efforts at epistolary fiction.

The note was in French, in a controlled, cursive hand. The syntax, however, wasn't nearly so precise as the handwriting. It wasn't that it was ungrammatical, precisely. It just wasn't as elegantly constructed as it could be. She could have done better than that, thought Penelope critically. No one would ever accuse her of being bookish, but she did have a knack for languages.

"Lady Frederick?" Captain Reid turned his horse's head, and Penelope hastily crammed the letter back into the pocket of her habit before turning on him a bright and beatific countenance. Perplexed at the sudden warmth of her smile, Captain Reid said quizzically, "We'll take the short way back, if you don't mind."

"No," said Penelope airily. "No, not at all."

Lapsing back into silence, she meditatively crumpled the piece of paper in her pocket. She ought, she supposed, to hand it over to Captain Reid. That would be the sensible thing to do. The responsible thing to do. Penelope snuck a sideways glance at her escort, at the granite profile beneath a battered hat. If she gave the note to him, that would be the last she ever heard of it. With another man, she might have used it as a bargaining chip, teasing out the transfer in exchange for information. She did not think that would work with Captain Reid. The note would disappear into his pocket just as it had disappeared into hers, and she would be left once again to the Residency drawing room, being bored to death one antiquated anecdote at a time.

It might be more rewarding to pursue one's own investigations. If only one knew who to pursue.

Await my coming, the note had said. Whose coming? There had been no salutation on the note, no closing courtesies, no direction on the back, nothing to indicate the author or the intended recipient. The man they had chased to the top of the hill might have dropped it before it could be delivered; it might be his arrival elsewhere that was spoken of. But would a Frenchman write such poor French?

He might, Penelope decided, absentmindedly gnawing on the finger of her riding glove. She certainly knew Englishmen whose grasp on their own grammar was wobbly at best—Turnip Fitzhugh came to mind—and she had only Captain Reid's word on the identity of the man on the hill. He might not have been a Guignon. He might have been a Smith or a Jones or a Fotheringay-Smythe.

Or a Fiske.

Like an echo, Penelope could hear Freddy's voice, thick with toast. *Fiske is coming to visit.*

Penelope frowned at the back of Captain Reid's head. Fiske looked nothing like the man on the hill, at least not what she remembered of him. The coincidence of phrasing was nothing more than that—a coincidence.

Or was it? Fiske had been a member of Freddy's regiment. To be more accurate, Fiske was still a member of the regiment to which Freddy had once belonged. The same regiment out of which, according to Henrietta, a ring of French spies had been operating.

What else had Henrietta said? She had been too busy sulking to pay much attention to Henrietta's tales of espionage and immorality.

Henrietta was always stumbling across spies. Henrietta's older brother, Richard, had gone about France under the sobriquet of the Purple Gentian, pinching French aristocrats from the Temple Prison and leaving amusing little notes under Bonaparte's pillow, while Henrietta's gallumping oaf of a husband performed the odd job for the War Office—presumably when they couldn't find anyone better, thought Penelope unkindly. She and Miles had never gotten along. Her insistence on referring to him as a gallumping oaf might, she was willing to admit, have had something to do with that, but if one were a gallumping oaf, one had to expect to be called that from time to time. Or all the time.

After years of flowery aliases and Purple Gentian this and Black Tulip that, it all tended to go in one ear and out the other, much like her mother's repeated admonitions about her behavior. Just this once, though, Penelope wished she had bothered to pay attention.

Taking advantage of the broadening of the path, Penelope edged her mare up alongside Captain Reid's.

"Freddy's friend Fiske." Penelope's tongue slipped slightly on all the alliteration. She soldiered manfully on. "You know him, don't you?"

Startled, he looked at her sideways. On horseback, they sat nearly eye to eye. He had, Penelope noticed, an exceptionally good seat. Her grandfather would have approved.

"Why do you ask?"

"Because he's flinging himself on our hospitality on the way to Mysore, and I want to know what I'll be obliged to endure over the dinner table. Well? What do you think of him?"

"I know him primarily by reputation," Captain Reid hedged. "You'd do better to ask your husband."

"In other words, you don't like him," said Penelope with relish. "Why?"

"I don't know him well enough to like or dislike him. We don't really move in the same circles. I," he added deprecatingly, "am not a great player of cards."

Fleetingly, Penelope remembered standing alone in Begum Johnson's drawing room, as the card room drew Freddy like a fly to dung. The only queen of Freddy's heart was the sort that did somersaults on green baize.

"I don't imagine you would be," agreed Penelope. "You bluff very poorly. Now that you've got all that out of your system, what do you really think? Come, come, Captain Reid. This is no time to develop a sense of discretion."

"Are you accusing me of prior indiscretions?" he asked smilingly.

"No more indiscreet than my own," said Penelope frankly, thinking of their conversation the night before. "Neither of us is framed for namby-pamby niceties."

Captain Reid bowed his head slightly, but not before Penelope saw his lips twitching. That, she thought triumphantly, was his Achilles' heel. No matter how much he tried to hide it, he had a sense of humor. "I stand well complimented." He fell silent, but it was a thinking sort of silence. After a moment, he said, "I meant it when I said I don't know Fiske well. The army chaps tend not to think highly of the politicals. It's one of the reasons," he added, looking off down the lane, "that we've had such bother with the Subsidiary Force."

"But you were in the army, too."

"The wrong army," said Captain Reid frankly. "I was in an East India Company regiment. It's not at all the same thing."

"Why not?"

"Stay here long enough and someone will be bound to tell you." As Penelope made a face at him, he relented. "Our troops are sepoys—Indians—rather than British soldiers. Even worse, we commit the social solecism of earning our commissions rather than purchasing them as a gentleman ought. Our officers, for the most part, are career soldiers, not gentlemen looking for a brief change of scene."

"In other words, like my husband," said Penelope. "Oh, for heaven's sake, don't look so stony. I'm not going to go repeat it to him. And for what it's worth, I agree with you. It's a remarkably silly system. I wouldn't trust Freddy to general his way out of a drawing room, much less a siege."

Captain Reid squinted thoughtfully. "It isn't always a disaster. There's Lord Lake, who's a decent strategist, and Lord Wellesley's brother, Sir Arthur, who's more than decent. And I imagine your husband would have no qualms about leading a charge straight into the heart of the enemy if the occasion arose."

"Yes," agreed Penelope, "shouting tallyho and swinging his saber all the way. He'd probably think he was out after a fox."

"Sometimes," said Captain Reid reflectively, "that's all that's needed, just making sure the men keep charging in the right direction. A fox or an enemy, it doesn't matter which, so long as he keeps them moving forward."

"Hmm," said Penelope, without much interest. "But Fiske . . ."

Captain Reid frowned at a pair of men trotting their way through the Residency gates. "Blast," he said. "They're early."

"So you did have an appointment!"

Captain Reid looked as though he didn't know whether to be exasperated or amused. "Is it just me you believe to be a terminal liar, or do you harbor the same suspicions of everyone?"

"Everyone," Penelope said promptly. "So few people have the backbone to say what they mean when they mean it."

"I believe other people call it tact," said Captain Reid dryly.

"In which I have already shown myself much lacking?" finished Penelope for him. "See? You do it, too. Only more obliquely."

"Was that a compliment?"

"It was meant as such," replied Penelope, offering back a phrase he had once used to her, by the side of the river Krishna. There was no answering flicker of recognition on Captain Reid's face. And why should there be? It was of no matter. Tossing her head, Penelope extended a languid hand to him. "Good day, Captain Reid. Thank you for the ride."

"You're welcome," he said, but he made no move to move on. Instead, he seemed to be debating something with himself. His fingers tightened fleetingly over hers. "Watch yourself with Fiske," he said.

And then, before she could question him further, he had released her, riding at a brisk trot along the gravel path towards the Residency proper. Blast the man! Penelope considered riding after him, but she doubted it would be of any use. He would only plead the pressure of his appointment. Sulkily, she surrendered her reins to one of the grooms and allowed herself to be helped from her horse. Reid knew something about Fiske that he wasn't telling. But what?

Ask your husband, he had advised her. Fine. She would. Looping the train of her riding habit up over one arm, Penelope stomped into the house.

"Freddy!" she bellowed.

It wasn't the regiment proper that Henrietta had mentioned as being the problem, was it? The regiment had been a recruiting ground for gentlemen interested in the practice of polite perversions. Could perversions be polite? Impolite perversions, then. It wasn't inconceivable that that was what Reid had known about and condemned. There was something of the Presbyterian minister about him, all stiff-faced morality. It made an interesting change.

"Freddy!" she hollered.

He wasn't in the drawing room or the bedroom or the tiny room that did service as a book room. Following a servant's direction, Penelope made for the back of the house, to the complex of rooms that made up the zenana quarters, although goodness only knew what Freddy would want there. According to the other wives, all the bungalows in the Residency had them, a suite of rooms designed to accommodate a *bibi,* or native mistress, along with the complex of companions and servants considered necessary for such an individual. "For the bachelors," Mrs. Dalrymple had explained primly, although Penelope doubted it was only the bachelors who had made use of such an arrangement.

True to the servant's word, she found Freddy in the corridor that connected to the old zenana quarters.

"You were looking for me?" he said, hastily drawing the door shut behind him.

"What in the world are you doing back here?" demanded Penelope, trying to peer around him. "You aren't planning to stick me into a zenana like the Resident's wife, are you?"

Freddy managed a sickly smile. "It takes a deal of imagining to picture you in purdah. There isn't a zenana quarter wide enough for you. What did you want me for?" he asked, looping an arm around her shoulders.

Penelope rested her head familiarly against his side. That was something to be said for Freddy; he made a very comfortable bolster.

At least, he usually did. Today, his chest was stiff beneath her cheek. "Why is your friend Fiske coming?"

"I told you. He's on his way to Mysore," said Freddy, steering her away from the zenana quarters.

Penelope let herself be steered. "Why Mysore?"

"Because that's where the regiment is. Shouldn't you be changing out of your habit?"

"Was he a member of that club you belonged to? The Hellfire one?"

Freddy's arm dropped from around her shoulders. "I don't know what you're talking about," he said stiffly.

Penelope backed into the bedroom door, using the momentum of her movement to push it open. "Of course, you do," she said, grinning up at him with her back against the door. "Lord, you're as red as a peony. Don't be all miss-ish, Freddy! I know all about your little orgies."

Freddy adopted a superior expression. "I doubt you know all about it."

"How much is there to know? An orgy is an orgy." Penelope's knowledge of orgies was limited largely to the fact that the Romans used to have them, but she doubted it took much imagination to figure out what they got up to. Depravity was depravity the world over, and generally not terribly creative. "Was Fiske a member of your little club?"

"It wasn't so little," muttered Freddy, resenting the slur on his branch of the Naughty Hellfire Club.

Men. So predictable. "Fine. Your *large* club, then."

Freddy scowled down at her. "Why so interested?"

"I simply want to know what to expect from Fiske," said Penelope loftily. "As your wife, it is my duty to entertain your friends." Ha! Let him pick fault with that one. Her halo was shining nicely. It was a sentiment of which even her mother could hardly disapprove.

"You needn't worry about entertaining Fiske," said Freddy, with some asperity. "I'll take care of him."

"Not orgies in the house?" murmured Penelope, gazing provocatively up at him from under her lashes.

Out of sheer habit, Freddy started to reach for her. But at the last moment he checked, sidestepping with an alacrity that almost made her lose her balance.

"You smell like horse," he muttered, not meeting her eyes.

Penelope walked her fingers up his shirtfront. "Call for some water and we can bathe." Freddy enjoyed the bath. It helped that there was always someone else on hand to clean up the spilled water after.

Freddy shook her off. "Not now, Pen," he said, striding towards the door.

Turning her head, Penelope delicately sniffed her shoulder. She didn't smell that bad. How did he think he smelled after a morning in the saddle? Not much like roses, that was for sure.

Penelope drew herself up to her grandest height. "Don't tell me you're actually *working* for once," she said caustically.

The suggestion of work horrified Freddy. Work smacked of trade and trade smacked of . . . well, people like Penelope's maternal grandfather. The sort of people one pretended not to know.

"I am the Special Envoy," he said indignantly.

"I know, I know," said Penelope snidely, turning away from him to unpin the coil of her hair in front of the cheval glass. "You're far too special to actually get anything done."

In the mirror, she saw the door start to swing before she heard the resounding slam. Penelope frowned at herself in the mirror. Arguments with Freddy were only productive when they ended in bed, something that they appeared to be doing less and less.

It was Charlotte who had expressed the hope that being exiled to India might be the making of Penelope's marriage. Penelope had scoffed at the notion at the time, but secretly, the idea had appealed to her. Going off to a strange place, with no one to turn to but each other—it did make a certain amount of sense, didn't it? Even if it had come from Charlotte, the most hopeless romantic since King Arthur's Round Table had ceased active recruitment. But it hadn't worked that way. They had done well enough on the boat. Freddy might have been distant in other ways, but he had always, always come back to bed.

On the boat, he hadn't had any other options.

Penelope frowned at her own face in the mirror. It wasn't a beautiful face, although men, cockeyed with port and desire, had often called it so. Her bones were too stark, her lips too wide, her nose too thin for beauty. She wasn't beautiful in the way Mary Alsworthy was beautiful, or even, in her own quiet way, Charlotte, with her porcelain prettiness. She ought, her mother had often said in disgust, to have been a boy. What she had—what she had always had—was nothing more than a pure animal instinct for attraction that drew men like dogs to a bitch in heat. As it had drawn Freddy.

Apparently, not anymore.

Untying the stock at her neck, Penelope felt a quiver of unease at the memory of that quick step away, at the way he had deliberately avoided looking her in the eye. He had scarcely looked at her at all.

Penelope forced a deep breath through her lungs, baring her teeth at herself in the mirror in an entirely unconvincing smile. No point in refining too much on Freddy's moods. He might simply be feeling the heat. Or was it only after she had asked him about Fiske that he had suddenly grown cold?

It was, wasn't it? Like Captain Reid, he knew something he wasn't telling her.

Since there seemed no opportunity to seduce any information out of either man, she would have to rely on Henrietta instead. Twisting in her seat, Penelope saw that the letters she had left on the breakfast table had been dutifully transferred to her writing desk, pending reply. The pile looked awfully thin, though. Henrietta's letter had been five sheets thick, closely written on both sides.

It wasn't there. The Dowager Duchess of Dovedale's letter was. Even the brief missive from her mother, left crumpled in the kedgeree that morning, had been carefully ironed into legibility and replaced among the rest of the post. But Henrietta's letter had been left out of the pile.

That was irritating. Penelope heaved herself up and swished her way out of the room, trailing the train of her habit behind her. The heavy wool pricked at her through her sweaty shift, but she didn't want to take the time to change; she wanted her letter and she wanted it now.

None of the servants, questioned in her halting Urdu, had the least recollection of having seen a folded packet of paper lying about on the floor or on a table or anywhere else at all. It was not, she was told with degrees of polite demurral by fifteen different servants, within their job descriptions. It took some time to find the person whose sole job appeared to be clearing the breakfast table. The letters had been removed, he confirmed, and placed on the writing desk. How many? After considerable back and forth, with some helpful interjections from those more accustomed to making sense of Penelope's attempts at Urdu, a count was reached. Three.

"But there were only two on my writing desk," said Penelope, with considerable frustration. Seeing the apprehension spread across the manservant's face at her tone, she waved a hand through the air. "It doesn't matter. I'm sure it's not your fault. Not . . . your . . . oh, bother. How does one say that in Urdu? It must have fallen somewhere after you put it there. Fallen down—*down*. Oh, never mind."

She should never have skipped her lesson that morning. It served her right for being all supercilious about the anonymous note-writer's French grammar, which was by far better than her Urdu. At least if the smothered smiles of the servants were anything to go by.

"Carry on!" she called in English, and swept back to her room with as much dignity as she could muster. There was no mystery to any of it. The movement of the fan must have blown Henrietta's letter off her writing desk. It was probably wedged under the armoire, or scattered page by page under the bed, and she wished she had never even started in on it with the servants.

Flinging herself to her knees, Penelope checked under the bed. Nothing. Save a spider who retreated as hastily at the sight of her as she did from it. Penelope dealt it a killing blow with a rolled-up newspaper and looked broodingly around the room, thwacking the flat of one hand with the rolled-up paper as she thought. The blasted thing had to be *somewhere*.

But no matter where she looked, Henrietta's letter was nowhere to be found.

Chapter Thirteen

S hifting, I accidentally kicked one of the albums off the bed.

It thumped, spread-leafed, to the carpet. Dropping the notebook I had been holding, I scrambled cursing off the bed. After uncounted hours curled up on the coverlet with a growing pile of Mrs. Selwick-Alderly's old notebooks, my limbs didn't want to move properly. My own notes, scrawled erratically with one hand, already filled a good half of the small spiral notebook I kept for those emergency occasions when a computer wouldn't be feasible.

Fortunately, the album didn't seem to be hurt. At least I had had the good sense to bump into one of the newer ones rather than one of the fragile old relics of Mrs. Selwick-Alderly's colonial wanderings. This one was made of sturdy modern material, with thick metal rings holding the plastic-covered pages in place. Murmuring apologetic noises to the abused plastic, I smoothed the cover closed, carefully checking for damage. None of the pages seemed to be bent, but something had fallen out. Plucking the sheet of paper from half-beneath the bed, I squinted at it curiously.

It wasn't a photo. But it also quite definitely hadn't been on the floor before. It was the beginning of a letter, written on thick, cream-colored stationery with Mrs. Selwick-Alderly's name embossed on the top. I couldn't see who it was addressed to; this must have been the second page, and only a draft, at that. It was heavily crossed out and interlined, in a way I would never have expected of my fastidious hostess. But she had clearly been in the grip of some strong emotion while writing the letter. The first full line, written ruler straight across the top of the page, read, *"To act on something that must cause those who love you so much unhappiness can only be accounted the most base self-indulgence."*

There it was again, that word, "self-indulgence."

I tried to remember why it sounded so familiar, why I could hear Mrs. Selwick-Alderly pronouncing it so clearly in my head. After a moment, the memory snapped into place. That was how she had referred to Colin's mother, condemning free spirit as merely another term for self-indulgence.

With renewed interest, I peered down at the piece of paper. The cross-outs made it hard to read, but the next line read, *"I should not have thought that even you could be so blindly selfish as to leave two grieving children deprived not only of a father, but of a mother, too. If you will not think of William, think at least of them and temper your own desires for the space of"*—she had crossed out at least five alternative word choices, finally settling upon—*"for a space in which reason and moderation might prevail. What seems imperative today may not be so tomorrow, and in the process, how many lives affected? I should not take it upon myself to interfere into your personal affairs upon a mere whim, but this—"*

Here the writer's words failed her in a sea of black ink. I could see the spiky *b, t,* and *l* of "betrayal" poking out among the general blackout, but the rest was unclear. Betrayal. It seemed an unusually strong word. There was stronger to come, under the wash of black ink. I squinted at the heavily scratched-out lines, trying to make out the letters. Was that "treason" there, a little after "betrayal"? I couldn't quite tell.

The letter picked up again in a calmer vein, as if the storm of emotion had washed itself out. *"If you must—as, indeed, I hope you will not—a space of time abroad would seem the wisest course."* Her pen had faltered on the word "wise," as though doubtful as to its use in that context. *"But I hope you will not. Do not make me ashamed to call you my—"*

A creaking sound down the hall jarred me out of my absorption. I banged my head against the mattress in my haste to stuff the letter back into the pages of the album, return the album to the box, and dispose myself innocently back among the Indian notebooks, breathing as quickly as though I had just been caught with my hands in my hostess's jewel box. Mrs. Selwick-Alderly might be indulgent enough about my foray in search of photos of an adorable, small Colin, but I doubt she would feel the same way about my reading her personal correspondence, especially correspondence such as that was.

I grabbed up a notebook at random and plunked it open on my lap, just in time. The door swung open on a widening arc, and a sleek brown head poked through.

"Oh!" I exclaimed, forgetting to try to look scholarly and absorbed. "Hi!"

Serena kept one hand on the door, as though unsure of her welcome. "I didn't mean to disturb you," she said, hovering in the door frame. "Please don't mind me. I just came to collect a pair of earrings from Aunt Arabella."

I half-scrambled, half-slid off the bed, my wool pants tugging up against my calves as I slithered down. "You're not bothering me at all. I was just about to call it a day anyway, before I overstay your aunt's hospitality."

As I said it, I realized it was true. The early dusk of winter had fallen, leaving it full dark outside, bringing into relief the cheerful circle of light cast by the bedside lamp. From across the way, I could see the dim reflection of a television screen through the window. It must be getting on towards dinnertime, at least. Judging from the profusion of cream-colored cardboard cards on the mantel, I wouldn't be surprised if Mrs. Selwick-Alderly had evening plans. She had let me stay behind to keep on researching while she went out once before, but I couldn't expect her to make a habit of it. No matter how nice she was being about it, it was still an imposition.

On an impulse, I asked Serena, "What are you up to tonight?"

Serena ventured a small, shy smile. "Watching *Emmerdale*?"

I wasn't entirely sure, but I rather thought that we might just have shared a private joke. It shouldn't have surprised me that Serena had a sense of humor—according to Pammy, she had been very clever in school—but I had never had a chance to see it before. Probably because

I was generally talking. Or Colin was there, and—let's be fair—when Colin was around, I didn't notice terribly much about anyone else.

"What would you say to a movie? There's the new James Bond playing at the theatre in Whiteley's. I guess that's pretty out of your way, though."

"No, I'd love to go," said Serena hastily, pushing her hair out of her face with both hands. "Unless—that is—unless you'd rather wait and see it with Colin."

"Not at all," I said firmly. "He doesn't need to see me drooling over Pierce Brosnan. It might hurt his feelings."

I got a full-fledged smile that time.

I waved my mobile in the air. "I'll just check for show times."

Our breath misting in the cold night air, we bundled into a cab. I almost never took cabs—a student stipend only stretches so far—so it felt wonderfully decadent to be coasting off into the night in a big black car to indulge in gratuitous entertainment in the middle of the week. The sharp air had brought a tint of bright color to Serena's thin cheeks. We scrambled into the back of the cab in a flurry of high heels and dropped gloves and trying to figure out who had accidentally sat on whose coat in the confusion of scooting across the black leather banquette.

We gave the cabbie the address and plopped back, with breathless laughter, against the back of the seat in the cozy, dark interior. We were going to the big multiplex in Leicester Square rather than the one in the Whiteley's shopping center, since we had already missed one and were too early for the other at Whiteley's. Besides, it somehow seemed more equitable to go to a theatre that would be equally inconvenient for both us, for Serena in Notting Hill and for me in Bayswater.

"I hope this one is good," I said, twisting to sit sideways with one arm against the back of the seat. "Thanks for saying you'd come with me."

"Did you find what you were looking for at Aunt Arabella's?" Serena asked politely.

"Sort of," I said. "I think so."

It might have helped if I could have said with any certainty what it was I had been looking for. Popular legend ascribed to the Pink Carnation various exploits in India, although neither the contemporary media accounts nor the scholarly sources had been terribly clear about what those exploits were meant to be. All that I knew was that the Pink Carnation was meant to have done something, somehow, in India. I had always wondered how he (back when I started my dissertation I had still assumed the Pink Carnation must be a he, arrogantly supposing that the Pink might even be a clever play on the phrase "pink of the *ton*" generally ascribed to dandies and the like) had managed that, when India was a six-month journey by boat. Each way. How would the Pink Carnation have had time to get to India, foil a dastardly French plot, unravel a league of spies, and then get back to Europe in time to meddle in Napoleon's coronation plans? It had never made any sense to me. Given the lack of such conveniences as telephones, fax machines, and FedEx, it didn't seem quite likely that the Pink Carnation would have been able to pass along orders remotely.

But it looked as though at least one aspect of the legend was being borne out. There had been a French spy ring in India and it had still been extant as late as 1804. For those non-historians out there, that in itself was a significant coup. Most people tend to just ignore India in the context of the Napoleonic Wars after 1799, assuming that once Napoleon got his unmentionables kicked in Egypt, that part of the world just ceased to be in play.

The system of flower names did seem to imply some sort of cohesive, overall organization, unless, of course, the Indian group was merely copycatting off their European counterparts. But who was organizing them? They might have been a part of the Black Tulip's empire, autonomous now that the Black Tulip had—presumably—gone to his reward. But the Black Tulip had specialized in petals, not in other flowers. I had the uneasy sense of having stumbled onto something far larger than I had anticipated and I had no idea at all where it was going.

If I were sensible, I would give the whole idea a miss. I would stick to the dissertation outline I had already submitted to my advisor, focusing entirely on the spies' European operations, without branching into the hinterlands.

But I was curious. Let's be honest, I was also looking for excuses to avoid writing up what I already had. Needing more research is always a brilliant reason to postpone actually writing your dissertation. After all, no one can accuse you of being lazy when you're working. There's a reason why you meet fifteenth-year grad students still diligently puttering away in the archives, amassing huge stockpiles of entirely undigested information. I knew one guy who spent nine years filling five file cabinets with notes without ever writing a single page of his dissertation.

Of course, there was no way I could justify my incursions into the Selwick photo albums as work. That was a different type of curiosity entirely.

"How are the Valentine's Day preparations going?" I asked in return. "The party, I mean."

The gallery for which Serena worked was throwing a big party for Valentine's Day, to showcase the works of one of their flagship artists, who apparently concentrated on deconstructing the Western tradition of romantic love. I hadn't recognized the name of the artist, but the price tags on his sculptures were enough to make my eyes go pop.

I'm a Pre-Raphaelite girl, myself. They did such a good job of painting red-haired women.

"You and Colin don't have to come if you don't want to," Serena said earnestly, once we had chatted about the mundanities of catering and guest lists and the pluses and minuses of having an event on Valentine's Day.

"Of course we do!" I exclaimed, a little too heartily.

Serena gave me a look. She might be insecure, but she wasn't stupid. It was probably painfully clear that my ideal Valentine's Day had more to do with champagne for two than squinting at abstract sculptures deconstructing the gendered Western notion of "love" (quotation marks theirs, not mine).

"I never say no to pink champagne," I added. That, at least, was true. And when it came down to it, I was just happy to have some-one to be with on Valentine's Day, whatever it was we did with it. I wished Serena had someone, too. Sadly, the Martin plan appeared to have been a damp squib.

Although he *was* coming to the gallery party, according to Colin. Under the influence of pink champagne, who knew what might happen?

"Pammy is coming, too," said Serena.

"Is she bringing anyone?" I asked curiously. Between Colin and the archives, I hadn't spoken to Pammy for a good few days. Given the way she went through men, she might be just about anywhere on the dating cycle since I had spoken to her.

"She's bringing a friend, she said," reported Serena, with a nice ap-preciation for the ambiguity of the remark.

"That could mean anything," I said in disgust. "I'll have to call her and ask. Oh, and did you know that Martin's coming?"

As an attempt at casual, it failed miserably.

Serena looked at me from under the shiny waves of her hair, with an expression of resigned tolerance that made me feel very, very young and very, very gauche. For a moment, she looked a great deal like her great aunt. "I don't fancy Martin," she said patiently.

"No?"

"No," she repeated firmly, adding, "but it was sweet of you to try."

Chagrined, I stared out the window as our cab nearly took the side mirror off a double-parked SUV. "What about Nick?" I asked, throw-ing Pammy to the wolves. Pammy could take care of herself.

"Nick," said Serena carefully, "doesn't fancy *me*."

"He certainly *likes* you," I said.

There it was again. That resigned curve of the lips, like the cover of old Judy Collins albums, where she's singing about being imprisoned behind the isinglass windows of her eyes. "No," she said. "It's just not on. Nick likes me as his friend's sister. That's all."

"*Mmmph,*" I said. If Miles Dorrington could learn to think of Hen-rietta Selwick as something other than a little sister, why couldn't Nick Whatever-His-Last-Name-Was take another look at Serena?

"No," repeated Serena quietly but firmly.

"Okay." Fortunately, the cab chose that moment to screech up to the curb, so in fumbling for the fare, the topic was dropped. While I was dropping pound coins on the floor of the cab, Serena efficiently paid the cabbie, rounding the fare off to the next number rather than falling prey to the American rule of fifteen percent. The cabbie, who must have heard my accent, looked disappointed.

I managed to reclaim my rolling change and get myself out of the cab without further incident, thinking soberly that I had to make myself stop treating Serena like a backward child, just because she wasn't as manically outgoing as most of the people of my acquaintance. For all that Serena's shyness made her seem younger, we were the same age. Depending on the date of her birthday, she may even be a few months older.

How had I come to start babying her like that? I guessed it came partly from knowing her through Pammy, who treated everyone, including me, like substandard preschoolers needing her firm hand and wise advice. There was also the fact that I'd wound up taking care of Serena on the second meeting of our acquaintance, holding her head over a toilet bowl at a party while she lost the remains of her supper. On top of that, there was Colin, who had all the protective condescension of any big brother for a delicate younger sister and who had strongly conveyed all of that to me. Not that any of those made a particularly good excuse.

It really was pretty presumptuous of me to try to give Serena advice about Nick and Martin, whom she had known far longer than I had. These were her people, not mine. When it came down to it, all of this was her world, not mine. She knew the streets, the people, the currency, the social cues in ways I didn't and probably never would.

There are times when I don't like myself much, and this was one of them. I felt like the worst sort of American stereotype, pushy and naïve all at the same time.

"Where do we go?" I asked with unaccustomed humility. Not wanting to brave the thronged street around the theatre, the cab had set us down some way from our goal.

Serena tugged her glove up on her wrist. "Just there," she said, nodding.

Despite the movie's having been out for a few weeks already, it was a popular showing, with people milling about in clumps as they filtered their way inside. Long posters hung on the side of the building, advertising the hero of the film in various dashing poses. I might like my nineteenth-century spies in knee breeches, but there was, I thought, really something to be said for martinis shaken, not stirred. "He's *so* cute," I said with a sigh, linking my arm through Serena's.

"Yes," she agreed distractedly, and I realized she wasn't looking at the poster.

Following her gaze, I could see a shock of red hair, visible among the shorter heads in the crowd. It was a different shade of red than mine, with more brown in it, cut in that casually expensive male style that looks as though someone just took a hedge trimmer to it. His teeth were very white against his ski-tanned skin as he smiled lazily down at his companion. His arm was slung cozily around her shoulders.

It wasn't Pammy—after umpteen years of school together, I would know Pammy from any angle—but it was someone of the same type, medium height, trendily dressed, with short, fluffy, expensively highlighted hair.

Of all the theatres in London we could have chosen . . . Damn. Damn, damn, damn. It was small consolation that now I didn't have to worry about choosing between Pammy and Serena; they both appeared to have been edged out before the competition even started.

I looked over at Serena and saw her watching me watching them. The Judy Collins look was back on her face, all resigned forbearance.

"See?" said Serena quietly.

It would be hard not to. I wanted to thump Nick over the head with an extra-large box of Milk Duds. Since that wasn't an option, there was only one thing to be done.

"Come on," I said. "Let's go get some popcorn."

Chapter Fourteen

"Whatever is that man doing with a bolster stuck down his dress?" demanded Penelope.

In the gardens of the Residency, a makeshift stage had been delineated by means of curtains and lanterns, illuminating a farce being played out by a local troupe of mummers, mostly in dumb show.

"That chap is a man, dressed as a woman, trying to sneak into a zenana," explained Daniel Cleave, leaning an elbow against the balustrade next to her. A slightly apologetic smile replaced the habitual look of anxiety on his fine-boned face. "Once you've seen these fifty times or so, you tend to get a sense of the plot. It will be the unwise horseman being fooled out of his clothes by traveling minstrels next."

"All his clothes?" demanded Penelope archly.

The mild-mannered civil servant blushed. "Just the outer ones, generally," he said. "At least, when there are ladies present."

On the stage, the bosomy imposter had managed to shoulder his way into the zenana, largely by dint of bowling over the eunuchs with his enormous chest, and was attempting to clutch a winsome zenana lady in his amorous embrace, in which he was considerably hampered by his bolster.

"Take it off!" hollered Lieutenant Sir Leamington Fiske from farther down the veranda.

The sentiment was echoed by his messmate, Ensign Jasper Pinchingdale, who punctuated his advice with a fist in the air that nearly sent him toppling over the railing.

Cleave, Fiske, and Pinchingdale had arrived two days before, bringing with them an escort of eight elephants, eleven camels, and one hundred and fifty servants. Freddy had been overjoyed to have the company of not one, but three new card players, although Mr. Cleave had proved a sad disappointment in that regard. He had, he had said, not the head for high wagers, and business to discuss with the Resident besides. So Freddy and Pinchingdale and Fiske had played cards, while Penelope had made a clandestine foray into Fiske's baggage without discovering anything more interesting than the fact that Fiske apparently thought it necessary to travel with enough medicaments to stock an apothecary's shop, with the emphasis on opium in every form one could devise.

One elephant had been devoted to carrying nothing but bottles of port, Madeira, and claret, although, from the way Fiske, Pinchingdale, and Freddy had been going, Penelope suspected its burden would be much lighter by the time they left Hyderabad for Mysore. Fiske and Pinchingdale had clearly been partaking liberally already, but of Freddy there was no sign. Showing a marked lack of interest in mummery, he had strolled back to their bungalow with the expressed intention of fetching Penelope's shawl for her. Since Penelope hadn't indicated any desire for it, she suspected that his marital solicitude arose out of a desire for a quick cigar well away from the disapproval of the ladies. Altruism was not a part of Freddy's makeup.

Below them, the buffoons had ceded the stage to a singer, who was singing in mournful tones in a language Penelope didn't understand at all. Grumbling, Pinchingdale and Fiske pushed away from the railing, wandering back into the Residency to avail themselves of more of the Resident's Madeira.

"Am I missing anything terribly exciting?" Penelope asked her companion.

"You should ask Reid to translate for you. His Persian is better than mine," said Cleave apologetically. "I deal mainly in Bengali these days."

She could see Captain Reid and the Resident standing a little way down the veranda, deep in conversation. The Resident wore his usual garb of a long, stiffened brocade robe over a pair of loose trousers.

With a small red cap on his head, and his narrow whiskers cut in the Persian style, he seemed as exotic and foreign as the keening lament of the singer or the scent of tropical flowers from the vast pleasure gardens he had helped to design. Next to him, Captain Reid looked jarringly normal. His evening clothes were as poorly tailored as his riding dress.

Over the past weeks, they had fallen into a habit of morning rides together. There had never been any official arrangement; it just somehow happened that Captain Reid always happened to be trotting past her bungalow at just the same time that Penelope was having her horse brought round. They were seldom very long rides—Reid always seemed to have appointments to get back to—but they had become more the cornerstones of her daily existence than she liked to admit.

When they did speak, they spoke of insignificant things; of the weather, or the scenery, or Mrs. Ure's latest act of extreme gluttony. Off-limits were Captain Reid's family, anything to do with Freddy, Hyderabadi politics, and the mysterious movements of French spies. She had never produced the note she had found and he had never said a word more about Guignon. They had never come to any sort of agreement on the topic; it had just sorted itself out that way, by mutual and tacit agreement. Those dawn hours, while Freddy still slept and the parched land rested from the sun, were like the territory outside a disputed castle, a place of truce rather than treaty.

She had never had a male friend before. Lovers, yes. Flirtations. But never a friend. It made an intriguing change.

Catching her eye on him, he smiled at her, a man-to-man, good comradely sort of smile. Penelope caught herself preening and made herself stop.

Mr. Cleave's light eyes flicked from one to the other with obvious interest. "Are you and Alex—friendly?"

The hesitation in his voice might have been just that, nothing more than the same diffidence that made him look so anxious in declaiming an ability to translate for her, but it seemed to imply something more. Penelope bristled.

"Captain Reid and I ride together," she said, more curtly than she might otherwise have done. "Horses," she clarified bitingly.

Deep color washed over Mr. Cleave's cheekbones. "I certainly never meant to imply—"

Penelope looked at him assessingly. "Didn't you?"

Having forced the retraction, she was more offended by the disclaimer than the initial assumption. Why shouldn't they be . . . friendly? Didn't he think she was attractive enough? Seductive enough? Penelope glanced sideways at Captain Reid. He stood directly beneath one of the lanterns that had been laced about the veranda. It struck red sparks off his black hair. What would it have been like had their morning rides been something else entirely?

Entirely misinterpreting the speculative expression on her face, Mr. Cleave rushed to defend his old schoolfellow from the calumny he felt he had accidentally brought upon him.

"Reid isn't anything like his father," Mr. Cleave said hastily. "At least, there have never been any whispers of it."

"Like his father?"

"Surely, you've heard—oh." Mr. Cleave broke off in considerable confusion. "You haven't, have you? Since you had made his acquaintance, I thought you must have known. . . . Well, never mind, then."

"You can't just 'never mind' me after that," said Penelope persuasively, leaning towards him in a way that made him go a very deep red. "I might make myself ill with curiosity. And you wouldn't want to be responsible for that."

"Oh, well." Mr. Cleave inserted a finger beneath his collar, as though his cravat had grown too tight. "It's just that the Colonel has a somewhat checkered reputation with women. It wasn't that unusual at the time," he added, accidentally heaping coals on the fire. "Many men took up with Indian women. But Colonel Reid—well, he was rather flamboyant about it. One of them killed herself. It was all," he said, with obvious distaste, "rather unpleasant."

"Not Captain Reid's mother?"

"Oh no," he hastened to assure her. "Not his mother. Jack's mother.

She was a Rajput lady, you see. Rather highly born. Her family dis-owned her when she took up with Colonel Reid."

"He must have been quite dashing in his day," said Penelope specu-latively, recalling a pair of twinkling blue eyes in a weathered face, volubly disclaiming any interest in games of chance. "A charming rogue."

In the corner of the veranda, Captain Reid grinned at something the Resident had just said. For a moment, Penelope saw a very fleeting re-semblance. Then it was gone, and Captain Reid was himself again, the very antithesis of roguishness. He might, Penelope suspected, have had his own share of charm had he not tried so very hard to suppress it.

"Not so charming for his wife—Reid's mother," said Mr. Cleave, flicking at a mosquito.

Penelope could see that it wouldn't have been. That, she thought practically, was the problem with charming rogues. They seldom con-fined their charm to one target.

"He was unfaithful to her?"

"Only at the very end," said Mr. Cleave, with painstaking justice. "Mrs. Reid was ill for some time. India didn't suit her."

He spoke as one who had seen it all personally. "How do you know all this?"

"My mother was quite close with Mrs. Reid. They came here to-gether as brides. This country is not kind to Englishwomen, Lady Frederick."

"Perhaps that depends on the Englishwoman," said Penelope tartly.

"My mother's health wasn't equal to it." There was no mistaking the bitterness in his tone. "India reduced her to a state of perpetual invalidism and provided her with none of the riches she was prom-ised. This is a country that makes some, but ruins untold others in the process."

Penelope brushed aside his philosophical musings. "What hap-pened to the boy? The one whose mother killed herself?"

"You mean Jack." He pronounced the name as though it were syn-onymous with pitch.

"And what does he do?" asked Penelope, amused. "Cattle-rustling? The odd bit of highway robbery?"

"I wouldn't be surprised," said Mr. Cleave, with more animation than she had seen him show so far. "He's—"

"Still telling tales, Daniel?" Mr. Cleave started guiltily, banging his elbow against the balustrade. Captain Reid cocked an eyebrow at him. "You're not still smarting over the incident of the toy soldiers, are you?"

Clutching his bruised elbow, Mr. Cleave flushed a bright red. "That was over twenty years ago, Reid! And they *were* my soldiers."

"You must forgive Daniel. He was an only child." The casual comment made the other man sound about five.

Penelope could feel him squirm against the stone balustrade. "Come, now, Reid," Mr. Cleave protested. "Jack was a bully, whichever way you look at it."

"Aren't we a bit old to be refighting schoolroom battles?" Captain Reid said lightly, but his expression didn't tally with his voice. Penelope had the impression that beneath his casual demeanor he was angry, deeply angry.

It would be rather nice, she thought, to have someone come to one's defense like that. It was impossible to imagine either of her brothers, aged twelve and thirteen respectively, doing anything of the kind.

Mr. Cleave's expression was painfully earnest as he looked up at his old schoolfellow. "It's not schoolroom battles that are the problem, Alex."

A palpable tension crackled between them. Penelope saw Captain Reid's lips press tightly together, closing over whatever it was he wanted to say—but wouldn't, while she was there to hear.

"Will you excuse me, gentlemen?" she said, whisking neatly between them. In her flat-heeled slippers, she was nearly as tall as Mr. Cleave. "My husband seems to have disappeared with my shawl."

Both gentlemen offered their assistance, as by rote, but it was clear that they both wanted nothing more than to be allowed to get on with their argument. Fair enough. Penelope was rather keen for them to get on with it, too. She wanted to know what they had to say. She swished past them with as much rustling, swishing, and fluttering as she could muster.

Once inside, she abruptly stopped swishing, gathering her skirts close to her legs to minimize the noise of her passage. Long windows, open for the circulation of air, looked out onto the veranda. Dragging over a chair, Penelope positioned herself beside one. If anyone asked, she was simply . . . resting her feet. No, inspecting her hem. Yes, that was it. A snagged hem was always a popular excuse. Scooting a little closer, she leaned her cheek against the white wainscoting.

At first, she heard nothing more interesting than the cry of the birds from the garden and the echo of Fiske's voice, slightly slurred by either distance or drink.

"Well?" said Captain Reid in a voice as hard as packed dirt. "What is it, Daniel?"

Cleave's voice, apologetic and anxious. "You know I wouldn't trouble you with this if it wasn't urgent. . . ."

"What does Lord Wellesley want?"

Cleave cleared his throat painfully. "I know he is your brother—"

"Perceptive of you."

"—But that doesn't change what he has become."

"What?" The word cut the air like broken glass. "What has he become, Daniel?"

Cleave's voice was so soft she could hardly hear him. "A traitor."

Oh my. Penelope nearly overbalanced into the open window. This was getting interesting.

Captain Reid sounded defensive, but not, Penelope thought, entirely surprised. "On what grounds?" he asked.

"You know who he was working for," said Mr. Cleave apologetically.

Who? This was the problem with eavesdropping, not that one seldom heard good of oneself, but that the people on whom one was eavesdropping were lamentably chary with proper explanations.

"He was working for Scindia," said Captain Reid flatly. The name was a vaguely familiar one. He might be, Penelope thought, something to do with the late war everyone had been talking about.

"He may have been nominally employed by Scindia, but he was working for General Perron," countered Cleave, giving the name a French twist. "And you know what that means."

Captain Reid's voice cracked like grapeshot. "Would you call George a traitor for working for the Begum Sumroo?"

"No. But—"

"But what?" said Reid harshly. "I fail to see how you can be a traitor to a country that never acknowledged you as its own."

"Why are you fighting so hard for him? He hasn't for you."

"Because we were children together. Because he's my brother. *Christ.* Do I need more reason than that?"

"That isn't all, Alex. If it was, do you think I would have troubled you with it?"

"If Wellesley asked you to, yes." There was no mistaking the contempt in his voice.

Mr. Cleave responded with a quiet dignity that was more than Penelope would have expected of him. "It's my duty, Alex. My obligation. I should have thought you would have understood that."

The silence hung heavy between them, all the more dramatic for the sounds of revelry from farther down the balcony. Penelope wished she dared to risk a peek out the window.

After a moment, Cleave resumed, in the tone of one determined to make the best of a bad business. "And there's more to it than that. We have—" Cleave's voice faltered, as though what he was about to say was distasteful to him. "We have reason to believe that Jack has been serving as go-between for the leaders of the French cause in India, lobbying on their behalf with rulers he believes might have cause to break with England. He's been offering them gold in exchange for allegiance."

"Gold from Berar."

"So you have spoken to him!"

The fight had gone out of Captain Reid's voice. Instead, he sounded bone-achingly weary. "No, Daniel, I haven't. Not since Christmas four years ago. I heard rumors about the treasure of Berar from other sources."

"What other sources?"

"If I told you, they wouldn't remain useful for very long, now, would they?"

"Is that your final word on the matter?"

"Am I on trial now, Daniel?" Captain Reid's voice was dangerously quiet, but even in her secluded window embrasure, Penelope felt the sting of it. "My record is as solid as yours and my word as good."

"No, no, nothing like that. Of course, I didn't mean—But what am I going to tell Wellesley?"

"Whatever you were bloody well going to tell him in the first place. I don't know, Daniel. I can't be your conscience." He gave a short, bitter laugh. "I'm my brother's keeper, not yours."

"Lady F!" A pair of gloved hands grasped Penelope about the waist, swinging her about to blast Madeira in her face. "What are you doing hiding away in here?"

"Just resting my hem," said Penelope nonsensically, wiggling away from Sir Leamington Fiske. There was little hope that they hadn't heard him out on the balcony. Raising her voice, she said, "You haven't seen Freddy, have you? I've been looking for him."

Fiske struck a heroic pose. He looked like a fish posing for a statue. "I'd rather feast my eyes on you."

"Watch out for indigestion."

Fiske blinked at her.

"Later," Penelope said soothingly, brushing a hand lightly against his sleeve. She had suffered Fiske's advances for the past week in the hopes of getting information out of him, and had gotten rather good at leading him on while ceding nothing. But right now she wanted to think. "Later."

"What's wrong with now?"

"Now," said Penelope charmingly, "I need to find Freddy. He was supposed to bring me my shawl."

Fiske released her with good grace. Penelope wondered if he was quite as foxed as he seemed. "When you find him, send him over to me, will you? We have a little wager that wants settling."

"I shall," promised Penelope vaguely.

Having told everyone she was going to find Freddy, it seemed that it was incumbent upon her to do so. She set off towards her own bungalow in a gray study, only half-aware of the rich scents of the night flowers, the now-familiar movements of servants moving about their tasks, the slither and rustle of animals in the underbrush.

As she walked on, she wondered whether she might have been wasting her time, these past two days, in attempting to wheedle confidences out of Fiske. Fiske, using every opportunity to fondle whatever came into reach, had implied a great deal, but confirmed nothing. When teased about French tastes, he had made a very crude joke about French letters. When Penelope had deliberately chosen to interpret that as a comment about correspondence, Fiske had made lewd comments about his prior correspondents. She had credited Fiske's lewdness to cunning. But what if he was simply lewd? The only French letters he received might well be the kind that came in boxes of twenty.

If everything she had overheard was to be credited, this Jack made a far better prospect for agitator than Lieutenant Sir Leamington Fiske.

Before Penelope could pursue that fascinating line of thought further, her attention was arrested by a familiar voice speaking in a decidedly unfamiliar way. It was Freddy's voice, low and intimate, murmuring something she couldn't quite hear. He sounded quite intent on whatever it was.

His voice had come from the unused zenana quarters at the back of the house. Semidetached from the body of the house, they opened onto their own enclosed courtyard. Untenanted, there was no reason for anyone to visit them, not even the servants. Penelope hadn't bothered to look inside since the Resident had first shown them around their new home, well over a month before.

What on earth did Freddy want in the old zenana quarters?

Wiggling through a gap in the shrubbery, Penelope shoved her way into the interior courtyard. There was no door into the encircling rooms, only cane screens that allowed for the air to circulate, while keeping out light and bugs. She could see thin slits of light through one screen, a sign that someone was very much in residence.

"Oh yes," said Freddy emphatically, obviously quite in agreement with the unknown person.

Lifting an edge of the screen, Penelope slid underneath. And stopped stumblingly short.

When she had first seen the zenana quarters, they had been empty and decaying, with patches of damp on the walls from the recent monsoon rains, falling chunks of plaster, and even a bird's nest in one corner of the ceiling. Now, gay hangings covered the walls, richly woven tapestries portraying lithesome ladies dancing in gardens much like the one Penelope had just left, sporting themselves beside the waters of cool fountains, or reaching into the air to catch a falcon on the wrist, while a lordly gentlemen in Jacobean costume sat in the shade of arched pavilions, the tip of a hookah resting between his parted lips. Silken cushions lay in careless piles upon richly woven carpets. A stringed instrument sat propped against one wall, the smooth wooden surface inset with precious mother of pearl. On a delicately carved table rested a filigreed carafe and glasses, cool in the warmth of the room, next to a display of honeyed sweetmeats piled in gluttonous array on a silver tray. Everything was rich and rare and lovely, a seduction of all the senses, from the haunting scent of flowers to the lilting song of a dainty songbird in a filigree cage, as pleasing to the eye as to the ear.

But nothing was quite so lovely or so rare as the woman in the middle of the room.

Her dark hair, perfect black, tumbled down her back, loosed more than held by the pearl band that circled her forehead. There were bangles on her arms and little else. Aside from the fall of her hair and the long necklace that fell between her breasts, she was entirely naked. She had the sort of figure Penelope had seen in temple friezes on their journey, all breast and hip, as smooth and round as well-worked ivory, carved to excite a man's lust. She was balanced on one leg, as graceful as an opera dancer. The other was wrapped around Freddy's right hip.

Freddy seemed more than happy with that disposition. His large hands were tangled in the wanton fall of her hair, his head thrown back and his eyes half-closed. His chest, bared by his open shirt, expanded and contracted in time to his uneven breathing. His companion rose farther up on tiptoe, bringing a delighted gasp to Freddy's lips and a contraction of his fingers in her hair.

Penelope emitted a squeaking noise.

She hadn't meant to. It just came out, like the last bubbles on the deck of a sinking ship.

An expression of extreme alarm crossed Freddy's face. She could see his eyes shift back and forth, mark the exact moment he had spotted her, standing at the back of the room. He stumbled violently back, sending his houri tumbling flat on her rump in a decidedly indelicate position.

Not quite so indelicate as his. The flap of his breeches dangled open, like a bad joke in a third-rate farce.

"Um, Pen." Freddy pinned a wobbly smile on his face. "Didn't expect to see you here."

Chapter Fifteen

"I don't expect you did," said Penelope distantly. "You might at least have secured the screens."

She looked contemptuously at the woman on the floor, who returned the expression with interest, no mean feat while lying entirely unclothed on one's back. But, then, thought Penelope with freezing scorn, she had probably had some practice at that.

"Um." Freddy had the grace to turn a deeper color of red, though he still contrived to look more affronted than affronting. Ignoring the woman at his feet, he cast Penelope a reproachful look. "Shouldn't you be watching the mummers?"

"Why should I, when there's such entertainment to be had here?" Without waiting for an answer, she said, in a cold, hard voice, "I want her out."

It was unclear how much English the courtesan understood, but she certainly understood that. Drawing a length of cloth over her nakedness, she sat back on her heels with the expression of one prepared to engage in a lengthy spot of squatter's rights.

"Now, Pen—" Freddy held out a conciliatory hand, the same hand that had, a moment before, been supporting some of the more rounded parts of the other woman's anatomy.

Penelope looked at it with an expression of pure loathing. "I want her out. Out *now*."

Freddy made a shooing motion—not to his mistress, to Penelope. "Let's discuss this outside, shall we?" he said hopefully, shoving his shirt into his breeches as he spoke. Penelope was surprised he knew how. She had only ever seen him remove clothing, usually in conditions of extreme haste. Not that he always removed all his clothing. Or hers. Sometimes . . .

Penelope yanked back her wandering thoughts. What did it matter? It wasn't as though she could stake her claim by a catalogue of the quantity and variety of his lovemaking. It wasn't a matter of earning one's position, so many tumbles to security.

Letting herself be herded through the screen, she said, in a tight voice, "You can't install a mistress in the same house as your wife. It's in poor taste, if nothing else."

"She's not a mistress," countered Freddy, with a bright-eyed enthusiasm that might have been either inspiration or afterglow. "She's a *bibi*."

"Calling it by another language," said Penelope, through clenched teeth, "does *not* render it any less offensive. I should have your balls for this. Oh, don't look so shocked. We both know you have them. And now," she said, flinging an arm in the direction of the screen, "so does *she*. And why," she continued, her voice rising dangerously, "am I the one standing outside like a . . . like a beggar, while that strumpet gets to lounge about inside?"

Looking nervously over his shoulder, Freddy made soothing, hushing noises, as though she were a horse who had just balked at a fence. "Don't cut up rough, old girl. This is just how it's done out here."

"Not in my house, it's not," Penelope said militantly.

"*Your* house?"

"Don't," warned Penelope. "Not when you've already spent *my* dowry. Possibly on drabs like her. How many have there been, Freddy? None on the boat, I suppose. You would have had to ship them in on little dinghies and that wouldn't have been terribly convenient. But in Calcutta, there were all those nights you were playing cards with Fiske. What were you really playing at, Freddy?"

It had been a bolt in the dark. Penelope hadn't expected confirmation until she got it, in the shifting of his eyes from hers, the working of his mouth as he tried to contrive a creditable explanation.

Penelope's stomach contracted as though she had been punched. Her tongue felt too thick for her mouth; she could feel it gagging her.

Freddy's hands moved in quick, impatient gestures as he worked himself into a soothing state of self-righteous indignation. "This is absurd," he blustered. "Why are we fighting about this? I'm married to you, however it came about. Anyone else is only a—"

"Diversion?" supplied Penelope, forcing her too-heavy tongue to move.

"Precisely," he said, nodding emphatically, pleased that she understood so well. "It isn't that you aren't, well, satisfactory, old thing—"

"Much obliged, I'm sure," said Penelope, white-lipped.

"—but a man does need a little variety. It's like having toast for breakfast every morning." Freddy warmed to his theme. "Toast is all very well and good, perfectly filling and all that, but sometimes you want a nice, big piece of ham."

"Which one of us is the toast?" asked Penelope. "Never mind. Don't answer that. Next I suppose you'll be wanting marmalade, too."

"I didn't mean it literally," said Freddy in a long-suffering way.

Penelope's voice was drier than burnt toast. "I know. Now that you've taken up the zenana, where am I to put my concubine?"

Freddy mustered a very credible "ha-ha," although he was still clearly suffering from the aftereffects of having been discovered in flagrante delicto.

"What makes you think I'm joking?"

Freddy delivered a stinging swat to her backside, a gesture with him that passed for affection. Lust involved other parts of the anatomy. And apparently other women, as well. "You're a good sort, all in all, Pen. You know how the game is played."

Penelope stood stiff and unresponsive as he slung an arm around her shoulders in a quick, careless hug, a curiously sexless gesture, the embrace of a comrade, not a lover. A lie, like everything else. They had never been comrades, only lovers. And now not even that. She could smell the scent of that woman on him, all flowers and musk, warm skin and sex.

"Yes," she said thoughtfully. "I do."

If Freddy had been a wiser man, he would have been very, very afraid.

Not being a wiser man, Freddy let out his breath in a gusty sigh of relief.

"I'll buy you some emeralds," he promised. "They'll look smashing with your hair. What do you say to that?"

"Smashing," Penelope echoed. "What a splendid arrangement for me—*she* gets all the work, and I get all the pay."

Freddy had the sense to look wary, as though he intuited that he had been insulted, but wasn't quite sure how and didn't like to inquire. "Quite so, quite so," he said with forced heartiness.

Gathering the rags of her dignity about her, Penelope took a step out of reach, towards the opening in the shrubbery through which she had entered a lifetime before.

"Don't be too long, will you, darling?" she said. "Fiske and that lot are looking for you. And we must keep up appearances, mustn't we?"

If Freddy recognized that her voice was several degrees colder than Norfolk in winter, he gave no sign. "I told Mother I could have done worse than to marry you," he said cheerfully.

High praise, indeed.

Penelope didn't wait to see where he went. She didn't need to. He had doubtless returned to his mistress—to pick up where he had left off? Or to apologize to her for his shrew of a wife, soothing her wounded feelings with promises of jewelry. What would he offer her? Sapphires? Rubies? Or would he buy them both emeralds, and get a discount for the bulk purchase, two women for the price of one? Penelope found she was shaking so hard she could hardly walk, shaking as though she had contracted a chill, even though there was a fine sheen of sweat on her skin, despite the pleasant cool of the evening air.

The worst of it was that there was nothing she could do. Oh, she supposed she could cry a headache, but why give Freddy the satisfaction? Penelope plucked with restless fingers at the fabric of her dress as she walked. She would have to go back and flutter her lashes and hang on Freddy's arm as though nothing at all were out of the ordinary, as if he hadn't delivered the crushing insult of installing a mistress under the same roof as his wife. The irregular circumstances of their marriage provided Freddy all the license he needed to do whatever he liked. "But I married you," he would say if she complained, and all the triple-chinned tabbies scattered in Residencies across India would agree with him that it was more than she had deserved. She was hoist by her own petard, whatever a petard might be.

The massive joke of it all was that nothing had happened on that fatal Twelfth Night nine months ago. Well, not precisely nothing. But Freddy certainly hadn't gotten what he'd been so ardently angling for. There had been kisses in plenty, kisses and illicit caresses, and fumbling at the hem of her petticoat that she had thwarted with a wiggle and a throaty laugh. She had looked laughing at the obvious evidence of desire outlined against the tight knit of his breeches, slipping away with a kiss and a promise—well, the promise of a promise. Just enough to keep him intrigued. She had left him cursing behind her, alternately cursing and pleading, hot for another assignation and not at all in possession of what he had come for.

But that didn't matter, did it? It wasn't what had happened or hadn't happened that mattered; the mere fact of her having been known to be inside a bedroom with him had been enough to damn her. She was used goods and Freddy was accounted a gentleman for condescending to marry her once he had already sampled the wares.

Penelope wished, with a burning intensity that balled her hands into fists, that she had allowed him under her skirts that night. She wished she had done everything people whispered of her and more. If she was a whore, shouldn't she at least have the pleasure of it?

Her nails cut purpled crescents into the skin of her palm.

She had left her gloves back in the bungalow, she realized. Never mind that. She wasn't going back for them. The thought of having to go back to the bungalow, knowing that that *thing* was under the same roof, made her stomach cramp with physical pain.

"Lady Frederick?"

Someone else was out walking in the night, walking with a ferocity that equaled her own, walking like someone trying to escape the devil—or with the devil in him.

Apparently, the entertainment didn't agree with Captain Reid either. Perhaps he had a *bibi* hidden away somewhere, too, thought

Penelope savagely, tucked away like summer ices stored in a nest of chipped ice, waiting to be taken out and licked to melting, all that fleeting sweetness hidden and hoarded and enjoyed in gluttonous wantonness in a cool and scented room.

Penelope found that she was shaking again, as with the ague.

His eyes narrowing on her, Captain Reid took a quick step forward. "Lady Frederick? Are you unwell?"

"You needn't concern yourself." Penelope rubbed her hands hard against her upper arms to warm herself, feeling the flesh cold and clammy beneath her palms. "It's only a flesh wound. Nothing mortal."

Captain Reid didn't seem convinced. "Is there anything I can do for you? Bring you?"

Her dignity? She didn't think she could get that back, not now, at any rate.

"I'd like to walk a bit. Walk with me, Captain Reid? It's too lovely a night to be wasted."

There was an edge to Lady Frederick's voice that Alex didn't like, but he fell obediently into step all the same, rather than leave her to walk alone. It was a lovely night, as she had claimed. There had been a ruined pleasure garden on the site where the Residency stood and James had taken it and enlarged it, adding groves of peach and mango, banana trees and toddy palms. Night-blooming flowers lined the paths, perfuming the air with their sweetness. Moonlight silvered the tall pillar of James's pigeon tower, turning it into something out of myth or fantasy, a ruined palace for a sleeping princess, to be wooed with birdsong and moonshine and borne triumphantly home on a palanquin woven of maiden dreams.

Lady Frederick's dreams were obviously not pleasant ones. Despite her lip service to the beauties of the scenery, Lady Frederick didn't seem to notice them. She moved by his side like a sleepwalker, unspeaking, unseeing, caught in a cage of her own thoughts. From time to time, she breathed in deeply, raising her hands to rub them against her arms like Lady Macbeth's trying to scrub out blood.

"Are you cold?" he asked. "Would you like to go back?"

Beneath lowered lashes, Lady Frederick's eyes glittered amber. "Why? Am I keeping you from your Lizzy?" she said silkily.

"My who?" Alex tried to figure out what she could be talking about and came up blank. "The only Lizzy of my acquaintance is my sister. I don't imagine she's missing me at the moment."

Lady Frederick stared up at him. A slow smile spread across her face. "I imagine she embroiders you lovely handkerchiefs."

Those blasted handkerchiefs. He'd had more than his fair share of teasing for those. They had been a birthday present from Kat years ago, marked in hair with his initials. Kat had not been amused when he had wanted to know why she hadn't just used thread. If he couldn't appreciate a sentimental gesture, she had told him, she certainly wasn't going to waste her hair on him, so there.

"No," he said. "That's Kat. My other sister. If Lizzy knows how to thread a needle, she's never shown it."

Lady Frederick touched a finger lightly to the corner of his lips. "You start to smile when you talk about your family. It suits you."

Her finger burned against his lips like a brand. Feeling as though he had just drunk too deeply of arrack, Alex stumbled a step back. "Lady Frederick—"

"Call me Penelope," she invited, strolling forward for every step he took back, like a tiger prowling after its prey.

It wouldn't, Alex thought, be all that terrible to be caught.

She was married, Alex reminded himself. And not to him.

"And scandalize society?" he said with a mildness he was far from feeling. Every sensible instinct he possessed screamed to sprint back towards the Residency before he did something he might regret. Unfortunately, his more sensible instincts were being rapidly shouted down by the rest of him.

Lady Frederick flung out her arms towards the deer park, with its silent audience of sheep and elk and blackbuck. "What society is there to scandalize?"

As if in agreement, a mynah bird gave an emphatic hoot from the branches of a nearby banana tree.

"Your husband," said Alex bluntly. Lord Frederick struck him as the sort who didn't have any interest in the contents of his own toy box until he caught someone else playing with them, at which point he would care very, very deeply.

"Oh, *Freddy*." Lady Frederick dismissed him with a word, but she stopped her forward progress with the abruptness of a child's toy pulled back on its string.

"I'm not on such familiar terms with him."

"Lord Frederick, then, if you please." Lady Frederick took his measure with a sidelong glance. "But I expect you don't. He doesn't please you at all." In a meditative tone that brought gooseflesh to Alex's arms, she said, "The question is, do I?"

He could feel the tension in the air around them like a premonition of danger. He forced his voice to hardness. "What is this about?"

Lady Frederick wasn't the least bit put off. Her eyes glinted yellow in the moonlight, tiger's eyes. "Me. You. A moonlit night. I can think of better uses for it than talking about Freddy. I can think of better uses for it than talking about anything at all."

She leaned up on her toes, erasing the few inches' difference in their height. He could feel the brush of her lace frill against his buttons, a startlingly erotic sound in the still night. Her breath whispered across his jaw, a promise of things to come.

An empty promise. It felt practiced. A seduction repeated by rote, no more personal than a tiger's kill.

Alex rocked back hard on his heels. "What are you trying to do?" he demanded.

"Seduce you, of course," said Lady Frederick—Penelope—tracing one blunt-nailed finger along his shirtfront. "Is it working?"

If she had looked any lower, she wouldn't have had to ask that. Alex wondered, with the bit of his brain that remained in proper working order, what in the devil was going on. One minute he had been pacing, brooding about Jack and Cleave and Wellesley, surely the least erotic subject known to man, and the next there was Lady Frederick—Penelope—shimmering among the moonflowers like a vision out of a Mussulman's heaven. All that was needed were a few piles of cushions and someone playing the zither.

"Is this a game?" he demanded hoarsely.

"It could be," she said, wetting her lips with her tongue so they glistened in the moonlight. "A very satisfying one."

Just the way she pronounced the word made him harden.

"You," he said, feeling like Odysseus tying himself to the mast and plugging his ears against the sirens, "have a husband."

"Not much of one." Beneath the seductive purr, there was a definite tinge of pique. Frowning, Alex pulled back. She clapped back on a bright social smile, like a comedienne donning a mask. "Marital fidelity is entirely out of fashion, you know. It wouldn't do to be less than à la mode."

Alex looked at her bright smile and her shadowed eyes and knew that she lied. "I don't believe that. And neither do you."

"Freddy does."

Beneath the pretended brightness, her voice was strained, as tense as her shoulders and the odd, watchful glint in her eyes, so foreign to honest desire. There had been rumors of late, in the bazaars, that the new Englishman had taken Nur Bai into keeping—not in hired quarters in the town, with all the inconvenience of having to obtain permission to enter the city after dark, but in his own zenana. Alex had dismissed the rumors as just that, rumors. It just wasn't done. Not when one had a wife. Discreet rooms in the town, yes. But not in one's own home. A man would have to hold his wife in utter contempt in order to contemplate a move like that.

Alex looked at Lady Frederick's pinched, white face and knew that he had been wrong.

"That's what this is about, isn't it? Not me, not the moonlight." He felt vaguely ill himself, with disappointment or disgust or both. Disgust, he told himself. Disgust at Lord Frederick's wanton cruelty. He had no right to disappointment. "*Christ.* I should have known."

"You'll blaspheme but you won't indulge in a spot of adultery? I call that hypocritical." Lady Frederick trailed a finger down his cheek, aiming for his lips.

Alex called it too much wine. Grasping her arm by the wrist, he held it suspended in the air between them. "Don't do anything you'll regret in the morning. He's not worth it."

Lady Frederick twisted her arm away, taking a step back. Her face was bitter in the darkness. "You mean I'm not worth it."

"You're worth ten of him," he said roughly.

Her lips twisted in a lopsided mockery of a smile. "Very kind of you, Captain Reid. Your condescension overwhelms me."

Condescension? If she thought that was all it was, she was more naïve than she looked. His body was screaming to reassure her that condescension was the last thing he had on his mind. It might even be called a kindness.

A sick sort of kindness, to use her pain as an excuse for his own desires. Do that, and he'd be even more of a cad than her ass of a husband.

"Go home—Penelope." He very deliberately employed her given name. "Go home and sleep it off."

Lady Frederick's mouth opened in soundless laughter. "You think I'm foxed? Trust me, Captain, I can hold my liquor better than that."

"Drunk on revenge," he corrected bluntly. "You'll feel differently in the morning."

"Will I?" she said, and her gaze swept him up and down, taking in every last detail, as someone anticipating thirst might drain the last drops of water from a dipper.

There was an odd, forlorn note in her voice that made Alex wonder, with a dangerous burst of exhilaration, if he might have gotten it all topsy-turvy, if it might not be at least a little bit about him and a little bit less about revenge. He made a move towards her, not towards Lady Frederick, but towards Penelope, forthright and honest and calling to him.

But he left it too late.

She turned, abruptly, missing the hand that had begun to reach for her.

"If you don't appreciate my company," she said flippantly, looking pointedly back towards the Residency, "I'll find someone who will."

Her back was towards him, the slim column of her throat held as high as it would go. She was every inch Lady Frederick again, as hard and glittering as the marble columns supporting the Residency veranda.

Alex tasted regret, as pungent as sour wine. Regret and pity.

Even though he knew she wouldn't thank him for it, he called after her, "Lady Frederick—Penelope."

She stopped at the sound of his voice, wary, waiting.

He couldn't bring himself to say what he really wanted to. "Don't sell yourself too cheaply."

He saw the flicker of her lashes as she glanced back at the shadow figures on the veranda. "That's the bother of it, Captain Reid. I already have."

Chapter Sixteen

I t was midnight, bleak and frigid cold, by the time I struggled up the Tube steps at Bayswater Station.

There was no self-indulgent cab on the way home from the movies. It was nearly midnight and Cinderella's coach had turned back into a pumpkin. Or a Tube train, as the case might be.

I huddled down into my coat and clamped my elbow over my bag as I navigated my way down Queensway. It wasn't entirely deserted— there were still lights on in the pub at one end of the road and the odd group of roving tourists—but the daytime crowds had gone and the shops were shuttered. Crumpled take-out wrappers and abandoned tourist brochures littered the street, bumping along in the wind like an urban version of tumbleweed. The whole stretch had the derelict feel of a party space after the party had gone.

The James Bond theme music was still playing in my head, bringing with it that rush one gets after a really good action movie. I wasn't ready to go home and go virtuously to bed. I wanted lights, people, conversation.

There wasn't much I could do about the first two, but I could manage the third. As I turned off Queensway, I fished my mobile out of my bag. It was a bit late to be calling, but that was the nice thing—well, one of the nice things—about having a boyfriend. You didn't have to worry about things like socially acceptable calling hours with them.

Scrolling down through my contacts list, I hit "Colin." It had taken me a while to program him into my phone, as though by presuming him permanent enough to be enshrined in my contacts list along with my parents, Pammy, and my favorite pizza place, I might somehow jinx the whole thing.

The phone rang twice, then three times, before Colin finally picked up. "Selwick."

I must have caught him in the middle of working on something, because his voice had a preoccupied sound to it and I could hear the *clack, clack, clack* of computer keys still going in the background. Or that might have just been the static on the line. Cell to cell does not always make for the best connection.

"Hi!" I shrilled, my breath coming in pants as I tried to walk, talk, and keep my head down against the wind all at the same time. "It's me."

"Me?" The *clack, clack, clack* had stopped at least.

"Eloise," I specified. I stopped short of adding "your girlfriend." Although I was pretty sure I was, we had never actually specified that bit. "How many women do you have calling you in the wee hours?"

"The hour isn't exactly wee yet," pointed out Colin, with that amused note in his voice that I loved so well. I could picture him settling back in his incredibly uncomfortable desk chair, wedging his mobile more snugly against his ear. "It's not yet midnight."

"Close enough," I chattered. "How's the book going?"

"Slowly." Colin was, or so he claimed, working on a spy novel. I wasn't sure what the plot was, but it seemed to have something to do with international mobsters operating out of Dubai. Or was it Moscow? He was very cagey about the whole project. "Are you outside?"

"Yup!" I hitched up the strap of my bag, nearly dislodging the phone from my ear in the process. "I'm just on my way back from going to the movies with Serena! We saw the new James Bond."

There was a pause on the other end of the line, followed by, "Oh." And then, "Was Pammy with you?"

It was a logical question. Pammy had gone to school—to different schools—with both me and Serena, so she was the natural connecting link. "Nope. Just me and Serena."

Silence.

"Hello?" I said, frowning at my cell. "Hello? Oh, good, you're still there. I thought the line had gone."

"I'm still here," said Colin, but there was something flat about it. I couldn't tell whether he was displeased or just preoccupied. Whatever it was, it wasn't the warm and fuzzy reception I had been hoping for.

I hate cell phones sometimes. It's impossible to pick up nuances of tone, especially with the wind driving your hair between your ear and the phone and the sound of your own breath rasping into the receiver.

I soldiered on, turning the corner onto Leinster Street. "Guess who we ran into in the movies?"

"Dr. Evil?"

Okay, it couldn't be that bad if he was making Austin Powers jokes. He was probably just checking e-mail while talking to me. I do that sometimes. It's awful of me and I know I shouldn't, but I do it anyway. "No. Your friend Nick. He was there with some little blond chicky."

"He usually is."

"It sucks for Serena, though." The wind was stronger as I turned down Leinster. I hunched my shoulders against it. "I was kind of hoping . . . I don't know."

"Hoping what?" I finally had Colin's full attention, but not in a good way. There was something sharp about the way he said it that put me instantly on edge.

I shrugged before realizing that he couldn't see it. "That she and Nick might hit it off."

"She's known Nick for years," said Colin flatly. "And weren't you just trying to set her up with Martin?"

Something about this conversation wasn't going quite as I had intended it. "Yes, I know, but . . ." Why did I suddenly feel like I was the one on the defensive? "She seems to have a thing for Nick."

Another horrible pause. Now that I was aware of them, listening for them, they sounded ten times worse. I could hear Colin exhale, his breath whistling down the line.

In the fake reasonable tone that people use when they're trying not to say what they're really thinking, he said, "Maybe you should just leave it be."

Since when had I become the villainess here? "I just thought it would be nice if Serena had someone of her own."

"It will happen when it happens."

And in the meantime, I'd have his sister as a permanent third wheel on our dates, if not present in fact, then in spirit.

I rammed my shoulder against the front door of my building. The door always stuck, but tonight I slammed it with even more force than necessary. "Oh, come on. These things don't just happen. Especially when people are too shy to make them happen for themselves."

"Are you saying that Serena needs you to find a bloke for her?"

Put that way, it did sound a little ridiculous. Not to mention condescending and more than a bit of an insult to Serena.

"I'm not saying she can't cope on her own." Oh, crap, that hadn't come out right, had it? I rushed on, "It's just that dating isn't easy. Everyone can use a little helping hand now and again."

"That's not a helping hand, that's a bulldozer."

I'm not the bulldozer; Pammy is the bulldozer. "Fine." I said tightly, kicking the door shut behind me. "I was just trying to be helpful."

"I'm not saying your intentions weren't good." Now that I was inside, the wind had stopped howling in my ears, but Colin's voice had gone as crackly as a brown paper bag. My building is a Victorian structure, a large town house turned into a series of flats. There's something about the old construction that stymies mobile reception. I like to think that it's the ghosts of disapproving Victorian spinsters going about gumming up everyone's lines.

A cute conceit, but not exactly useful when one is in the middle of a tense conversation with one's boyfriend.

If I went down to my basement flat, I would lose him completely, so I stood there on the upper landing, letting my bag drop to the floor as I rested an elbow against the ancient radiator where everyone's mail got dumped every day. I could feel the damp heat of it against my legs.

"Then what are you saying?" The scent of mold made my nostrils twitch. I scrubbed the back of my hand against my nose.

With only a single bulb hanging drunkenly from the ceiling, the foyer seemed even dingier than usual, with its ancient blue carpet and peeling blue wallpaper. We'd had our first kiss in this foyer, Colin and I, crackling radiator, mold and all.

Colin was clearly not in a kissing mood at the moment. "I'm just saying you should let it go."

"You mean you don't want me meddling in your sister's life." Fine. I got it. It was his family and it wasn't any of my business. And maybe it wasn't.

No, I corrected myself. Under normal circumstances it wouldn't be any of my business. But it became my business when a good half of our already limited time together had to be shared with his only sibling. He couldn't have it both ways.

"You just don't know what you're dealing with. Our family is"— Colin struggled for the appropriate adjective—"unusual."

"I would never have gotten that." Although, come to think of it, everyone thinks his family is unusual. True, the Selwicks did have that whole spy thing going, but everyone kept swearing right and left that that was all in the past.

So what else was there? I remembered those albums, and my conversation with Mrs. Selwick-Alderly about Colin's parents. Even if Colin's mother had run out on his father, that wasn't precisely unusual these days. Sad, but not unusual. My friend Pammy was the product of not one, but three broken homes, and look how she turned out.

"Serena's had a hard time."

For heaven's sake. Not that again. Yes, I knew, Serena had had a bad breakup the previous year. But, then, so had I. If Colin wanted to compare bad breakup notes, I thought that public infidelity, at *my* department Christmas party, no less, was right up there with some jerk using Serena to get to her family archives. It's always fun heading back to the history department on a Monday morning, knowing that about half the department have seen your boyfriend—your very official boyfriend of two years' standing—kissing someone else in the cloakroom of the Faculty Club, while the other half may not have witnessed the deed, but have all heard about it. With embellishments.

It had been painful and humiliating and I had done some nasty things with voodoo dolls, but you didn't see me starving myself into a size zero and sobbing into my Cheerios over it a year later.

The more I thought about it, the more militant I felt. What had happened to the good old stiff upper lip? I was beginning to get more than a little fed up with the whole poor-Serena-the-martyr narrative. To be fair to Serena, it was never a line she had tried to play. It was all coming from Colin.

Being a protective big brother was one thing, but this was something else.

Which was why I said, in an intolerably bossy tone, "At some point, you're going to have to stop coddling her."

Stupid. Stupid. Never ever use the phrase "have to" with a boy. Or anyone else for that matter. It's the fastest way to end a conversation. Or a relationship.

"Let's just drop it, shall we?"

"You're angry with me, aren't you?" I said unnecessarily.

Silence. I stared at a curl of wallpaper that had started to peel away from the wall. The underside had turned an ugly mustard yellow. I could hear the creak of Colin's chair as he tipped it back on its hind legs. "It's been a long day."

"Right," I said. I knew I should ask him why, ask him how his day had been, change the subject, but I couldn't make my lips form the words.

"I'll see you on Valentine's Day," Colin said. He didn't need to sound quite so grim about it.

"Okay," I said, in a small voice. "I'll see you then."

At Serena's party. There was no escaping it, was there?

Pressing the "end" button on my mobile, I dragged myself down to my basement flat, hauling my bag by the strap so that it bumped along the steps behind me like a child's toy.

After that, I only wished I knew what kind of Valentine's Day it was going to be.

Chapter Seventeen

P enelope hadn't imagined that it was possible to feel any lower than
she already had, but she did. She felt lower than an untouchable,
lower than the scraps missed by the sweepers in the streets.

The lights on the veranda stung her eyes, painfully bright after
the soothing shadows of the gardens. The lantern light seemed to cut
straight through her clothes. It sliced through the battle armor of paint
and jewels to the huddled, whimpering creature crouching underneath. It was all she could do not to slink off to a burrow somewhere
and lick her wounds in echoing silence. But she didn't have the luxury
for that.

A hand snaked over her shoulder to push open the drawing room
door for her. Penelope could see a sliver of brown wrist showing against
the edge of a white cotton glove. Penelope wrapped her own ungloved
hands in the gossamer folds of her skirt, feeling her wedding band slip
on her ring finger, too large without her glove to hold it in place.

"I can get that," said Penelope tartly.

"I know you can," said Captain Reid, and there was something in
his voice that made Penelope cringe.

He wasn't supposed to pity her. He wasn't *allowed* to pity her. He
was supposed to madly desire her so that she could swirl away laughing, with a cunning comment and a tap on the cheek.

Look how well that had turned out for her last time. With
Freddy.

"Thank you for your escort, Captain Reid," she said in a voice that
effectively killed off any further conversation. She swished past him

without meeting his eyes. It was bad enough hearing the pity in his voice. She didn't need to see it as well.

Her husband, such as he was, had already found himself a pack of cards and someone to play them with. Freddy, Henry Russell, and two others were engaged in a spirited game of Pope Joan. He looked up abruptly as Penelope sauntered by and gave her an overly hearty smile. It felt like a bribe, so many pats on the head for good behavior in public.

Well, she didn't feel like behaving.

"Do try not to lose the rest of my dowry, dearest," she said in a voice that tinkled as sweetly as the cut crystals hanging from the chandelier.

Freddy slapped down a card, his blue eyes telegraphing a warning. "I wouldn't"—*slap*—"be too worried. I'm feeling in a winning mood tonight."

Penelope let her eyes drift deliberately towards the small knot of officers at the other side of the room. "Funny," she said. "So am I."

Lieutenant Sir Leamington Fiske and his friend Pinchingdale hailed her with flattering enthusiasm. Penelope leaned into their compliments like a beggar crowding close to a fire, hating herself for doing it. She shouldn't need the flattery of second-rate roués to soothe her pride. But she needed to do something to gouge the pity out of Captain Reid's eyes. She didn't need him, not one bit. It was just that he was the first person she had run across after . . . well, after that. She shied away from the memory of that lush room with its equally lush occupant. It might just as well have been Pinchingdale, or Fiske. Anything in trousers would have done.

As if to prove her own point, Penelope laughed very loudly at something Pinchingdale had just said. She had no idea whether it was meant to be funny, but she supposed it must have been, because Pinchingdale puffed out his chest in a gratified way and reached for her hand, her scandalously ungloved hand.

Penelope slapped him away with an arch little flutter that was more a "come hither" than a "go hence." "Naughty, naughty," she crooned, and checked over her shoulder to make sure that Captain Reid was watching, watching her have an absolutely brilliant time, desired and desirable, crowded with amorous attentions.

When had it become about making Captain Reid jealous? She could see Freddy's color rising, but the victory was an empty one. It wasn't Freddy's blood she wanted to make boil, but Captain Reid's, and he was watching her in an entirely too-detached way, as though he knew exactly what she was doing—and felt sorry for her.

Very ungentlemanly, that. He wasn't supposed to understand what she was doing, he was just supposed to succumb to it.

Dimly, Penelope acknowledged that she had missed a step somewhere. The whole point of seducing Captain Reid had been to make Freddy jealous. That was all right. To seduce Captain Reid out of revenge was perfectly fair and just; to want him because she wanted him . . . that would be adultery.

"Mr. Pinchingdale." Penelope broke into a very long story involving an inheritance that ought to have been his but for the perfidy of his cousin in refusing to die at a convenient moment. She curved one hand to simulate a cylinder and shook it suggestively. "I find my glass is empty."

"Far be it from me to contradict so charming a lady"—Pinchingdale, who fancied himself a rake, positively oozed oil as he took the opportunity to possess himself of Penelope's ungloved hand—"but I see no glass in your hand." One by one, he peeled back her fingers to reveal empty air.

With the flat of her hand, Penelope pushed playfully at his chest, sending him staggering. "My point precisely, dear Mr. Pinchingdale. Somewhere in this room, a glass simply yearns for my lips."

"Fortunate glass!" exclaimed Mr. Pinchingdale. "Might one hope that the provider of the item might also feel the touch of your lips? As a form of . . . bounty." From the direction of his gaze, it was another form of bounty he had in mind.

Not that Penelope was all that bounteous in that area. Not like the girl on the floor of the zenana, who had positively jiggled with overabundance.

Penelope cast him a look to smolder by. "That depends on the . . . bounty of your offering, Mr. Pinchingdale."

"Bartering your favors, Lady Frederick?" inquired Fiske, as though the idea rather pleased him.

"My favors, like everything else, belong to my husband," countered Penelope, blowing a careless kiss at that individual. "The laws of England are quite explicit in that regard."

Fiske hitched a hip against an octagonal table that wobbled with his weight, sending a small statue bobbling for balance. "I wouldn't have thought you one to abide by the letter of the law, dear lady. Not from what I've heard of your . . . career."

Penelope gritted her teeth and smiled. He was referring to her marriage, of course. Her infamous, thoroughly reported, thrice-damned marriage. Of all the manifold indiscretions in her long and heedless existence, who would have thought that that particular one would lead to this? Driving Percy Ponsonby's phaeton into the Serpentine had been far more satisfying.

On the other hand, it did provide her an opening. Leaning forward, she made a show of settling the statuette into position, running her hand suggestively over its curves. "Nor, from what I've heard of your career, do you care overmuch for the strictures of the law, my dear, dear Sir Leamington."

Fiske continued to leer, but it had a somewhat perfunctory quality to it. Between his absurdly high shirt points, his eyes were watchful. "And what have you heard of my . . . activities, dear Lady Frederick?"

Penelope arched an eyebrow and her back. "Alarmed?"

Fiske bared his teeth. "Interested." With a show of nonchalance, he added, "I saw you and our young Daniel in tete-à-tete earlier this evening."

"Daniel? As in the lion's den?" Not an inapt description of the company. In the corner of the room, the worthy Residency matrons were glowering at her from behind their fans, sharpening their claws on her reputation.

Didn't they know she was immune to that sort of thing? Penelope smiled brilliantly at them, eliciting a wholesale retreat behind their fans. Mr. Cleave was also watching, with a concerned expression on his face that suggested he was debating with himself whether it was incumbent on him to intervene on her behalf. Penelope winked at him, partly to reassure him, partly to annoy the fan brigade.

As for Captain Reid . . .

The Bible had all sorts of interesting things to say about adultery. And coveting one's neighbor's ass.

Penelope turned back to Fiske with a toss of her head. "I should have thought there would be other Biblical locations more to your liking. Sodom and Gomorrah, perhaps. I hear they're lovely this time of year."

Fiske was not amused by her Biblical exegesis. "As in Daniel Cleave. Has Mr. Cleave been telling tales about me?"

Penelope batted her eyelashes with exaggerated innocence. "Are there tales to be told?"

Something in her expression must have reassured him of her ignorance, because Fiske smiled a cat-and-canary smile, a smile of deep, private satisfaction. "You would be surprised at the tales I could tell."

Penelope leaned forward so that her bosom pressed against the yielding neckline of her gown. The sapphire pendant of her necklace dangled in the hollow between her breasts. It had been a present from Freddy, a morning gift. She could see Fiske's eyes following the glittering bauble. She shifted to give him a better view. "Try me."

"You offered Pinchingdale a kiss for a glass. What do I get in return for information?"

"That," murmured Penelope, her breath stirring the hair at his temple as she leaned forward to whisper in his ear, "depends on what you have to offer."

Fiske smiled an infuriatingly superior smile that made Penelope itch to slap him. "Is that what you told old Freddy?"

It was an effort to keep her voice low and sultry. "And what would you say," she whispered, "if I were to tell you that I already know?"

Fiske wasn't smiling anymore. Good. "What do you know?"

"About your little club. Among other things." Penelope made her voice as suggestive as she knew how, which was very, very suggestive, indeed.

"Right." Obviously, it meant something to Fiske. He dropped the leer and his voice. "What do you want?"

What was it that Henrietta had said the spy called himself? A fuchsia? A frangipani? No, another flower. After the conversation she had overheard on the balcony, Penelope thought it exceedingly unlikely that it was Fiske whose coming they were supposed to await, but it was worth a go. One never knew where a stray shot might hit, especially with such men as Freddy called his intimates. Ammunition was cheap.

Undulating towards him, Penelope tapped a finger against the roughly engraved ruby stickpin protruding from his cravat. "I find myself exceedingly partial to marigolds."

Penelope's gentle tap bowled him over backwards. Fiske rocked backwards and kept going, flailing for balance, with a look of startled alarm that might have been owing to the marigolds, the Madeira, or the fact that the table against which he had toppled wasn't nearly equal to holding his weight. His mouth opened and closed in his favorite guppy imitation.

"Marigolds?" he croaked, latching on to Penelope's arm to steady himself.

Penelope stumbled but held firm, arm to arm, practically in embrace. "One would do," said Penelope, watching him closely. "If it were the right one."

Freddy had had enough. With a prolonged scraping noise, he shoved his chair back to the table, grabbing Penelope by the arm as one might a wayward child.

"Will you excuse us, Fiske, old thing? I need to have a word with my *wife*."

Brilliant. Freddy would choose just the right moment to remember his conjugal duties.

Penelope favored him with a smile dripping with acid. "Oh, is that what I am? It is, isn't it? Funny, how easy that is to forget."

Freddy manhandled her across the room, onto the balcony, where the mummers had long since packed up their props. Insects cruised idly through the guttering light of the remaining lanterns. "What was he telling you?"

Penelope slapped at a mosquito as it attempted a landing on her arm. "Darling, I hadn't thought you cared. Are you afraid he'll reveal all your little secrets? Or perhaps," she added meditatively, "your not-so-little ones. Pity, the way those have of coming out. Or sometimes falling down flat on their arse."

"You," said Freddy through clenched teeth, "are embarrassing me."

Penelope drew herself up to her full height. "You generally do that for yourself. I would imagine my contribution would be negligible."

"You were flinging yourself at my friends!"

Personally, Penelope would have called it less of a fling and more of a shimmy, but she doubted syntactical precision was Freddy's primary concern.

She ran her tongue across her lips in a deliberately sultry manner. "What's sauce for the goose is sauce for the gander."

Freddy's lips tightened with annoyance. "You've got it backwards. You're the goose. *I'm* the gander."

"More like a rooster, strutting your cock in every walk," flung back Penelope, with deliberate crudeness.

Freddy's hands formed an automatic fig leaf over the area in question. "Don't be absurd."

Penelope followed up her advantage, like a boxer closing in on an opponent. "You needn't bother coming to bed tonight. I don't want you there."

"Did you think I was planning to?" Freddy's blow snuck under her guard, hitting her where it hurt. Penelope stiffened as though slapped. Softening, Freddy held out a hand, his voice taking on a wheedling note. "Now, Pen—"

Penelope jerked out of his reach. Was that all he thought she was worth? A fist to the ribs and then a pat on the head like a dog? That was Freddy for you, always convinced he could charm his way out of anything with a minimum amount of effort for himself. "Don't 'now, Pen' me. Go ahead. Go play with your little strumpet. But don't object if I amuse myself as I see fit."

When charm didn't immediately succeed, sullenness invariably followed. Now was no different. Freddy dropped the smile, his brows drawing together in a threatening way. "Don't push me, Pen. Or I'll—"

Penelope laughed contemptuously. It was like being kicked by a cocker spaniel. "What? Divorce me?" They both knew how impossible that was. "Or just deny me your conjugal companionship? I assure you, it will be no great loss." She looked pointedly at the placket of his breeches.

"Don't worry. You'll be free of me for the next few weeks." When she looked at him blankly, he made a gesture of exasperation. "Berar? The hunting? I told you about it."

No, he hadn't. He must have told *her*. The other one. The thought that she was interchangeable, just another woman in his bed, made Penelope's temples ache, like the beginning of a migraine. They didn't even look anything alike. They didn't speak the same language, for heaven's sake. How hard could it be to keep them straight?

How many others were there?

In a tone of exaggerated patience, Freddy said, "The First Minister invited me to Berar for the hunting. Fiske, Pinchingdale, and I will be gone a fortnight."

Penelope remembered the First Minister's sinister, rotting face. What was it Captain Reid had called him? An asp? There was a story going around that even snakes wouldn't bite him, for fear of dying of his venom. Penelope wondered, briefly, whether she ought to warn Freddy off, to repeat any of what Captain Reid had told her.

She looked at her husband, golden and arrogant in the lantern light, and felt a familiar surge of irritation. He was so sure of himself, so bloody sure.

Fine, then, thought Penelope, with a fine fit of Irish temper. Let him make his own bed and lie on it. With whomever he pleased.

"Enjoy," she said flippantly. "Do try to shoot the birds and not yourself."

She didn't ask where he intended to sleep. She found that she didn't want to know.

She stood on the balcony for a long time, the night breeze making her skin prickle beneath the fine sheen of nervous sweat that had formed during her fight with Freddy. In the distance, the blackbuck roamed through the Resident's preserve while mynah birds called to one another through the scented trees. She had been left in possession of the field, but she had lost the battle.

Penelope's ungloved hands tightened around the balustrade. Who was she fooling? It was a battle she had never had the slightest chance of winning. She had thought, for a time, that she might bind Freddy to her by sheer force of fascination—but she obviously hadn't been fascinating enough. In this setting, she felt stunningly provincial, in a way she had never felt in London or Bath, too gangly in her form, too garish in her coloring, too blunt in her speech. *You're worth ten of him,* Captain Reid had said. Out of pity, Penelope reminded herself. He hadn't wanted her either. At least, not that way.

By the time Penelope returned to the drawing room, Mrs. Ure had eaten all the sweetmeats and dragged herself home to bed; the crowd at the card table had flung in their hands, settled their debts, and gone home; and all the rest had evaporated away to their own beds or other pursuits. Only the Resident and Captain Reid remained, discussing some matter of business at the deserted card table.

Penelope heard the words "guns" and "missing" before the Resident noted her presence and rose hastily from the table.

"Lady Frederick! I had thought you had gone home."

"I was enjoying the view from your balcony." How ironic that after her long series of indiscretions on balconies, her experience on this one should be so entirely chaste. It was decidedly déclassé to be caught lurking on balconies with one's own husband or, even worse, by oneself.

The two men exchanged a look.

"If you will excuse me," said Captain Reid, to his superior.

"Of course." The Resident nodded his thanks, and before Penelope could protest that she didn't appreciate being passed around like a parcel, he gave her a perfunctory smile and a "Good night, Lady Frederick," leaving her alone with Captain Reid.

They faced each other across the debris of the night's entertainment, the guttering candles, the dropped sweetmeats, the spilled wine.

"There was no need for you to offer to see me home," Penelope said belligerently. "No one appointed you my guardian."

"I'm not offering as a guardian," he said tiredly, and Penelope noticed that, unlike the other men, he didn't seem to have been drinking. It was past three in the morning and he would be up and riding by six. If she hadn't been fool enough to proposition him, she would be riding with him. "I'm offering as a friend."

"Oh." For once in her life, Penelope found herself entirely at a loss for words. "Thank you." The words felt foreign to her tongue. She didn't say them often.

"No need for thanks," he said practically. "It isn't far."

Maybe not in yards, but Penelope felt as though she had just gone a much longer distance than that. Her head hurt too much to parse it out. She was more grateful for the escort than she cared to admit. The Resident, with a fine sense for self-preservation, had placed Freddy in the bungalow farthest from the Residency proper. Without her gloves and shawl, Penelope felt oddly bare. Considering the depth of her bodice, it was absurd to feel quite so unclothed just from the lack of a little kid leather on her hands, but she did.

It made her feel very young and very unsure of herself, which was all, she told herself, pure bollocks. She hadn't been unsure of herself when she was young, and now that she was an old, married matron, she ought to be even less so.

"Did you ever find your missing guns?" she asked, just to say something.

"My—? Oh." Whatever Captain Reid had been thinking about in the moonlight, it had been just as absorbing, and not entirely pleasant. He shook his head as though to clear it. "No. No, we haven't." He grimaced. "It's something of a sticky situation, with everyone swearing right and left that he's done what he was supposed to do." They paused within striking distance of her bungalow. "You should be all right from here."

The old Penelope would have cast him her sultriest look and asked mockingly if he didn't consider himself man enough to see her to her door.

The strange, new Penelope who appeared to have replaced her didn't do anything of the kind. She just took a step back, nodded her head once, and said stiffly, "Thank you." Like a gawky schoolgirl, she jerked her head towards the front of the house. "Will I—see you tomorrow morning?"

It was too dark to make out his expression, but there was something comforting about the way he stood there, steady and solid.

"I'll be where I always am," he said.

Penelope drew in a deep breath, feeling more herself again. She would have missed her morning exercise, that was all.

"You'd better get some sleep then, hadn't you?" she tossed over her shoulder, and scrambled up the steps to the veranda.

It felt good to get the last word. It felt even better to know that Captain Reid was still standing there, watching her, making sure she got safely home. Such as it was.

Someone had considerately left a single candle burning in the bedchamber, sending wobbly shadows undulating across the untouched bedclothes. There were no piles of clothes on the floor, no husband sprawled snoring across the center of the bed. True to his word, Freddy had taken himself off to bed elsewhere.

Penelope couldn't bring herself to care.

Contorting her arms around her back to try to reach the tiny row of pearl buttons at the back of her dress, Penelope tried to reclaim the hurt and indignation she had felt earlier in the evening, but the closest she could come was a sense of mild exasperation, with herself as well as Freddy, and an overwhelming relief that he would be away for at least a fortnight.

A fortnight of early morning rides.

With an impatient tug, Penelope gave up on the buttons and yanked the dress up over her head. A pearl button skittered across the floor. It wasn't a real pearl anyway, so it was no great loss. There were dozens of others like it, rather like Freddy. Penelope carelessly tossed the dress into a corner of the room and turned her attention to the pins in her hair. Drawing out the anchoring pin, she shook her hair free, enjoying the sound of its rustling around her shoulders—and heard an answering rustle from the side of the room.

Frowning, Penelope peered into the wavy surface of the mirror, where the satiny fabric of her discarded dress had begun to ripple, like moonlight on the water. Penelope stilled in the act of reaching for the clasp of her necklace. She really hadn't had that much to drink.

Penelope put out a hand to steady the mirror, but the dress continued to rustle, undulating in waves on the floor. A forked tongue flicked out from beneath the embroidered hem.

In the wavering light of the single candle, a cobra wiggled itself free of the folds of satin and began coiling upwards on its speckled tail, its beady eyes fixed on Penelope.

Chapter Eighteen

I n the mirror, the snake's obsidian eyes fixed on Penelope, its pointed tongue flicking in and out of its mouth.

Something about the beady eyes in that wrinkled face, with the hood arching to either side reminded her of the malevolent, ruined face of Mir Alam, the man even a snake wouldn't bite.

Too bad it wasn't Mir Alam in the room instead of her. The two reptiles could have had a reunion.

Penelope held herself very still, rather hoping that the snake might take her for a piece of furniture, of no more interest than the post on the bed or the legs of the chair. It was not, she feared, the sort of creature with whom one could come to an amiable arrangement. The snake blocked both the door to the veranda and the door to the hall. She would have to run directly across its path either way and she was willing to wager it could strike faster than she could run.

What did one do about a cobra? Not scream or run or flail, she knew that much. Not that there was any danger of that. Her body had frozen out of sheer instinct and seemed to be intent on turning into a pillar of salt on the spot. Did snakes eat salt? Penelope dismissed that thought as immaterial. What she needed was a scythe, a sword, even a poker or a shovel. But there was nothing of the kind, not even one of Freddy's ivory-handled canes. The servants were all asleep. There would be no one to hear her if she screamed for help. No one except the snake, of course, who was uncoiling in her direction with a slow determination that Penelope found distinctly unnerving.

Freddy kept a pistol in the dresser drawer.

Penelope's fingers tingled with nervous energy. It wasn't much, but it was a chance. If only he had left it where it was supposed to be. It would be just like Freddy to flounce off on a whim, leaving her alone with a cobra. Please, God, Penelope thought, let him not have taken the pistol with him.

Keeping her eyes on the creature in the mirror, Penelope felt blindly for the drawer handle, wincing at the screeching noise the drawer made as she drew it open. Venom dripped off the snake's fangs, or perhaps that was just the sweat beading off her brow, clouding her vision. Her shift clung damply to her chest as she inched her fingers forward, trying to keep her back as painfully still as any dowager might demand. She could feel the drops of sweat trickling down her spine. Each seemed to take an eternity to travel its way down, vertebra by vertebra, each drop assuming mammoth proportions.

By a miracle, the pistol was where it was meant to be. Penelope didn't need to look to know what it was, or to feel the familiar weight of it in her palm. She didn't dare avert her eyes from the creature in the mirror, swaying gently on its tail as the light of the single candle cast its shadow against the far wall, as ominous as any mariner's nightmare of ship-devouring serpents.

Keeping her elbow stiff, Penelope drew the pistol out of the drawer. It was primed and cocked, and she gave silent thanks that, whatever Freddy's other flaws, he kept his firearms in good order. It was, he felt, one of the marks of a gentleman, like good horseflesh and shiny boots and a well-dressed wife.

One shot. That was all she would get. Penelope conjured the memory of old targets, playing cards hung from a line in the back garden, with her father cheering her on while her mother lurked disapproving behind bedroom drapes. Under her father's tutelage, she had shot the pips out of playing cards, but that had been before London, before society demanded that she replace pistol with fan as her weapon of choice. The target had been smaller then, she reminded herself, and the cards had swayed in the breeze just like the snake.

Penelope swallowed hard, her tongue clinging stickily to her palate. It felt like forever that she had stood there, locked in silent battle, but it couldn't have been more than sixty seconds by the clock, the space of two drops of sweat making their slow journey down her spine. He who hesitates is lost, once more into the breach, and all that rot.

As she pivoted, fast and furious, she spared a moment's thought to regret that she hadn't kissed Captain Reid in the garden that night, with all the moonflowers blooming. It was, after all, in the manner of a last meal.

Affronted, the snake reared up on its tail, hissing its outrage with all the venom in its scaly little soul.

Penelope didn't bother to pray. As the cobra arched straight for her, she closed one eye, picked her mark, and pressed the trigger home.

Standing outside the bungalow, Alex watched to make sure Penelope got safe inside, thinking thoughts that made him a very inappropriate sort of chaperone. A candle flickered into light through the slats of the screens, casting her silhouette against the wall, tall and graceful. There was no answering male shadow. Lord Frederick was presumably otherwise occupied for the night.

In the bungalow, Penelope was shaking out her hair, dropping pins carelessly as she went. The shadow Penelope lifted her arms above her head to reach the last pin, poised like a dancer on a temple frieze. The vagaries of reflection turned her dress to mist, to nothing more than a smudge along the supple lines of her body.

His entire body tightened at the sight. Christ, but she was—not beautiful. Sensual. Desire embodied in female form. It had taken every ounce of will he possessed not to take her up on what she was so blatantly offering in the garden that night. One moment more and they would have been locked together, with his lips on hers and his fingers in her hair and that would have been that.

Grass-stained clothes and crushed moonflowers—and ruined reputations and a broken marriage, Alex reminded himself. Lord Frederick might be an ass, but that didn't mean he had to be. She deserved better than to be used so. Penelope. The name suited her much better than Lady Frederick. It fit her, stubborn, brave, resourceful, and just as abandoned as that other Penelope had been, left behind to ward off her suitors while her husband sailed off to dally in the company of seductive sorceresses and assorted sirens.

It was foolish to wish that he had said yes instead of no in the garden, foolish and selfish.

Rubbing one hand against the beginnings of a headache, Alex forced himself to turn away and to think instead of Jack and Cleave and the unwelcome intelligence Cleave had brought. It had been generous of him in its way, all the more so knowing how very much Cleave disliked Alex's brother and had since they were all children together. By going to Alex, Cleave had offered him a chance, a chance to find Jack and warn him—of what? That Wellesley had a price on his head? If Jack were involved in the sorts of activities Cleave implied, then that certainly wouldn't be news to him. Alex mocked himself for his credulousness. It was more likely that Cleave hoped he might use the ties of family to prevail upon Jack to turn himself in, and with him precious information on his contacts and activities.

It wasn't necessarily a bad bargain that Cleave offered—for Cleave. Cleave would get the promotion he so ardently desired; Alex would get a pat on the back and the district commissionership that not all his father's charm had managed to wrangle for him; and Jack . . . If Cleave's employer were honorable, Jack might get the option of exile or imprisonment rather than a noose around his neck. Some bargain.

Damn him. Damn Jack, damn Cleave, damn Wellesley, damn their bloody father for never bloody thinking before he hopped from romance to romance and bed to bed, leaving in his wake this legacy of bitterness and muddled loyalties.

As if in agreement, a sound like a rumble of thunder echoed in his ears.

Only, it wasn't thunder. It was the muffled report of a gun. And it had come from inside the Staineses' bungalow.

Alex sprinted for the veranda, his imagination churning with nightmare images of Penelope, sprawled dead on the floor, red blood spreading across the white muslin of her gown, bubbling up at the corner of her lips, while those wicked amber eyes stared forever dulled at the punkah swaying rhythmically back and forth above. There had been murder in Lord Frederick's eyes when he had hauled his wife away from Fiske earlier that evening. Staines wouldn't be the first man to imagine himself wronged and to settle it with a bullet.

Using the balustrade as lever, Alex vaulted over the side, pushing the cane screen roughly aside. Inside, he saw Penelope, her hair all about her shoulders, dressed in nothing but a shift. She was upright. She was standing. She was alive.

Thank God.

After his imaginings, it was relief enough to see her upright, breathing, alive, whole and unmarred, with no bullet holes charring her skin. Her hair blazed like flame around her white face. In one hand, she held a pistol from which a plume of smoke still trailed.

Alex looked abruptly at the floor. But there was no sign of the lady's husband, dead or otherwise. No blood, no brains, no powder-singed cravat. Instead, there was the jumbled body of a snake, the spotted scales shining faintly against the darker boards of the floor.

"The devil," breathed Alex, and, indeed, the smoke tasted like brimstone in the back of his throat. It didn't take any great herpetological knowledge to identify the body as that of a cobra. The bullet must have gone in somewhere just beneath the eyes, leaving the distinctive hood intact.

Alex looked involuntarily at the gun in Penelope's hand. That had been either a bloody brilliant shot, or a devilishly lucky one. He wasn't sure he could have done it, not in that uncertain light and with the odds of failure what they were.

Penelope casually hefted the pistol, twirling it to make the silver facing glisten in the candlelight. "I told you I was a good shot."

"That," said Alex flatly, "is a cobra."

"You mean that *was* a cobra," corrected Penelope giddily, tossing the spent weapon onto the bed. She missed. The heavy piece of metal glanced off the side of the mattress, clattering to the hardwood floor.

There were bright patches of color high on each cheekbone and her shift clung damply to her body, even though the night was cool. Her amber eyes glinted feverishly in the light of the single candle, cursed gems at the heart of a haunted mine.

Alex crossed the room in three long strides, grasping Penelope by the arms. "Did it touch you? Bite you?" he demanded tersely, scanning her fevered face.

Her bare arms were clammy beneath his hands, damp with a sheen of sweat that gave the lie to her cocky grin, the grin of a soldier coming out of a cannonade, powder-grimed but whole. "I didn't give it time."

Alex felt a lopsided smile quirking across his own face, product of fear, adrenaline, and goodness only knew what else.

"Wise decision," he said, and kissed her.

Her arms clamped around his neck as though he were her only escape from drowning, a desperate, clinging grip that gave the lie to her devil-may-care demeanor. Wrapping his arms around her, he could feel the way her body was shaking through the sodden material of her shift. She trembled as though she were suffering from an ague, with convulsive shivers that trembled through her whole body.

"It's all right," he murmured between kisses, stroking soothingly up and down her back. "It's dead. It's gone."

Pulling his head down to hers, she blotted out his reassurances with her lips, kissing him with an openmouthed fervor that made Alex's ears ring and the rest of his body to respond in an unmistakable and inappropriate way. His better self tried to intervene, reminding him that this was not what he had come for, that he was meant to be comforting her, not—well, whatever the rest of him was thinking.

The clamoring in his ears grew louder.

It took a moment for Alex to realize that the noises weren't in his head; they were coming from beyond the door and getting louder by the moment, as footsteps clattered in the hallway and agitated voices rose in inquiry. It wasn't surprising that the shot would have roused the household. What was surprising was that Alex had completely forgotten to think about that before putting the mistress of the house in a decidedly compromising position.

Pushing with both hands against his chest, Penelope extricated herself from his embrace.

"Stay here," she ordered.

Alex wasn't quite sure where she expected him to go. Into the armoire, perhaps? The evening was starting to take on all the classic attributes of farce, but for the deadly collection of scales jumbled on the floor.

Penelope whisked blithely around the snake. Yanking open the door, she thrust her head through the gap. "I'm all right!" she shouted down the hall in ungrammatical Urdu. "It was just a snake. It's dead."

That apparently occasioned a certain amount of comment. "It's dead," Penelope repeated. Sticking her head back inside, she demanded, "How do you say 'go back to sleep' in Urdu?"

Feeling rather dazed, Alex told her.

Penelope repeated it with considerably more force. He could see the taut muscles in her upper arms as she held on to the edge of the door, her entire body quivering with a frenetic energy that Alex recognized all too well from his brief stint in the Madras Cavalry. She was soaring on the sheer, exquisite pleasure of being alive, of having survived. In an hour, Alex thought darkly, feeling his own crazy euphoria beginning to dissipate, she would probably have a crashing headache.

"There!" she said, slamming the door and grinning at Alex. "That's taken care of them." Her bosom swelled against the neckline of her shift as she drew in a deep breath of pure anticipation. "It's just us again."

"About that," Alex said, in the mildest voice he could muster, keeping his hands firmly at his sides. "Where is your husband?"

The question had the desired effect. Penelope stumbled to a halt, like a mare clipping her foot against a fence. She cast Alex a quick, startled glance before her old mask clamped back down.

She crossed her arms across her chest. "As you can see, he's not here."

"I see." He should have known. Lord Frederick would be with his mistress. "I'm sorry."

Penelope drew herself up defensively. "I'm not. Oh, don't look like that! Ours was never a love match."

"What was it then?" Alex asked, willing her to provide him with an excuse, and just as strongly willing her not to. Honor and desire battled for supremacy, and desire was having by far the better of it.

Biting down on her lower lip, Penelope looked away. It would have to be her lip, already swollen from their kiss. Her mouth was too wide for fashion, generous, flexible. Alex thought it was perfect.

"Boredom," she said, with a shrug. "Expediency. Bad timing." She looked up at him, her eyes brilliant. "But it brought me here."

There was no mistaking her meaning.

Alex tried to make light of it. "To snakes in your bed."

Penelope wasn't having any of it. "To all this," she said, her sweeping gesture taking in the cane screens, the moonlight spilling across the floor, the shadows of trees like filigree. She took a step forward, her bare feet moving soundlessly against the floor. "To you."

Alex could feel his Adam's apple bobbing up and down as he swallowed. "I won't be your revenge," he said levelly.

"What if it's not about revenge?"

"Then what?" demanded Alex, taking a step forward, without realizing that he had. "Boredom? Expediency?"

A whisper away, Penelope's lips curled as if at a shared joke. "Bad timing," she said in a way that made it feel as though it were very good timing indeed.

Alex found himself grinning back, a reckless, devil-may-care grin that matched hers.

Reckless. Careless. Like his father's.

The grin froze on Alex's face, even as his hands automatically closed around Penelope's waist. Cold reality crowded in on him, breathy icy prickles down his neck. Who knew what sort of unanticipated outcomes might arise from tonight's careless carnality? Gossip, scandal, a marriage broken, a child to be raised under another man's name. He could present arguments against each of those outcomes, specious arguments, designed to comfort his conscience and license his roving hands, but there was still Penelope to be thought of.

As if there could be anything but Penelope to be thought of, with the material of her shift fragile beneath his fingers, damp lawn melting into damp skin, with her eyes glinting up at him, her lips curving into a smile that promised pleasures more wicked than words.

"Where were we before?" Penelope asked, sliding her body up against him. In the shadowed room, the scent of flowers rose from her skin like a drug.

Alex dragged in a deep breath of air, trying to force himself to think, to reason, to do the responsible thing. Penelope might claim she wanted this—with words, smile, lips, hands; oh Lord, the hands; he couldn't let himself think about what she was doing with her hands, or he would be lost—but how would she feel in the morning, when the potent brew of anger, fear, and lust had run its course? Jack's mother had followed his father willingly, and look where that had got them.

He wouldn't hurt Penelope that way. He wouldn't let her hurt herself that way. In the morning, it would all seem different; in the morning, when the cobra corpse was tidied away and the scent of the flowers had burned away with the dawn.

"No." He wrenched himself back, away, prying his fingers away from her skin. "I can't do this."

Penelope stared at him, frozen, a statue of Aphrodite caught in the middle of a seduction, or Lot's wife turned to salt at a particularly intimate moment. Shock, dismay, confusion chased one another across her face as she stared at him, her empty hands suspended in air.

"Wha—" She shook her head, but the words didn't seem to come out. For once in her life, Penelope Deveraux Staines was rendered completely and entirely without words. He could see her trying to comprehend, trying to figure out how they had gone from there to here, and failing entirely. He wasn't entirely sure he understood himself. "You—I—what?"

She was owed an explanation. He didn't have one. At least, not one he could cram into coherence.

"I just . . . I can't do this."

Penelope's cheekbones suddenly seemed very prominent and there were hollows under them that had not been there before. "Do what?" she demanded, never letting go of his gaze, daring him to say it out loud. "What? Make love to me? Take me to bed?"

"Your husband's bed." That was the crux of it. There was no way around it. Damn it, it was for her own good.

Penelope turned on him a glare of truly ferocious proportions. "Don't say his name."

Alex's lips tightened. Managing, by heroic effort, to keep his voice level, he said, "I am in his house, in his room, with his wife. What am I supposed to say?"

His words had an incendiary effect. "Is that how you think of me? As someone else's chattel? *His* house, *his* room, *his* wife?" Penelope mimicked. "Nothing more than an appendage of Lord Frederick Staines, Special Envoy to His Majesty the Nizam?"

Alex looked at her in surprise at the vehemence of her reaction. "You know it's not."

Penelope drew a breath in sharply through her nostrils. "It is, isn't it? Just another piece of baggage to be carted about from place to place, preferably shoved into a palanquin where it won't bother anyone. Perhaps you might ask Freddy if he'd be willing to let you borrow me. You'd do the same for his horse, wouldn't you? Or his pistol, or his sword, or his snuffbox, or his—"

"Don't," he said roughly, breaking into her matter-of-fact catalogue of Lord Frederick's possessions, before it could go on and on, through neck cloths and stickpins and pantaloons. There was something in her face that unnerved him. A bleakness so staggering that he felt all his anger collide and crumble against it. "Good God. I had no idea you felt that way. Penelope—"

Anger turning to concern, he reached for her, but she jerked away from his hand, pushing past him so abruptly that the force of her passage sent him staggering against the bed, clipping his shins on the baseboard. Off balance, Alex grabbed blindly at the mosquito netting, but his hand passed through empty air, and he landed heavily with one hand against the mattress.

Where was the bloody mosquito netting?

Across the room, Penelope pivoted on her heel to face him, like an entire artillery regiment about to go blazing into battle.

"Well, I'm not his bloody pistol," she announced, bright patches of color burning in her hollow cheeks. "Or his horse, or anything else belonging to Freddy bloody Staines. It's *my* body, *my* life, *my* choice. Not his and certainly not yours."

It would have been a very effective oration, but Alex was distracted by the mosquito netting, or rather the lack of it. The bars were bare. The fine film of mosquito netting that usually hung from the poles, shrouding the bed in folds of fabric, was missing. There was something about its absence that niggled at him.

"Well?" Penelope demanded, one foot tapping against the bare boards of the floor. "What do you have to say?"

Alex squinted up at the bare poles where the mosquito netting should have hung. "What happened to the mosquito netting?"

"The *what*?" Penelope stared at him as though he had just grown an extra head.

"The mosquito netting," said Alex.

"The mosquito netting," Penelope repeated, her voice dripping with a nicely calculated mixture of derision and incredulity. "You are asking me about the mosquito netting."

"Yes," replied Alex, goaded. "The transparent thing that usually hangs from the bed."

Penelope tossed her head, sending the strap of her shift sliding down one shoulder, revealing the upper curve of one breast. "It was off when I came in. At least, it must have been. I don't remember moving it. I didn't think about it." Nor should he, her tone seemed to imply.

"One generally wouldn't." A horrible suspicion was beginning to coalesce in Alex's mind, blotting out other, lesser concerns. His troubled eyes met hers. "When was the last time you saw it in place?"

Penelope shrugged, sending her shift plunging still lower. "You needn't pretend an interest in my sleeping arrangements," she said caustically. "We've covered that quite thoroughly already."

Alex gave her an exasperated look. "This isn't bloody about that." Before she could launch whatever sarcastic comment was cruising to her lips, Alex said hurriedly, "What happened with the snake? Where was it when you first saw it?"

Turning sharply away, Penelope yanked her strap back into place.

"There's nothing to tell. I tossed my dress onto the floor and it must have landed on that hideous thing. It got annoyed. I shot it."

"But how did it get here?"

"I think we should name it," said Penelope flippantly. "It seems disrespectful to just refer to it as 'it.' How about Marmaduke?"

Irritable with frustrated desire, Alex snapped, "I'm not calling the bloody snake Marmaduke!"

Penelope raised an eyebrow at him. The strap of her shift had begun to slide again.

Flushing, Alex looked away. "Fine. Did you consider that, er, Marmaduke might not have made his way here of his own accord?"

"Are you suggesting that Marmaduke didn't want to see me?" Penelope lowered her lashes suggestively, but underneath them, her eyes were wary. He knew she knew what he was driving at. But Alex spelled it out anyway.

"What I'm suggesting is that someone else was quite eager for Marmaduke"—did they really have to keep calling it that?—"to make your acquaintance."

Tilting her head back, Penelope looked Alex square in the eye. "Why not just say it? You think someone wants me dead."

Chapter Nineteen

"Yes."

He didn't bother to sugarcoat it. Penelope gave him points for that, at least. "Other than you, you mean," she said provocatively.

Alex rubbed a hand across his brow, before letting it fall heavily to his side. "I don't want you dead," he said wearily. There were shadows under his eyes and in them, too. Despite herself, Penelope could feel some of her indignation draining away. He looked at her and said simply, "But someone else does."

She was not prepared to cede the point that easily. Any point. "Cobras *are* indigenous to India," she pointed out.

"They are."

"And they do occasionally wiggle their way into houses." Penelope folded her arms across her chest, daring him to contradict her.

He dared. "But they generally don't bother to remove all the mosquito netting. That suggests a degree of premeditation that is beyond, er, Marmaduke's powers."

"I won't have you slandering Marmaduke. He has excellent taste in victims." Unlike some people, her tone implied.

"It's not his taste I'm worried about. Let's not beat about the bush, Penelope." Her pulse gave a little jump at the intimacy of her name on his lips. Stupid pulse. Penelope scowled. Alex scowled right back, never giving an inch, not letting himself be deflected. "Who wants you dead?"

"You certainly do know how to flatter a lady. Can't we just concentrate on my brilliant marksmanship? You never did compliment me on that shot, you know."

It was not one of her more effective attempts to change the subject.

"I don't want you dead," he said shortly.

Penelope had received more fulsome comments in her time, but never one that had moved her more. She felt warm all over, despite the cooling sweat on her arms and chest. It was a warmth generated inside, not out. It was an entirely unfamiliar sensation. It made her very, very nervous.

"Does that mean you want me alive?" Penelope said in the sultriest voice she could manage, sarcasm dripping from every syllable.

Alex just looked at her, waiting. Bloody single-minded man.

Bloody single-minded man who wanted to keep her alive. One could forgive a certain amount for that. There weren't that many people in the world who cared whether her skin was intact or not.

But, then, this was Captain Reid, protector of the world, defender of treasonous siblings and small kittens. He would have done the same for the cobra.

Well, maybe not the cobra.

"Oh, all right, all right." If he was determined to discuss the cobra, they would discuss the cobra. Penelope plonked herself down on the edge of the bed, feeling the mattress give around her. It wasn't that she wanted to keep him there talking. Not in the slightest. She angled her head up at him. "We all know that you weren't too keen on having me here, but I don't think you're trying to kill me—"

"Thank you."

Ignoring him, Penelope went on ticking off people on her fingers. "—Henry Russell wasn't too pleased when I turned down his overtures, but a little bit of rejection hardly rises to the level of snakebite."

Alex didn't rise to the bait. His mind was elsewhere, on politics, not dalliance. "You made an enemy of Mir Alam."

"Nearly a month ago," countered Penelope. "If he really were set on getting his own back, I doubt he would have waited that long. Revenge tastes better hot."

"That's debatable. Mir Alam waited several years before taking his revenge on some of his enemies here in the capital, and I don't believe he enjoyed it any the less for the wait."

"Even so," said Penelope stubbornly. "I doubt that talking out of turn at a durbar is cause enough to elevate me to the top of his enemies list. I imagine I'm somewhere down near the bottom, somewhere below the man who trimmed his mustache too short."

"That would be a capital offense," agreed Alex, before adding, "What about Lord Frederick?"

Penelope squirmed slightly against the white coverlet. Something about the question gave her a decidedly queasy sensation, although she wasn't sure whether it was the implication that her husband wanted her dead or simply the sound of his name on Alex's lips. "What about him?" she asked belligerently. She didn't want to talk about Freddy with Alex.

Alex sighed.

With an airiness she was far from feeling, she said, "Of course, you are ignoring the obvious solution, which is that the netting was just taken down for cleaning and the snake crawled in through the drainage sluice on his own scaly initiative."

"He couldn't fit through the drainage sluice."

"The door, then. The window. This house is positively riddled with permeable passages."

"You said it wasn't a love match."

Penelope balled her hands into fists in her lap. "If every marriage of convenience ended in murder, the graveyards of London would be packed to capacity. Freddy might not love me, but that's no reason to murder me! I'm rather convenient for him, really."

"How so?"

Penelope gave a bitter laugh. "He can dally all he likes without fear of consequences. It isn't as though anyone else can force him into marriage."

Damn, damn, damn. Penelope wished she could suck that betraying "else" right back into her mouth, but it was already too late for that. Alex was wearing his thoughtful expression again, looking at her as though he had just fit the last piece into a puzzle.

Desperate to refocus his attention, Penelope said hastily, "Freddy's mistress, on the other hand, might justifiably desire to put a period to my existence. Does she speak English?"

If Alex was surprised, he didn't show it. "Excellent English. And French, too. She was mistress to Guignon, among others."

"Guignon," repeated Penelope softly. "The man we chased to that tomb."

"You mean the man I chased, while you followed," Alex's voice was mild, but there was something guarded behind it. At another time, Penelope might have pursued that, but she was preoccupied with something far more pressing. What if it wasn't all rubbish? What if Alex was right, and the snake had been deliberately released into her room? She didn't want to think that Freddy wanted to kill her, or even his mistress—although she couldn't help but admire her initiative if the woman had tried—but there was someone who did have a far more powerful motive than piddling little affairs of the heart.

"It's Fiske," said Penelope with resolution, lifting her head an abruptness that made the bed wobble. "It's Fiske who wants to kill me."

Alex blinked. "Fiske? He seemed to be having a rather good time in your company earlier tonight. I don't think murder was what was on his mind," he added dryly.

"Until," said Penelope, "I mentioned the Marigold."

Even if a maddened French spy was trying to murder her, at least she had the satisfaction of doing what she might once have thought impossible: rendering Captain Reid completely and utterly speechless. She hadn't even had to jump into a river to do it.

"I take it you know of him, too?" she said brightly. "I imagine that was why you were chasing Major Guignon up to that Frenchman's tomb—not for his onion soup recipes."

"Raymond's Tomb," Alex corrected numbly. "And Guignon was a pastry chef, not a cook. How in the devil do you know about the Marigold?"

Penelope let out a snort of repressed amusement. "This fearsome French military man was a *pastry chef*? Oh Lord, whatever will they do next? Boot-blacks leading their engineers? Tailors sailing their ships?"

"Vive la Republique," agreed Alex absently. "Why Fiske? How in the hell does he come into it? And how in the *bloody* hell do you know about the Marigold?"

Penelope regarded him with approval. There was nothing more annoying than miss-ish reservations about not cursing in front of a lady. "I have my sources," she said airily. "And I know that your Guignon was expecting the arrival of a contact who would set certain plans into motion."

Penelope briefly considered telling Alex about the note she had found and just as quickly discarded the idea. No point in raising unnecessary questions about how and where she had come upon it and why she hadn't thought to bring it to his attention before. Of course, Penelope told herself self-righteously, that was when she hadn't quite realized what it was. And how was she to know back then that Alex was to be trusted? It had all made perfect sense at the time.

Penelope looked up to find Alex staring at her as though she had grown a second head. "What are you?" he demanded dazedly.

Penelope positioned herself to best advantage, bosom forward, shoulders back, chin tilted. If he wanted to know, there it all was, on display.

"Exactly what I seem," she drawled.

Alex regarded her thoughtfully, examining her face, as though taking her apart, feature by feature, until the mechanics were laid bare beneath.

"Somehow I doubt that," he said, and Penelope had the sense that he was referring to more than just spies. But he didn't pursue it further. "How—," he began, and then broke off, shaking his head. "No. Scratch that. So there really *is* a Marigold, then?"

"Of course," said Penelope with great conviction, exuding superiority even though the only authority she had for it was Henrietta's letter, which she still hadn't managed to find.

"I had heard rumors, but it seemed . . ."

"Too silly?" Penelope laughed at the expression on his face. "I know a Gentian, a Carnation, and a short-lived Calla Lily. Nothing is too silly. It's all the notices in the paper. Ever since the success of that Scarlet Pimpernel fellow years and years ago, they all play up for the reviews, tossing flowers about in the hopes of getting into the illustrated papers. You'd be amazed what people will get up to."

"Including your friend Fiske?" said Alex, bringing them doggedly back to the matter at hand.

"Not my friend," corrected Penelope. "Freddy's. I had thought— well, no need to get into that, but let's just say I had almost decided to absolve him, but his reaction to a casual little mention of marigolds was decidedly damning."

"Casual?"

"Well, maybe not that casual," Penelope admitted. "But I certainly got a reaction. He nearly toppled over."

Alex looked frowningly at her. "Don't you think a real Marigold— if there were one—would have better sense than to react so violently to the mention of his name?"

"In general, perhaps. But I caught him off guard," said Penelope smugly. "He certainly didn't expect anything of the kind from *me*. In Fiske's eyes, I was nothing more than a . . . a walking set of bosoms. He certainly won't make that mistake again."

"That may not be a good thing," murmured Alex, scrupulously avoiding staring at her chest. "You were probably safer when he thought of you, er, that way."

Penelope brushed that aside, well away on her own train of thought. "It does all make sense, when you think about it. He decided to end the danger by ending me. But he couldn't be seen murdering his best friend's wife."

"Of course not," Alex said. "I could see where that would be difficult for him."

"Not at all good *ton*," agreed Penelope caustically. "So he had to find a way to eliminate me that would look like an accident. Hence, the snake."

Penelope marveled at her own cleverness. It was a perfectly beauti-ful theory. Even the Pink Carnation couldn't have done better.

Her stubborn companion, on the other hand, didn't seem nearly as impressed. "Would he have had time?"

"Of course!" said Penelope. "He left the party at least a full hour before I did, maybe more. How long can it take to plant one little cobra?"

"Not so little," said Alex soberly, his gaze flicking to the snake corpse still cluttering up a portion of Penelope's bedroom floor.

Penelope had to admit that the sight of it did serve as a slight check on her high spirits. But it was no matter. Forewarned was forearmed and all that. Fiske was a measly little toad and she could certainly deal with *him*.

"One of us should search his room," she said with great decision. "He'll be away all this next week, so it should be easy enough." At Alex's quizzical look she elaborated. "He and Freddy are going to Berar. For the hunting."

The mention of Berar acted on Alex as Marigold had on Fiske. "Where are they going?" he demanded, looming over her in a way that made her tilt her head back at a very uncomfortable angle.

"To Berar. Oh, do sit down! You're making me dizzy, hovering like that."

Alex leaned over her, disregarding her instructions about looming. "Are you sure he said Berar?" he demanded.

"Quite sure," said Penelope, lifting her hand to her mouth to stifle a yawn. "The point is that he'll be gone."

Alex looked at her tight-lipped. "The point is that he'll be in Berar." After a moment, he said abruptly, "Have you heard of the lost treasure of Berar?"

"It sounds like a bedtime story," Penelope commented, leaning sinuously back against the pillows. She looked up at him from her supine position. "I don't suppose you're planning to come to bed and tell me."

Clasping his hands behind his back, Alex wandered over to the window. "During the siege of Gawilighur last year," he said, as much to himself as her, "a vast treasure belonging to the Rajah of Berar mysteriously disappeared."

"Into someone's pockets, no doubt," volunteered Penelope from the bed. "There's nothing mysterious about that."

Alex turned to face her. "Yes, but whose?" he said spiritedly, and Penelope thought how very oddly domestic it was, he by the window, she in the bed, chatting like an old married couple. As she and Freddy never had. "Someone claiming to be called the Marigold has been going around, offering people chunks of that lost treasure in exchange for their support in a rising against the English."

"The machine you have put together," murmured Penelope.

"What?"

"Nothing," said Penelope, lifting a languid hand from the coverlet. "Just something I read somewhere. Go on."

Alex stopped by the edge of the bed. "There's really no 'on' to go. That's it. If your Fiske—"

"Not my Fiske."

"—is the Marigold, and the gold of Berar is still in Berar . . ."

Penelope pushed herself up to a sitting position. "He's going to fetch the gold! To make good on those payments and set the wheels of his machine in motion."

Alex sat down again on the edge of the bed. "So it would seem."

Leaning forward, Penelope grasped his upper arm. "Then we have to follow him."

"That would—We?"

"We," repeated Penelope firmly. "Goodness only knows what a botch you would make of it without me."

"Can we fight about this in the morning?" suggested Alex mildly, starting to rise. "It is very late."

Grabbing him by the hand, Penelope tugged him back down. After years of driving her own pair in the Park, her arm muscles were in peak condition. Alex subsided onto the coverlet with a startled *oomph*. "And let you sneak out while I'm still asleep. Oh, no, no, no." He had the good grace to look guilty, confirming that he had been planning to do precisely that. The man couldn't lie to save his life. All the more reason he needed her along on this journey. "I'm going with you."

Alex cocked an eyebrow, but he didn't make the mistake of trying to get away again. "Would it be very trite to say, no, you're not?"

"Ridiculously trite. And completely pointless."

"It's a long ride over rough terrain."

"We've traveled over rough terrain together before."

"Yes—with more than fifty servants, a cook, and a separate dining tent! I'll be sleeping rough, in the fields most likely and taking only what can fit into my saddlebags."

"I'm not afraid of privation."

"You've never experienced it."

There was too much truth in that for Penelope's comfort, but she didn't let that daunt her. "You're wasting time," she said instead. "If I don't go with you, I'll go without you. Which would you prefer?"

"I won't be bringing my groom," he said.

Penelope's amber eyes slanted up at him. "Good. Then I shan't bring mine either."

Chapter Twenty

W hen he arrived at the main gate, Penelope was waiting for him.

In her dark blue habit, she looked like a smudge against the landscape, a dark splotch against the pale stone of the walls. Not yet dawn, the sky was dark, the air still held its nighttime chill, and the sentries in their box were little more than smudges themselves, patently uninterested in the appearance of anyone whose purpose was not to relieve them from their posts.

Alex checked when he saw Penelope waiting for him, fighting a craven desire to turn right around and ride out the back way.

They had never resolved the question of her presence, at least, not to their mutual satisfaction. As far as Alex was concerned, he was going to Berar alone. He had said so. Repeatedly. And when that failed, he had resorted to a knave's trick; he had told her he planned to leave at dawn. So here he was in the predawn dark, his saddlebags packed and his provisions ready, and here was she.

It was too bloody late for a fight. Or did he mean too early? He had never been to bed. He assumed she hadn't either. Even so, there was nothing fatigued about her straight-spined stance as she sat her horse, waiting for him with the alert composure of a seasoned general watching for an enemy attack.

Eschewing the coward's way out, Alex spurred forward. Penelope calmly clucked her own mount into motion, moving from her vantage point by the side of the gate to meet him in the open space beyond.

"No," he said.

"Good morning to you, too," Penelope said coolly, bringing her horse into step with his. "Going somewhere?"

Alex pulled abruptly to the side, far enough in the shadow of the walls to put them out of range of the sentries' incurious gaze. He reined up, turning to face her. "You know very well where."

"You were going to leave without me." It wasn't a question.

"Yes." He had meant to leave it at that, but found he couldn't. He caught himself groping after explanations, excuses. He shouldn't need them. They had been over all this the night before. Even if they hadn't agreed. With an exasperated sigh, Alex rubbed a hand over his blood-shot eyes. "We discussed this."

"We clearly came to different resolutions." Penelope leaned back in her saddle. "Let me make this clear. I don't care about traveling rough or riding hard or any of those things. I would far rather be in the saddle than in the Residency drawing room."

"It's not that I'm worried about," Alex said reluctantly. "Although I don't think you'll like the saddle sores after the second day of continuous riding."

"Then what? My reputation?" Seeing the confirmation in his face, Penelope laughed, a laugh like cut glass, all brilliant glitter and jagged edges. "Darling Alex. Darling, innocent Alex, I haven't any reputation left to lose. I divested myself of that a long time ago. Why do you think Fiske and that lot dare to treat me as they do? If I'm to have the opprobrium, I might at least have the freedom."

It made Alex's teeth grit to think of Fiske or any of his dissolute companions daring to sit in judgment of Penelope. Including her husband.

"Fiske treats most women as fair game," he said sharply. "Not just you. If it is discovered that we were traveling alone together, it will be a very great deal of opprobrium—for a very small space of freedom. Are you sure you want to make that trade?"

"It is my trade to make." Her face lit with a sudden, irresistible smile. Like the sun coming out from beyond the clouds, thought a dazzled Alex unoriginally, as she turned the full force of her considerable charm in his direction, saying deliberately, wheedlingly, "What can possibly be wrong with a lady hastening to join her husband, escorted by a dour and reliable member of the Residency staff? I think it's terribly romantic, don't you?"

He smiled reluctantly. "Is that what you told your ayah?"

"Yes, with strict orders not to tell anyone at all. Which means she will tell absolutely everyone. By dawn, the story will be all around the Residency. So you see, if I return now, it will cause more talk than if I go."

Alex wasn't quite sure he agreed with that logic, but he let it go. "And if I leave without you?"

"I will follow," she said without hesitation. "Loudly. Conspicuously. Embarrassingly."

She wouldn't, really. If she followed, it would be silently and purposefully. But she would follow.

The devil of it was, he wanted her there. Which was, in his fatigue-fuddled brain, all the more reason why she shouldn't be there. It was several days' ride to Berar, days of riding together, foraging together, bunking together. It wasn't the riding or foraging he was worried about.

As if reading his mind, Penelope said caustically, "You needn't be afraid for your virtue. Who is Sir Galahad to be swayed by such a minor siren as I?"

"I'm not Sir Galahad," said Alex tiredly, seizing on the least of the points. "And I don't remember him having much trouble with sirens."

Was Sir Galahad the one who slept with the king's wife? Or was that another one? Either way, he wasn't a knight of any table, round or otherwise.

"Odysseus, then," said Penelope carelessly. "Whoever you imagine yourself to be, you needn't fear that I'll force my attentions upon you. You made your feelings on that score quite clear." As if suddenly impatient with the whole discussion, she set her heels to Buttercup's sides. "Are you coming? Or am I going without you?"

He had done the right thing by refusing her offers the night before.

He had done it for her own good, to save her misery and regret. Then why did he feel like such a heel?

Alex hastened to catch up with her. "You don't know where you're going."

It was only a pro forma protest and she knew it. He was not going to leave her to wander the countryside of Hyderabad by herself. Alex's stomach experienced a sinking feeling, like a rock cake settling to the bottom of his gut. Bunk mates it was going to be. In separate bedrolls.

Penelope cast him a superior look. "How hard can it be?"

Harder than she knew.

"Without map, compass, or more than a rudimentary knowledge of the language? Just as a broad guess, I would say very."

Penelope ducked her chin and looked up at him from under her lashes. "I like a challenge."

And then she was away ahead, deliberately leaving him in her dust.

Stifling a cough, Alex shook his head, smiled wryly, and followed along behind, prepared to head her off should she take the wrong pass. She deserved to be allowed to make her point. Up to a point, that was.

She put on a good show, but he could see from the tension of her shoulders that she was still geared for battle. That was his Penelope, always ready with a shield in one hand and a sword in the other, prepared to come out swinging. Swinging, shooting, jumping into a river. The memory made him grin, despite his fatigue. Watching her plunge into the river had taken a good year off his life, but he couldn't help but be impressed by the sheer, brash courage of it. It wasn't many women who would plunge into a river in full spate after a drowning man or shoot down a cobra by candlelight. The woman he had first met, in a drawing room in Calcutta, might have been an entirely different creature, a construct of his own preconceptions and prejudices.

Yet, beneath all that bravado, there were times when she seemed as fragile as glass, protected from shattering only by that thick layer of nonchalance she cast up around her like a shield. *You needn't fear that I'll force my attentions upon you*, she had said, as though it weren't entirely the other way around. He recalled the bleak expression on her face last night, in the garden, when he had come upon her on her way back from her bungalow. Bleak and lost, lost in a way that had nothing to do with maps or compasses or geographical terrain.

It hadn't been a love match, she had said. Even so, he remembered the way she had followed after Lord Frederick that night after the river, watching his shadow through the wall of the tent like a beggar at a lighted window. He had never seen anyone look quite so alone as Penelope had that night.

What had they been to each other back in London? Had she thought she loved him then? Alex supposed Lord Frederick was charming enough, if one didn't know him well. He was titled, polished, not entirely dull-witted. Even a clever woman could make the mistake of falling in love with a handsome face.

He hated the thought of her with Lord Frederick; he hated the thought that Lord Frederick still held the power to wound her so. For all that Penelope had tried to banish the topic, Lord Frederick had been all around them the night before: his house, his room, his bed. In that room, at that moment, it had been impossible to know whether Penelope's attentions, physical and otherwise, had been truly for him, or whether he was merely a weapon wielded in a rearguard action against her husband, gouging out the memory of her husband's mistress by bringing another man into her husband's bed. It was not a particularly flattering thought.

He had hurt her, too, he realized, in turning her down. Just how much, he hadn't suspected until that moment by the gate, when she had spurred her way forward ahead of him.

How to explain that it wasn't the lack of wanting that was the problem? It wasn't just physical desire, even though that was the sole currency by which Penelope appeared to measure her own worth. It would be easier if it were. The reality was much more complicated and much more worrisome. He appreciated her as a companion; he admired her as a comrade; he wanted her as a lover.

All innocuous enough each on its own. Put together . . . Christ.

What a coil. His father couldn't have done better. She was the wife of a man who was technically his superior, a visitor to his province, a lady under his protection. It was the devil of a time to finally discover just what it was that had made James decide to risk his job and his neck for the love of Khair-un-Nissa, or his father's Rajput concubine to put knife to chest when his father had strayed, this fierce, possessive, overwhelming something.

Oh, hell. Not just something. He might as well call it by its name. Love. Such a mild term for such a destructive force.

It wasn't supposed to be like this. He had decided long, long ago that when he fell in love, it was going to be appropriate. Orderly.

He had had it all figured out. Once he had established himself in the political service, settled in his own district with a reasonable sufficiency with which to support a wife, he was going to set about looking among the daughters of his father's peers for a pleasant, sensible sort of girl, preferably one raised in India, who knew the land, the language, and the people, who wouldn't cherish any false expectations about the sort of life he would be able to provide for her. Simple as that. They would marry, raise a family, and that would be that, all open, aboveboard, and legitimate. Legitimate was very important.

The only one of those qualifications Penelope fit was that she was female.

Yet, there it was. And, for all his good resolutions, he had hurt her last night and he didn't know how to put it right.

"That was a damned fine shot last night," he said awkwardly, trotting along beside her. Compliments, his father always swore. A sure way to any woman's bed. Not that her bed was his goal, of course. "Taking down that cobra."

If Penelope was softened, she didn't show it. "It took you long enough to acknowledge it."

That was truer than she knew.

"You were too busy complimenting yourself to let me get a word in," said Alex bracingly.

"If I don't, who will?" She had meant it to be flippant, but didn't quite carry it off. Penelope looked away, gesturing at random at the passing fields. "This landscape reminds me of the Highlands, all craggy, with those bursts of green."

"The Highlands?" Alex, having never been, looked skeptically around them. It still looked like Hyderabad to him. "I shouldn't think they have many mangos there. Or banyan trees."

"Haven't you been? I thought your father was Scottish."

"At a remove," said Alex. He grinned reminiscently. "Although he can muster a fairly convincing brogue when he's in his cups. And he does insist on singing the most appalling collection of sentimental Scottish ballads at the slightest provocation."

"I shall remember that," said Penelope, and Alex turned his mind away from the thought that it was highly unlikely his father and Penelope should ever cross paths again.

Why should they, after all? he asked himself harshly. No matter how he might feel about her—and he very carefully shied away from naming that feeling—they were from different worlds, he and Penelope, and they would return to them.

Eventually.

But that eventually would come no matter how far away it might feel now, in the no-man's-land of the back roads of the Deccan. Penelope came from title, wealth, privilege. He came from a long line of charming scoundrels, outlaws in all but name. There were Reids dotting the English-speaking world, adventurers, wanderers, gamblers. Dreamers. In Alex, that had all been tempered by the stern strain on his mother's side.

At least, so he had thought. Perhaps he wasn't quite so immune from the flighty fancies of his father's family as he had imagined, lusting after the impossible and spinning tales designed to make it true.

"My grandparents fled Scotland after the '45," said Alex abruptly. "They were Jacobites. Traitors, as your side would have it."

"Oh, so it's my side now?" mocked Penelope. "I'll have you know that my very own uncle was court-martialed for his part in the rising in Dublin in '98. It was quite embarrassing for my mother. She tried to pretend she wasn't related to him."

Penelope's lips curved with a malicious satisfaction that gave Alex a fair inkling as to the nature of her relationship with her mother.

"How embarrassing for your mother," Alex said dryly. Nice to know that there were other people with treasonous siblings out there.

Jack. Another matter he didn't want to think about. They were piling up, like sandbags at a siege.

Penelope raised an eyebrow, every inch the debutante. "Of course, Lord Edward Fitzgerald was involved in the rising, too, so there was at least *some* social cachet to it."

Alex choked on a laugh. "Indeed?"

Penelope nodded serenely. "A grandson of the Duke of Richmond and Lennox, no less. It was the only saving grace as far as Mother was concerned."

"She wasn't at all concerned for her brother?"

Penelope shrugged. "As far as my mother was concerned, once her surname changed, so did her family. I never met my uncle, nor any of my cousins, for that matter. I gather there are a number of them."

Alex had never met his cousins either—there were scads of them back in Charleston, uncles and aunts and cousins and so forth—but there had always been letters, scores of letters back and forth between his father and his father's siblings, marking marriages, births, deaths, feuds, reconciliations, fortunes lost and won. The letters were frequently torn, crumpled, months, even years late, but still they came; just as George wrote dutifully to Lizzy, and Kat sent scathing commentary and embroidered handkerchiefs to him.

The only one left out was Jack, and that was of his own accord, not for want of attempts to drag him body and soul back into the warmth of the family circle.

"Did your family mind?" Alex asked curiously. "Your coming here?"

Penelope clearly found the question an odd one. "Why should they? My brothers scarcely noticed me when I was home. And my mother was primarily concerned that I use the opportunity to strike up an acquaintance with Lady Clive."

It had been a wrench for his father to send his Lizzy and Kat to England two years before and just as much of a wrench to go and join them and leave Alex and George behind. He had fussed over all of their departures like a mother hen, clucking and brooding. Penelope's picture of complete indifference was as alien to him as—well, as the rest of her London world.

It was impossible for him to imagine a world without the solid foundation of a family's affection. No matter how far any of them roamed, that was home in the end, one another, even when they drove one another mad.

No wonder Penelope clung even to the unreliable attentions of a Lord Frederick Staines if that was all she had left behind. So much for the so-called civilized world. The thought of the household Penelope described, the emptiness of it, chilled Alex to the bone, despite the sun that was already making its presence felt as dawn gave way to morning.

Alex chose his words carefully, keeping his tone light. "I take it you're to embroil yourself only in aristocratic treasons?"

Penelope smiled narrowly. "Precisely."

It was definitely time to change the subject. "Have you eaten anything this morning?"

She squinted against the sun. "Not that I recall."

Alex nodded, back on solid ground again. "We should stop now anyway, give the horses a rest."

"And ourselves, too?" said Penelope delicately, as though trying to tease out of him an admission of weakness.

Alex grinned at her. "Yes. I don't know about you, but I could use a soft stretch of ground and a long drink of water. It's too damn hot to stay this long in the saddle without a break."

Turning his horse off the road, they picked their way carefully across the uneven ground, stopping in a quiet grove shaded by mango and banyan trees. At the center of the grove sat the remains of a shrine, with Gothic arches in a cinquefoil pattern. The roof had fallen in on one side and tree branches poked through the ruined masonry, but it filled its purpose. It was quiet and shady and there was grass for the horses.

Penelope levered herself off her horse with a distinct sigh of relief.

"Sore?" asked Alex, reaching up to help her down.

"Not at all," lied Penelope, shaking her head so briskly that she caught him a blow with the brim of her high-crowned hat. "Just hungry."

"If you explore my saddlebags, you'll find tiffin," Alex suggested. His voice was hoarse from the dust of the road. He cleared it self-consciously. "And water."

"Brilliant," said Penelope, flashing him a smile to match. While he set their mounts to grazing, tethering them to the remains of a Gothic-looking arch, she rooted about in the bag he had tossed her. "I'm surprised you trust me to go through your things," she said conversationally, her head bent over the bag.

"We are a team, aren't we?" said Alex in a rallying tone. "Comrades in arms. Partners in adventure."

Penelope shook back her hair, holding aloft one of the metal tiffin containers. "Messmates, even."

Mate had been an unfortunate choice of words. But, then, comrade in arms wasn't much better.

"Toss that over here," Alex said heartily. Too heartily. Next thing, he would be pounding her on the back and calling her "matey."

Food. That was what he needed. A nice, filling meal and then a long, uninterrupted sleep. Alone, he specified, before his unregenerate imagination could get any unfortunate ideas.

Too late.

Penelope tossed, perfectly gauging the trajectory and distance. Alex gave a brief, instinctive nod of appreciation as he caught the tin neatly between his hands.

Penelope ducked her head back over the saddlebag, and began industriously piling up a small stack of metal containers on the blanket Alex had spread out across the ground. "What are you feeding us?" she demanded.

Alex passed her the opened tin. Penelope stuck her index finger in, conveying a whopping fingerful to her mouth.

"Mmm, goo," she said, making enthusiastic sucking noises.

"Aubergines," Alex corrected, shifting uncomfortably. Utensils. He ought to have thought of utensils. Who knew that the omission would cause such pain? "There should be spoons at the bottom of the saddlebag."

He sounded, he thought with disgust, like someone's governess, prim and starchy. Although as far as he knew, it would be anatomically impossible for any governess worthy of the name to be suffering the precise problem he was suffering at this moment.

Fortunately, Penelope chose that moment to dig back into the saddlebag, giving Alex a much-needed moment to compose himself, before triumphantly producing two somewhat battered spoons and one fork. She tossed them onto the blanket before peering back into the saddlebag. "Am I to take out all of this, or must we husband our resources?"

"We should be able to buy our food going forward," said Alex, busying himself opening a second container. He managed a tired grin. "Failing that, you can shoot it."

"I hope you like the taste of cobra," said Penelope blandly. "It's my specialty."

"If you shoot it," Alex promised extravagantly, "I can cook it."

They dug into their food with more hunger than ceremony. It was pleasant in the shade. Peaceful. The leaves of an overhanging banyan tree cast restful shadows across the blanket. Around the side of the shrine, Alex could hear the gentle whifflings and slurping noises as the horses grazed, taking their own nourishment as their owners ate theirs.

Cleaning off her spoon with a lick of her tongue, Penelope wiped it carelessly on the side of her habit before dropping it back in the saddlebag.

"How long, do you think, before we get to Berar?"

"We could get there fairly expeditiously," said Alex, cleaning his own spoon far more meticulously with a clean square of cloth. "Traveling as we have." Penelope preened at the implicit compliment. "I imagine your . . . Lord Frederick and his friends will be traveling far more slowly. The grooms told me they were going in a proper procession, elephants and all."

"And stopping for leisurely meals, too, no doubt, knowing Freddy," said Penelope, leaning back on her elbows to squint up at the shifting canopy of leaves overhead. "Afternoon naps, even."

"I wouldn't mind one of those," admitted Alex ruefully, rubbing a hand against the new growth of his chin. There had been no time for sleeping or for shaving. The bristle of new beard was already beginning to shadow chin and jaw in physical demonstration of how long it had been since he had last woken up in his own bed, with his own shaving kit. He didn't want to count the hours. It would only make him more tired.

Penelope put out a finger to lightly brush the bristles on his jaw.

"You must be exhausted," she said, tracing her way up along the side of his lips.

Catching her hand, Alex lifted it to his lips, pressing a kiss against the palm.

Chapter Twenty-One

Alex flushed, dropping her hand. "I'm sorry," he said hastily. "I didn't—"

Leaning forward, Penelope silenced him with a kiss. If he had any objections, he didn't voice them. It would have been hard for him to do so. His mouth and hands were otherwise occupied. He tasted of stewed aubergine, with a slight hint of cloves. Mmm, tasty, thought Penelope, and enthusiastically gave herself up to osculation and aubergine.

Alex's hands remained for just a moment too long on her elbows before he regretfully withdrew.

"Wait," said Penelope laughingly, as he drew back, away from her. "Where do you think you're going?"

He raised an eyebrow. "A safe distance away."

His tone was light, but she could tell he meant it. Penelope sat up straighter, dragging her skirts close around her knees. "To stop me from attacking you, I wager," she said acidly, feeling the sting of his words like lemon juice on an open cut. Poor, beleaguered man, pursued by the relentless advances of an amorous matron. She doubted anyone would feel sorry for him.

"Change the pronouns around and you'll have it right," he said wryly. "You can't think, after all this time, that I don't want you—"

"You give a convincing impression of it," grumbled Penelope.

"—But it would be a cad's trick to dishonor you," he finished. "It wouldn't do to serve you so."

It was on the tip of Penelope's tongue to tell him that he wouldn't be the first. But she couldn't, not when he was looking at her so gravely, as though he actually gave a care for how she might feel, for something other than the fleeting press of her body against his in a convenient corner.

So she schooled her sarcastic tongue and said simply, "I know. That's why *I* want you."

Despite himself, he grinned. "Because you can't resist a challenge?"

He looked so much younger when he smiled, thought Penelope, young and carefree. It lifted away the anxious lines beside his eyes. That was one of his most redeeming qualities, Penelope decided, that sense of humor that popped out no matter how hard he tried to be stern.

"You're not that much of a challenge," said Penelope dampeningly.

But, then, what man was? Penelope had pursued her fair share over the years, straight from ballroom to balcony. None of them had put up much of a fight.

It was a poor substitute for riding to hounds, where at least the fox had the courtesy to keep running. She had canoodled in corners with a variety of uninspiring specimens, seeking that momentary thrill that came of desire and the defiance of convention, two birds with one stone. There had been Turnip Fitzhugh, handsome, endlessly good-natured, but as simple-minded as a child; Martin Frobisher, good with his lips but too fast with his hands; Freddy. All good-looking, all self-assured, all with lineages far more distinguished than hers, but not any of them men Penelope had given serious thought to marrying. They were playthings, short-lived pastimes, like the block castles she used to build only in order to smash. There had been precious little liking involved and even less affection; that she had reserved for her female friends, for Henrietta and Charlotte and the crusty old Dowager Duchess of Dovedale.

It was hard to imagine Alex on one of those balconies she had frequented with such reckless abandon. He was dark where her previous conquests had been fair, serious where they had been flippant, irritatingly observant where they had been comfortably oblivious. If one were to judge from past conquests, Alex wasn't at all in her line.

And it wasn't just because he was a challenge.

"Because I like you," she blurted out, and realized that for once it was true. It was a rather unsettling revelation. "You're . . . , well, you."

Not just a body on a balcony, not just a pair of lips to blot out boredom, but Alex, Alex who argued with her and watched out for her and woke absurdly early in the mornings to ride with her every day, whether he had the time to do so or not.

Perhaps this wasn't such a good idea after all.

Alex didn't seem to think so, either. His dark eyes were intent on her face, watching her in that way of his, as though he were learning her from the inside out, peering into every little dark nook and cranny of her soul. There were plenty of those to choose from. Dark nooks were one of Penelope's specialties.

He might have wanted her last night, in the still of the bungalow, with the lingering scent of moonflowers on the breeze, but not in daylight, when he saw her again for what she was, brash, impetuous, with her face gone unfashionably tan and curry stains on her habit. He was undoubtedly mustering the words with which to turn her down politely.

Penelope suddenly, very desperately, didn't want to hear them.

She jumped to her feet, leaning over to gather up the empty tins. "Or we can just ride on," she said brusquely, not looking at him.

A lean brown hand closed around her wrist. Penelope regarded it blankly, as though not quite sure what it was doing there, alien against the white lace frill of her sleeve. Slowly, her breath catching somewhere in the vicinity of her corset, she lifted her eyes to Alex's face. What she saw banished any doubts she might have had. In his eyes blazed a reflection of the desire she felt in her own.

Nothing more needed to be said. Without a word, he drew her down beside him on the blanket, the blanket that had seemed so prosaic only moments before, but now presented the prospect of a host of exotic and illicit possibilities. Penelope plunked down hard on her knees, catching at his shoulders for balance as she tilted her head down to kiss him, enjoying the unusual advantage of height.

"Are you sure?" he murmured, his teeth tugging at her earlobe, even as his hands moved intimately up and down her torso.

In answer, Penelope pushed hard at his shoulders, sending him toppling back onto the blanket, narrowly missing sheer disaster with a fork. She followed him down, bracing herself on her elbows and scattering kisses across his upturned face as he busied himself with the buttons on her riding jacket. The fabric parted, and his hands slid beneath, burning through the linen of her blouse, drawing her down on top of him with drugging kisses that made the noon sky dim to dusk and the rustling of the tree leaves blur in her ears.

Penelope wriggled her hands beneath his shirt, feeling the hard edges of muscle beneath, delighting in the way they contracted with each labored breath, with a flick of her tongue against the hollow of his throat and an exploratory expedition taken by her lips along his collarbone. His body felt very different from Freddy's. His frame was more compact, more economical, with none of the extra layer of flesh lent by too-indulgent living, only skin stretched spare over muscle and bone, broken by the odd ridge of an old scar.

He drew her back up to kiss her mouth, one hand tangling in her hair, drawing her face down to his. The long skirts of her riding habit bunched between them. Her lips still joined with his, Penelope wiggled impatiently against him, trying to displace some of the layers of fabric separating them. Her breasts tingled through the linen of her shirt, her corset cover lightly abrading her nipples as she moved. Penelope could feel Alex's hands working at the folds of her skirt, moving beneath the heavy fabric to the bare skin underneath. Impatiently, she rocked against him, their mouths locked tongue to tongue as his hands found the bare skin above her garters. The sensation of his hands on her thighs was all the more erotic for the layers of heavy wool cascading around them.

Whimpering, Penelope tried to push downwards, towards his questing fingers, but his hands closed around her thighs, holding her poised in all the inarticulate irritation of suspended desire. She could feel his thumbs at the soft junction of her thighs, maddeningly close to, but not quite touching the area she so ardently wanted him to reach.

Well, two could play at that game. With unsteady hands, Penelope scrabbled at all the excess fabric, prospecting through a wilderness of bunched-up blue wool for the front of Alex's breeches. It didn't take his quick, indrawn breath or the constriction of his hands around her thighs to let her know she had found the right place. Penelope gave a husky laugh of triumph as she yanked at the front flap with a fine disregard to buttons and stitches.

Raising the stakes, his thumb brushed against the swollen place between her legs. Penelope delicately curved her fingers around his shaft and applied the just right amount of pressure to make all the blood travel from his brain to another location entirely.

"Christ!" Alex groaned, with what was left of his verbal faculties. "You're wicked."

"I try," Penelope said, then gasped, her back arching as he did some rather wicked things of his own, revealing that while he might not have had much experience with corset ties, he did have a healthy working knowledge of the female anatomy. Penelope emitted a little mewing noise, as her body contracted of its own accord. Lord. It had taken her weeks to teach Freddy to find that spot. Her knees were feeling wobbly. They didn't want to hold her up anymore. There were black spots in front of her eyes and her swollen nipples rubbed painfully against the lining of her corset. She felt like a ripe fruit, about to burst out of its own skin. Every inch of her was overripe and aching, bursting for completion.

She squirmed away, out of the reach of his teasing fingers. She wanted him inside her and she wanted it now.

"No more games," she rasped, her knees tightening around his hips. Holding his shaft in one hand, she lowered herself slowly down on top of him, her lips parting in an involuntary gasp as she felt him inside her.

"No games," he agreed, and there was a wild note in his voice that matched her own, as his hands closed around her bare buttocks, pulling her down as he drove up into her, hard and fast.

Penelope felt herself convulsing around him, the waves of pleasure coming one on top of the other, all the stored-up desire of the past few days pulsing out between them. She could barely hear the echo of her own hoarse cry in her ears for the thrumming of her blood. Still caught in a dizzy spiral of pleasure, she was only vaguely aware when Alex's hand closed desperately about her waist, lifting her unceremoniously off him as he rolled over to spill his seed in the grass.

Flushed, disheveled, they lay gasping like pugilists who had just fought a difficult bout, each in his own corner. Penelope sprawled in the center of the blanket where Alex had dropped her, propped up on her elbows, feeling her chest work up and down against her corset as her breathing returned to normal and some of the hectic color faded from her cheeks.

Across the blanket, Alex rolled to a sitting position, his hands going self-consciously to the flap of his breeches. His shirt was untucked, his breeches' flap flopping, his hair rumpled, and there were angry red patches at the open neck of his shirt where she might just have gotten a little bit carried away in the heat of the moment.

Penelope suspected she didn't look much better. Her hair was scraggling down on one side of her head, her jacket was still open, and she was sitting in a patch of wet. Why was it that the act itself was so wonderful, but the sequel invariably so awkward?

"Well," she said brightly. Licking her sore lips, she surreptitiously stretched the muscles in her thighs, feeling the stickiness between her legs.

"Well," Alex echoed uncertainly, watching her with obvious concern. She could see his eyes go to her open jacket, then the rumpled blouse underneath, and a mottled red flush spread slowly beneath his tan.

She could tell what he was thinking, that he might at least have had the courtesy to wait to remove her clothes. Penelope could have told him she didn't mind. In fact, the extra layers had added a certain spice to the whole adventure. Like the bit of clove stuck between her back teeth. Hmm. How had that gotten there?

Struggling to her feet on legs that weren't entirely steady, Penelope shook out her skirts. "Oh, Alex, don't look so Friday faced! I'm not going to call you out to defend my honor."

After a startled moment, he grinned back, levering himself up off the ground. "A good thing, too. You're the better shot."

Reaching for her, he helped her do up the last two buttons of her habit. His fingers, so deft on the reins, fumbled with the tiny, cloth-covered buttons. He had not, Penelope surmised, had a great deal of practice with ladies' clothing, unlike Freddy, who could get a lady out of her corset in about five seconds flat. Looking at the bowed top of his dark head as he squinted over her buttons, she felt a painful wave of fondness. Or maybe that was just the pressure of the close-fitting jacket around her ribs.

His fingers lingered on the last button, his knuckles brushing her chin. Glancing up, she found he was looking at her searchingly. "Are you sorry?" he asked.

Penelope raised both eyebrows. "Are you?"

His hands shifted from her stock to her shoulders, smoothing the woolen fabric. "Only if I've done anything to cause you distress."

This conversation was causing her distress. Penelope wished he would just kiss her again. She didn't want to have to talk about it all, parsing emotions and meanings; she just wanted to enjoy it. But she had some respect for Alex's tender sensibilities, so instead of just shrugging and yanking him down for a kiss, she smiled reassuringly up at him.

"Those were not noises of distress you were hearing," she said pro-vocatively. "In fact, quite the contrary."

Alex dropped a kiss on her nose, presumably because it was there. "That wasn't what I meant."

"I know. But it is what I meant."

"So you're using me for my body, then." He tried to make a joke out of it, but didn't quite succeed.

"What's the use of pretending to anything else? We both know how this has to end." Penelope rested her palms against the light material of his shirt, feeling the rise and fall of his breathing beneath her hands. "Can't we just enjoy it for what it is?"

"What about your husband?"

"He doesn't matter," said Penelope, and meant it. Freddy could go hang. It wasn't about revenge anymore. What it was about, she wasn't quite sure. All she knew was that she wasn't ready for it to end. "How long do we have until we reach the others?"

"About four days. Perhaps less."

"Can we—would you—" Penelope cleared her throat. "Can't we just take these days as our own? No strings, no reproaches, no regrets. Just this, nothing more."

"I don't like it." Penelope could feel his chest rise and fall as he dragged in a deep breath. Looking down at her, he managed a wry sort of smile. "But I'd rather have a little bit of you than none of you at all."

Light-headed with relief, Penelope beamed giddily at him. She hadn't realized she was holding her breath until she let it out. "You won't regret it," she assured him. "But there are rules. No mentioning Freddy. No talking about what will happen after."

"No future," finished Alex grimly.

"You," said Penelope reproachfully, "think far too much. Don't. Wouldn't you rather be in the present? The future is only a series of possibilities, the majority of which may never come about. But this—this is here and now and sure."

Alex took her hands, his thumbs stroking against her palms. "You might tell yourself this now, but how will you feel four days from now?"

"That's still four days from now. If there were a future," said Penelope, as much for herself as him, "there would be all sorts of other things to worry about, like where we were to live and who wants the window open and whether we ought to send the children back to school in England or keep them here." It was unnerving how quickly hypothetical images could become concrete in one's head. Penelope shook them away and went resolutely on, her voice shriller than usual, "Marriage isn't all the sentimentalists claim it to be, you know. You would worry about my spending and bemoan my flightiness and deprecate my low relations—"

"In this case," broke in Alex calmly, "I believe I'm the one with the low relations. And you're not flighty. Impulsive, certainly, but not flighty."

Penelope blinked. Freddy had said . . . But that didn't signify. By her own rules, she wasn't allowed to think of Freddy. "Oh. Well. But you do see my point, don't you? This way, we can just appreciate each other for what we are, without having to worry about all those other bits. It's really the best of all possible worlds, when you think about it." She smiled up at him, her hands smoothing upwards from his chest to his shoulders. "Just us, just here, just now."

Alex's limber mouth twisted into the sort of smile a man might wear as he gallops knowingly into the cannon's mouth. Rueful. Resigned.

"Do you have any apples to offer while you're at it?" he said wryly.

"Does that mean you'll be a fallen man with me?"

"If we're going to be thrown out of the garden, we might as well enjoy it while we're in it," he said philosophically, as his head dipped again towards hers. A breath away from her lips, he added, "But I draw the line at fig leaves."

Chapter Twenty-Two

For three days, Penelope had her Eden without fig leaves. She was exhausted, dirty, and saddle sore. She couldn't remember when she had last been so happy. She learned to skin rabbits and made an enemy of a monkey and discovered the hard way that an overripe mango was exceedingly messy to eat.

They traveled slowly, camping early for the night and spending little of it in sleep. True to their agreement, neither mentioned the end of the journey, but it was there nonetheless. It lent a heightened awareness to everything and kept them awake long after fatigue would otherwise have driven them to slumber, determined to eke out every moment given them. It was a precious, finite time and they both knew it. Leaves were greener, food spicier, the light brighter; everything clear, clean-edged, perfect, down to the last choking cloud of dust from the road. Even charred meat, product of Penelope's unsuccessful foray into fire-top cookery, had its own peculiar savor.

As they neared the border of Berar, the real world that they had pushed aside began to crowd back in upon them. They both did their best to ignore it, but Penelope could tell it was there. It was there in the way Alex would sometimes start to say something and then move rapidly away. It was there in the controlled violence with which he would scuff out the smoldering remains of their campfire, belaboring the fragments with his boot until there was nothing left but ash. It was there in her own short bursts of temper, her impatience with a girth that wouldn't tighten and a fire that wouldn't kindle. Even the landscape echoed the sense of impending loss; the farther they went from

Hyderabad, the more desolate their surroundings became, littered with deserted villages, burned houses, and trampled fields; legacy of the recent fighting in the area between British and Mahratta troops. By the third day, they began to come across carts with broken wheels and shattered crockery, the detritus of parties of refugees who had painstakingly picked their way south, away from the ruins of their homes. There was even a small skeleton.

Penelope, who had thought herself proof against maidenly tremors, had to avert her eyes. Pariah dogs had been at the child's corpse. They buried it in a shallow grave, piled with stones to discourage the dogs, before moving on.

Penelope could feel reality pressing in on them. She shut her eyes and pushed back against it with both hands, desperately trying to keep it at bay.

As they rode along yet another back path, between fields that showed the recent ravages of military engagements, Alex broached one of the forbidden topics. "You never did tell me how you knew about the Marigold." He raised an eyebrow. "Unless your hus—unless the special commission was all a pretense, and you've really been on the trail of the spy all this time."

"I'm just sleeping with you to winkle out your secrets," said Penelope kindly. "It's what we secret agents do."

She liked the image of herself as a secret agent. Why hadn't she ever thought of that before?

Because she had been too busy making meaningless mischief to consider embarking on anything constructive. Besides, if she had gone to Henrietta's brother and told him she wanted to be a spy, he probably would have sprinted in the other direction. He had been on the receiving end of one too many of her practical jokes over the years to repose any confidence in her ability to follow orders neatly.

"What have you found out?" Alex asked, amused.

"Only that you make strange snuffling noises when you sleep on your back. And you take up more than your share of the bedroll."

"*Snuffling* noises?"

"You know. Like this." Penelope did a very successful imitation of a pig with adenoidal issues. Her horse sidled at the noise and Penelope reached forward to stroke her between the ears. "There, there, darling, not you. You're a perfect lady."

Alex rolled his eyes in masculine disgust.

"At any rate," said Penelope more prosaically, "I heard about the Marigold from a friend of mine. Another friend managed to get entangled in the activities of, well, a sort of club that Freddy was involved with."

"I think I know the club you mean," murmured Alex. There was something in his voice that made Penelope look sharply at him, but his eyes were fixed on the road ahead, his profile perfectly bland.

"Don't tell me you're a member, too," said Penelope with a laugh. "That I *won't* believe. But did you know a man named Arthur Wrothan?"

"I do know Wrothan," said Alex slowly. "I'm surprised you know of him."

"Did," corrected Penelope. "You did know him. He's dead."

"I can't say I'm sorry to hear it."

"I'm sure you aren't the only one," said Penelope, adjusting the brim of her hat against the sun. "Wrothan caused a great deal of bother to some very important people. He was running a spy ring out of the Hellfire Club, using it to pass along secrets to the French."

Alex nodded. "And that's why you looked to Fiske. Fiske was a member of Wrothan's group in Mysore."

He said the last with the conviction of someone who didn't surmise, but knew.

"For someone who wasn't a member, you seem to know an awful lot about it," teased Penelope.

There was no answering smile. "Their group touched upon a . . . a friend of the family."

"A girl?" asked Penelope sharply, surprised by the sudden rush of jealousy she felt.

"Yes. It's not a pleasant story."

"Oh, for heaven's sake, Alex, if you haven't learned by now that I'm not miss-ish, there's no dealing with you. If you start trying to protect my tender ears, I'll . . . well, I'll think of something."

"I'm sure you would. All right, then. There was a girl I knew— *no*," he elaborated. "Not in that way. She was the daughter of one of my father's corporals and she must have been all of fourteen at the time. She looked young for her age, too, still in pigtails and pinafores. She and my sister Lizzy had made mud pies together before they became too old and grand for it."

Penelope smiled reminiscently at the memory of some of her own mud pies. The fact that the last of them had only been last year and her mother had practically gone into a decline at the sight of her dress was entirely immaterial.

"Her situation was complicated," Alex was saying, "by the fact that her mother had been a local woman."

"I gather that's not all that unusual," said Penelope, remembering what Mr. Cleave had told her of Alex's past.

Alex's eyes met hers. "No," he agreed. "Not unusual at all. But her father wasn't an important man, or a wealthy one, and some men viewed Annie as easy pickings."

"What does this have to do with the club?" Penelope asked, although she was beginning to have a fair idea. It gave her a slightly sick feeling in the pit of her stomach that had nothing to do with the murky water she had drunk earlier.

"Did you know that your friend Fiske has the pox?"

"No." Penelope blinked, surprised by the seeming non sequitur. "But it doesn't surprise me." With Fiske's rollicking habits, syphilis couldn't have been far behind. She was only amazed that Freddy had managed to come through his own carousing free of disease.

"Many people believe that, er, concourse"—it was rather adorable, thought Penelope, after three days of rampant concourse, to see how he stumbled over pronouncing the word—"with a virgin will cure the French pox."

"It's certainly more pleasant than a mercury treatment," said Penelope at her very worldliest.

"Except for the virgin," pointed out Alex, and Penelope suddenly, sinkingly realized just how the pieces fit together.

Penelope's thighs must have involuntarily tightened, because her mare chose that moment to go fussy. Calming the agitated animal gave her a respite to school her face and her thoughts.

"Was Freddy involved?"

Alex's silence was all the answer she needed.

"Of course, he was," she answered herself. "It would be just like him. He would have thought that she was fair game."

Like a chambermaid or an orange seller or any one of the other categories of female that registered on the male mind merely as available flesh. Penelope hadn't been born into that category, but she had done her best to put herself into it by her behavior. Even then, there were lines that couldn't be crossed, at least not without severe repercussion. Like marriage. When it came down to it, no matter how murky her bloodlines or how poor her behavior, she was still a baronet's daughter, and that meant something in the bizarre code that governed the behavior of the young rakes of the *ton*.

She had never realized before, in all her days of chafing at chaperonage and thumbing her nose at convention, just how great were the protections that hedged her about or how fortunate she had been to have them.

She couldn't even imagine what it must be like, at fourteen, to be dragged into a dark cavern of a room full of men, men everywhere, men leering and pawing and shouting bawdy comments, with candles guttering and incense smoking and no one to help or protect you. To hear the horrible tearing sound of your own clothes rending and know there was no recourse. To have strange hands holding you down while a stranger pushed between your legs, brutally, without affection; all his cronies cheering him on. To know that your screams and struggles did nothing more than to excite them and that, in the end, there was nothing to do but turn one's head and try not to cry.

"What happened to the girl?" she asked with a catch in her voice.

"She died," said Alex bluntly. "She and her child, both. They were both riddled with the disease."

"How . . . sad."

"It's a common enough story," said her lover matter-of-factly. "It's one of the reasons my father sent my sisters home to England. They would probably have been safe enough—my father's situation is very different from that of poor Annie's father—but they'll have a more assured future there."

"How many siblings do you have?" asked Penelope, seizing on the change of subject.

"There are only five of us," said Alex, adding, with lines of amusement that deepened beside his eyes, "though sometimes it just feels like more. I have a twin sister and then the three others."

"You have a *twin*?" It was hard to imagine two of Alex, especially a female version.

"Kat. Technically, she's the elder. She elbowed her way out twenty minutes ahead of me."

"Good for her," said Penelope. "I believe I would like her. She sounds like a woman of great decision and character."

"That's one way of putting it," said the fond brother.

"What of the other three?"

"Lizzy is the youngest. She's only seventeen. George is three years older."

"And then there's Jack in the middle," supplied Penelope, watching him closely.

"Yes. Jack."

There was no point in beating about the bush. "I heard your conversation on the balcony that day."

Alex looked as though there were a great deal he wanted to say, none of it pleasant. "Two hundred years ago, they would have burned you as a witch," he said bluntly.

"It's the red hair," said Penelope, holding up the end of her braid to admire it. Over the past few days, she had lost enough hairpins to make any other style unfeasible. "Unmistakable sign of, er, *concourse* with the devil, don't you agree?"

Alex scratched at the stubble on his chin. "Since that places me in the role of the devil, I'm not sure I should."

"No," agreed Penelope. "You're not the one wearing the horns in this situation."

Damn. Damn, damn, damn. She realized her mistake the moment the words were out of her mouth. She had crossed that unspoken boundary they had carefully constructed around them, blocking out the unpleasant realities of the situation. Any mention of cuckoldry was strictly forbidden. The question of adultery bothered Alex far more than it did her, even though he wasn't the one wearing the horns.

Penelope rushed on, hastily substituting one unpleasant topic for another. "Do you really think your brother is in league with the French?"

"Cleave seems to think he is," said her lover tersely, but Penelope knew it wasn't his brother driving his lips into a thin line. He was having one of his attacks of conscience again.

Penelope poked him in the arm with the butt of her whip. "That's not an answer."

Alex twisted conspicuously in the shadow, scanning the sides of the road.

"What are you doing?"

"Looking for a stake." As Penelope stuck out her tongue at him, Alex relaxed back into his saddle, looking far more like himself. "I don't know," he said honestly. "Nothing would give me greater pleasure than to believe that Cleave is mistaken, but the evidence all militates otherwise. Cleave doesn't like Jack—"

"I'd say he out and out detests him," contributed Penelope cheerfully.

"—but he wouldn't lie about him. He's too . . ."

"Mewlingly honest?"

"Yes, that. And Jack's career hasn't precisely been designed to quell those sorts of suspicions. Not that it was his fault," Alex added hastily. "I suppose Cleave has told you about Jack's mother?"

"About her suicide? Yes. But I don't see what that has to do with it."

"Daniel always was a hopeless telltale," said Alex inconsequentially. "Even when we were little. It wasn't her suicide that was the problem, but her nationality. According the East India Company's laws, no one without two European parents can enter the military or the civil service. Jack was damned before he started." He scrubbed a hand through his hair, looking very tired and more than a little fed up. Penelope had the feeling he had been over this particular argument many times before. "What choice did he have but to go over to the other side? At least they didn't turn him away because his blood wasn't pure."

Penelope held up an imperious hand to signal a stop. "Wait. No, not you," she informed her horse, before turning back to Alex. "Are you saying that if your mother hadn't been English—"

"Welsh."

Penelope dismissed that with a shrug. Wales had belonged to England since the fourteenth century or thereabouts. Or was it the twelfth? Charlotte would have known. Whatever it was, it had been a very long time. "Same difference. If she hadn't been, then you wouldn't have been able to do what you're doing now?"

"None of it," said Alex. "Unless it was in a decidedly under-the-table capacity. There are ways around it. General Palmer's son, William, served here, under a British commander in the Nizam's army. Since it's technically the Nizam's force rather than the East India Company's, the usual prohibitions don't apply. But Jack went into Scindia's army, where he came under the command of General Perron."

"A Frenchman," Penelope cleverly surmised. Alex's French pronunciation was surprisingly good. She wondered if that came from his schooling, or the now-defunct French force in Hyderabad.

"The very thing. Not only a Frenchman but a banner-waving, liberty-tree-planting enthusiast for the Revolution. He changed the troop's colors to the *tricolore*." Alex's expression was wry. "Jack told me he thought I should understand why the concept of *liberté, égalité,* and *fraternité* had particular resonance for him."

"Ouch."

"He's—well, he's had a hard time," said Alex.

Penelope wasn't impressed. "So have many people, and they don't go about joining revolutionary armies."

"It wasn't really a revolutionary army. It was a perfectly normal army with a revolutionary general." Alex strove for a lightness he obviously wasn't feeling. "Otherwise, it would be just the same as if he had gone to serve for the Nizam or any other ruler in India."

"Hmm," said Penelope, but let it go. "You are missing something, you know. Even if your brother is a raving revolutionary, he can't be the Marigold."

"Why not?"

"Fiske," said Penelope with assurance. "If Fiske is the Marigold, your brother can't be."

The brief glow of hope faded from Alex's face. He shook his head. "Fiske wouldn't be able to undertake a project of this magnitude alone. If the Marigold really is, as I've been told, trying to raise all of the Mahratta territories and Hyderabad against the English, it will take more than one man." A grin lightened his dark features. "Even a man on an elephant."

Penelope's amber eyes glinted with shared amusement. Fiske's triumphal entry into Hyderabad had been wonderfully ridiculous, especially with his friend Pinchingdale clinging to the side of the howdah, his face a green that boded ill for anyone walking below.

For a moment, they grinned at each other in perfect harmony, both enjoying the memory of the absurd spectacle Fiske had made.

Alex looked away first.

"And there's something else," he said with the air of a man determined to come clean at all costs.

"You want an elephant!" guessed Penelope.

"Do you remember that man we chased up to Raymond's Tomb?"

She would have to be pretty thick not to remember something that had happened a mere three weeks ago.

"Vividly," she said with a toss of her braid.

"That wasn't Guignon. That was Jack."

Chapter Twenty-Three

"Hunh," said Penelope, which felt like a perfectly reasonable response at the time. She liked the way it sounded, so she repeated it. "Hunh. Right."

She tried to remember what the man had looked like, but she had only a blurry impression of dark hair that glinted red where the sun struck it and a flurry of hooves that belonged, not to the man, but to his mount. He had a very good seat, she gave him that much. And a decidedly dashing air about him. At the time, she had ascribed that to being French, which just went to show how expectation could inform appearance.

She looked measuringly at Alex. Dashing really didn't come into it. Reliable, yes. Competent, yes. Incredibly good company when he wanted to be, yes.

Dashing, no.

"I don't know why I lied," Alex confessed. "Habit, I guess."

Penelope cocked an eyebrow, a skill that had taken ages to learn, but had paid off in spades over the years. "Are you in the habit of lying for him?"

"Not like that," said Alex quickly. "Just little things when we were younger, food missing from the kitchen, broken bric-a-brac, that sort of thing. . . . He didn't thank me for it," he added.

"Then why did you do it?"

"I'm his big brother. It's part of the job. And I knew that my punishment would be lighter than his would have been."

He didn't explain why and Penelope didn't ask. She doubted it would be presuming too much to assume that the son of the deceased Mrs. Reid received a very different sort of treatment from status-conscious servants than would the by-blow of the Colonel's concubine.

It would, she thought wistfully, be rather nice to have that sort of champion. She had had one of a sort when her grandmother had been alive, exerting a leavening presence between the dissimilarities of her parents, scolding or condoning according to her own pattern. Her father might have taken up the role, but he had been too indolent to do so, preferring to spend his time with his racing forms and his breeding books, abandoning Penelope in the end to her mother and the thousand and one boring strictures that Penelope systematically set out to flout.

Penelope straightened in the saddle. Not that she needed a champion, of course. She was perfectly capable of fighting her own battles—or unearthing her own spies, if it came down to it.

"Is there really a Guignon?" she asked, at random.

"Very much so. I have it on good authority that he's been skulking around the province again. That's why his name came so easily to mind."

"I wouldn't have thought you had it in you to lie so effectively," said Penelope admiringly.

"You were distracted," said Alex generously. "And on uncertain terrain. I had the advantage of you."

In one thing, she still had the advantage of him. After an internal wrangle, Penelope said brusquely, "While we're coming clean, I have a confession to make."

"If you tell me you're the Marigold, I won't believe you."

"I, um, found something at the tomb that day. A little piece of paper. It was a message, presumably from the Marigold, advising the recipient to await his coming for the great work to be set into motion. Or something like that. I can't remember the exact phrasing."

Alex scrubbed his hand against his eyes, looking unutterably bleak. "That proves it, then. Cleave was right."

"You don't know that Jack dropped it." Odd to be talking about a man she had never met on first-name terms, and a nickname, at that.

But, then, it would be even odder thinking about him as Mr. Reid. Lieutenant Reid? Penelope had no idea what sort of titles they handed out in Scindia's armies.

"Then who did? The pixies?"

"French pixies," agreed Penelope. "Back in Hyderabad without leave. Shall we stop soon? It will be dark before long."

The real world would be with them soon enough. Penelope refused to spend their last night together on depressing reflections that could only cause one of them pain. This was their last night in Eden and she intended to make the most of it, even if the snakes were already beginning to slither about in the underbrush and half-eaten apples littered the ground beneath the tree, conveying their cursed burden of partial knowledge.

She didn't need to explain what she meant. He knew. Without another word, he nodded ahead. "If I recall, there's a lake not fifteen minutes from here. We can camp there."

They plunged determinedly into mundanities: where to camp, what to eat for dinner. Alex teased Penelope about her cooking and Penelope retorted that if she wasn't such a good shot there would be nothing for them to eat, and so the yards passed on, and with every hoofbeat, Penelope could hear echoing in her ears, *It's over, it's over, it's over*.

Not yet, she told herself fiercely. Not yet.

The lake was a small one, tucked away in a copse of banyan trees, the water thick with lily pads bearing brilliantly blue lotus flowers. Penelope's riding habit had begun its life as a similar color, but three days of dust and grime had turned it into a mottled gray.

"I smell," said Penelope with disgust, turning her head to sniff at her shoulder. Wearing the same habit for three days in very hot climatic conditions did not do wonders for one's personal hygiene. She wished she had thought to bring a change of clothes, or at least of linen.

Undaunted, her lover drew her to him, uttering those romantic words, "So do I."

"Yes, worse than me," agreed Penelope pertly, and kissed him hard on the lips, before pushing away. She yanked at the buttons on her habit. "I am having a bath, and I am having one *now*."

Alex cast a critical eye over the dark water of the lake, made darker by the dropping dusk. "You don't want to jump into that. You don't know what's in it."

"An apt metaphor for life, I imagine." Dropping to her knees, Penelope wiggled her fingers in the water to test the temperature. The water felt like heaven against her heat-swollen hands. "One I've never heeded."

"Let me." Taking a cloth, Alex dipped it into the water, wrung it out, and applied it to Penelope's sticky shoulders.

"Mmm," sighed Penelope, tilting back her head, as the cool water trickled down between her breasts. She could feel it mingling with the sweat that already dampened her shift. "Heaven."

Raising her hands in the air, she waited for him to peel her shift off her body. The night breeze felt heavenly on her sweaty body. The mosquitoes weren't quite so heavenly, but Penelope was prepared to be philosophical about that. Penelope could feel her skin prickling from the air and the water and pure, undiluted anticipation. Desperately wanting his mouth on her breasts, she thrust her chest out, but perversely, maddeningly, he continued his own set course, dragging the damp cloth down the hollow of her belly, stroking across each hip, before—

Returning to the lake to dip the cloth again in water.

"You really are quite maddening," she informed him hoarsely.

On one knee, Alex's dark eyes glinted up at her. "Am I?" he said, decisively wringing out the cloth. The touch of the damp fabric against the inside of one ankle made Penelope shiver. He worked the cloth slowly up the inside of her leg, his eyes intent on hers.

Penelope swallowed hard. "But in a very nice way," she amended, as the cloth worked its way up the other side, pausing, tantalizingly, just between her legs, brushing and retreating. She bit down hard on her lip, stifling a gasp, as he worked the cloth up between the delicate folds, the moisture of her body mixing with the cool of the lake water while the twisted piece of fabric worked back and forth against a point of extreme sensitivity.

"Very, very nice," she said breathlessly.

Alex moved lower, his lips following the path of the cloth, and Penelope thankfully gave herself over to thinking of nothing at all.

It was only long afterward, after making love and eating supper and making love again, as they lay together beneath a single blanket, the small flame of their fire reflecting off the waters of the lake, that Alex ignored his own advice and ventured into dangerous waters of quite another variety.

"We should reach the border tomorrow," he said casually. Too casually.

"Is there any way of making the border move back?" asked Penelope drowsily. "Just a few miles would be nice."

"I'm afraid not." Alex's voice was serious. They were clearly going to have A Talk, whether she wanted to or not.

Penelope buried her head in his chest and wished they could stay this way for always. Without talking about it.

"What happens next?" Alex asked, as she had known he was going to.

"You know what happens," said Penelope, although she found it far harder to do so than she had three days before. Almost four days now, she corrected herself. She wouldn't want to cut their time together short by so much as an hour. "You have your work in Hyderabad. Freddy and I will eventually return to London."

"Do you want to go back?" Alex asked seriously.

Penelope bit her lips. "No," she admitted.

Funny, that the prospect should seem such a bleak one. Only a month ago, she would have been glad to go back to London, to take tea with Henrietta and Charlotte again and listen to the familiar rantings of the Dowager Duchess of Dovedale. But she was becoming accustomed to India. She liked it. She liked the strange, spicy food and the sunshine that turned her face to freckles and the curious, gnarled faces of monkeys that scowled and chattered at her from between the branches of the trees.

And she liked Alex. She liked him too much. But that didn't bear thinking about, so Penelope didn't. Or, at least, she tried not to. She had always been very good about not thinking about things. It was much easier to act, as rashly as possible, trusting to the resulting ruckus to blot out any danger of reflection or introspection.

Shifting, Alex wrapped his arms more comfortably around her. "You know," he said, his vocal chords burring against her ear. "There are ways."

"Ways?"

"I've been thinking about it," he said thoughtfully, "and India is a large country. If you were to retire to the hills for your health—"

"—You could come with me?" It was a pretty fairy tale, but that was all it was, no more realistic than one of Charlotte's novels. She didn't have a fairy godmother to wave a wand and make it all turn out right.

"Yes."

Penelope shook her head against his chest. "And leave here? You wouldn't." More matter-of-factly, she added, "I wouldn't want you to. You would hate me before long if you did."

He paused just a moment too long before answering, long enough to know that her words had struck home. "I wouldn't hate you." But he didn't sound quite as certain as he had before.

Penelope tried not to sound as desolate as she felt. "Resent me, then. It's close enough. Either way, you would be unhappy. And I would be unhappy for making you unhappy and then we would both be unhappy, and where would we be?"

Together, prompted a dulcet little voice in her head.

"Miserable," she finished, more forcefully than she had intended. "Stranded out in the hills in disgrace with nothing to do but snap at each other."

Alex's hand stroked softly up and down her arm. "Does the disgrace bit bother you?"

Since he had asked it honestly, Penelope did him the courtesy of actually thinking about it before answering, rather than shooting off the flippant answer that came too easily to her lips.

"No," she said at last, twining her fingers absently through the dark hair on his chest. "I've been in disgrace before. I'm very good at being in disgrace," she added, and was rewarded by the rumble of a chuckle beneath her ear.

"Then, why?" he asked.

There was something about being in the dark with someone that made one say too much, too frankly. "It's not my disgrace that matters. I don't mind ruining myself, but it wouldn't do to drag you down along with me."

"It wouldn't be you doing all the dragging," said Alex mildly. She felt the brush of his lips against the top of her head. "I do believe there are two of us involved."

"Wouldn't it?" retorted Penelope. "Without me, there would be no dragging to be done."

"You might as well say that without the sun there would be no sunstroke. And yet we couldn't do without it."

Was he saying that he couldn't do without her?

"It's all a moot point, anyway," grumbled Penelope, stirring restlessly against her human bolster, "because I'm not ruining you, and that's that."

After three days, he knew her well enough to know when she couldn't be swayed. "Fair enough," he said at last, adding, provocatively, "but I call that ungenerous of you."

Penelope levered herself up on an elbow so she could look down at him, her braid falling over one shoulder. "Oh, ungenerous, am I?" she taunted.

And then neither of them said anything at all, for quite some time.

There was a curiously ferocious quality to their lovemaking, as if it were a competition to see which of them could elicit the greater response from the other. It was as though they were trying to scour their mark into each other, like lovers' initials charred into the trunk of a tree, relic of a lost romance. Teasing, taunting, titillating, they grappled together long after the fire had burned down to embers and the night-blooming flowers on the lake had opened their petals to the night sky, perfuming the air with their too-sweet fragrance.

Afterwards, Penelope lay awake, feigning the regular breath of sleep. Beside her, she could sense that Alex was doing the same. His shoulders were too stiff and his breath too shallow for anything but pretend sleep. Besides, he wasn't snuffling.

She would miss his snuffling. She would miss the circuitous arguments over whose turn it was to scour the dishes and the long-winded, nonsensical conversations about nothing in particular. There were more things to miss than she had ever imagined there could be, a thousand Alexes, forking a snake out of their bedroll with a long twig, smiling up at her as he skinned a rabbit, dipping a hand into the lake to test its waters, doing, fixing, arguing, being.

What would it be like to take him up on his offer and be like this always? For a moment, the image drifted tantalizingly in front of her, as sweet and insubstantial as the scent of the flowers on the lake.

Nonsense, Penelope told herself roughly. It was all pure nonsense.

It was the sort of harebrained daydream Charlotte might have come up with. What sort of happiness could they have, with Freddy forever looming over them? He would be within his legal rights to storm in and haul her back by her hair, from wherever they might choose to hide. Both the law and public opinion would back him. Even if they did succeed in getting successfully away, any children they might have would be bastards, shunned from polite society. They wouldn't bear the same sort of systematic barriers that prevented Alex's half-Indian siblings from entering their chosen professions, but there were legal disadvantages to bastardy, as well as the social ones.

Besides, how would they live? Her own dowry had long since disappeared into Freddy's ample pockets; any money she had came from him. If Alex had anything other than his pay, she would be greatly surprised. It wasn't that she needed luxury. She could do just as well without the jewels and expensive muslins. She was happier in boy's breeches than a satin gown. But one needed something to live on. They couldn't eat charred rabbit forever, however idyllic it might seem for the space of an enchanted tryst. Desire would fade, in time, and leave only disenchantment in its wake. He *would* grow to hate her in time. Sacrifice didn't ennoble; it only embittered.

Not that the alternative was terribly attractive. Penelope rolled over onto her side, resting her head on one arm. It was useless to think that they could go on as they were back in Hyderabad. She might be willing to do it, cuckolding Freddy with the same abandon with which he had cuckolded her, but Alex wouldn't. It was only the very oddity of their circumstances that had won her these past four days, as remote from the world as any fairy-tale princess's overgrown palace.

She could, she knew, make his control snap if she tried hard enough. In a fit of madness, they might make love against the pillars of Raymond's Tomb or tumble together in the prickly discomfort of the hydrangea bushes in the Residency gardens. If they were lucky, they might not even be caught. But it wouldn't bring them closer. Instead, every stolen physical encounter would drive a deeper wedge between them, killing off the easy companionship that had begun to mean so much to her. As matters stood, she could have him as lover or friend, but not both.

There was justice for you. She had taken Freddy without caring, just because. Now, when she cared, she couldn't have.

Justice was highly overrated.

Penelope woke up with a headache pinching the flesh between her brows. There was no morning kiss or playful banter. They avoided each other's eyes as they dressed. They were like two prisoners sharing the same cell on the morning of an execution, waiting for their names to be called.

It was noon before they reached the main road to Berar. They were close enough now to the probable location of the treasure that it made sense to follow Fiske's party more closely.

Squinting down to road, Penelope saw a cloud of dust in the distance. Alex raised the spyglass he kept in his saddlebag. "That's our boy," he said, squinting through the glass knob. And then, "But why are they going in the wrong direction?"

Freddy's caravan was on the move, but it was moving the wrong way. They might still be a fair way down the road, but it didn't take close observation to tell that the cavalcade was traveling towards them, away from Berar.

"They can't have been there and back already!" Penelope exclaimed.

"No," said Alex with conviction. "We didn't dawdle that much. They were supposed to stay for a full two weeks' hunting."

Penelope could tell that he didn't like the situation any more than she. "Do you think Fiske got his hands on what he came for and persuaded them to turn back?"

"It's hard to see how," muttered Alex. "A whole visit arranged— they're dealing the First Minister a considerable insult by rejecting his hospitality."

"Unless the First Minister is involved," suggested Penelope, twisting in her saddle as a new idea struck her. "Or he never invited them in the first place. Fiske might have made up the invitation."

"Did it ever occur to you . . . ," Alex began with difficulty. "That is, have you ever thought—"

"Yes?" Penelope raised an eyebrow, waiting.

"That it might not be Fiske but your husband?"

Penelope had to blink several times before she could be sure that she had heard him properly. "My husband *what*?" she asked, in a hard voice.

"Your husband was in the same regiment as Fiske. He was a member of that same club. He took as mistress the known consort of a French officer."

And it was Freddy who had told her about the First Minister's invitation to Berar. Penelope remembered that letter of Henrietta's that had so mysteriously disappeared after she had left it by Freddy at breakfast. And, from very far away, she could see a small orange-cloth flower being pressed to the courtesan's lips and tossed—straight into Freddy's lap.

"Nonsense," she said coldly. "It's Fiske. Just because you don't like Freddy—"

But that was treading too close to dangerous territory. "You're wrong," she said instead.

Alex didn't quite meet her eyes. "For your sake, I hope I am."

"Why?" said Penelope flippantly. "Are you afraid that if he were executed for treason you might be stuck with me permanently?"

Alex's startled gaze caught hers. "Pen—"

Penelope applied her heels to her mount. "If they're already on their way back, there's no point in following them, is there?" she said rapidly. "We'll have to intercept them instead."

And she was off down the road before he could say anything more.

An elephant lumbered in the center of the party, preceding a long line of donkeys and pack mules, but this time, Fiske wasn't on it. She could see him riding in front of the party, cleverly staying ahead of the dust cloud. There was another man beside him, but it wasn't Freddy. Beneath his fashionable hat, Penelope recognized the curly head of Mr. Jasper Pinchingdale. Barring the inevitable dust of travel, both men were as fresh and clean as though they had stepped out of their dressing rooms. That, she supposed, was what all the pack mules were for. Penelope scanned the mass of animals and men for Freddy. She spotted Aurangzeb, being led by Freddy's groom, but of Freddy himself there was no sign.

"Ahoy, there!" she called, waving a hand playfully above her head.

Neither Fiske nor Pinchingdale recognized Penelope at first, with her dirty face and her hair in a long plait down her back.

Penelope swished her braid and grinned at them, a practiced, gamine grin. "I'd wager you didn't expect to see me here."

"Lady Frederick?" gasped Mr. Pinchingdale, losing his grasp on his urbane sophistication and nearly on his horse as well. Next to him, Fiske was doing his very best guppy imitation. Penelope wasn't fooled. A guppy Fiske might be, but he was a deuced dangerous guppy.

Penelope spread a dazzling smile impartially between the two of them. "I've come to surprise Freddy. I bullied Captain Reid into escorting me." Her tone reduced him to a superior sort of servant, which was, she had no doubt, how Freddy chose to view him. He would as soon suspect her of canoodling with one of the footmen. "It's no fair that you gentlemen should get all the fun of the hunting."

Their frozen stares was enough to make Penelope start to feel more than a little self-conscious. All right, so she might be a bit bedraggled, but how did they think one would look after riding four days? Not everyone spent five hours a day on her toilette.

Abandoning them as a bad job, Penelope craned to look over their shoulders. "Where is Freddy?"

She didn't miss the look Pinchingdale and Fiske exchanged, or the quick slide of Pinchingdale's eyes to a palanquin being carried by four bearers a little way behind them. So that was it, was it? Penelope felt her smile curdle on her lips. That explained why Aurangzeb was riderless in the middle of the afternoon. Trust Freddy to bring his mistress with him on a simple little hunting trip. That was Freddy for you. He liked to be supplied with all the creature comforts. Home away from home, as it were.

Well, too bad for him.

Swinging off her horse, she tossed the reins to a groom. "In the palanquin, is he, lazy old thing?"

"Um, Lady Frederick," began Pinchingdale awkwardly. "I don't think—"

Oh, he didn't, did he?

"Don't worry," said Penelope gaily. "I'll soon roust him out."

Under the frozen gaze of Fiske, Pinchingdale, all four bearers, sixty-odd servants, and one elephant, she yanked open the curtains of the palanquin.

Freddy was inside. But he wasn't resting. And he wasn't with his mistress. His hands rested neatly on his chest. His legs were stretched straight out in front of him, boots blackened and shining. But his once-handsome features were swollen and distorted and there were two gold coins where his eyes had been, weighting the eyelids shut.

Pinchingdale cleared his throat. "I was trying to tell you. Lord Frederick is dead."

Chapter Twenty-Four

A bell was tolling, but it wasn't tolling for Freddy Staines. It was tolling for me.

When my doorbell rang, I was still sprawled across my bed with one of Mrs. Selwick-Alderly's notebooks propped against my knees. With a jolt, I tumbled out of the early nineteenth century, landing with a crash back in the twenty-first. It was Valentine's Day and I—I took a quick glance at the neon travel clock balanced on the suitcase that did double duty as a night table—was running late.

"I'll be right there!" I hollered, flinging Freddy and Penelope and the whole lot of them aside.

Rolling off the bed, I brushed futilely at my hair with one hand as I stuck a foot into a shoe and yanked at the heel strap with the other, trying to lurch towards the doorway and get my other foot into my other shoe all at the same time. Don't laugh. We've all been there.

It wasn't the fact that I undoubtedly had bed-head or that I'd just put my foot in the wrong shoe that was making my stomach lurch as though I'd gone on the wrong sort of amusement park ride. It was the man on the other side of the door. We hadn't exactly ended our last conversation on the most positive of terms. It had been two whole days, and I had spent most of that time veering between self-justification and self-loathing, alternately assuring myself that I was absolutely in the right and kicking myself for being an insensitive ass.

I mean, Serena was his sister, so what right did I have to dictate to him how he should or shouldn't behave to her? But I really had only been trying to help.

I'd been over that same patch of mental ground so many times that I felt like I'd worn a groove into my brain.

"Coming, coming, coming!" I called, lurching through the tiny hallway that doubled as a kitchen. Fortunately, my flat is about the size of a postage stamp. By the time the last word was out of my mouth, my hand was already on the doorknob, yanking open the door to reveal a tall, blond man holding a single red rose.

"Hi," I said breathlessly.

Colin took in the hair standing straight up on one side of my head and the shoes I had managed to shove onto the wrong feet. The laugh lines on either sides of his eyes deepened.

"Napping?" he guessed, holding out the rose.

"Reading," I corrected, accepting the flower. He didn't look angry. Or sulky. He just looked . . . normal. Like a man about to take his girl-friend out for Valentine's Day. "I was a million miles away."

"Welcome back." Taking the flower from my hand, he dropped it neatly into my sink (yes, my hallway/kitchen is that small) and gathered me into his arms for a proper hello kiss.

I took that to mean we were okay.

I'll never understand boys, historical or modern. Here I had been, tormenting myself for the past forty-eight hours, convinced I had irreparably damaged the best thing I had going in years, and Colin had probably hung up the phone, gone to sleep, and not bothered thinking about it again. Not that I was complaining, mind you. I'd much rather make love than war. Or something like that.

Tottering on my mismatched stilettos, I clung to his shoulders. "Sure you want to go to the party?"

"No," he agreed, resting his forehead against mine. "But we should probably put in an appearance."

Right. It was Serena's party. Damn, damn, damn. Open mouth, insert foot. I didn't want to open that whole can of worms again. Worms plus foot would be very uncomfortable to swallow.

"Of course," I said brightly. "It will be fun! Just let me grab my bag."

Bright red and patterned in iridescent scarlet and hot pink beads, the bag was my concession to the occasion. "Don't say it," I warned

Colin, as I saw him eyeing the bag with a look of masculine bemusement that looked like it was about to mature into a snide comment.

He held up both hands. "I wasn't going to say anything."

"It was a present from Pammy." Left to myself, I don't buy hot pink. Hot pink anything.

"Of course it was."

I stuck out my tongue at him as he gallantly stepped aside to allow me to precede him through the door. His gallant gesture was self-defeating since I then had to wiggle back around him so I could lock the door.

We exchanged notes on our week as we made our way to the Tube. On Valentine's Day night, hailing a cab was completely out of the question. All around us, there were signs of Valentine's Day in progress; harried-looking men in sports coats hurriedly buying cellophane-wrapped flowers at the gas station/convenience store a block from my flat; groups of girls in tottery heels and defiantly red dresses, pink-cheeked in the February cold, trip-trapping their way towards the Tube; couples, in various stages of coupliness, meandering arm in arm or side by side or, in one case, one stalking several feet ahead, the other scurrying behind. Across the street, the gates of Hyde Park had already been locked, but the Park wall made an excellent place for blind dates meeting, agitated last-minute text messaging, and more than a bit of concerted smooching.

I tried to remember where I had been for Valentine's Day last year and wished I hadn't. Oh, right. Some things weren't really worth remembering. Last Valentine's Day, a mere two months after catching my then-boyfriend in the cloakroom of the Harvard Faculty Club with an art history student nearly ten years his junior, I had still been alternating between rage and despair. I had gotten sloshed on white chocolate martinis with two friends at the fancy dessert place in Harvard Square and stumbled home in a state of embarrassing inebriation to carry on a long and unhappy conversation with my mirror. Not the sort of memory one cares to dredge up, except by way of contrast.

I leaned into the hand resting on the small of my back, thought of the rose lying upside down in my kitchen sink, and breathed a silent prayer of thanks that I hadn't managed to screw everything up with that ridiculous phone call two nights ago.

By the time we arrived at the gallery, I had my halo firmly in place. As far as relationship issues went, one needy sister was a fairly small cross to bear. I was going to be on my very best behavior and not make any fuss about sharing my Valentine's Day with Serena. And who knew? It might even be fun.

Relinquishing our coats, Colin and I made our way, arm in arm, into Serena's gallery. It was one of those terrifyingly posh modern places where they hang a single canvas per wall and the asking price per artwork is roughly the same as a down payment on a one bedroom flat. Not that they would do anything so indiscreet as affix a price tag to anything. That was for shops, not galleries. Instead, a tastefully clad assistant (i.e., Serena) would glide helpfully over and talk up the finer points of the piece until the question of purchase was reached after a decent interval of art appreciation, the intimation being, of course, that mere money could never be the point when Art was at stake, as though selling were somehow only a byproduct of the gallery's proper mission of Encouraging Art.

"Isn't your mother an artist?" I asked idly, as we strolled into the main gallery, having scooped up glasses of pink champagne from a tray by the entrance. The glasses were either genuine crystal or a very good facsimile. It was a far cry from red plastic tumblers in someone's apartment in Cambridge.

"A painter," confirmed Colin, nodding to an acquaintance in passing. "Some of her paintings are down at Selwick Hall. You've seen them."

"The Italian scenes?"

"Like Canaletto on speed," Colin agreed calmly.

I had thought they were quite good. "Did she get Serena this job?" I asked, guessing.

"No." Was it my imagination, or did Colin's lip actually curl? "Her husband did. He also works in the art world."

Yep, that was definitely a curled lip, like curdled milk in smile form.

No one warns you, in college, that when you date someone you run a good chance of dating his family as well. This was a new experience for me. Grant, the evil ex, had been one of those oddly rootless types one finds frequently in the Ivy league. Grant had left the Midwest for Princeton at eighteen and never looked back. I knew he had a large-ish family back in Michigan, with multiple brothers and sisters and even a few nieces and nephews floating around, but in the whole two years we had dated, I hadn't met a single one of them. He had spoken to his mother on the phone for half an hour once every month, regular as clockwork and about as intimate.

Colin, on the other hand, came not only with a full complement of interesting ancestors, but plenty of living ones, all of whom kept intruding on the scene in one way or another. I couldn't decide whether to be entertained, or very, very afraid. My mother would probably opt for the latter. She has very strong feelings about certain of my father's relatives.

What was the stepfather doing dredging up jobs for Serena, when, from what I could gather, Serena wasn't on speaking terms with either him or her mother?

"What do you think of the show?"

Not wanting to set off any more red flags about his family—I had done enough of that the other night—I let it go. For the moment. I could always ask Serena later.

I squinted at a very large bronze that might be either Europa being seduced by a bull, a squashed globe, or an interpretive exposition on global poverty in a postmodern world (that last comes from the little plaque in front of the sculpture). Personally, I didn't see it. But it could have been worse. Crosses in urine, toilets masquerading as installation art, rooms constructed entirely of balloons that popped when you stepped on them.

Compared to the exploding balloon exhibit, I could cope with Zeus as commentary on global poverty.

Leaning comfortably against Colin's arm, I took the measure of the room. "It's not as bad as I thought it would be."

"It helps to have low expectations," my boyfriend agreed, looking doubtfully at his pink champagne before taking a gingerly sip.

Across the room, I could see Serena, pink-cheeked with champagne, in an animated discussion with a man in a black cashmere turtleneck and something that wasn't quite a beret but wanted to be. They seemed to be deeply enmeshed in agreeing over the merits of a statue that looked to me like a squashed hamburger without the bun.

"We're philistines, aren't we?" I said, looking up at Colin.

"Irredeemably," he agreed cheerfully, taking a more confident swig of his champagne. Apparently, he had concluded that just because it looked pink didn't mean it tasted pink.

My heart squeezed with a rather embarrassing rush of affection for him, which I covered by hastily babbling, "The posters aren't bad, though. I rather like them."

Someone, possibly Serena, had come up with the idea of hanging huge art posters in the empty spaces on the walls, as a pictorial representation of the history of love through art. They had played around with the colors, of course, framing the classic images in funky hot pink frames and coloring some of them with a neon wash in multiple variations, like those Andy Warhol prints, but it still made a nice effect. Among other favorites, I recognized Botticelli's Venus, Fragonard's *Love Letter,* and Francisco Hayez's *The Kiss.*

There were darker images at play, too: Waterhouse's *Ophelia* twining wildflowers in her hair; the Lady of Shallot floating down to many-towered Camelot as singing in her song she died; Dicksee's *Belle Dame Sans Merci* tempting her knight at arms to his pale and loitering fate. The Belle Dame's unbound locks were a bright, unmistakable red. Red, like my hair, or like that of Penelope Staines, nee Deveraux. All around me, in the bright posters hanging like feudal banners in the walls, red-haired women were coming to bad ends, and all for love. It was an unexpectedly sobering observation.

I looked at them all, trapped in their several fates, and thought about Penelope, trapped in her own spider's web, like Rosamund in Queen Eleanor's tower, or the Lady of Shallot in her doomed barge. A sad soul, Mrs. Selwick-Alderly had called her, and as I read on, I was beginning to understand why.

It was, I thought, dangerously easy to get swept up in other people's expectations, pulled into patterns based on the person you had been five, or even ten, years ago. Look at Serena. On her own turf, she seemed happy. Confident, even. She was still too thin, but in her blush pink cashmere dress, with a glass of champagne in one hand and a gloss in her hair, she looked elegant rather than sickly. With a deftness I would never have imagined of her, I watched her guiding potential patrons neatly in the direction of unsold pieces, sorting out some confusion about the canapés, and soothing the ruffled feathers of a man whose name had been left off the guest list. But put her within five feet of her brother, and she suddenly became an awkward adolescent again, all open wounds and raw emotions.

Not that I should talk. Over on the other side of the room, under the poster of *Belle Dame Sans Merci*, I spotted my friend Pammy, decked in a hot pink crocodile-skin sheath. We will ignore the fact that I am pretty sure there is no such animal as a hot pink crocodile. Pammy is a law unto herself, in more ways than one. And I was just as bad as Serena—or Penelope. Put me in a room with Pammy, and I was in sixth grade again, standing shyly at the sidelines of the middle school dances, while Pammy pulled boys over by their ties. No matter how old we got, to a certain extent our relationship would always be a replay of our respective roles from middle school. There were times when it was comforting, like a tattered old shoe, but other times when I found myself behaving in ways that I didn't like and didn't respect, all on the strength of those old patterns.

Speaking of people I neither liked nor respected . . . Standing not far from Pammy, I recognized Joan Plowden-Plugge, Colin's next-door neighbor from Sussex, the one with the ungodly crush on Colin. She was wearing red, of course. It looked smashing with her faux blond hair.

Making a face, I pointed Joan out to Colin. "Where's her broomstick?"

"I'm sure she left it in the cloakroom. Serena got her to agree to write up the show for *Manderley*."

That was undoubtedly a coup for Serena. *Manderley* was a very respected arts journal and they seldom had much to do with anything more modern than William Morris. It was also a pain in the you-know-where. I didn't want to have to be nice to Joan. It was Valentine's Day. Fortunately, Joan appeared to be occupied for the moment with a large glass of pink champagne (which clashed beautifully with her dress) and a shaggy-haired man with trendy rectangular glasses, who I assumed had to be another arts journalist.

Next to them, Pammy had got her hot pink fingernails into Nick. She was doing her twinkly laugh at him, the one that goes with the hair flip and the eyelashes at half-mast. Nick was flirting happily back, and I wondered what had happened to the blonde I had seen with him at the movie theatre. Whoever she was, she didn't seem to be in evidence.

Serena was conspicuously not looking at them, talking to black-beret man with an intensity that suggested she knew very well what was going on behind her and was making a concerted effort not to notice. I looked around for Martin, but if he was here, he wasn't in evidence. Probably moping in the cloakroom, or drunk-dialing his ex.

Useless, I thought irritably, wondering whether we ought to wander over and intercede. Colin had found an old university friend, with whom he was having a grand old time bemoaning the depraved mentality that would take a decent bubbly and tint it pink.

"Nothing short of vandalism!" the friend was saying, holding up the glass to the light in illustration.

It seemed a shame to extricate him, just when he was having fun.

Fortunately, intercession appeared from another quarter. I watched with interest as a newcomer made his way from the cloakroom straight towards Serena. She had her back to him—and, incidentally, to Pammy and Nick. A potential love interest? Or simply a determined customer? It might be either.

The man was on the older side, but so was Serena's most recent ex. Like her evil ex, this man was in his late thirties or early forties at a guess. But there the resemblance ended. Where the evil ex had been on the broader side, solidly built, this man was tall and willowy, with the sort of slender grace one associates with old movie stars premiering across from Grace Kelly. His clothes were as expensively casual as the evil ex's had been deliberately formal; his cashmere sweater, black wool slacks, and sports coat all screamed Italian tailoring. His winter tan brought out the bright blue of his eyes. Definitely not the sort of man one would kick out of bed. If one went for the older type, that is. Which Serena quite definitely did.

On the other hand, the cost of his clothes suggested that if he wanted to place a three-foot-high squashed hamburger cast in distressed bronze in the center of his living room, he could very well afford to do so.

As the boys moved on from bubbly to the canapés, I watched as the new arrival tapped Serena casually on the shoulder, with the easy intimacy of someone who felt he had every right to do so. Curiouser and curiouser, as one of my favorite characters might say.

Serena had been so busy ignoring Nick and Pammy that she never saw him coming. She started visibly, spilling champagne in a sparkling stream down the front of her dress, droplets catching on fuzzy bits of cashmere where they glittered like sequins under the bright track lighting.

But even that couldn't quite account for the look of distress on her face, or the way she backed away from him as though he were a poisonous serpent come to bite her. She pointedly ignored the cocktail napkin he held out to her, liquid dripping from the bottom of her glass onto the distressed wood floor as she stood staring at him from eyes that suddenly looked far too large for her thin face.

Who was he?

He looked familiar. He did. But I couldn't place why. He wasn't the evil ex. I should know. The evil ex had asked me out, and not, honesty compels me to add, for the sake of my personal charms. He had asked me out for the same reason he had dated and dumped Serena: in the hopes of getting closer to answers about the elusive—and potentially lucrative—Pink Carnation.

"Who is that?" I hissed, poking Colin in the arm.

"Huh?" said Colin, breaking off mid-sentence. He had been saying something about rugby. At least I assumed it was rugby. It was all gibberish to me, although his friend appeared to be agreeing heartily with whatever it was.

Fortunately, a tray of hors d'oeuvres came around and the other man—Berry? Budgy? It had been something like that—made a flying tackle for a tiny square of high-piled tuna tartare with a rosemary sprig sticking out of it, like the flag of a hostile power laying claim to a small island. It might be raw fish, but sustenance was sustenance and Budgy was obviously hungry. I could see the same maneuver being repeated all around the room by equally ravenous husbands, boyfriends, and dates, all who had been promised refreshments and served fish food.

Taking advantage of his companion's momentary distraction, I jerked my head towards the other side of the room. "Who is that? With Serena?"

"Where?" he asked, absently rubbing his wounded arm.

I pointed.

Colin's expression went from friendly to stony in an instant. It was a truly awe-inspiring transition.

"Damn," he said.

That was certainly informative. "Well?" I prompted. "Who is he?"

Drawing in a long, irritated breath, Colin folded his arms across his chest. "That," he said succinctly, "is my mother's husband."

Oh.

"Oh," I said.

"Yes," agreed Colin grimly. "Oh."

No wonder Serena was looking vaguely green. I only had the sketchiest knowledge of Colin's recent family history, but from the little bits and pieces people had dropped, I had gathered that (a) Colin's father had been diagnosed with some sort of cancer; and (b) Colin's mother had decamped with another man, with whom she now lived in Italy.

From what I gathered, Serena had definitely been a daddy's girl. She couldn't have taken kindly to the immediate addition of a replacement. Especially when the replacement had to be a good decade younger.

I looked at the man standing next to Serena with renewed interest, trying to work out how old he must be in relation to Colin's mother. She had looked awfully young in those pictures in Mrs. Selwick-Alderly's albums, but even if she had been a teenage bride, she must be at least in her late forties by now, a good decade older than her second husband. No wonder Colin and Serena were so cagey about her second marriage; it must have been incredibly embarrassing having to introduce a stepfather as close in age to them as to their mother.

Not to mention that it had never been made entirely clear to me whether the second husband had made his way onto the scene before or after their father's death. The impression I had gotten, although I couldn't say with any authority how, was that Colin's mother had bolted at the first hint of a lingering illness, abandoning her husband at his most vulnerable moment.

To be fair, though, Colin had never actually specified anything of the kind. That was all me reading between the lines. For all that he clearly wasn't thrilled to see his mother's husband in England, it sounded as though Colin had at least remained on speaking terms with his mother. When his mother had been involved in a car accident in Siena a few months ago, he had gone haring off to Italy to make sure she was okay, and I knew he had spent at least part of the Christmas holidays with her and the second husband. So the story couldn't be that bad. Either that, or Colin had simply shrugged his shoulders, wrestled with his own demons, and taken the practical approach in coming to terms with his one remaining parent. Knowing Colin—or at least, beginning to know Colin—I could well believe that, too. If he had been the sort to hold a grudge, we wouldn't be out together tonight.

That thought made me feel very warm and fuzzy and prepared to take a generous approach to the rest of the world.

I linked my arm through Colin's, letting my full weight rest against his side as I whispered, "Should I go rescue Serena?"

He considered it for a moment and then shook his head. "She's going to have to get used to speaking to him sooner or later."

As I watched, Colin's mother's husband turned to say something to a man on the other side of him, bringing his face fully into view. And as he did, that elusive resemblance clicked into place.

I *had* seen him before, but not in the flesh. He was considerably older now, taller, more filled out in the chest and shoulder, with a deeper tan and the beginning of a hint of gray in his smooth dark hair, but it was unmistakably the same man I had seen pressed between plastic in the pages of Mrs. Selwick-Alderly's photo album.

The man married to Colin's mother was Mrs. Selwick-Alderly's grandson Jeremy.

Chapter Twenty-Five

Freddy's hair looked obscenely golden against the swollen ruin of his face.

That wasn't Freddy. It couldn't be. Not that inert, bloated form, from which the stench of corruption was beginning to rise in the warmth of the October day. Freddy was—oh, Freddy was a dozen things, but none of them this.

This was someone else's stinking flesh, not Freddy's. Not Freddy who had always been so particular about his toilette. Even on the long voyage from England to Calcutta, he had been meticulous about bathing, using cologne to mask the deficiencies caused by a dearth of fresh water. Freddy would never have allowed his hair to go unbrushed, his features to be distorted, his flesh to decay. At any moment now, he was going to stroll up behind them, making a moue of distaste at the stinking lump of mortality in the palanquin, and say something like, *Must we?*

But it wasn't Freddy's voice Penelope heard behind her, it was Alex's, quietly asking, "What happened?"

"It was a snake." Even Jasper Pinchingdale's usual bravado was muted by the presence of death, although his formulaic hush didn't quite mask an undertone of irritation. It was obvious that he considered it a glaring social solecism for his host to go and die on him in such an abrupt and inconsiderate manner.

"A banded krait," oozed Fiske's voice, too close to Penelope's ear. "His syce found it when he went to wake poor Freddy this morning. It must have crawled into his tent with him while he was sleeping."

"Surely someone must have heard something." That was Alex's voice again, coming from a very long way away, as of someone she had known long ago. "A cry. A gasp. Something."

It was Fiske again, shedding innuendo like a snake's scales. "Freddy preferred to set his tent a bit apart."

Penelope heard her own voice, flat and emotionless. "He had brought his mistress with him, hadn't he?"

There was a rustling behind her, the sound of embarrassed men shifting from foot to foot. "Lady Frederick——," Pinchingdale began awkwardly.

"Hadn't he?" Penelope repeated.

It was Fiske who answered her, his voice arch. Whatever his feelings for Freddy, he was delighting in her discomfort. Fiske was the sort who never forgave a slight and Penelope had slighted him by rejecting his advances in Calcutta. Leaving aside the whole matter of marigolds. "Regardless of who else might have been—ahem—present earlier in the evening, Freddy always made sure his tent was otherwise untenanted by the time he was ready to slumber. But you would know that, wouldn't you, Lady Frederick?"

She did. Freddy had never seen the point of continuing intimacies after sex. He preferred to remove to his own bed, where the sheets were crisp and pure and pristine.

Freddy. Freddy, Freddy, Freddy. It was all too much like him for doubt, every last, damning detail. No matter how little her eyes believed it, this thing, this thing in front of her, was what had been Freddy. There wasn't any other Freddy to come striding out of the bushes, casually demanding her attention. Whatever there had been of him that marked him as himself was gone, leaving nothing but flesh in its wake, already dotted with decay.

The gold coins covering his eyes branded molten circles in her eyes. Penelope shut them hard, wincing against golden discs, circle after circle after circle, like a wedding ring, or a brand, burning against the undersides of her eyelids.

Groping out blindly, Penelope braced her hands against the edge of the palanquin, fighting against a sudden wave of dizziness. Against the closed lids of her eyes she could see Freddy. He was smiling at her, as he first had, all those months ago at Girdings House, his hair as glossy as his boots, his cravat a miracle of engineering, his cheeks flushed with cold, port, and that indefinable eau de rake that Penelope found more compelling than any combination of virtues. Like a cat to catnip, Henrietta had once exclaimed, half in jest, half in despair, and so it was.

She had seen him and wanted him. She had wanted him as a child might want a shiny gold coin, not because she had any particular use for it, but because it glittered and it was pretty and other people didn't want her to have it. It came flooding back to her now, across the ten-month divide, that knee-weakening brew of lust and hurt feelings and pure boredom that had driven her to smile back, a slow, challenging smile, and then, with a slight flick of her head, to draw him out with her into one of the many alcoves with which Girdings House abounded.

It seemed a different world, that frosty winter's day at Girdings House, where the world was clothed in shades of icy blue and the only snakes were the ones in satin dresses, wielding feathery fans to hide their fangs. She had been smarting still over Henrietta's marriage, that precipitate union that had thrust her abruptly out into the cold, a perennial third at their table for two. Charlotte's clumsy attempts to fill the void had been more irritating than soothing. And even Charlotte, second-best though she might be, was drifting away from her. Penelope wasn't stupid. She could read the writing on the wall in the way that Charlotte looked at the new Duke of Dovedale, all breathless adoration, like a puppy wriggling to be petted.

In the midst of it all, there had been Freddy, as tall and golden as the graven idol of a primitive people. Freddy, who had looked at her with admiration, turning his compliments flesh with his lips and hands. She had known it was nothing more than that, just hands and lips and empty compliments, but at least his lust was real, concrete, hers. She could feel it in the way his breath quickened beneath her touch, the way his eyes followed her as she left the ballroom, in the way she could bring him running with one flick of a finger, to freeze his extremities in a January garden for the sake of nothing more than a kiss and the lure of more.

For that brief period, he had been hers. Hers. She had so desperately wanted something of her own, even if it was only fool's gold, base metal beneath a shiny veneer.

Selfish, that was what she had been. Selfish, heedless, thoughtless. All the epithets her mother had hurled at her came back to drive stinging craters into her flesh. She had killed him. She had killed him as surely as if she had poisoned him herself. But for her, Freddy would still be safely in London, drinking himself sick at White's and making unwise purchases of horseflesh at Tattersall's.

Freddy had never wanted to come back to India. London was his world. Had Penelope left well enough alone, Freddy would have lived to become a jaded old man, the sort who pinched young girls' cheeks and generally died in ignominy in the arms of a whore and had to be hustled home so it could be pretended he had died in his bed. Freddy would have liked that. Penelope fought a hysterical urge to laugh, pressing her balled fists against her mouth to hold the laughter inside.

Someone caught at her hand and pressed a glass into it. Penelope's fingers automatically closed around it. Liquid splashed against metal, like water lapping at the banks of the river Hades.

Without looking to see who it was, Penelope said, "I killed him. I did it."

A strong, brown hand closed around her own. "Drink."

For a moment, Penelope stared at it, that hand, so familiar and suddenly so unfamiliar. Only hours ago, she had rubbed against it with breathless pleasure as it had stroked the curve of her cheek. Only a day ago, she had leaned into that touch, as though there were nothing more to be wanted from the world. Bile rose in her throat, with sudden and inexplicable revulsion.

Penelope wrenched her hand violently out of his. The contents of the glass spattered down the front of her habit, brandy mingling with the grime to create trails of mud like dirty tears. Dirty. Corrupt. Spoiled.

"Penelope—" His voice was low, concerned.

"Go away," she said harshly. "I don't want you here."

What had they been doing while Freddy was dying? Last night, Fiske had said. She might have been in Alex's arms while the krait was slithering into Freddy's tent, sinking her nails into Alex's back while the snake was sinking its fangs into Freddy's flesh, crying out her pleasure while her husband contorted with pain. The full magnitude of her betrayal came tottering down on her like a fallen temple. She felt herself swaying beneath the weight of it.

Alex caught her before she could fall, his hands on her elbows, but his touch was an impersonal one. "Let's get you something to sit down on," he said, in a voice meant as much for the others as for her.

He was Captain Reid again. That was all right. She could deal with Captain Reid. It hadn't been Captain Reid with whom she had—no. Not now. She couldn't think of that now.

Around them, Penelope could hear the sounds of scurrying, as people bustled about trying to make accommodation for the bereaved widow. Had they done the same for Freddy's mistress? Penelope felt her stomach heave with bile and loss.

"A snake," she said, to no one in particular, sitting down heavily on the stool provided for her. Someone had hastily tossed a blanket over it, giving it the appearance of a makeshift throne. "A *snake*!"

The bastard would have to go and die in a way guaranteed to cause the maximum discomfort and inconvenience to everyone around him.

Looking down at Lord Frederick's mortal remains, Alex couldn't find it in him to think any of the proper, pious thoughts attendant upon the passage of mortality. Instead, he was cognizant of a strong sense of irritation. He wanted to take the corpse up by the lapels, shake him, and demand to know just what he was thinking, publicly carting his mistress about with him. Didn't the man give a damn for the embarrassment it might cause his wife?

A moot point now.

Irritation was good. Irritation kept other emotions at bay: messy, dangerous emotions, like guilt, relief, worry. Easier to vent his irritation on Lord Frederick for those things he had done while still alive.

Alex's mind refused to quite grasp the crux of it all, that Lord Frederick Staines, the bugbear of his twilight imaginings these past months, was well and truly dead. Gone. No more. Leaving his wife, technically, free.

Free for what?

Alex looked down at Penelope where she sat heavily on the stool provided to her, head bent, air escaping through her pursed lips as she breathed determinedly in and out. Her face was an unpleasant waxy color, her eyes unfocused as she tried to get the workings of her body back under her own control. On her bent head, an uneven line of scalp showed where she had parted her hair, twisting back and forth like a snake in burning grass.

"Yes," echoed Alex slowly, "a snake."

"A krait," corrected Fiske, in his odious voice.

Penelope looked blankly up at him. Her face might be wiped clean of expression, but her curiously colored eyes were as agitated as the churning interior of a volcano. Get sucked in there and a man would be burnt to nothing more than bare bone. "It doesn't much matter which one it was, does it? It did its job."

Fiske regarded her speculatively. "What an interesting way you have of putting things, Lady Frederick."

Penelope didn't answer. Instead, she braced her head on her hands, fingertips pressed hard against her temples, her palms shielding her eyes. Below, Alex could see the rise and fall of her chest, as though she were struggling for breath.

"She's had a shock," Alex said shortly. "You shouldn't have let her see him."

"She shouldn't be here."

For once, they were in agreement.

"She wanted to surprise her husband," said Alex, between clenched teeth.

"Oh, Freddy would certainly have been surprised," said Fiske, drawing his handkerchief between his fingers. "I am surprised you agreed to it."

"What was I supposed to do? Let her go by herself?"

Fiske's protuberant eyes wandered in seeming idleness from Alex's angry face to Penelope's bowed head. "Heaven forbid that Lady Frederick be balked of any of her desires."

Those desires were the last thing either of them needed to think about, considering that she had—that they had ... Well, what they had been engaged in, perhaps at the very hour of Lord Frederick's death. Not that it would have changed anything. No matter what the circumstances, Lord Frederick would still have gone off to Berar; the snake would still have found a way into his tent. He and Penelope had nothing to do with that. Nothing at all.

Alex only hoped Penelope would see it that way.

Bugger bloody Frederick bloody Staines. Bugger himself, while he was at it. One week. If Alex had only managed to keep his hands off her for one blasted week, it might all have been different. No guilt, no tainted associations. There was nothing to be done about it now, of course. Nothing to be done but to get Penelope someplace quiet and let her carry on grieving as best she could.

"Very gallant, Fiske," said Alex curtly. Turning to Penelope, he added, in a gentler voice, "Do you need to lie down?"

Penelope's eyes shifted sideways to the palanquin where Freddy lay in perpetual rest.

Her braid swung violently against her back. "No! No." Pressing her palms against her knees, Penelope addressed herself to Fiske rather than Alex. It made Alex feel like as much of a ghost as the late Lord Frederick Staines. Penelope looked right past him as though he didn't exist, saying forcefully, "I want Freddy buried from the Residency. In the English cemetery. He deserves that, at least. He deserves better than to be buried by the side of the road like a dog in a ditch."

If Fiske were taken aback by her vehemence he didn't show it, save for one startled blink. "Of course," he said smoothly. "Naturally."

Standing, Penelope looked from one man to the other, her eyes opaque circles in her pale face. "We'll have to go quickly, then, won't we? So he doesn't—"

"Of course," repeated Fiske.

Penelope wobbled, but she stood alone, deliberately ignoring the arms both men thrust out towards her. "Then there's no time to lose, is there?"

Alex made as if to catch her arm. "Shouldn't you lie down?" he remonstrated.

She jerked away from his touch so abruptly that she nearly over-balanced. "No," she said harshly, in a voice like sandpaper on stone. "I don't want to lie down. I don't. I don't."

She wouldn't look at him, Alex realized in dismay. Wouldn't touch him.

"You have had a shock," he began carefully.

Penelope laughed, an ugly laugh, like a burning house crackling as it crumbled at the joints. "Not so great a shock as Freddy had."

Without waiting for either of the men to respond, she marched off in the direction of her horse.

"You heard the lady," said Fiske, He touched his handkerchief delicately to the sides of his lips. "The widow demands we ride."

The widow looked like she was about to snap in two, but loyalty to Penelope prevented Alex from saying so to Fiske.

Tight-lipped, Alex watched as a groom helped Penelope onto Buttercup. There was no point in arguing with her in this sort of mood; better to let her ride off the worst of her shock. It was just shock, Alex told himself. She would be fine by and by, Penelope. She was tough. Resilient. Stubborn.

Why didn't he feel reassured?

Since there was nothing else he could do, he caught the eye of the groom. Alex recognized the man, one of the Residency's staff. Alex angled his head towards Penelope, signaling the groom to stay close. Not that it made much difference, but it made him feel better. Like he was doing something for her.

"Quite a spot of bother, this," said Fiske beside him. "Not exactly one for the dispatches, eh?"

"Spot of bother," Alex repeated slowly. Well, that was one way of putting it. The bearers assigned to Lord Frederick's palanquin re-shouldered their mortal burden. Knowing that Lord Frederick's corpse lay in the midst of the caravan gave it the air of a funeral cortege, rather than the hunting expedition it had been.

Unless the game had never been grouse.

A snake might very well have crawled into Lord Frederick's blankets. But for a snake to fatally bite Lord Frederick a mere three days after a cobra had been discovered in his and his wife's bedroom was too much of a coincidence to stomach.

There were too many bloody snakes for coincidence.

Too many bloody snakes, and too many two-legged reptiles who might have planted them. It needn't even have been a real snakebite. The double-pronged thorn of the kikar tree, dipped in poison, would replicate the shape and symptoms of snakebite, with none of the irritating element of chance involved in using the genuine article. A brief prick, and the sleeping victim would be doomed even before he awoke. All that would be left to do would be to take the body of a dead snake and place it by the victim's wound, where it could be conveniently "discovered" the following morning. It was a fairly fool-proof strategy. Anyone spotting the deadly snake would be likely to take a bludgeon first and ask questions later. By the time the hullabaloo died down, the snake would be well and truly dead. As dead as Lord Frederick Staines.

Alex's skin crawled despite the heat. Who had killed Lord Frederick Staines? And what did that mean for Lord Frederick's bereaved wife?

Fiske was the most obvious culprit, Fiske, who was watching Penelope mount her horse, his mouth going in and out in that fish-like way of his. He looked smug. But, then, he always looked smug. It would have been easy enough for him to arrange for that cobra in the Staineses' bungalow—but they had assumed before that the cobra had been meant for Penelope, to prevent her revealing Fiske's putative identity as the Marigold. Lord Frederick might have known, or found out. Or a cautious spy might simply have deemed it expedient to root out both husband and wife, agreeing with English law that the two were, in essence, one body.

Unless it wasn't Fiske at all.

If Penelope were to be believed, someone had tried to kill Lord Frederick before. Alex could almost have smiled when he remembered how Penelope had originally sought to lay the blame for that at his door, accusing him of attempting to murder her husband. Almost. The syce would have been the most logical suspect in that instance, as the man with the opportunity to weaken the girth and send Lord Frederick tumbling. It had been the syce, Mehdi Yar, who "found" the snake in Lord Frederick's tent that morning. There was just one problem with that theory. Alex would have been willing to swear that the groom had been one of Wellesley's plants, an informant planted in Calcutta by no less an authority than the office of the Governor General himself. In that case, why would Wellesley's plant kill off Wellesley's own chosen envoy?

Unless, of course, Wellesley's plant had caught Wellesley's envoy red-handed in a spot of double-dealing.

Alex's head ached with more than heat. Lord Frederick Staines as the Marigold? It was impossible. He had just got to India four months ago. But that wasn't quite true, was it? Lord Frederick had been in India before, at a time of extreme turmoil, in the center of a set known for their dissolute and self-serving behavior. It was Penelope herself who had told him that Lord Frederick's old mate, Wrothan, had been running a spy ring out of his Hellfire Club. The two had been as thick as thieves in Mysore. The phrase might be more than just a metaphor.

Alex positioned himself in the column of riders a little way behind Penelope, near enough to keep an eye on her.

She had never explained how she knew quite so much about the Marigold. Did she—

No. The idea was absurd. It was impossible to imagine Penelope as a cold-blooded assassin, planting a cobra in her own room, arranging her husband's death, either as a double-dealing agent for Wellesley or as a representative of whatever this bloody flowery cabal might be. It wasn't that he thought her incapable of it; it just wasn't in her style. If she had wanted to kill her husband, she would have done it simply, cleanly, with a bullet through the breast, not this convoluted charade of snakes and poison. Subtlety wasn't among Penelope's vices.

Alex's heart twisted at the thought of her, his impetuous, impulsive, passionate Penelope.

His recently bereaved Penelope. Penelope who might still be in danger from whoever had killed her husband. Alex made himself stop mooning and forced himself to concentrate. The snakes were still out, and there were more of them than he cared to count. Penelope might not be one for the subtle and convoluted, but Alex knew someone who was.

So had Lord Frederick. Intimately.

Alex maneuvered his mount forward, next to Fiske's. Fiske was riding beside Penelope, and Alex signaled him to fall back, leaving Pinchingdale by Penelope's other side. Getting Fiske away from Penelope was only a pleasant by-product of his real purpose. With Lord Frederick dead, Fiske was the de facto senior member of the original expedition, the one most likely to have the information Alex needed.

"Is that woman still in the camp?" Alex asked in an undertone, or at least as much of an undertone as one could manage and still be heard, surrounded by thudding hooves and creaky baggage ropes.

"Woman?" said Fiske blandly.

The man knew very well who he meant. "Nur Bai."

Another person who might well want Lord Frederick dead, for personal reasons, professional reasons, or both. There had been rumors during her time as mistress to Major Guignon that she had become so on the instruction of Mir Alam, but where her ultimate loyalties lay were known to no one but the lady herself.

"Oh." The syllable oozed through Fiske's perpetually rounded lips like an eel's. A poisonous one. "So you knew about Freddy's little bit of fun."

Little bit of fun? He doubted Nur Bai would appreciate the sobriquet. If Lord Frederick had called her that, no wonder there was a snake in his bed.

"He wasn't exactly subtle about it." That had come out a little more vehemently than intended. Alex hastily wiped his face blank. "Is she gone?"

"I can't imagine why she would still be here." Fiske pursed his lips.

"She seemed a practical enough daughter of the game to me. Can't very well service a corpse, can she?"

"Thank you for that lovely image," Alex said dryly.

Fiske laughed. No, giggled. A high-pitched, fluting giggle. Alex looked at him with a mix of disdain and incredulity he couldn't quite suppress. And this was the man they had suspected of being a master spy, responsible for the cold-blooded murder of his former messmate?

Perhaps. Even as he hee-hawed, Fiske's pale eyes were as hard as ice and twice as cold.

"If you're looking to replace old Fredders," Fiske said carelessly, his tone at odds with his eyes, "I doubt you can afford her."

With an effort, Alex kept his voice pleasant. "I simply wanted to make sure there would be no awkward encounters between Lord Frederick's mistress and his wife. His widow."

He could hear Penelope's voice in his head, accusing him of thinking of her only as Lord Frederick's wife, his chattel, like his horse or his stock. But that was how Fiske would think of her, as an object, a category. Better for Fiske to keep thinking of her that way, as Lord Frederick's widow, his relict, someone of no further importance—and, especially, of no further danger to him.

"No cat fights, eh?" Fiske looked as though the prospect rather pleased him. "Oh well. The dusky beauty appears to have cleared out, as far as I can tell."

Alex nodded stiffly. He would have to check for himself, of course. "Good." And, then, just to make sure he had a plausible reason for his concern, "We don't want any discredit to redound to the Residency from this affair."

"No," said Fiske thoughtfully. "One wouldn't want to embarrass oneself with any of one's . . . affairs."

Before Alex could react, the other man raised a languid hand and cantered forward to reclaim his place beside the ominously silent form of Lord Frederick's widow.

Chapter Twenty-Six

"And then old Freddy tripped over the hem of his robe, and pitched right into the ceremonial brew!"

Fiske giggled as his latest how-I-remember-Freddy story barreled to a rollicking close. Pinchingdale obliged with a hee-haw. Even the new widow permitted herself a small, ironic smile, directed into the campfire, as though she could see her husband reflected in the flames, facedown in a butt of mead, sputtering, bare shins thrashing in the air.

Alex sat on the edge of the group, near them but not part of them. Their first night on the road had turned into an informal wake for Lord Frederick Staines, each man vying to tell more outrageous stories of the dead man's exploits: his fearlessness on the hunt; his successes on the field of battle (more sartorial than military if the stories were anything to go by); his popularity with the ladies, his clubs, his friends, his family, his tailor.

It was a world foreign to Alex, but not to Penelope. She didn't so much as blink at the introduction of names like Badger Throckhurst. Apparently, she knew Badger. He had had a mishap with a punch bowl and Freddy—Lord Frederick—had made money off it on some sort of long-standing wager in one of the umpteen London clubs to which he belonged, the names of which meant nothing to Alex, but a great deal to Fiske and Pinchingdale, who belonged to them, too. It was Penelope who had contributed that story, her voice rusty from disuse and rough with brandy, drunk neat from Fiske's flask.

This was good for her, Alex knew. Good for her to talk about her husband's life, to remember him as he had been, with other people who had known him and, more importantly, liked him. Under the influence of the fire and the brandy and the stories, the pasty color had left her cheeks. There was still an odd fragility about her, as though she were held together by a brace of pins that might drop out at any moment, but a muted version of her old sarcasm had replaced the stony calm in which she had ridden all afternoon.

Except when it came to Alex. The few times he had ventured a comment, the blankness had returned to her eyes and she had looked right through him, as though he weren't there.

He stopped trying after the first few times.

This was what she needed, he told himself. It was only natural for her to look to her husband's memory, to try to come to terms with his death. She might not have loved her husband, but he had been her husband, and his death had come as a shock. She needed time to come to terms with it. It shouldn't matter who was comforting her, so long as she was comforted.

That was his official line. In truth, he gritted his teeth every time Fiske opened his mouth and he had to swallow a scowl every time the loathsome man brought a smile, no matter how anemic, to Penelope's lips. He squirmed every time she reached to take the flask from Fiske's hands, her lips touching where Fiske's lips had touched.

Alex was supposed to be the one comforting her, not Fiske. Especially not Fiske, the very man who might be the cause of her husband's death. It was bloody ridiculous, even if there had been no other considerations involved. Alex was supposed to be the one she turned to in her time of need, the one she looked to across the campfire, the one from whose flask she drank. All right, so he didn't have a flask. It was the idea of it that counted.

How in the hell did his bloody father do it? Women fell for the old Colonel right, left, and center, forsaking home and hearth just for a chance at his smiles. And here he was, with just one woman in the whole wide world whom he wanted, and for all the attention she paid him, he might as well have been another log on the fire, here today, gone tomorrow. Disposable.

He might try to salvage his hopes by putting it down to shock and grief, but Fiske's casual reminiscences opened a whole vista of problems Alex had been too blinded to consider. Yes, Penelope was finally free. But free to what? This world Fiske evoked, this world of restricted clubs and even more restricted parties; this was Penelope's real world, her real home, only a six-month voyage away. With Lord Frederick gone, what reason did she have to stay in India?

Alex knew what he wanted the reason to be.

He also knew how pitifully unlikely it was. In all their gilded days together, there had never been any talk of love.

The important thing, Alex reminded himself, was keeping Penelope safe. He might not be able to make her love him, but he could keep her alive. It was something, at least. Pathetic, but something.

He waited until both the fire and the conversation had died down, tongues slowed with drink and fatigue, heads and eyelids beginning to droop. Penelope slowly rose from her seat, stretching joints made stiff with sitting.

Alex jumped into the waiting silence before she could begin the general exodus to bed.

"Lady Frederick," he said, doing his best to sound casual, formal, distant, nothing more than a representative of the Residency that had once housed her husband. "I wondered if I might have a quick word."

"I am tired," she said, stony-faced, looking past Alex rather than at him. "I believe I shall go to bed."

"It is rather important." Alex tried to keep the frustration he felt out of his voice. He wanted to grab her by the arm, shake her, make her look him in the eye. This wasn't about them, he told himself. It was about Penelope and her safety. It was for her, not for him.

Fiske unfolded himself from his place by the fire, raising a languid arm to block Alex's path. "The lady said she was tired, Reid."

Since when had Fiske appointed himself Penelope's protector? The gall of it all set Alex's teeth on edge.

"My hearing is still perfectly good," he said tightly, watching Penelope slip away from him behind the barrier of Fiske's arm. He didn't like where they had set up her tent. It was too far on the edge of the camp, too easy for an assassin to access.

"If your hearing is not at fault, it must be the subtleties of civilized conversation that you miss," oozed Fiske.

Civilized? This was the man who had brutalized a fourteen-year-old in a mock pagan ceremony for the sheer depravity of it, and he had the nerve to call Alex uncivilized? Alex burned with important anger as he looked at Fiske's smug, overbred face, lips peeled back from crooked teeth in a lazy smile.

It was far too tempting to knock those teeth loose from that smug smile, but that was just what Fiske wanted. He wanted Alex to lose his temper. The moment he attacked Fiske, Fiske would have him up on charges faster than he could blink.

Alex swallowed his simmering anger and forced himself to speak levelly. "I simply wanted to make certain that we have no further incidents with snakes on this journey," he said shortly.

Fiske's face was the picture of innocence. "Why should you think we might?"

Alex leveled a long, assessing look at his unwanted traveling companion. "I find that reptiles tend to travel in packs."

Abandoning the consuming task of sniffing his brandy, Jasper Pinchingdale lifted his curly head in alarm. "Do they?"

He clearly hadn't registered the insult to himself. It was better that way.

"I doubt we need to worry," said Fiske carelessly. "So long as all the usual precautions are taken."

Alex smiled without humor. "You can be assured that I intend to see that they are. Good night."

It was an empty threat. Short of detailing one of the bearers to stand watch by Penelope's tent at night—which he had already done—there was very little he could actually do. The men he had spoken to in the cavalcade, Residency employees all, had informed him that Nur Bai had indeed left the caravan, breaking off with her own retainers and with the proclaimed intent of carrying on to Mir Alam's hunting lodge in Berar. That didn't mean she actually had. Nor would it have prevented her from leaving half a dozen of her creatures scattered among the traveling circus that made up the camp. With hundreds of servants and bearers, it was nearly impossible to evaluate all the inhabitants.

All Alex could do was make sure Penelope was on her guard.

The placement of her tent might be a danger, but it was also a boon. He waited until Pinchingdale and Fiske were safely immured in their own canvas constructions before slipping over to the edge of the encampment. He knew she was awake. A candle burned within, casting her silhouette against the canvas. She didn't seem to be undressing or reading or doing much of anything at all. She simply sat, her head bowed over her folded hands, pausing, from time to time, to take a long swig from the flask she had coolly walked off with when leaving the fire. Fiske's flask. Alex might have worried about poison, but that Fiske had drunk from it, too. No man poisoned his own well.

Feeling like an idiot slinking through the shadows, Alex fell to his knees beside the tent flap, angled so that the bulk of it hid his body from the rest of the camp.

He tugged on the flap. "Psssst," he hissed. Then, when she didn't answer. "Penelope."

Penelope's nose poked out of the fold. Her nose and one eye. One very bloodshot eye. It did not regard him favorably.

"Don't," she said stonily. "Just don't."

It took a moment for the implication to hit, and when it did, Alex rocked back on his heels. She couldn't possibly think that he was there for . . . Oh.

"This isn't about that," he whispered hastily.

The flap opened a little wider, just wide enough for Penelope to give him a freezing stare.

"About what?" she said, in a tone designed to reduce to nothing anything between them that might ever have been a something. She followed it up with the equally chilling "Why *are* you here?"

Because I love you didn't seem like the appropriate answer.

Alex could smell the brandy on her breath. It was the only warm thing about her. All the anger, all the self-loathing she had obviously been feeling had found an outlet. Him.

"I was worried about your well-being," he said with dignity.

"Well, don't be." The tent flap started to fold down.

This was not how this was supposed to go. Alex made a quick move to block the fall of canvas. "Have you given any thought to that damn snake?"

Penelope looked at him with something akin to loathing. "What do you think I've been contemplating? My toenails? Of course, I've thought about the snake. Again and again and again. What do you want me to do, find an asp to clutch to my breast?"

"Um, no." Taken aback by the unexpected attack, Alex hastily regrouped. "You might still be a target, Penelope. What if someone tries to pull a similar trick with you?"

In the uncertain light, Penelope's face was all bones and hollows, like a skull. She smiled a singularly unpleasant smile. "And what if they do? Good night, Captain Reid."

The tent flap swung emphatically down. The discussion was closed.

Only it wasn't, damn it.

Alex tugged at the canvas. The flap held firm, clearly anchored by something on the other end. A flat voice emerged from inside the tent. "Do that one more time and I will start screaming. I mean it."

Alex didn't doubt she meant it.

Fine. She needed time alone. He could accept that.

"Just be careful," he hissed, and crawled off to his own tent, checking first to make sure that the sentry he had planted near Penelope's temporary lodging was well in place. That would have to do for tonight. By morning—well, surely by morning—Penelope would have seen sense. Alex couldn't have produced a definitive definition of what he meant by sense, but he was fairly sure it had something to do with resuming speaking to him and taking elementary precautions for her own safety.

Penelope did neither of those things. When the morning dawned, she was there with the others, clothed in a habit that had been miraculously cleaned overnight by the staff, her hair brushed and pinned. She took her place at the front of the rank, between Fiske and Pinchingdale, both of whom treated her with an exaggerated solicitude that would have made Alex laugh if only Penelope had been laughing with him. Instead, she treated him just as her husband had once done; with the chilly indifference of the aristocrat to a subordinate, speaking to him only when necessary and, even then, addressing her comments past him rather than to him.

This wasn't Penelope.

Watching her, straight-backed in the saddle, hair brushed and coiled, he remembered her with sweat streaking lines through dust on her face, profanely attempting to put together a fire under his tutelage, jumping into the river after a groom, stealing his horse and riding it, hairpins flying.

That had been Penelope. This was Lady Frederick as he had first met her in Calcutta, hard-edged, sharp-tongued, warding off the world from behind a shield of sarcasm and devil-may-care bravado, and desperately unhappy behind it. She was the first one in the saddle in the mornings and the last to dismount, leaping obstacles with a recklessness that smacked less of her usual bravado and more of a shattering lack of concern with whether she lived or died.

Alex gritted his teeth and bided his time, despising himself for his own helplessness. What was he supposed to do? Take her in his arms and—what? he mocked himself. Kiss her tears away? Remind her that she had never liked the rotter anyway? Offer her sex as a substitute for grieving? Charming behavior, that would be, worthy of Fiske at his best. Alex was only surprised that Fiske hadn't tried it.

It drove him mad to think that their time together might have been nothing more than an interlude to her. A few days before, he would have been willing to swear that it hadn't been, but the steady offensive of indifference drove him to distraction, and to decidedly ignoble emotions.

He was not, he discovered, nearly so self-sacrificing as he had believed himself. If he were, he would have been ready to nobly respect Penelope's unspoken wishes, pretending that nothing of an intimate nature had ever occurred between them. But he couldn't. He couldn't just pack her off to England, to ballrooms full of Fiskes and Freddys. He worried about Penelope, about her health, her safety, but his worry wasn't entirely unmixed with what Alex could only view as selfish self-interest. He couldn't seem to help caring about her, and if she wanted to repudiate that, she would have to do it from her own mouth.

It was three days before Alex found an opportunity to speak to Penelope alone, free from the perpetual presence of her twin shadows, Fiske and Pinchingdale. They had paused to wait out the hottest part of the day in the shelter of an abandoned caravanserai, napping as their inclination and status required: Fiske and Pinchingdale in the tents their servants had scurried ahead to set up for them; the members of the caravan disported in whatever bits of shade they had managed to wrangle from their fellows.

Penelope's tent had been set up with the rest, but she didn't make use of it. As Alex rubbed down a profusely sweating Bathsheba, he saw Penelope disappearing around the side of the ruined building, the train of her abused riding habit dragging dustily in the earth behind her.

Without thinking, Alex tossed the cloth to a groom and followed.

There must once have been a courtyard in the center of the building, where tired travelers might refresh themselves. The fountain was empty, the foundations cracked and dry, and weeds pushed up between the flagstones. Rosebushes grew wild on one side of the courtyard, twining up the arched frames of empty windows, and wild herbs grew fragrant underfoot.

Penelope sat on the edge of the ruined fountain, the skirt of her habit flowing like water around her. With her hair fallen in a long, red rope over one shoulder and the unpruned rosebushes climbing all around her, she looked, thought Alex, like a princess in a story, waiting to be woken by a prince's kiss.

Alex grimaced. If only it were that easy. With his finesse, he seemed to have turned her into a frog. A very angry, fighting frog.

Hearing the brush of his boots against the foliage, she looked up sharply. For a moment, Alex surprised her in an expression of open confusion; her face looked softer, younger than it had for days. She swallowed convulsively and hastily pushed herself up off her perch, pulling her skirts together to brush past him.

She couldn't even muster a hello? One hello after all they had shared?

"Wait." The word was torn out of his chest, less a request and more a command. Softening his voice, he said, no less urgently, "Damn it, Penelope. Why won't you talk to me?"

"We're talking now, aren't we?" she said, as though it were a matter of supreme indifference to her, and made to brush past him.

Alex blocked her, feeling like a cad, but too desperate to care. "That's not what I meant."

"Fine," she said flatly. She turned to pluck at a leaf on the rosebush, shiny and sharp-edged. "Talk."

Having received his mandate to talk, Alex found that both his tongue and his brain had ceased normal function. He had held so many conversations with her in his head over the last few days that it was hard to know where to start—or what had actually been said and what hadn't.

But since he couldn't leave her standing there waiting indefinitely, "I worry about you," he said lamely.

Wrong approach.

"You shouldn't." A thorn pricked her finger, leaving a crimson blot of blood in its wake. Penelope regarded the tiny dot of blood dispassionately. Rubbing her hand against the skirt of the habit, she shrugged. "I'm no concern of yours."

That was precisely the opposite of what he had wanted to hear.

"Yes, you are," said Alex urgently, wishing he had the guts to deploy something more than words. "I—"

But he couldn't say it. It was an impossible time to tell a woman he loved her, all but over the corpse of her husband.

"Captain Reid, Captain Reid," said Penelope, in that tone of polite mockery he was beginning to learn to hate. It was the same one she used with Fiske and Pinchingdale, as delicately deadly as a stiletto. She wouldn't even bloody use his first name. "There's no need, you know. Just because we—"

Alex flung up a hand in an instinctive gesture of negation. Whatever she was about to say, he didn't want to hear it. He didn't want what they had had together reduced to the most base of carnal terms. It had been more than that. Hadn't it? His lungs ached as though he had been running a mile.

Penelope's eyebrows lifted, but she respected the unspoken barrier. With a shrug—a shrug as dreadful as the words she had been prevented from uttering—she said, "I hold you under no obligation to me."

It was a clear dismissal.

Alex stood his ground, searching her face for signs of the woman who had accompanied him to Berar. "But I do. I brought you here."

Penelope laughed lightly. It rang with a false note in the quiet garden. "Trussed and bound?" she said contemptuously. "No. Everything I did, I did of my own accord. You had no part in it."

Right. That was quite enough of that. It was one thing letting her grieve, another thing to be relegated to the position of hired stud, put out to pasture after his turn in the paddock. It had been his affair as well as hers and she could bloody well remember that.

"Didn't I?" he said provocatively. "I seem to remember two being involved in some of those activities."

She hadn't expected that. She turned on him with the sort of freezing stare designed to reduce a man to gibbering apology, a slow spark of anger kindling in her eyes, like gold to the flame.

With a nonchalance he was far from feeling, Alex plucked a petal from a rose, rolling it between his fingers so that its musky fragrance permeated the air between them. "Forgive me. I wasn't aware you were the only one allowed to refer to it." He paused before saying, deliberately, unforgivably, "You weren't so cold four days ago."

"Four days ago," Penelope said, through clenched lips, "Freddy wasn't dead."

"It's not fair hiding behind Freddy," Alex said harshly. The mashed remains of the rose petal crumbled through his fingers. "You had precious little time for him when he was alive."

Penelope stared at him in shock. "That's not—you can't—"

"Did you love him?" Alex demanded. He hadn't meant to say it, but once it was out, there was no taking it back.

Ugly laughter rasped through Penelope's throat. "Does it matter? Now?"

"Did you?"

Heedless of thorns, Penelope turned and banged a fist into the vine-covered wall. "No! Is that what you wanted to hear? No, I didn't love him. I never loved him. I never even *liked* him. I married him out of—out of boredom. I married him on a bloody whim, and do you know what happened? He died of it. There. Happy now?"

Blood seeped down her wrist where a thorn had torn the side of her hand, but she seemed not to notice.

"No," Alex said soberly.

What could he say? That he wanted her to be happy? The sentiment seemed absurd in the face of her wild-eyed despair. He hadn't realized quite how much emotion she had been holding tamped down beneath the fragile social crust of the past few days.

Tentatively, like a skater shifting out onto uncertain ice, he said, "You weren't even there when it happened. It's not your fault that Lord Frederick died."

Penelope's hands balled into fists in the folds of her habit. "You don't know the first thing about it," she said with withering scorn. "You don't know at all."

"Try me," he said, keeping his voice hard, granite to her granite, rough and unyielding.

It worked.

"If you must know, I compromised him," she said defiantly.

Alex had never heard anything so absurd. "I should have thought that *he* compromised *you*."

Penelope glowered at him. "He wouldn't have if I hadn't given him ample opportunity."

Alex looked at her flushed and angry face and thought that several things made a great deal more sense. "Is that what they told you?" he asked softly.

Penelope made an impatient gesture, brushing aside his words. "I announced to the world at large that we had been in a bedroom alone together. I did, not Freddy."

"On purpose?"

"By accident," she admitted grudgingly. "But the result was the same. He had to marry me. He would never have come out here but for me. And it bloody well killed him."

"Penelope—"

Ignoring him, she clenched and unclenched her bloody hands, pacing the paving, wearing a circle into the stones. "I was the one who drove him to India."

"What did you do?" demanded Alex softly. "Hit him over the head with a truncheon? Drag him onto the boat *trussed and bound*?"

"I made him come out here," Penelope repeated stridently. "I made him come out here and it bloody killed him. I killed him. I killed Freddy."

"A snakebite killed him," Alex said bracingly. "You can't blame yourself for that."

"Can't I?" Penelope's face twisted. "I've been a disaster since the day I was born. Just ask my mother; she'll tell you."

"Mothers aren't always the most reliable sources."

"Ask Freddy then. Oh, wait. You can't, can you?" Penelope's face screwed up but she got it under control again, saying roughly, "I'm a walking blight and if you have any sense you'll get well away from me before I curse you, too."

Alex shook his head gently. "I could never do that," he said, and realized it was true. He was in too deep. For the first time, he understood the doomed lovers of the epics, taking steps that had always seemed monumentally stupid to him before, flinging aside reputation, pride, honor, all for that elusive chameleon called love.

Apparently, Penelope had never understood it either. "Why?" she shot back at him, every word a taunt. "Do you just like playing with trouble? Or are your heroic instincts acting up again?"

Alex watched her, like a hunter stalking a hind. "There's nothing heroic about it."

Penelope snorted. "I know you. Gallant Captain Reid who can't bear to leave a stranded kitten in a tree." Alex had never, to his recollection, even seen a kitten in a tree, but Penelope was off and running, her words tumbling out faster and faster, higher and higher pitched. "For heaven's sake! Your brother stands condemned of treason in front of you and you still bend over backwards to shelter him."

Her voice broke on the last words. Alex, who had been prepared to take umbrage, stopped, arrested by the unprecedented sight of tears trickling down Penelope's cheeks. She fought a losing battle for control over her own body. He watched as her face contorted, her hands clenching and unclenching, as her whole body shook with the sobs she refused to give in to.

"I compromised my husband," she spat out hoarsely. "I cuckolded him. I dragged him out here to die. Yes, die." Turning her head, Penelope dashed angrily at her wet cheeks with the back of her hand. Blood and tears mingled in pinkish stripes across her face. The effect was gruesome. She screwed up her face, sucking up snot through her nose. "Let me tell you this, Captain Reid. Some people aren't worth the saving. Get out while you still can."

She looked like something designed to frighten small children, eyes narrowed to slits, cheeks puce, face contorted. Alex took a step towards her. "No."

Penelope pushed against him with both hands, blood, tears, and snot dripping unheeded down her chin. She pushed again, harder, her voice taking on a hysterical edge, "*Go,* damn you! Damn you, damn you, damn you. What in the *hell* are you doing here with me? Do you just like being kicked again and again? Or are you saving up for a halo?"

"You bloody fool," Alex said tenderly, and took her in his arms. He rubbed his hands soothingly up and down her back, feeling her muscles jerk with suppressed tears and halfhearted protests. She drew in a ragged breath against his chest, snuffling up snot and choking on a sob. Alex pressed his cheek against the top of her head, her sun-warmed hair warm against his skin and smelling only slightly rank from a day without washing. "You bloody, bloody fool. You've got it all cock-a-hoop. Don't you realize I—"

"My, my," intruded an all-too-familiar voice, at just that inopportune moment. Booted feet slapped decisively against the ancient paving. The sound brought Alex's head up with a snap, but not soon enough. "What have we here?"

Chapter Twenty-Seven

"Comforting the widow, Reid?" inquired Lieutenant Sir Leamington Fiske.

Penelope stumbled as Alex's hold abruptly loosened, leaving her cold and exposed. She felt battered, disheveled, and entirely adrift.

Fiske assessed her ravaged face with an appraiser's eye. "Zounds," he said softly. "Tears. How touching. Are they real?"

Alex stepped between Penelope and Fiske, shielding her with his body. "What do you want, Fiske?"

With deliberate insolence, Fiske thrust his hands into his pockets and lounged back on his heels. "It might be more to the point to ask what you want with a woman so recently bereaved, Reid."

Penelope had never seen Alex so angry, not even on the memorable occasion of the cobra. No, not even when she had accused him of embezzling funds from the Nizam's treasury.

"Question my motives all you like," he said sharply, every word cracking like a pistol shot, "but never impugn the honor of the lady."

He meant it, Penelope realized, with mingled awe and horror. He really meant it. Although how he could mean it, when he knew what she . . . when she and he . . . Penelope blinked away a morass of muddled memories, hands and lips and tangled blankets and snarled hair by the campfire in the dawn light. Honor. This wasn't just plucking a kitten from a tree; it was scaling a rickety branch for a stranded tiger, stupid and noble and pointless and certain to end very, very badly.

She wanted to grab at his arm and shout at him not to be a fool, but it was too late. A crushing sense of inevitability descended on Penelope as she watched Fiske's lips spread in a slow, knowing smile.

"Honor?" Fiske emitted a sharp bark of laughter. He nodded insolently towards Penelope. "No offense, my dear. We all know how you came to marry poor Freddy."

"Would you care to take that back?" suggested Alex conversationally.

Fiske crossed his arms across his chest. "Why should I?"

Alex's lips twisted into a grim smile. "Allow me to provide you with the reasons."

Penelope wished she could pretend not to understand what was meant by that, but there was no way anyone could, especially not a trigger-happy, honor-mad army man who had fought duels in the past over matters so slight as a disagreement about the set of his lapels. Her head pounded and her chest ached and her throat burned, but somehow, through the drumming of her blood in her ears, she heard her own voice, raised in remonstrance.

"Don't," she said sharply. She pushed out from behind Alex, placing herself between the two men. "Just—don't."

Fiske smiled lazily down at her, as though it hadn't been her honor he had been calling into question a few moments before. "Too late for that, old girl," he said patronizingly. "Matter of honor and whatnot."

"Yes," said Penelope fiercely. "My honor. Which, I believe, we have already agreed isn't worth fighting over." It hurt to voice it, but it needed to be done. She managed a tortured smile and drew herself up in her best imitation of her usual demeanor, mad hair, blood-streaked face and all. "So we're done here, yes?"

Alex looked over her head as though she hadn't spoken. "You'll name your seconds?"

"Blast you!" Penelope struck at his arm. "There won't be any firsts! How many times do I have to say it? I won't have you fighting over me. It's not worth it."

Fiske looked benevolently down at her. He was thinner than Alex, but taller, willowy where the other man was more compactly built. He would have the advantage of reach in a fight with swords. "Maidenly qualms, my dear? I wouldn't have thought it of you."

The derisive amusement Fiske injected into the word "maidenly" brought Alex forward on the balls of his feet, ready to settle with his fists what he had already proposed doing with his sword.

Penelope drove an elbow into his ribs before he could get past her. She could hear the indrawn hiss of his breath, but she didn't look at him. She couldn't. Focusing all her attention on Fiske, she said shortly, "I won't ruin another man's life—whether it's yours or his. Fight if you must," she added, with hard-won flippancy. "But not over me."

With the peculiar instinct of men the world over to scent a good fight, their raised voices had attracted spectators.

"Who is fighting?" asked Jasper Pinchingdale eagerly, strolling into the courtyard, followed an assorted entourage of grooms, bearers, and functionaries, whose actual function remained a mystery to Penelope.

"No one," said Penelope forcibly.

Neither Fiske nor Alex—nor, for that matter, Pinchingdale—paid the slightest bit of attention to her. Regardless of her role in the inception of it, at this stage, she was nothing more than an insignificant intruder into the matters of men.

Penelope felt a cold sweat breaking out beneath the heavy wool of her habit. Why didn't anyone else seem to realize that this was a dreadful idea? That men could die this way?

That Alex could die this way.

Penelope wanted to thump them all. How could they be such idiots? Wasn't one fatality enough for any journey?

Unless, of course, someone wanted another fatality.

The prospect hit her like a punch to the gut. Penelope's head buzzed with confused suspicions and inchoate fears. The Marigold. She had forgotten all about that. It seemed like a million years ago that she and Alex had discussed Fiske's potential culpability in the predawn dark of the bedchamber she had shared with Freddy. All of that seemed very far away, but it wasn't, and Alex knew it. It had been Alex who had warned that Freddy's death might be more than an accident, and urged her to be on her guard.

Why couldn't he listen to his own advice?

The two opponents exchanged a long, level look. "We can settle this back at the Residency," said Alex in a hard voice.

Fiske readjusted his gloves. "I shall look forward to the sport."

"How very sporting of you," said Alex dryly.

"I'll put odds on you, old man," said Pinchingdale to his messmate, brightening at the prospect of a bit of blood and bookmaking. Remembering his purpose, he added, "Just came to tell you that we seem to be all packed up and ready to go. Proper beds at the Residency tonight!"

Fiske's mouth opened and closed like a guppy's. "Except for those of us who wake at dawn."

With an inconsequential comment to Pinchingdale, he pointedly turned his back on Alex. Whatever it was he had said, it must have been amusing. Penelope could hear Pinchingdale's arrogant laughter floating away with the sound of their retreating footsteps.

From the entryway, someone signaled to Alex, undoubtedly about one of the hundred tasks to do with getting the cavalcade back underway. Alex held up a hand, indicating that he would be along in just a moment.

Turning to Penelope, Alex looked at her searchingly. "Are you all right?" he asked gently.

All right? Had there ever been a more idiotic question in the history of the world?

Every emotion she had ever had boiled and churned and spilled over like acid, burning through whole layers of skin, leaving her naked and exposed and vulnerable. She felt as though her guts had been dragged out through her nose and left lying all over the cobblestones.

"You idiot," she fumed. "You pigheaded, mule-brained, feeble-minded man. You walked right into that like—like an idiot sheep to slaughter. Did you ever stop to think that he might have done it on purpose?"

"Yes," he said calmly. Penelope gaped at him. Taking advantage of her momentary speechlessness, he added, in a voice that brooked no dispute, "Fiske can't be allowed to say such things about you with impunity."

"Why not, when it's true?" demanded Penelope frantically. "Others have said worse."

Alex's face set in lines of pure granite. "Not anymore."

He appeared to be missing the point. Images of Freddy, waxy-skinned and lifeless, flashed through her head, oddly intermingled with images of Alex, Alex sprawled like a dropped doll on a patch of trodden ground, mouth slack, eyes hollow. They were all muddled together in her head, death after death after death, and all on her account. She had thought she could save him by staying away. Why, oh, why had he been fool enough to seek her out?

Balling her hands into fists at her sides, Penelope said fiercely, "I won't, won't, won't let you kill yourself for me."

She knew she had lost even before he spoke. He grinned down at her, an endearing, boyish grin that made her throat lurch with the presentiment of future pain. "What makes you think I'll lose?"

Idiot!

Penelope didn't even attempt to answer. If she had possessed Charlotte's vocabulary, she would have excoriated him in a thousand different ways, each more scathing than the last. But she didn't. She walked right past him, listening carefully to the slap of her own boots against the paving stones, willing the sound to expand and expand until it drummed out the shrill buzz of raw panic that roared in her ears and battered against her chest.

This was worse, far worse, than finding a cobra waiting for her by her dressing table. Then she had been calm. There had been no one's life but hers to account for, and she held that life cheap. No great loss to the world if she were to shuffle off this mortal coil. Henrietta and Charlotte would mourn her for a week—when they eventually found out—and Freddy, were he still alive, would have celebrated her memory by going on a spree with his mistress.

But, Alex! Steady, reliable, careful Alex. What had he been thinking? Was it part of the same madness that had seized his brain when he had allowed himself to take up with her? She had battered at him and battered at him and battered at him until he had; less a seduction and more an assault, sapping and razing his defenses, turning him inside out for her own selfish gratification.

Penelope swallowed hard, fighting the image of Freddy lying in the palanquin, dead and cold, with gold coins where his eyes should have been. As she watched, the bright gold hair darkened slowly to black, like a shadow creeping over the moon, and the coins shrouding his eyes blackened and tarnished and charred until they, too, were black, black and empty. It would be Alex lying there instead and no matter how she tried to shake him he wouldn't wake up, he wouldn't ever wake up, and it would all be her fault.

With an effort, Penelope took hold of her rising panic, forced it down, hunching over her horse's neck until Buttercup sidled and knickered reproachfully. She forced herself to lighten her·seat, but the leather of her riding gloves stretched tight across her knuckles as she gripped the reins. The duel had to be stopped, that was all there was to it. She wouldn't let Alex die as Freddy had.

Chewing the inside of her lip, Penelope rode along beside Fiske and Pinchingdale, grateful for the broad hat that shielded her face as mile passed mile. The Resident might be the answer, Penelope thought determinedly. It was his jurisdiction. He would have the power to stop the duel.

Unless he didn't want to. Penelope's hopes, which had begun to rise, abruptly crashed again. The Resident was a man, after all, and there was no telling how they would react to perfectly logical requests. Honor must be served and a duel provided good sport.

Even if the Resident did stop the duel, it would go poorly for Alex. Duels were technically illegal—in England, at least. Penelope had no idea whether the rule extended to India. If it did, Alex might find himself facing disciplinary action or demotion for having embroiled himself in such an affair. All the sordid details would have to come out, Fiske's insinuations, Alex's reactions. It would look bad for him. It would look even worse if it ever came out that it was all true. Adultery was a crime, too, and public opinion, with all its usual perversity, would run on the side of Freddy, simply because he was dead. Freddy. He always had had a miraculous ability to wallow in muck and come out shining golden. Death hadn't changed that.

Strange, that the thought of him still evoked such bitterness in her. She had thought death would have conquered that, transmuting bitterness to grief and recriminations to guilt. For a time it had. But like an alchemist's experiments, the transformation had proved illusory.

There was no point in thinking about Freddy, she told herself harshly. He was dead. It was Alex who needed to be kept alive.

Perhaps she could lock him in his quarters and prevent him from appearing at the appointed time.

No. He would hate her for it, and Fiske would gloat at Alex's supposed cowardice in fearing to meet him. Besides, knowing Alex, he would calmly and methodically find a way out. He was too competent by half.

Far better, she could confine Fiske in *his* quarters. A crazy smile tugged at the corners of Penelope's lips. It made the muscles in her face hurt. She had got out of the habit of smiling. But it felt good.

The plan was just crazy enough to work. Penelope snuck a glance sideways from under her hat brim. It would be a double revenge, preventing Fiske from meeting Alex and tainting him with the imputation of cowardice at the same blow. It was perfect, and so much easier than trying to immure Alex. It wouldn't take much. Some poppy juice in Fiske's after-dinner brandy, a whispered suggestion of an assignation—and then the key turning in the lock, leaving him to sleep it off till well past dawn.

Penelope felt herself buoyed by a new sense of purpose and resolution. She might have killed Freddy, but she could save Alex. Even if he wouldn't necessarily thank her for it. Well, too bad for him, she thought, with a stirring of her old imperiousness. At least he would be alive to not thank her.

It was dark by the time their cavalcade passed under the great gate of the Residency. Alex was nowhere to be seen—presumably preparing for a meeting that would never take place, Penelope thought with satisfaction. She submitted to being lifted down from her horse by Fiske, simpering at him for all she was worth.

"Penelope!" someone cried out, and Fiske, whose hands had lingered longer on her waist than strictly necessary, nearly dropped her.

The slight form of a young woman raced down the steps of the Residency, holding up her skirt with one hand and waving the other in animated greeting, her blond curls frothing in front of her face with her joyful progress.

Penelope squinted in the uncertain light. Heavens, what with Alex and snakes and Freddy's death, her mind was beginning to go. She was starting to hallucinate.

The hallucination skidded to a halt in front of Penelope, grabbing Penelope's gloved hand in an affectionate clasp.

"Oh, Penelope! I'm so glad to see you!" exclaimed Charlotte.

If she was a hallucination, she was a surprisingly corporeal one. Penelope inched her fingers out of Charlotte's clasp.

"What—?" she began.

Lady Charlotte Lansdowne—no, the Duchess of Dovedale now, Penelope reminded herself—beamed at her, glowing like the royal fireworks all going off in unison. "We're on our way to Mysore, so Robert can show me where he lived. We've been to Calcutta already on the way, and some lovely little villages, and seen such sights and ruins. And aren't the elephants wonderful? I hadn't thought they could be nearly so big," said Charlotte all in rush, bouncing up and down in her enthusiasm.

Her very evident happiness hit Penelope like a door in the face.

Confronted with Penelope's stony countenance, some of the glow faded from Charlotte. She looked searchingly at her old friend. "Pen, what's wrong?"

"Freddy is dead," Penelope said brusquely.

Charlotte's hand flew to her mouth, which had formed a perfect *O*. "Oh, Pen."

"'Oh, Freddy,' more like," said Penelope, with deliberate callousness, even as she hated herself for doing so. Venting her anger at Charlotte was like kicking a kitten. "He's the one in the box."

Charlotte's lips folded closed over what was clearly about to have been another *Oh, Pen*. Penelope wished she wouldn't do that; even if the intent behind it was good, it had always grated on Penelope's nerves like nails on a slate.

Instead, Charlotte turned to a servant, and said, with charming diffidence, "Please, might we have some tea?" before turning back to Penelope with obvious concern in her big, cloudy eyes. When had Charlotte acquired that unconscious air of command? More had changed than just a ring on her third finger.

The source of it all stepped out from behind her, coming more staidly down the steps. "You might want something a bit stronger than that," said Charlotte's husband.

Penelope eyed him warily. Back in England, they had not gotten along. He had blamed her for the infatuation of his friend, Tommy Fluellen—heavens, it wasn't as though she had asked the man to follow her around—and she had made no secret of her conviction that his designs on Charlotte were less than honorable. So he had proved her wrong. It had seemed a sure-enough proposition at the time.

Respect for the dead—or at least respect for a death, since he had no respect for Freddy—tempered whatever residual resentment the new Duke of Dovedale might have held for her.

"I am sorry for your loss," he said.

"No, you're not," said Penelope baldly. "You had nothing but contempt for Freddy."

"Like you," blurted out Charlotte. Coloring to her eyebrows, she clapped her hands over her mouth. "Oh, Pen. I didn't mean—that is . . . Oh, dear. But it's just that you did criticize him. Rather a lot." She hastily shut her mouth before she could put her foot down it any farther.

With friends like these, who needed poisonous snakes? It didn't help that Charlotte was right.

"And you never criticize your husband?" she said frostily.

"Only when I deserve it," said the duke, genially enough, but there was a hint of steel under it, and an unspoken warning in the way he threaded his arm around Charlotte's waist.

Penelope wanted nothing more than to fling herself down on the steps and bang her fists against the cold stone until her hands cracked and bled. She wanted to howl like a child in a temper tantrum, stamping her feet and shouting that it wasn't fair. Why did everyone else get cosseted and coddled and protected while she was left to fend for herself? It was always the lumpy part of the porridge for old Penelope.

Fleetingly, Penelope remembered the way Alex had looked in the caravan courtyard, striking out for her honor. But that wasn't really for her, any more than those days on the road had been an expression of anything more than the desires of the moment. Alex was in the habit of playing protector. And he didn't like Fiske.

"You called for tea?" said Penelope tightly.

The duke's arm dropped from around his wife's waist.

Penelope didn't miss the private look that passed between the two. It made her feel like a spoiled child in the presence of indulgent adults prepared to humor her so far as might be necessary to ensure general tranquility. Penelope's throat tightened. It would have hurt less if she hadn't known herself to be behaving like a spoiled child.

Her husband had just died. Didn't that count for anything?

She could almost hear the mocking laughter. *Like you*, Charlotte had said, silly, absentminded Charlotte, who always saw more than was convenient and didn't have the good sense to hide it. And it was true, all of it. When it came down to it, she didn't like Freddy. She had never liked Freddy. But she had married him anyway. Somehow, that made it all worse.

"Shall we?" said Charlotte timidly, threading her arm through Penelope's and supporting her steps, as though she were an invalid. Considering that Penelope was a good head taller than Charlotte, it was a particularly futile gesture. If Penelope went over, they would both go splat.

"Why not?" said Penelope bitingly. "One must never underestimate the restorative powers of tea."

She let Charlotte lead her into the Residency, into a small parlor on the side of the house, pleasantly cool in the peaceful dusk. The visiting duchess had already made the room her own, novels piled carelessly on a side table, a journal marked with a red ribbon lolling open on the settee. The tea was waiting for them, all the proper accoutrements laid out neatly on an octagonal table. Charlotte busied herself preparing the tea, waiting until the leaves were steeping before saying tentatively, "Do you want to talk about it?"

Penelope prowled restlessly back and forth, heedless of the caked mud being transferred from her hem to the Resident's prized Persian carpet. "I want it all to go away. I want to go to bed and wake up and find that none of it ever happened. That's what I want."

"Your marriage or Lord Frederick's death?"

"Both."

"Oh, Pen."

"Don't 'oh, Pen' me!"

Charlotte sat down abruptly in a chair. "I'm sorry. I didn't mean . . ."

Penelope pressed her eyes tightly together. "I know. I do know. It's just . . . hard. All of it."

She looked at Charlotte sitting there so placidly. Charlotte, who had found her Own True Love—one could practically hear the capital letters every time Charlotte looked at her husband. But Charlotte had believed in her duke, even when circumstances had militated against him, and others, including Penelope, had advised her not to trust him farther than she could throw him. Charlotte had earned her happy ending.

If circumstances had been different, might she and Alex—no. She wouldn't let herself start thinking rubbish. It might be all flowers and poetry in Charlotte's world, but it wasn't in hers.

Once she rescued Alex from the idiocy of this duel, that would be the end of it, all obligations over on both sides. She had bullied him into dallying with her, and he had defended her out of duty. There was no point in falling into Charlotte's fantasy land and deluding herself that it might ever be anything more.

A wild laugh tore out of Penelope's throat. "I did something you wouldn't approve of," she blurted out, rounding towards her friend in a swirl of heavy fabric. "I committed adultery."

There it was. No euphemisms. No pretense.

Penelope could tell Charlotte was horrified, even though she made a valiant effort to hide it. "I never thought you and Lord Frederick were well-suited," she said diplomatically, before adding hastily, "not that I hoped he would get bitten by a snake, of course."

"You don't understand. I was with Alex—Captain Reid—while Freddy was dying. I didn't know—I had no idea—"

Charlotte lurched forward in her chair, her innocent face earnest. "But you couldn't have known. Oh, Pen. How could you possibly have foreseen that something like that might happen?"

It was on the tip of Penelope's tongue to tell her about Fiske. But she shrugged the impulse aside. Matters were complicated enough. "Bad things happen. If I hadn't caused him to be exiled to India, he wouldn't be dead."

"Bad things can happen anywhere," said Charlotte earnestly. "He might just as well have fallen off his phaeton or tripped into the Serpentine or been bludgeoned to death by footpads. You certainly didn't mean any of this to happen when you—well, you know."

"Just because I didn't mean him to die from it doesn't make it any less my doing."

"Everyone dies eventually," said Charlotte, looking down into the clouds created by the milk in her tea. In a barely audible voice, she added, "No matter how much one wishes otherwise."

Not even Charlotte could muster that much sympathy for Freddy. With a jolt, Penelope realized that Charlotte was not thinking of Freddy, but of her parents. She spoke of them so seldom that it was easy to forget how deeply she had been attached to them.

Feeling beastly, Penelope plopped into the chair next to her friend's. "I'm sorry, Lottie."

"Don't be." After a moment, Charlotte looked up from her tea, her eyes as bright and curious as a sparrow's. "Do you love him?"

"Who?"

"Captain Reid," said Charlotte, as though it were entirely obvious. Perhaps it was.

"I don't know," said Penelope bleakly. "I don't know what love is."

All she knew was that she couldn't let him perish on the field of honor tomorrow morning. It would be worse than what she had done to Freddy, worse than anything she had ever done or could do.

"Do you know," said Charlotte, addressing herself to the sugar bowl, "I believe that's the closest I've ever heard you come to making a declaration of affection."

"Over my husband's corpse," said Penelope darkly.

Charlotte sighed. "You never do do anything in the ordinary course, do you?"

Chapter Twenty-Eight

Freddy managed to be quite as much bother in death as he had been in life.

James Kirkpatrick, the Resident, went gray when he heard the news, tugging at his carefully cultivated mustachio as he murmured the proper words of condolence, his mind all the while obviously already working over the phrasing of diplomatic dispatches. How did one tell Wellesley that his pet had perished in the wilderness four days north of Hyderabad?

Penelope didn't envy him the task, although she would gladly have traded his for hers, the letters Charlotte had reminded her were due to both Freddy's mother and her own.

It fleetingly occurred to her that she would never be able to go back to London. Well, not never. But not for a very long time. She had no desire to spend her remaining days shrouded in widow's weeds, to face the anger and accusations of Freddy's family and the opprobrium of her own, returning to the family home where her mother would have free rein to vent at her all the rage of her thwarted ambitions.

No, she couldn't go back to London. What was odder was that the thought brought with it no regret.

England and their respective families seemed very far away. In the confused days after Freddy's death, Penelope hadn't thought about that. She hadn't thought about a lot of things. It was the Resident's task to remind her, ably seconded by Charlotte, who fluttered and fussed and produced enough tea to keep the servants permanently engaged in emptying chamber pots. There were funeral arrangements to be seen to—sooner, rather than later, as the Resident intimated with charming delicacy.

"You mean he's beginning to rot," Penelope said bluntly, to which the Resident had replied, with a diplomat's tact, "In hot climates, funerals tend to be held sooner than those to which we are accustomed. As it has already been several days . . ."

They arranged for the funeral and a myriad of administrative details, as Henry Russell made notes and a variety of functionaries were sent back and forth on various related tasks. Alex was sent for at one point, something about official representations of Freddy's death to the Nizam and pacifying Mir Alam for the non-arrival of his guests, but the servant sent on that errand returned with the news that Captain Reid had gone into the town and hadn't left word when he would return.

Securing his second for the meeting the next day? Penelope wondered where Fiske had got to.

The Resident said something, loudly, and Penelope realized that they were all looking at her, waiting for her to respond to a question that had been asked twice, or even three times.

"I'm sorry," Penelope said. "I'm afraid I was elsewhere."

A look of insufferable understanding passed between Russell and Kirkpatrick. "No matter," the Resident said kindly. "If you would prefer to retire . . ."

Penelope stiffened her spine. "No. No. Carry on."

She knew they were watching her, waiting for signs of the anticipated breakdown, the grieving widow's grieving. It would be the womanly and proper thing to do. But she had had her hysterics already, in the caravan courtyard the day before. She had had four days to walk through her shock and guilt and despair. All she wanted now was to get it done with, to have the arrangements arranged and Freddy safely in the earth.

"I have ordered a room prepared for you in the Residency," the Resident said delicately, as they rose after what seemed a very long time.

It was a kindly gesture, even if misplaced. It served her current purposes perfectly. It would be easier to incapacitate Fiske if she was spending the night beneath the same roof.

"Thank you," she said demurely, as they passed through a high-ceilinged room that lay still and dark in the evening cool. "I shall take supper in my room."

She could sense the approval from her entourage. It was the sort of thing a grieving widow was supposed to do. It also left her free to hunt down Fiske.

"I shall see that—," the Resident began, and broke off to dart forward as Charlotte, who had been walking a little way ahead, suddenly launched herself into the air, flailing her arms madly for balance.

"Oooph!" she said descriptively, as the Resident caught her neatly around the waist, preventing her from pitching over.

As Charlotte grimaced at him apologetically, Penelope discreetly rolled her eyes. Charlotte had a habit of collisions with inanimate objects; her mind and her body seldom kept company together on their various wanderings, leaving her prone to tripping over anything that wasn't wise enough to get out of her way first. Rolled-up carpet edges and small tables were not known for their self-preserving instincts.

"I'm so sorry," Charlotte said brightly. "I seem to have tripped over . . . Oh. Oh, dear."

Her fair skin went waxy in the uneven light of the candles. The Resident hastily stepped between her and whatever it was, shielding Charlotte's tender sensibilities. He also obstructed Penelope's view.

Charlotte swallowed hard. "Oh, dear," she repeated.

Penelope elbowed her way forward. There, in the flickering light, she saw the body of a man sprawled facedown on the Turkey rug. It was hard to tell what color his hair had been; it was matted with the blood that seeped from the gash in his skull. There was a ring on his outstretched hand, large and flashy with the incised lines of a lotus flower riven onto a ruby surface. Penelope recognized it as belonging to Fiske. Freddy had owned a similar one, insignia of the club to which they had both belonged.

That past tense suddenly sounded particularly significant.

"Call Dr. Ure," said the Resident sharply. He bent over the body.

When he straightened, there was an expression of inestimable relief on his face. But all he said was, "He breathes."

There were pounding feet, behind them, the sound of bodies being dispatched and arriving.

As for Penelope, she was conscious of a distinct and ignoble sense of relief that someone had put Fiske out of commission before she had been required to do so. A man with a head wound couldn't very well put in a dawn appearance on a dueling field.

"He might be breathing now, but for how long?" demanded Jasper Pinchingdale loudly, shouldering his way to the front of the group. "That's the devil of a nasty head wound. And who did it?"

"Perhaps he fell," suggested Charlotte innocently.

"And struck himself on the head with a candlestick in falling?" said Penelope, relief taking vent in sarcasm.

The candlestick lay on the ground beside Fiske. It was a silver candlestick, of sturdy construction. The fluted edging bore a disquieting smudge of some dark substance. Based on the dent in Fiske's head, it did not take more than rudimentary intelligence to discern what it might be.

Charlotte bit her lip at Penelope's tone. She covered her confusion by leaning over, scooping up a scrap of white fabric that showed pale against the dark red patterns of the carpet.

"You dropped this," she said politely, holding it out to the Resident.

"I?" Taking it from her and turning it over in his hand, the Resident shook his head. "No. It's not—"

His voice broke off. Following his gaze, Penelope could see what he had seen. Three neatly marked initials, embroidered in hair, set into the white cambric. The large *R* in the middle dwarfed the smaller initials on either side, but there was no mistaking what they were.

On the Resident's face, Penelope could see the reflection of the sick feeling that was currently rising from the pit of her stomach.

Pinchingdale plucked the piece of cloth from the Resident's hand.

"Reid," he breathed. "It would be."

"What?" said Charlotte.

"Reid. *Captain* Reid." His exaggerated pronunciation turned the title into a mockery. Pinchingdale shook the scrap of cloth at the Resident. "It is his handkerchief, isn't it?"

"They are his initials," said the Resident carefully. "That does not, however, mean . . ."

Balling the handkerchief in one fist, Pinchingdale flung it to the ground beside his friend's body. "It is Reid. I know it is." He swore, viciously. "He's the one who did this to old Lemmy."

"I don't see . . . ," Charlotte began hesitantly.

"Captain Reid couldn't have done it," interrupted Penelope. "He isn't even here."

"Wasn't he?" Jasper Pinchingdale kicked violently at the square of fabric on the floor. "His handkerchief says otherwise."

"Nonsense," said Penelope stridently. "Anyone might have dropped that handkerchief. Anyone can see that."

"With his initials on it?"

Penelope set her arms akimbo. "If Captain Reid had meant to strike anyone, he would have done it fair and square, in the face, not snuck up on him and hit him over the back of the head."

"Fair and square at twenty paces?" said Pinchingdale nastily. "Didn't anyone here know? Reid and Lemmy were due to duel tomorrow morning."

The Resident looked up sharply. "Is this true?"

Penelope glowered at Pinchingdale. "They had words earlier today. But only words."

"A challenge," corrected Pinchingdale. "I was there."

"Over what?" asked the Resident, adding, slowly, "Reid has never struck me as a dueling sort of man."

Pinchingdale didn't say anything. He just looked pointedly at Penelope. He kept on looking at her until it was abundantly clear just what was meant.

The Resident pressed his eyes closed for a moment, looking very, very weary. He, too, had nearly thrown away everything for love, not so very long before.

Pinchingdale knew he had won his point. In a voice high with triumph, he said, "I was Lemmy's second. I was waiting for word from Reid's second. But the coward never sent one."

"Because there was no duel," Penelope said tightly.

"Because he intended to incapacitate Lemmy a different way!" shot back Pinchingdale.

"That is absurd," said Penelope coldly.

"Not absurd enough, I'm afraid," said the Resident wearily, looking down at Alex's handkerchief as though the weight of the world rested in its well-laundered folds. He looked to Pinchingdale. "Reid will be taken into custody as soon as he returns from wherever he may be."

"And tried for murder," insisted Pinchingdale.

"It does seem rather hard to be tried for murder when one hasn't murdered anyone," Charlotte contributed. "For it to be a murder, doesn't someone have to be dead?"

"Murder?" The portly Dr. Ure, who had just arrived, took a hasty step back, nearly overbalancing himself. Penelope was reminded of a child's toy, rocking back and forth on its rounded base.

"Just a flesh wound," said the Resident soothingly. "He seems to be unconscious. But alive," he added, with a pointed look at Pinchingdale.

The doctor knelt down beside Fiske's body and the men all clustered around. Penelope wondered how long the examination would keep them occupied. How long before someone came up with the clever idea of sending a search party out after Alex? Someone needed to get to him first.

"I believe I need to lie down," Penelope said loudly, making a show of tottering. She had never done it before, but after three Seasons in London, she had seen more than her fair share of faux swoons. She wafted her hands dramatically in the air. "All of this . . . so soon after Freddy . . ."

"Of course." The Resident was all solicitude, eager to get her out of the way so he could deal with the latest crisis.

Charlotte knew better. She tagged along after Penelope down

the hallway. "You're going after him, aren't you?" she said in a stage whisper.

Penelope cast her a look of extreme irritation. "Not so loud!" she hissed back. "And, yes. Someone needs to warn him."

"But what will you do?" asked Charlotte breathlessly.

"Find out who did it," said Penelope, with more confidence than she felt. "It will be easier done without Alex mewed in a cell somewhere."

"I think it would be his room, actually," said Charlotte apologetically. "House arrest."

"Dungeon, house." Penelope dismissed the difference with a flick of her wrist. "It all amounts to the same thing in the end. I won't have him hanged for something he didn't do."

"How do you know he didn't?"

"He just didn't!" Penelope snapped, driven past endurance. "He wouldn't."

She wouldn't have let that go for a minute, but Charlotte seemed to take that as a perfectly reasonable explanation. "What do you need me to do?"

Penelope frowned at her second-oldest friend, moved by a powerful mixture of shame and gratitude. Unworldly Charlotte might be, irritatingly optimistic, infuriatingly vague, but when it came down to it, she always came up trumps. It was both endearing and infuriating.

"I don't deserve you, do I?" Penelope said gruffly.

Charlotte beamed up at Penelope, her eyes suspiciously bright. "Will you need anything? Food? Supplies? Money?"

Penelope hastily turned away. This was no time for sentiment. Besides, she had no doubt that Charlotte would do something to irritate her in about five minutes and then they could be back to normal again.

"We shouldn't need food or supplies," said Penelope, ignoring the question of money. Freddy had been generous with his gifts, but stingy with providing funds. She had been well dressed and cash poor. "If this goes well, I expect to return in triumph, thumbing our noses at that vile toad of a Pinchingdale person. If it doesn't"—No. That wasn't to be thought of—"if it doesn't, I'll think of something."

"Good luck!" Charlotte flung herself at Penelope for a quick, fierce hug, from which Penelope emerged feeling as though she had just been strangled by a kitten.

"Thank you," said Penelope.

She needed all the luck she could get.

"The falcon has returned to the nest? What sort of absurd message is that?"

The unwitting object of Penelope's concern strode into a jewel box of a garden designed to look like something out of the pages of an illuminated manuscript. He raised an eyebrow at the man in the midst of it all, who was posing as though determined to be just as ornamental as his surroundings. Lanterns twinkled like stars, their pierced sides creating an elaborate filigree of light and shadows over the stone flagging of the courtyard.

The storybook illumination was only ruined by the grin threatening to break through the other man's deliberately serene countenance.

"It got your attention, didn't it?" said Tajalli, reclining comfortably on a pile of cushions arrayed beneath a canopy in one of the many courtyards that dotted his father's rambling city palace.

Beside him, a fountain tinkled gently, the constant flow of water creating a pleasant sense of coolness against the residual heat of the day. It also served the more practical purpose of muffling their conversation from any would-be eavesdroppers. It was an old trick, and one Alex had learned from Tajalli early on in their acquaintance.

So with assurance that his words would be heard by no one but the intended recipient, Alex said tartly, "Just what falcon might you be referring to?"

Tajalli smiled reassuringly and took a slurp of sherbet. "Not Jack."

Alex scowled, plopping down onto the cushions across from his friend. He didn't appreciate being quite that easy to read. "Who, then? Guignon? I knew about that already. Mah Laqa Bai told me he was back in town."

"But she won't have told you this." Abandoning his languid pose, Tajalli leaned forward. "He goes tonight to Raymond's Tomb to meet with the man who has been promising to all and sundry largesse from the treasure of Berar."

"You mean—"

Leaning back against his cushions, Tajalli smiled smugly. "Your Marigold."

"How do you know this?"

"How do you think?" Tajalli angled his head sideways, indicating his father's house. Of course, everything around them for an acre in either direction belonged to his father, so the gesture was purely a symbolic one, but Alex took the point.

"He won't like your telling me."

Tajalli gave him an impatient look. "He doesn't know I'm telling you."

Alex doubted that. There was very little that escaped Akbar Khan. The man had been at the game longer than any of them, including James. He was a master of court politics and all the darker arts that went with it.

"What time?" If Tajalli's father knew—as he must have known— that the information would be relayed by his scapegrace son, there was every reason to suppose that this might be a blind or, even worse, a trap. On the other hand, Tajalli wasn't his father's son for nothing. If the information had been acquired by more devious means, it could very well be an honest and valuable lead.

It was a gamble, like everything else in life, and one Alex couldn't afford not to take. Not with Wellesley's pet Cleave peering into dark corners and Jack in it all up to his stubborn neck and possibly beyond.

"Late. Midnight."

It would be. So much for sleep. Alex pushed aside thoughts of his putative dawn meeting with Lieutenant Sir Leamington Fiske. It wasn't the time for that now.

As if reading his thoughts, Tajalli said blandly, "I heard you just returned from Berar."

Alex was sure that hadn't been all he had heard. "I never made it all the way there. We had a casualty along the way."

"Ah, yes. The Special Envoy." Tajalli's father's spies had been busy. He made a lazy gesture that set the pearls on his wrist glimmering like condensed moonlight. "As I recall, he won't be any great loss. What did he do, fall off his horse again?"

"He was bitten by a snake." Alex suspected his friend knew that already. "Potentially one of the two-legged variety."

"Why?"

"I wish I knew."

There were too many suspects, too many possibilities, among them the most mundane of all, the possibility that the snake might have simply been a snake, acting of pure snakeish instinct.

Tajalli proffered a dish of sugared sweetmeats. "Someone might not have wanted him to reach Berar?"

Alex waved away the sweets. "Is that idle speculation, or do you know something?"

Tajalli dodged the question. "Me, idle?" he said laughingly.

He worked very hard to give the appearance of being so, but Alex knew few men quite so active, or quite so well informed. "Far less than you would have me believe. What do you know?"

Tajalli helped himself to one of the rejected sweets. "He had taken Nur Bai to his bed, hadn't he?"

Alex leaned forward, on the alert. "That much was common knowledge. Is she still working for Mir Alam?"

"Would she neglect a source of income?" Swallowing the last of the sweetmeat, he said more definitively, "Let's just say that it wasn't just your man's personal charms that enticed her to take up a position in his bed."

"Several positions from what I've heard," murmured Alex, his mind elsewhere. If Nur Bai was Mir Alam's creature, then the whole trip to Berar took on an entirely different complexion. It was a work of genius. No one would suspect a snakebite of being other than what it was, and even if they did, no one would think of holding the First Minister or the Nizam accountable for an event so far outside the capital. With the typical English disregard for the zenana, no one—short of James, whose own position was too precarious to force an inquiry—would make the connection between Lord Frederick's mistress, his death, and the First Minister.

Alex looked up at his friend, blinking at the swaying shadows as a chance breeze set the lanterns in motion. "But why would Mir Alam bother? Why Lord Frederick?"

"A blind?" Tajalli suggested sagely. "Something to distract your Residency while the Marigold does his work?"

"Hence the timing," said Alex slowly. "The meeting tonight, while the Resident is busy with the preparations for Lord Frederick's funeral."

Tajalli spread his hands. "Possibly. It is all merest speculation."

Levering himself up, Alex smiled wryly down at his friend. "Your 'possibly' makes a good deal more sense than any of my probablys."

"You won't stay?" Tajalli indicated the cushions. "There is some time left until midnight."

"Thank you, but no. I have other matters that need settling." The pesky matter of a duel to arrange. Some things, he didn't particularly feel like sharing, especially since he had a feeling that Tajalli's reaction would involve a certain amount of polite incredulity and impolite derision. His own reaction would have been the same had their positions been reversed. "Good night. And thank you for the . . . news."

The wind rocked the lantern forward, sending a pattern of shifting shadows across Tajalli's face. He looked, for a moment, like another person entirely, a stranger, and an alarming one.

"Think nothing of it," he said.

With one last nod, Alex saw himself out, leaving the perfumed perfection of the garden for the squalor of the streets beyond. The contrast never ceased to amaze him. From the street, the beauties cultivated so carefully within the walls of Tajalli's father's compound could only be guessed and wondered at; the high white walls formed a complete barrier between the pleasure gardens within and the thoroughfare without.

Bathsheba had been tended to and was wordlessly returned to him at the gates. Mounting, Alex made his way through the city, so familiar to him by now, all its twistings and turnings and scents and sounds, as much at night as by day. He had ridden this same route time and again before, visiting Tajalli or other friends for evening entertainments in the city, even though the city was technically banned by night to the denizens of the Residency, short of special permission to the Nizam.

It was all familiar, but tonight there seemed to be a shadow across the moon, something hanging in the air, lurking over him. Lord Frederick's death? Penelope? The prospect of a duel? Tajalli's so fortuitously supplied information?

He would have to make arrangements with Fiske before setting out for Raymond's Tomb. Alex heaved a heavy sigh. He hadn't the first idea what he was supposed to be doing; he had never put himself in a position to fight a duel before, or even to second one. It had always struck him as a profoundly silly and wasteful practice, the plaything of a leisured class with more time than sense. Honor was something one kept close by one's side, not a commodity to be bandied about on the point of a sword. At least, not until it became a matter of Penelope's honor rather than his.

He could send a message to Ollie Plowden over at the Subsidiary Force, he supposed, ask him to second him. Ollie would know what needed to be done, who was meant to be contacting whom.

It had been an impulse of the moment, that challenge, wrung out of him by the expression on Fiske's face as he regarded Penelope, looking at her in a way he had no right to look. All the frustration and anger Alex had felt, all the impotent rage at the shade of Freddy Staines and at the strange Fate that flung Penelope into his path only to dance her out of reach, had found a vent in that red-rimmed moment, when all the injustice of it all reduced itself to a contest of strength, sword to sword, like the trial of ordeal of old.

Too bad it wasn't really that simple. Once the moment had passed, it was impossible to delude himself that the world would right itself simply because he beat Lieutenant Sir Leamington Fiske at a contest of arms. Fiske would still go about spreading his poison about Penelope. And Penelope . . . Alex rubbed the back of his hand across his eyes, feeling the ache of an incipient headache. He had no idea what she would do.

She wouldn't fling herself into his arms and thank him for defending her honor, that much was for certain.

He had felt a momentary surge of hope at her obstinance in forbidding him to fight, but his irrational optimism had been forced to give way before the cold weight of reality. Just because she didn't want him on her conscience didn't mean she wanted him for anything else.

It was a grim thought. Alex grimaced to himself as he rode along the last stretch towards the Residency. The feeling of foreboding that had settled upon him as he left Tajalli's grew heavier. His father would claim it was the Sight, legacy of some witch back along the family line. Alex called it instinct, and instinct was warning him that something was decidedly wrong.

He checked his pace, feeling to make sure his pistol was by his side even as he leaned forward to scan the shadows along the road for followers.

He never expected the danger to come from ahead.

Before he had time to do more than feint for his weapon, a rough hand grabbed his stirrup and an imperious voice called, "Halt!"

Chapter Twenty-Nine

"What in the blazes?" Alex demanded. "Penelope?"

"Ouch," complained Penelope, shaking out her hand where he had kicked it. "A fine welcome for your official rescue party!"

"What do you expect when you leap out of nowhere and grab someone's foot?"

It was a fair point, but one Penelope didn't intend to acknowledge.

"Stop quibbling and listen," she ordered. "Someone struck Fiske in the head. Everyone thinks you did it. They plan to put you in custody and bring you to trial."

She congratulated herself on an intelligent and succinct rendering of a complicated situation. Alex stared at her as though she had grown a second head.

"Would you care to run through that again?" he said very carefully.

Penelope held up one finger. "Fiske—assaulted." A second finger. "Your handkerchief—next to him." A third. "You—blamed." She unfurled the rest of her fingers and waved them through the air in front of his horse's nose. "Clear enough?"

"As mud," said Alex blankly. "My handkerchief?"

"Next to the body—I mean, Fiske."

"But I wasn't there."

"I told them that."

"Someone assaulted Fiske," Alex repeated.

"Haven't we just been through that?" Penelope said impatiently. "His crony Pinchingdale is baying for your blood. He wants you arrested as soon as you set foot back through the gates of the Residency."

An expression of intense irritation passed across Alex's face. "Damn!" he cursed uninventively. "Of all the evenings . . ."

"Did you have other plans?" inquired Penelope caustically.

Sparring was easy. Sparring kept uncomfortable emotions at arm's length. Sparring kept all of Alex's attention focused on her.

Alex looked down at her, the branch of a tree casting a long shadow across one side of his face. It was a long way down from horseback to where she stood, one hand on his horse's bridle. Penelope was beginning to get a crick in her neck from looking up at him.

"I might as well tell you," he said after a very long moment. Good. If he hadn't, she was going to have had to beat it out of him, and that wouldn't be pleasant for either of them. "If my sources are correct, the Marigold intends to venture abroad tonight. To Raymond's Tomb."

"Unless Fiske was the Marigold," provided Penelope. "In which case, the Marigold won't be going anywhere. We'll soon find out."

"We?"

Penelope had already reached her decision. "Give me a hand up, won't you? It wouldn't do to be late."

Alex ignored her outstretched hand. He frowned down at her. "Penelope, if I'm under some sort of cloud back at the Residency, I can't just run away. And you can't help me run away. There's a word for that. Accomplice."

For a bright man, he could be terribly thick sometimes. It was all that honor; it clouded his thinking. "We aren't running away. We have an assignation to keep. At Raymond's Tomb. *Think*," she said impatiently. "If you can return with the Marigold's head on a platter, do you really think that anyone will have the nerve to blame you for Fiske? You'd be a hero. And have an alibi," she added, as an afterthought.

"And if Fiske was the Marigold?"

"Well, then, the Resident can't very well complain about your bashing his head in, can he? It would be practically an act of patriotism."

"Remind me to hire you as my advocate at trial," he said. "Fair enough. But there's no need for you to go with me. It's not too late for you to go back."

Penelope bared her teeth at him. "Trying to get rid of me, Captain Reid?"

"Never," he said quietly. "But I shouldn't like to see you hang either. Obstructing the King's justice is a dangerous business."

"Have you ever known me to shy away from danger?"

A slow, rueful smile spread across Alex's face as he looked down at her. Penelope felt an unaccustomed ache in her chest. It was a new and not entirely comfortable sensation. Charlotte would undoubtedly call it love. Penelope preferred to leave it nameless.

"No," he said. "Not even when you ought."

With that, he held out a hand to her.

Penelope looked at it and looked at him. He didn't offer any explanations, and she didn't demand them. If she did, he might change his mind. It never did do to look a gift horse in the mouth. And she wanted this, so very badly, one last adventure together, one more journey as partners, even if not quite such intimate partners as they had been before.

Taking his outstretched hand, Penelope clambered up behind him, wrapping her arms around his waist as he slid forward in the saddle to make room for her behind.

Penelope couldn't remember ever riding pillion before. She squirmed, trying to find a more comfortable spot. There wasn't one. Her one consolation was that it was almost undoubtedly as uncomfortable for him as it was for her. On the other hand, he at least got the satisfaction of being able to handle the reins. Not to mention that his view included more than an expanse of someone else's back.

It was an odd feeling, being so entirely reliant on another person, a body's breadth away from the reins, blinded by his back, forced to trust his judgment and skill to lead them safely forward. She had never allowed anyone else to take the reins for her before, even when Freddy protested that he should bloody well be able to drive his own phaeton.

Penelope resisted the urge to poke him in the back and demand that they switch places. He knew where they were going and she didn't. And, when it came down to it, it was Alex. He wasn't going to take it into his head to leap them over a fence just for the fun of it and send her toppling off backwards or ride off on a tangent just because the mood took him. Penelope gritted her teeth, swallowed her protests, and linked her arms around Alex's waist, feeling the muscles move beneath his jacket as he leaned forward to urge his mount into motion.

Denied the distraction of sight, Penelope's other senses seemed sharper than usual. Every movement was magnified by proximity as Alex gently urged Bathsheba from a walk into a trot, forcing Penelope to tighten her hold on his waist, her skirt ruched up around her thighs, the angle of her legs mimicking his as she pressed close for balance, missing stirrup and reins.

She could smell the shaving soap Alex used and the slight tang of perspiration, redolent with memory. He smelled a good deal cleaner than he had after three days on the road, but still smelled like himself. He smelled like he had that first afternoon in the lee of the abandoned shrine, or that last morning, before they found Freddy, or any number of afternoons, mornings, or evenings, hands, lips, eyes, arms.

It was a strange thing, desire. Strange to ride behind someone in silence on a grim and deadly errand, and be rendered weak by a whiff of soap; strange to retain the memory of touch, so strong that even such impersonal and enforced contact could bring back a shiver of anticipation, as though the foolish flesh still anticipated treats the conscious mind had already deemed unwise. Penelope didn't care whether it was wise or not; she still wanted him, despite Berar, despite Freddy, despite knowing that in the eyes of the world her widowhood was meant to have rendered her as stiff as stone in continual contemplation of the memory of the man who had been legally licensed to share her bed. Not that Freddy would have denied himself any of the usual pleasures had the situation been reversed. But she doubted anyone else would see it that way. Including Alex.

Penelope leaned her cheek against his back, feeling the scrape of his wool jacket against her skin. There was no mistaking the way his muscles tensed every time she adjusted her position.

She could make Alex desire her, she knew that. She certainly had enough experience in that department. But desire was no substitute for what she really wanted. It was no substitute for affection.

Once, she had believed it might be, that it was the closest she might come, but she knew better now.

Not that the knowing helped. It just made it worse. At least one could manufacture lust; it was a simple enough formula. Some organs were more susceptible to manipulation than others. Unfortunately, the heart did not fall into that category. Penelope's usual weapons dangled blunted from her hands, an entire arsenal of tricks without a single one to accomplish the thing she wanted. It made her feel itchy and restless and irritable, a thousand times worse than being denied the reins.

At least Alex seemed equally restless. She could feel him gearing up to speak long before he did, with that uncanny knowledge provided of being pressed chest to back, with every breath and movement common property.

Well, there was something about a long ride in the dark that prompted reflection. They had a good deal of unfinished business left after their encounter that afternoon. Penelope held herself alert, waiting to hear what it was that Alex had to say.

At long last, he came out with, "I wonder who attacked Fiske."

So much for grand declarations of thwarted desire.

"It could be anyone," said Penelope nastily. "Someone he cheated at cards, a servant he kicked, a woman he propositioned. He wasn't exactly the sort to accumulate friends."

"But why would any of those people leave my handkerchief next to him?"

That was what had been bothering him for the past mile?

"Maybe they didn't like you either," suggested Penelope. "Oh, I don't know. Maybe you dropped it there yourself days ago and it was pure happenstance. Maybe you loaned it to someone and he dropped it. You loaned one to me at one point."

"Are you saying that you hit Fiske and tried to frame me?"

"If I had, would I tell you?"

He was smiling. She couldn't see his face, but she knew it all the same. "Probably. Just to rub it in." His tone turning serious again, he added, "There are too many potential wrongdoers roaming about. It *could* be nearly anyone. If Fiske weren't the Marigold, but knew who the Marigold was . . ."

"Your brother," Penelope said. From the way his muscles tensed, she could tell her guess had hit home. It was better than a truth serum, sitting as they were. "That's what you're afraid of, isn't it? That it's Jack."

She expected Alex to try to deny it, to leap to defend his brother as he had with Cleave. Instead, he said, in a voice so low she could hardly hear it, "It is a possibility."

The depth of the potential betrayal shook Penelope all the way to her cynical core. It was one thing if this Jack wanted to go about working for the French or whoever it was he was supposed to be serving, but quite another to stab back at the brother who had defended him, protected him, and shielded him at the cost of his own career and reputation. The brother who, contrary to all common sense, loved him.

If she ever met this Jack, he had better watch out.

"No," Penelope said abruptly, so abruptly that the horse's gait faltered before falling back into rhythm. "No. It isn't your Jack."

Alex's shoulders hunched forward. "I wish it were that easy. There's no getting around it. My brother is neck deep in treason. All I can hope is that he had nothing to do with this particular piece of treason. But there isn't much hope for it. And we'll all go down with him."

"Don't be absurd," said Penelope bracingly. "No one can hold you accountable for your brother's treasons."

"Can't they?" Alex said wearily.

If her arms hadn't already been around him, Penelope would have put them there, to comfort him. Not that she had much experience in the comforting department, but she felt an inexplicable need to try. She could hear the Dowager Duchess of Dovedale in the back of her head, hooting at her for going soft. Well, what if she had? It mightn't be so awful to care more for someone else than for herself for a change.

Alex said, with difficulty, "If matters had been different—"

"What?" prompted Penelope, sitting up straighter behind him. "What?"

Whatever it was, it was too late. Alex shook his head, staring off over Bathsheba's neck, off towards the horizon where Raymond's obelisk could already be seen, glowing palely in the moonlight.

"Never mind." With false brightness he said, "It won't be long now. A few more minutes and we'll be there."

If matters had been different *what?*

"We'll see this thing through, one way or another," he added, and Penelope had the feeling that he was speaking to himself rather than her.

Through with Jack, or through with her?

They rode in silence for the last stretch up the hill, each occupied with his own thoughts. As they drew level with the temple, Penelope noticed a strange light spreading across the ground. It was coming from above, from the moon, or even from a lantern held at normal lantern level. The light came from below, as well, from the floor of the temple where one of the stone slabs appeared to have pulled away, leaving a well-lit cavity below.

Poking Alex in the arm, Penelope pointed. Alex nodded. Penelope's eyes met his and she knew he had reached the same conclusion. That was how his brother had so expeditiously disappeared that day when they were chasing him. The whole time they had stood on the hill, pacing back and forth and scanning the horizon for traces of him, he had been cached away just below.

Penelope's jaw clenched. If Wellesley didn't flay Alex's little brother, she might just do it for him.

"Down?" mouthed Penelope, pointing at the hatch.

It was quite a sophisticated little hidey-hole. Rather than a simple ladder, stone stairs jutted downwards, roughly hewn, but sturdy for all that.

Putting up a hand to counsel caution, Alex dropped to his belly, pulling himself forward against the stone of the temple floor. Following his example, Penelope did likewise. Propelling oneself by one's elbows was harder than it looked. Her muscles ached as Penelope dragged herself painstakingly forward, wincing every time the material of her dress rasped against the stone flags.

After what seemed an age, she drew abreast with Alex, and peered over the edge of the cavity, down the stone steps. Something glittered darkly at the bottom, like the carapace of a bug. Shiny. Metallic. It took Penelope a moment to realize that it was guns. Pile upon pile upon pile of guns. All the guns the Nizam had been promised. The guns she had accused Alex of stealing. The guns that the commander of the Subsidiary Force swore he had purchased, but had never arrived. Guns enough to arm a rebellion.

Among the jumbled piles of weaponry stood a man. He stooped over to inspect the pile nearest him, unwittingly leaving his back unguarded. Whoever he was, it was clear that his usual role must not be a particularly martial one. His shoulders angled forward in the habitual slouch that came of too many hours at a desk. His head was uncovered, his hat in his hand, a nicety usually wasted on criminal dens, but habitual to him.

Penelope, who had thought she had seen all there was to see, forgot herself so far as to gape in frank astonishment. She forgot that she was lying on her stomach. She barely registered Alex's bug-eyed confusion. She simply stared, mouth open, unable to comprehend what she was seeing.

The man didn't need to turn around for Penelope to know him, but turn around he did. He seemed as nonplussed at the sight of them as they were by him.

"Alex?" the man gasped.

To which Alex mustered an incredulous *"Cleave?"*

Chapter Thirty

"What?" demanded Penelope, but no one paid any attention.

Alex swung to his feet.

"Cleave?" he repeated incredulously, staring down through the hole at an angle that gave Penelope a pain in her neck just watching it. "What are you doing here?"

Without a word to her, he started off down the stairs, leaving Penelope standing there, behind. Rolling her eyes at his back, Penelope scrambled after him, looping the skirt of her riding habit over one arm to get it out of the way. In the other hand, she had firm hold of her pistol. Alex might be willing to go clambering down barehanded into a potential den of thieves, but she wasn't that trusting. Or that naïve.

But the man at the bottom of the stairs didn't make any move for a weapon. It was Daniel Cleave, standing beside a lantern balanced on a packing crate. Rather than a hardened criminal, he looked like a fifth former caught smuggling sweets from the headmaster's study. He looked quite as startled to see Alex as Alex had been to see him.

There was no one else in the long, low room.

"Alex?" he echoed, although Penelope would have thought that they had more than adequately established who everyone was. The two men had only known each for twenty-odd years, after all. "I thought you were in custody."

"I would have been. Had I made it back to the Residency." Alex's face was completely unreadable in the uneven lamplight.

Taking a step back, Cleave gestured ineffectually around the piles of munitions that filled the long, rectangular chamber. "Quite a sight, this."

"Indeed," contributed Penelope.

Cleave's gaze darted in her direction. "Lady Frederick?"

Oh no. They weren't starting all that again. With an impatient gesture, Penelope said, "I know who you are and you know who he is, but what in the devil"—it felt good to curse, so she decided to repeat it—"what in the devil is all this?"

Cleave looked at her with shocked rabbit eyes. Treachery was one thing, profanity quite another.

"These are guns," Alex said softly. "Guns that were meant to be delivered to the Nizam. Aren't they, Daniel?"

"Wellesley will be pleased at this, at least." Cleave rubbed a hand across his forehead as though it pained him. "The missing guns could have been something of a bother diplomatically."

"More than a bother if they fell into the wrong hands," said Alex thoughtfully. "How did you know to find them here?"

"A tip," said Cleave vaguely, before Alex's meaning caught up with him. "You can't think—you don't think . . ."

"I don't know what to think," said Alex frankly. "I heard the Marigold was meeting here tonight with a local contact."

"So did I. What are you doing here?" challenged his old schoolmate. "Did Jack—"

"No."

"Dash it all, Alex—," began Cleave, and then blushed as he remembered Penelope's presence.

"Don't mind me," said Penelope with a wave of one hand. "I'll just amuse myself playing with the weaponry."

Alex's lip curled.

Cleave looked alarmed.

"They, er, they might be loaded," he said hesitantly. "Not that I would know. I just got here, you see."

A man could stutter and stutter and still be a villain. He could blush at a curse and still be a traitor. But was Daniel Cleave? He did seem to be exuding guilt the way a rose did fragrance, but he always exuded guilt, as though he felt it necessary to apologize to the world for his very existence.

"I received some intelligence," he said, with more confidence this time, raising his head to look Alex in the eye. "I heard a report that Jack—"

Alex made a swift, instinctive move of negation.

Cleave winced, but he refused to back down. "It's no use, Alex," he said apologetically. "You can't go on protecting Jack from the consequences of his own actions. I can make sure that you're not implicated, but . . ."

"How do you know I'm not?" said Alex tautly. "You can't have a rotten apple without tainting the whole bushel."

"Oh, for heaven's sake," said Penelope crossly. "Yes, you can. None of us are responsible for our family members."

Alex looked at her sideways. "Or spouses?" he said softly, so softly that Cleave didn't even hear it.

"Whatever the case, you're about as likely to commit treason as . . . as Queen Charlotte," Penelope blustered.

Alex raised an eyebrow. *"Queen Charlotte?"*

"Little. Royal. German," said Penelope. "I'm sure you've heard of her."

"Well said, Lady Frederick," said Cleave heartily, tugging at his cravat with nervous fingers. "And now I suggest that we report back to the Residency. This is no place for a lady."

Penelope folded her arms across her chest. "Then it's a good thing I'm not much of a lady, isn't it?"

"Even so," said Alex.

Even so? What sort of a phrase was "even so"? The sort of phrase that said absolutely nothing, that was what it was.

Alex compounded his foolishness by adding, "Cleave can show you back. I'll wait here."

Penelope didn't budge. "And leave you to the mercies of goodness only knows how many French spies? I think not."

"They're named after flowers. How frightening can they be?"

"Very," interjected Cleave, but no one paid the least bit of attention to him.

"If you face them, I face them," said Penelope, knowing she was talking about far more than French spies. "Mr. Cleave can go."

"And leave you unchaperoned?" Earnestly, Mr. Cleave said, "No, I couldn't do that. I'll stay, Lady Frederick. Reid can escort you back."

"I'm a widow. I don't need chaperonage," snapped Penelope. "And I fail to see why I should be any safer from Captain Reid's advances on a dark road than I would be in this room. Unless you intend to suggest that there are hitherto unrecognized amorous properties to the presence of large quantities of gunpowder?"

"I didn't mean—," Mr. Cleave began, but whatever he had meant or hadn't meant was lost in the horrifying sound of footfalls overhead.

Without saying a word, Alex grabbed Penelope by the arm and hauled her back into the lee of the stairs. It was really quite impressive. One moment she was standing at the foot of the stairs, the next she was jammed against Alex's side in an impromptu alcove created by a keg of musket balls on one side and the stone side of the stairs on the other.

Cleave made a move to extinguish the lantern, but he was too slow. A pair of scuffed boots appeared on the stairs. They seemed too small to support the girth of the man who followed them. It was a belly that wobbled its way down into view, a massive belly, buttoned into, but not contained by, a blue wool coat with tarnished brass buttons. The coat might once have been of some military order, but now was barely clinging to its usefulness. Beneath the straining wool, the man's legs looked absurdly skinny, rather like a chicken's, if chickens wore boots.

The rest of him did little to counter that impression. An impressive wattle fell over his neck cloth, the fifth of several chins, and the remaining reddish hair on his head had been combed straight up in a futile attempt to disguise its thinning, like the crest of a rooster.

"Guignon," Alex mouthed, his face so close to hers that Penelope could feel his breath on her lips.

Penelope inclined her head to show that she had understood,

angling her face away in a desperate bid at self-preservation. She was sure the signs of heightened awareness must be written all over her face, in the color in her cheeks, the quickening of her breath, the odd tingling of her lips, as though that accidental exhalation had been the prelude to a kiss. She had kissed him too many times in the past. She knew exactly how it felt and her treacherous body was intent on reminding her. Penelope found herself painfully aware of Alex's arm clamped tightly around her waist. Admittedly, his arm was only there as a means of keeping her pressed back out of sight, but her body wasn't interested in insignificant details. It just registered arm. Alex's arm.

What was it that Charlotte had said? That she could never do anything in the normal course? Naturally. That would be why her body decided that being cornered by a French spy—a French spy who could probably squish them both in one go just by sitting on them—was an excellent time to contemplate a little bit of light dalliance.

The Frenchman clumped his way down to the bottom of the flight. Spotting Cleave, he raised a hand in a genial greeting. "Ah, you are here. Good. I hate the waiting, me."

Next to her, Penelope could feel Alex stiffen into complete immobility as his eyes narrowed on his old schoolfellow.

Cleave's eyes slid sideways towards the corner in which Penelope and Alex were hiding. "I think we should go upstairs. The air in here. Close, you know." Cleave tugged at his collar in illustration. He did, indeed, seem to be feeling the heat.

"You do not want to check the inventory?" Guignon lumbered down the last few steps. His belly wobbled like a bowl of blanc mange as he indulged in a hearty chuckle. "I should not be so trusting, me."

Sound sense on the Frenchman's part, thought Penelope. Trusting often got one in trouble, as she could tell from the stunned expression on Alex's face as he stared at his childhood playmate. Bewilderment warred with disbelief on Alex's countenance as Guignon dealt Cleave a hearty slap on the back that sent the younger man staggering forward. Penelope found herself wanting to squeeze his hand, to touch his cheek, to offer some small gesture of comfort, whatever it might be. She wanted to wrap her arms around him and drag his head down into the crook of her shoulder and promise him that at least she was always what she was, no matter how the rest of the world dissembled and betrayed him. But she couldn't. They were mewed in their corner like mice in a hole. Any movement might be fatal.

There was still always the chance that Cleave was what he claimed; that it was Guignon he had lured to the cavern under false pretenses; that he had lied to the Frenchman, and not to them. Penelope found herself hoping, for Alex's sake, that it would be so.

Lord, she must be going soft in her old age. Much more of this and she'd find herself thinking like Charlotte, all hearts and stars and fluffy bunnies.

"It all seems to be accounted for," said Cleave stiffly, making a doomed attempt to herd the Frenchman back towards the stairs. "As you promised."

Guignon bumped Cleave out of the way with one casual wiggle, making an expansive gesture that encompassed the pile upon pile upon pile of munitions stacked against the stone walls. "An impressive sight, *non*? Musket, powder . . . *Par dieu!* Who are they?"

"No one," Cleave said hastily. "No one at all."

Penelope did her best to look like a musket. Alex seemed to be doing a bit better with his stone pillar impression, but it was still not enough.

"You cannot fool me so easily," said Guignon. "*That*"—he nodded to Alex—"is not a keg of powder. And *that*"—his gaze traveled appreciatively over Penelope—"is most certainly not—"

Penelope rose smoothly to her feet. "A loaded gun?" she said sweetly, training hers on his midsection. It was the largest target in the room, after all. As an extra precaution, she added chillingly, "All of the others are empty. I can shoot you long before you load."

Guignon appeared to take her threat at face value, which was a very good thing, since Penelope wasn't at all sure whether any of the muskets, rifles, and assorted instruments of destruction were loaded or not. Instead of reaching for the nearest firearm, he turned to Cleave, with a look that would have turned Medusa herself to stone.

With great dignity, he looked the other man in the eye, and pronounced, "You have betrayed me, Monsieur."

Cleave opened his mouth in an immediate negation—and snapped it shut again as Alex stepped forward, his gaze as hard as Guignon's. Harder, even.

"You've betrayed one of us," Alex said. He said it in a conversational tone, but Penelope could hear the rough edge beneath. They had grown up together, she remembered. Played together. Studied together. He held tightly to his loyalties, as did Alex, and every betrayal was like a little fall of man. "Which one is it, Daniel?"

Cleave looked from one to the other, from Guignon's threatening bulk to Penelope's pistol and back again. "I didn't—I mean—dash it, Alex! I had to. I had no choice."

His voice was low and pleading. From the corner of her eye, Penelope could see Alex wince, as though pierced by a sudden, acute pain. And then it was gone and his face was under control again, but for a certain bitterness around the lips that hadn't been there before.

"Had to?" Alex repeated. Shrugging, Guignon seated himself heavily on the bottom step, removed a squashed pastry from his waistcoat pocket, and proceeded to rip off a hearty bite. "Had to do *what*?"

Cleave looked away. Penelope could see his Adam's apple bobbing up over the edge of his cravat as he swallowed hard. "This," he said in a low voice. "These."

"You," said Alex, in a hard voice. "You were the Marigold."

"There is no 'were' about it," contributed Guignon, spitting puff pastry as he spoke. With his accent thickened by a mouthful of doughy treat, it came out more as *dere eez noo werr*. "M. Cleave *is* the Marigold."

"And the attack on Fiske?" demanded Alex, his eyes never leaving his old friend. "That was you?"

Cleave's head moved in a barely perceptible nod.

"My handkerchief?"

Cleave pressed the back of his hand to his lips. "It was the handkerchief gave me the idea," he said, in a barely audible voice. "I had one among my things. Kat"—he faltered on the name of Alex's sister before pulling himself together—"Kat had given it to me. She said she had made you too many anyway. Not that it would have been hard to take one from you. I had—have—a man in your household. I would never have let them hang you," he added desperately. "You have to believe that. It was just until—just until this was all over. And then I would have done everything I could for you, I promise."

"Forgive me if your promises carry little weight at the moment," said Alex dryly, and Cleave turned a deep, unbecoming red.

Penelope heard her own voice, as though from very far away. "You planted that cobra in my room, didn't you?"

"I didn't mean—" Cleave took a stumbling step back in reflex as Alex tensed like a spring waiting to uncoil.

"You left a cobra in Lady Frederick's room," said Alex, in a voice so low and deadly that even Penelope shivered at it.

"Not me," said Cleave hastily. "Mehdi Yar. The groom. He did it. And it was never meant for you," he added, turning anxiously towards Penelope. "It was meant for Lord Frederick. It never occurred to me that—"

"We might share a bed?" Penelope said dulcetly.

Cleave blushed.

Penelope drew in a shuddering breath as a host of seemingly unrelated incidents tumbled into place. "And when that didn't work," she said, watching him closely, "you tried again. On the road to Berar. You knew no one would connect you with it, because you weren't there. That was the groom again, wasn't it?"

Cleave nodded.

"You planted him in our household in Calcutta," recalled Penelope. "Even then you were planning this. But why? Why kill Freddy?"

"I didn't really *want* to kill him," said Cleave hopefully.

"Fine way you have of showing it," said Alex, and Penelope knew that he was remembering, as she was, a certain cut girth.

Cleave swallowed hard. "It was Fiske, you see. He said he'd told Staines. No one would have believed Fiske, miserable little opium eater that he was, but Staines? He was the son of an earl. Who wouldn't believe him over me?"

"Believe what?" Alex's voice was like granite.

Penelope was beginning to feel slightly sick to her stomach. She couldn't have said quite why. It might have been the way Guignon was enthusiastically reducing his pastry to pulp. Or it might have been the half-eager, half-sheepish expression on Cleave's face as he tried to explain why he had systematically set out to murder her husband. The incongruous boyishness of it made Penelope's stomach turn.

"He had found out about—well, that I—you know."

"No," said Alex in a deadly tone, "I don't know. Would you care to enlighten us?"

"That I was selling secrets," Cleave blurted out. "Nothing dangerous," he added defensively. "Just little things that wouldn't hurt anyone."

The Frenchman snorted.

Penelope entirely concurred.

"Little things," repeated Alex flatly.

"What else was I to do?" demanded Cleave shrilly. "You know what the East India Company's idea of pay is like."

"The rest of us manage somehow. Without resorting to treason." Alex's voice was drier than dust.

Cleave bristled. "You don't know what it is to have a sick mother to support."

"No, only four siblings," murmured Alex, but Cleave didn't seem to hear him.

"Her medicines are so dear. And the doctor's visits and the carriage—she can't be expected to walk—and the paid companion. It just goes on and on and all of it costs money. Money! Do you know how much my father left me? Nothing. Just his sword and his name—and only one of those was salable," he added bitterly. "He died a hero's death, fighting for the Company, and what did the Company ever give us in return?"

"A job," said Alex softly. "A livelihood."

Cleave laughed bitterly, his pleasant features twisted. "Some livelihood. India broke my mother's health and took my father's life. I was owed something. *She* was owed something."

"So you decided to take it," prompted Alex.

In the corner, the Frenchman's jaws opened in an earsplitting yawn. True confessions were evidently not his idea of entertainment.

"Fiske saw me." Cleave looked anxiously from side to side as though expecting to find Fiske there, watching. "He saw me passing information to Wrothan, damn him. He started demanding payment in return for silence. Just little amounts at first, but it added up over time. I'd meant to get out, to stop doing it, but I had to get in deeper, just to keep making Fiske's payments. And then—" He drew a shuddering breath. "Then they told me about the treasure of Berar. I had my way out. If I could only get my hands on the treasure, I would be free."

"And the little matter of the planned rebellion?"

Cleave seemed to have forgotten the Frenchman's presence. He spoke only to Alex, his mild face more animated than Penelope had ever seen it. "That was the genius of it! It never had to happen. Without the gold, the princes would never rise. And I—I would have the gold. I was even going to give the bulk of it over to the government and claim I'd found it," he added with pathetic eagerness. "I would have been rewarded—a hero! Don't you see? All I have to do is get my hands on the gold and it will all come about."

Guignon looked up from trimming his fingernails with a pastry knife. "There is no gold."

"Jewels, then. Treasure. What does it matter? It's all the same thing."

Simply, as though to a very slow student, Guignon said, "There is no treasure."

Cleave's face was a study in incomprehension. "No—what?"

"No treasure," repeated Guignon, without the slightest bit of hesitation. "There never was any." He gave a Gallic shrug. "Oh, there might well be a lost treasure of Berar, but we never had it. It was just a carrot, to dangle before the princes, like mules, you see? The mule trots faster for the promise of reward."

Cleave's face drained of all color. He swayed slightly, catching on to the back of a packing crate to steady himself. "You mean it was all for nothing. All of it. Nothing."

"Not nothing," said Guignon genially. "It was all for a very good cause."

His words brought back the memory of a piece of paper found lying on the pavement above, a paper that Cleave must have crafted in his persona as Marigold. The French had been poor, but the revolutionary rhetoric had been remarkably fluent.

"'And the tree of Liberty shall blossom again in the courtyards of the East,'" Penelope quoted softly.

"Precisely," said Guignon, with great satisfaction. "What is a little lie to a grand end?"

In substance, it wasn't all that different from the rationalization for his own actions Cleave had expressed only moments before. But something pushed him over the edge. It might have been his own words quoted back at him. It might have been the Frenchman's air of smug superiority. It might have been the brioche crumbs that landed square in one eye. Whatever it was, Cleave snapped.

"You thrice-damned, frog-eating bastard!" he breathed out through his teeth, and snatched up one of the muskets, barrel first.

A look of mild apprehension appeared on Guignon's epicene face, but before it could ripple down his layers of fat into movement, it was too late. Cleave swung the musket like a mallet.

The stock connected with Guignon's head with a sickening crunch that made Penelope jump back a step. Penelope went careening into Alex, who was attempting to make a grab for Cleave. Alex staggered sideways as Penelope stumbled against him, putting out a hand to keep them both from falling together off an inconveniently placed keg of ammunition. The rim of the keg hit Penelope in the waist with sickening force.

Dizzy, Penelope clutched at the side of the tub, feeling her gorge rise as the series of strange sounds in the background crystallized into meaning. Guignon was on the ground, but Cleave's arms still rose and fell, the blood-stained stock of the musket rising and falling with them, spattering flecks of blood as he panted, "Bastard, bastard, bastard!"

Alex grabbed at him from behind, catching the other man's arms high over head as Cleave struggled to be let free, panting and sobbing and babbling words that Penelope could hardly hear over the ringing of her ears and the labored sound of Alex's breathing as he fought to hold Cleave steady.

With the strength of the mad, Cleave wrenched free, turning on his old friend with a frenzied look in his eye. The musket lifted.

The sound of a shot reverberated through the room.

Chapter Thirty-One

T he shot had not come from Cleave's musket.

Cleave's bloody musket tumbled harmlessly to the ground, as they all stared in confusion at one another. Penelope glanced down at her own pistol, still in her hand, still cool.

As the sound of the report died away, one booted foot stepped down onto the top stair. It was a well-used boot, scuffed along the sides, and it posed—there was really no other word for it—on the stair as though its owner were well aware of the effect it would have.

From where she stood, Penelope could only see the side of the stairs, but Alex had a clear view upwards, and she could see his face change as the newcomer descended, step by well-calculated step. Unlike Guignon, this man's frame was athletic, with the well-developed leg muscles of a man who spends a great deal of time in the saddle. His coat fell carelessly open over a travel-stained linen shirt.

He held a smoking pistol in one hand.

"That's a hell of a way to say hello," said Alex.

Visible nearly up to his neck, the other man tucked the spent pistol carelessly away in his belt.

"You looked like you needed the help," he said, and came fully into Penelope's view.

His reddish brown hair had been tousled into a careless style reminiscent of the current London mode, but Penelope would have been willing to wager it was less by design and more by exertion. He had high, clean-cut cheekbones, a square chin, and a quirk in one brow that looked as though it were habitual.

Penelope knew exactly where she had seen him before. It had been in the marketplace in Hyderabad, smiling a rogue's grin as he tossed his *biryani* to a beggar and sent them on a fool's chase all the way to Raymond's Tomb.

"I had hoped *not* to see you here," said Alex pointedly.

"Warmest greetings to you, too, brother," said Jack Reid.

He paused on the second-to-last step to survey the field below, grimacing as he looked down over the piles of munitions to the bloody mess that had once been Louis Guignon.

Jack made a clicking noise with his tongue. "Messy, Daniel, messy," he said reprovingly. "I can't leave you alone for a moment, can I?"

Against her better instincts, Penelope followed his gaze. There wasn't much left of Louis Guignon, at least, not of his face. Cleave had done a very thorough job with the butt of the musket.

Cleave took a stumbling step backwards, staring in horror at his handiwork.

"I didn't," he babbled. "I didn't mean—"

"I doubt your intent means much to Guignon at this juncture," said Jack, gracefully descending the stairs. "But I owe you a debt of gratitude, for all that. Major Guignon's presence would have been a decided nuisance at this juncture." He surveyed the gruesome scene with a critical eye. "Better you than me."

Cleave backed away. "I didn't mean—"

"Yes, we heard that already." Jack looked quizzically at Penelope. "And this is?"

Alex didn't waste time with introductions. His face was bleak as he looked at his brother, so full of naked pain that it hurt Penelope to look at it. "So you are involved in this."

Jack's smile was a masterpiece of mockery. Despite herself, Penelope couldn't help but feel a certain kinship for Alex's black sheep brother. She had smiled that way often enough herself. "Didn't Daniel tell you? No? I thought not. We are colleagues, Daniel and I. Traitors in arms, as it were. Aren't we, Daniel?"

Cleave's sudden pallor provided all the answer they needed.

Contempt etched across Alex's face like acid as he turned to Cleave.

"And yet you condemned Jack for it. You would have thrown him to the noose to save yourself."

"That was different," stuttered Cleave, with a fluttery movement of his hands. "He actually believes in all this! I was only in it—"

"For the money," Jack filled in genially. "As it happens, so am I. But you are right. There is a difference. You see"—he paused, waiting until he was sure all their attention was upon him—"I am not being paid by the same people who are paying you."

With a quirk of the eyebrows, he leaned back against the wall, patiently allowing them time to puzzle it out. Cleave stared at him, open-mouthed. Alex's face was a study of wonder and relief.

"You aren't working for the French," said Penelope flatly, since no one else seemed capable of doing it.

"Brilliantly well spotted," drawled Jack. Penelope felt some of her sympathy for him begin to evaporate.

"Who?" Alex asked hoarsely. "Who are you working for?"

"I can't name names of course. Not with him here." Jack smiled genially at Daniel Cleave, who seemed to be intent on climbing backwards into a packing crate. "We wouldn't want the information getting into the wrong hands now, would we?"

"I knew you couldn't," Alex said roughly. "Not treason."

Jack raised an eyebrow. "Don't go all sentimental on me, brother mine. Your side pays better than the other."

"You lied to me," said Cleave blankly.

"Don't feel so special," said Jack airily. "I lie to everyone. And a good thing, too, or my presumed allies would have my guts for tiffin."

"Not just your allies," said his brother darkly. "Does Father know about this?"

"I see no reason he should," said Jack coolly. "I wouldn't have told you if you hadn't made such a bloody nuisance of yourself."

"A nuisance." Alex appeared to be having trouble getting the words out of his mouth. "*I* am the nuisance."

"You have a remarkable facility for getting in the way."

"I was trying to save your reputation," said Alex through gritted teeth.

"My reputation, as you care to call it," replied Jack, "is all that keeps me alive in this snake pit I've tumbled into."

"Then climb out of it," said Alex harshly. "No one asked you to play with snakes."

"Didn't they? Not everyone can walk the straight and narrow, *cher frere*. Especially when they're not allowed onto the path."

"Touching," said Penelope rudely. She was still smarting from that "well spotted." Not to mention that the man had no business beating up on Alex, who had been jumping through hoops of fire on his ungrateful behalf. "You poor, deprived man. You only have a brother willing to sacrifice his own future to save your sorry hide. My heart bleeds for you."

"Brilliant," said Jack, with a clipped diction that was painfully reminiscent of his brother's. "Just what was needed. A Greek chorus. Or are you meant to be posing as my conscience?"

Penelope looked Alex's brother straight in the eye. "I never take on thankless jobs."

"Then why are you here?"

Before Penelope could answer, Alex interjected, in a very tired voice, "What was meant to happen here tonight, Jack?"

"If you hadn't interfered, you mean?" Having gotten his little dig in, Jack went smoothly on. "There are plans afoot for coordinated risings across India. I, as you can imagine, am but a very small cog in this large wheel. Guignon, known in the business as the Gulmohar—"

"A flower," Alex explained, for Penelope's benefit.

Penelope found herself leaning towards that small attention like a flower towards the sun and abruptly made herself look away.

The little byplay was not wasted on Alex's odious brother, who looked very pointedly from one to the other before resuming.

"As I was saying," Jack continued coolly, "Guignon was responsible for Hyderabad. The munitions stored here were to be used for a local rising against the English, with the connivance of several of the leading members of the durbar. As you might imagine, I have quite an interesting little list of names in my possession."

"Including mine?" said Cleave dully.

Jack bared his teeth in a grin. "Your name is on a different list." Turning to his brother, he elucidated. "Our Marigold over here was meant to coordinate between the various sectors, pushing some forward, urging patience on others, promising bribes all around. How does it feel, Daniel, old boy, to have been the pin in the grenade that could have set all India aflame?"

"I wouldn't have done it," said Cleave defensively. "It wouldn't have happened without the gold. And I would have given the gold to the Governor General. So it would all have come out right in the end."

"You just keep telling yourself that," said Jack soothingly. "I'm sure it makes a lovely bedtime story. Puts you straight to sleep at night, doesn't it?"

"It's all true!" Cleave insisted. "Without the gold—"

He broke off as the hideous reality of it all assailed him.

"They would have risen on the mere promise of gold," said Jack softly. "Just as you did. A token here, a token there. That was all that it took. For them as for you. Pity for Guignon that he had to be the one to break it to you."

Cleave swallowed hard, his eyes snaking over towards the two kegs that mercifully concealed Guignon's fallen form from view. "I killed him. I—I've never killed anyone before. But I killed him."

"Never killed anyone before?" asked Jack with all the exasperation of a professional dealing with an untalented amateur. "What did you think happened when you passed on those coded messages? Tea parties?"

"That was . . . different."

Jack's lip curled. He regarded Cleave with undisguised contempt. "Just because you didn't spatter their brains yourself?"

Cleave went an unpleasant shade of green, swaying slightly where he stood. Penelope could almost bring herself to feel sorry for him.

Almost.

How many men had he killed? Even leaving aside those shadowy figures who might or might not have been condemned to early graves by the intelligence Cleave had passed along to the other side, there was still Freddy, Freddy who would have been alive but for the misfortune of learning Cleave's close-kept secret. Cleave had killed Freddy, and he would have killed her, too, had he believed her a threat.

When it came down to it, Penelope wasn't entirely sure that cobra in her room hadn't been meant for her, no matter how Cleave chose to recall it. Penelope tried to remember what they had discussed that night on the balcony, and couldn't, other than that some of it had been about Alex. But if she had said anything that had triggered Cleave's sense of self-preservation, he would have sent the groom to do his work for him and then murmured about tragic accidents afterwards. He would probably even have convinced himself that he had never meant it to happen.

"Did you hit Fiske over the head?" she asked coldly. "Or did the groom do that for you, too?"

"I think not," said Jack Reid. "If Mehdi Yar had done it, Fiske would have been dead as planned. The Frangipani seldom misses his man."

Cleave looked at him blankly. "The what?"

"You didn't know that, did you? You thought you were simply slipping a bit of extra to a servant to do your dirty work for you." Jack shook his head. "No. Mehdi Yar is an old hand at the game. That's not his real name, of course. He's been at this so long, I doubt even he remembers what his name once was. Frangipani suits him as well as any."

Alex was looking decidedly grim around the lips. "In other words, Mehdi Yar is yet another spy."

"Our superiors weren't entirely sure that Daniel could be trusted to keep his nerve, so they sent Mehdi Yar to keep an eye on him. If you had showed any signs of weakening, an . . . accident would have been arranged."

"He went off to Hyderabad when I sent him," argued Cleave. "How he could he watch me from there?"

"But you followed him, didn't you? And I'd wager it was because of a message he sent you."

The dropping of Cleave's jaw was answer enough. "He'll kill me, won't he?" he said after a minute. "When he finds out what happened here tonight."

"If we don't shoot you first," said Jack idly.

Penelope couldn't tell whether or not he was serious.

Alex sent him a hard look. "No one is shooting anyone. I believe there's a way out of this. Justice may not be best served by it, but at least fewer heads will roll."

"Pity," said Jack. "I enjoy a good rolling head. It was why I originally joined up with the other side."

Ignoring him, Alex turned to Cleave. "You have to turn in Mehdi Yar."

"But he'll denounce me. He'll tell them I'm the Marigold."

"No," said Alex succinctly. "We'll put it about that Guignon was the Marigold. Our authorities won't quibble. They'll simply be happy to have the Marigold out of the way. You might even get that reward you so badly wanted," he added dryly.

Cleave had the grace to flush.

"There is a quid pro quo, I imagine," his brother drawled.

"Naturally," said Alex. He looked to Cleave. "In exchange for our silence, you maintain yours. Not a word about Jack, one way or the other. As far as anyone was concerned, he wasn't here tonight. And neither were you," he added, looking full at Penelope for the first time in a very long time. "Cleave and I came alone. We cornered the Marigold. He fought back. We prevailed. In the struggle, he gasped out the name of a confederate. If Mehdi Yar attempts to implicate Cleave, it will be taken as sour grapes, revenge for capture."

"All very neat and tidy, brother. As usual." Jack turned to Cleave, who looked more dazed than anything. "You will have to leave the country, of course. If Mehdi Yar doesn't finish you off, someone else will."

"That is part of the deal," said Alex. "You go back to England. You stay in England."

"But . . . ," Cleave began.

"You'll have your life," said Alex in a tone that extinguished all further protest. "Perhaps even your pension. It's more than you could otherwise expect."

As if to underline the finality of it, he gestured towards the stairs, indicating that Cleave should precede him.

"I'm sure your mother will be delighted to see you," commented Jack, as they began to mount the stairs. "She might even have found a nice girl for you."

Cleave's look of consternation would have been amusing but for the trail of dead bodies in his wake. It was a bit much to cut up stiff about a few dances when one had, until recently, been lobbing snakes into people's bedchambers.

Penelope found it hard to muster much sympathy. By all rights, Cleave ought to have been shackled, bound, not walking freely up the stairs of his own accord, his life and his reputation intact. Alex had been more than generous. But that was Alex, wasn't it?

It wasn't all generosity, though. Penelope could see the logic behind it. If Cleave were brought to trial, he would waste no time in implicating Alex's brother. In that event, one of two outcomes was certain. If Jack maintained his cover, he would hang as a French spy. If the truth came out, the English wouldn't kill him, but the French probably would. Once again, Alex was pulling his little brother's fat out of the fire.

He probably wouldn't fare too badly out of it either. They could blame Guignon for the attack on Fiske—Cleave would have to back Alex up on that, or risk exposing himself. The capture of the so-called Marigold would probably merit a promotion for Alex as well as a reward for Cleave. It was the perfect solution all around.

The only person left out in the cold was Penelope.

Outside the night was cool, the air fresh. Penelope hadn't realized quite how fetid it had become below until she breathed the clear, cool air above. The stars were out, glittering like diamonds from the Golconda mines, like the jewels for which Cleave had been willing to perjure himself and sell his country.

There was something a bit flashy about their brightness, a bit mocking. Penelope looked away, following the others away past the obelisk that marked a former French commander's passing, down the crest of the hill to where they had tethered the horses. By tacit agreement, the two brothers had disposed themselves on either side of Cleave, ready to grab him should he lose his nerve and try to bolt. For all their differences, there was a bond of long understanding between the two that made Penelope feel like an outsider or, worse, an interloper.

Funny, the things one took for granted. That whole long journey back from Berar, she had taken it as a matter of right that she should have Alex's undiluted attention, watching her, looking out for her, worrying about her. She had taken it so for granted that it had seemed like nothing to shrug it aside, in the smug assurance that she could rebuff him and rebuff him and rebuff him and he would still come back for more. But this—Penelope glanced sideways, watching how like his brother he moved. They might be dissimilar in other ways, but they couldn't hide the similarity in gait, in inflection, in tone, all those relics of a childhood in common. This was Alex's real world, and it was a world in which she had no place.

For a wonder, Alex's horse was where they had left her, with the addition of Jack's gelding, which was eyeing Bathsheba with an expression uncannily reminiscent of his master's. Cleave, shrunken and dazed, couldn't remember what he had done with his horse, and a vague squint from side to side did little to refresh his faulty memory.

"She's probably run halfway back to the Residency by now," he said, as if it were a matter of supreme indifference. Penelope noticed that Cleave kept rubbing his hands against the tails of his coat, like Lady Macbeth and her damned spot. She doubted he even realized he was doing it.

"You'll have to ride pillion with Alex," said Jack to Cleave, with barely concealed amusement. "I would offer," he added mendaciously, "but I'm going off in the opposite direction. It wouldn't do for me to show up at the Residency. Officially, I don't exist, you know."

"You do exist," said Alex tiredly. "You're simply not here."

"Oh, right," said his brother. "Such an easy mistake to make."

Folding her arms across her chest, Penelope looking challengingly up at him. "You've dealt very neatly with everyone else," she said, in a high clear voice. "What of me? What are my orders?"

Alex looked down at her, and a rueful smile creased his lips. "I would be a fool to order you anywhere," he said. "I've made that mistake before."

The word "mistake" set a series of warning bells ringing in Penelope's ears. Rue hadn't been quite the reaction Penelope had been angling for. She gathered her resources for one last offensive.

"You don't have to order," said Penelope. "But you might consider asking."

She held his gaze and her breath, feeling the world slow and still around them as she waited for his answer. Their companions seemed as remote as the silent obelisk on the hill above them. They might have been there alone, in the middle of the Hyderabadi night, with only the skeptical stars keeping score.

"Asking what?" said Alex, and the entire fragile structure came crashing down around them.

Penelope didn't know what. But he was supposed to. If he didn't know, she couldn't tell him.

As if matters weren't bad enough, Alex's brother chimed in. "I have a question," he said, looking down at her from all the height of his saddle. "Who are you?"

Penelope crossed her arms across her chest, venting all her irritation on the nearest convenient target. Jack made a very convenient target. He might as well have had a bull's eye painted across his chest. "Shouldn't so accomplished a double-dealing agent already know?"

"For whatever reason, you didn't make it into my last dispatch." Jack's eyes slid sideways to his brother. "Although I believe I may have heard something of you from another source."

Alex hastily intervened. "This is Lady Frederick Staines."

"*Was* Lady Frederick Staines," Penelope corrected.

"The name doesn't change," said Alex softly, and cupped his hands to help boost her into her saddle.

Looping Bathsheba's reins around her wrist, Penelope looked down at him. "But everything else has," she said pointedly.

Releasing his hold on the bridle, Alex stepped back. It felt like more than a step. It felt like a renunciation.

But all he said was, "I know."

I know. That was all he could find to say? *I know?* Penelope had never more resented the ambiguities of the English language.

Alex's brother raised a hand. "Well, that's my cue," he said cheerfully. "I'm off. Lovely to have met you, Lady—er."

Self-loathing settled on Penelope's chest like a weight of heavy stones. Why should Alex's brother bother to recall her name? It wasn't worth knowing. She wasn't worth knowing. She had spoiled her chance with Alex just as she spoiled everything else.

That didn't mean she was going to let him have the last word.

With bitter bile bubbling in her chest, Penelope ignored Alex and vented her spleen on the departing rider instead, calling derisively after him, "And what am I to call you, sir? Mr. Um?"

Checking his horse, Jack twisted sharply in his saddle. His rogue's grin seemed to hang in the air behind him, like the curve of a sickle moon.

"You can call me the Moonflower," he said, and cantered away into the moonlight.

Chapter Thirty-Two

"Would you like to travel on to Mysore with us? A change of scene might do you good." Charlotte perched on the end of a settee, her hands wrapped around a cup of chocolate. Unlike Penelope, Charlotte had remembered to wear her sun hat. In the light from the windows, her skin was as porcelain pure as it had been in a Norfolk winter. She looked at Penelope with evident concern. "Somewhere away."

"You are probably right," Penelope said wearily. "But—"

Charlotte looked at her over the rim of her cup. "But?"

Penelope tilted her cup from side to side, watching as the congealed chocolate left a wash of dark sediment in its wake. She drank her chocolate without sugar, strong, dark, and bitter. But today, she didn't really feel like drinking it. It was wasteful, she knew, cavalierly tossing aside so dearly bought a luxury. But she was good at tossing things aside. She had practically made a profession of it. Friends, husband, lover. Some clung anyway, despite her best efforts, like the tracks of grainy chocolate adhering to the bowl of the porcelain cup.

Alex hadn't.

Since they had ridden back to the Residency with Cleave three days before, she had scarcely spoken to him. In the hullabaloo surrounding the so-called Marigold's capture and death, Penelope had been discreetly pushed to the side. According to the official version, she had been prostrate in her bed at the Residency, overcome with grief like the good little widow that she was. It made Penelope want to gnash her teeth. Unfortunately, tooth gnashing was about the only outlet open to her. There was no way she could voice any of the highly sarcastic things she was dying to say without ruining the story Alex had gone to such trouble to concoct—a story that neatly wrote her out of the entire narrative.

She had never felt so insignificant or so powerless in her life, and that counted her days with Freddy. At least, then, she had been able to kick up a fuss, create a scandal, anything to draw attention to herself, however briefly. But, now, all her old weapons were blunted.

That was the problem with caring. One starting worrying about consequences and what people thought of one and all sorts of other irritating things. It made her feel uncertain. Shy, even. She, who had never felt shy in her life. Even as an infant, she had bawled louder than any other baby in the county.

Perhaps Charlotte was right. Perhaps she did need to get away. She could amuse herself in Mysore by scandalizing Charlotte and picking fights with her duke. There would be more officers with whom to flirt, gardens in which to conduct assignations, an endless round of the same old dissipation, without purpose or meaning.

Without Alex.

Stupid, stupid, stupid, she told herself, gulping down the remains of her tepid chocolate in one joyless gulp.

She was the one who had set the terms. She was the one who had kept him at a distance. She had done her best to push him aside in those dark days after Freddy's death. And even before that, she had been the one who refused to speak of the future, to acknowledge anything other than the pleasures of the moment. She had made her bed, and she would have to lie on it.

Alone.

"I'm just not sure I'm ready to go," she said brusquely, avoiding Charlotte's eyes. "And you and your duke are far too happy. It's irritating. I don't think I could endure that for six months at a time."

Without bothering to put down her chocolate cup, Charlotte reached out to squeeze Penelope's hand. Her hand was as small and soft as a child's, with none of the calluses that marked Penelope's palms. "You will be, too." She sucked absentmindedly at the droplets of chocolate that had landed on the back of her other hand, adding, with typical Charlotte honesty, "Eventually."

Penelope levered herself up from the settee, shaking her hand free from Charlotte's. "I don't think I can ever be as happy as you until I can become as good as you. And that," she added definitively, turning away from the settee, "is never going to happen."

"I don't think you need to be good to be lovable," said Charlotte, tilting her head thoughtfully to one side. "You just need to be you."

"Thank you," said Penelope dryly.

Charlotte colored. "I didn't mean it like that. What I meant was that you're lovely just as you are." Rallying, she added defiantly, "And Captain Reid clearly thinks so, too."

"Who said anything about Captain Reid?" said Penelope, stretching languorously, as though she hadn't a care in the world, when what she really wanted to do was grab Charlotte's hand and demand to know whether Charlotte really thought he thought she was lovely and, if so, why. With details. In triplicate.

"You did," said Charlotte, with inimitable Charlotte logic. "By not saying anything at all."

"I haven't mentioned Bonaparte either," said Penelope sarcastically. "Would you care to read anything into that?"

"Why not just tell him you love him?" suggested Charlotte.

"Bonaparte?"

Charlotte cast her a reproachful look. "Captain Reid."

Penelope turned to give Charlotte her best derisive stare. And froze. Behind Charlotte, framed in the doorway, stood a man in ill-cut clothes with a suntanned face and close-cut black hair.

"Penelope?" There was a rustling noise as Charlotte twisted on the settee, followed by a faint "Oh."

Penelope had heard the expression "speak of the devil" before, but she had never thought that it would work quite that literally. The bitter chocolate congealed in an undigested lump in the back of her throat, blocking any possibility of speech. That was probably a good thing. Penelope didn't trust herself to speak judiciously. Not right now.

Of course, right now what she most wanted to do was murder Charlotte.

After eleven years of friendship, Charlotte had developed a very sound sense of self-preservation where Penelope was concerned.

"I'm just going to go for a walk now," said Charlotte a little too loudly as she scurried towards the door. "A very long walk."

Penelope was going to kill Charlotte. Slowly. Painfully. Just as soon as she got back from her very long walk. If Charlotte had any sense, it would be a very bloody long walk indeed. Preferably all the way to the Outer Hebrides. On foot.

Alex moved politely to the side to let her pass, somehow managing to nod in greeting without ever moving his eyes from Penelope. That unbroken stare was distinctly unnerving.

"Captain Reid." Charlotte bobbed a hasty curtsy and whisked herself around the door frame.

A long, drawn-out "Bye-eee" trailed down the hallway after her.

If Charlotte didn't watch out, that was going to be her very last bye-eee, thought Penelope grimly.

It was calming to concentrate on murdering Charlotte. It removed at least part of her mind from Alex, who might or might not have heard that very unfortunate little conversation about certain emotions that one might or might not be feeling.

"Penelope." Alex took a slow step into the room.

Something had to be done. A diversion. A preemptive strike. Anything to diffuse the dreadful tension that suffused the room like strong tea.

"Hello," Penelope croaked.

As a preemptive strike, it lacked a certain amount of force.

Alex continued his slow progress into the room, his face giving nothing away. He wasn't terribly good at dissembling, but he did a brilliant imitation of a granite boulder.

Squaring her shoulders, Penelope took strength from the reminder that, Charlotte's romanticism aside, anything that had been between them was long since over. They were sophisticated adults, prepared to deal with each other in a sophisticated way—and why was he staring at her feet?

Oh. There were drops of brown goo plopping slowly onto her slippers.

Penelope hastily set her empty chocolate cup down on a teak table and drew in a deep, bracing breath through her nose.

"Captain Reid," she said forbiddingly. Had she said that already? She couldn't remember. But it certainly staved off any discussion of love.

His lips twisted up on one side. "So formal?" he said.

Damn. He had heard, hadn't he? Damn, damn, damn. "You might as well be a stranger," she snapped. "I've scarcely seen you for days."

That had been a tactical error. She sounded . . . jealous. Clingy. In short, like a woman in love.

But her former lover didn't press his advantage. Instead, apropos of nothing, he announced, "I've been made District Commissioner for a parcel of the ceded territories."

"Well, huzzah for you," said Penelope rudely. And since that might have been a bit too churlish, even for her, she added grudgingly, "I'm sure no one could have deserved it more."

"Thank you." He was still watching her—like a worm on a hook, thought Penelope unpleasantly. Couldn't he just squish her and put her out of her misery already? No, this was Alex. He would shy from squishing. He would try to do it humanely, and in the process hurt her far worse. She didn't want to be disposed of humanely. She would rather be able to resent him after.

"So you'll be leaving, then, I take it?" she said tartly. "You must be eager to brush the dust of Hyderabad off your heels."

"Some dust more than others," he said.

Here it came, thought Penelope. The thank-you-for-a-lovely-interlude. The you-were-highly-diverting-while-it-lasted. The it-was-wonderful-but-it's-over. Drop me a letter once every three years, and have a nice life.

"Dust is dust," said Penelope brusquely. "The same the world over. If you've come to say good-bye, say it."

But he didn't.

"Your friend seemed to think you have something to tell me," he said.

So he had heard that. Damn, damn, damn. Damn bloody Charlotte with her irksome habit of blurting out the first thing to come to her lips. Damn her for putting herself in this position in the first place. But she hadn't entirely. She hadn't spoken of love. She had never spoken of love. That was all Charlotte.

Even if Charlotte did happen to be right.

"Why should I?" Penelope said shrilly, feeling like a drowning man clutching for a rope.

Or her pride, as the case might be.

She had been far calmer when she had been within inches of drowning in the Krishna. That had been as nothing compared to this, compared to the clutching, clawing panic she felt now.

Penelope abruptly turned her back on him, feigning interest in the window, although she couldn't have said with any assurance what lay beyond the glass.

"I have nothing to say," she said in a tight little voice. "If you have, I wish you would just say it and get it over with. I'm sure we both have other things to do this afternoon."

Alex's hands grasped her by the shoulders and turned her bodily around to face him. Up close, his face wasn't expressionless at all. The expression on display appeared to be intense irritation.

"Damn it, Penelope," he said harshly. "Don't play games. Do you?"

"Do I *what?*"

Alex just looked at her. He didn't need to say anything. Just the look was enough.

Penelope jerked her head back defiantly. "What is it to you?"

Alex choked on an incredulous laugh. "Don't you know by now?" he demanded. "If you don't, you're the only one who doesn't."

"Now who's playing games?" shot back Penelope, but it came out decidedly less vigorous than she had intended it.

Alex met her gaze without hesitation. "No games," he said. "No evasions. If you don't know by now that I have a severe case of being-in-love with you, you're the only damn one in the compound."

"'A severe case,'" Penelope mocked, a rash surge of hope lending venom to her tongue. "Like the measles?"

"An apt comparison," he agreed, but Penelope could see the little twitch at the corners of his lips, and felt her heart lift absurdly at the sight of it. "The symptoms are roughly the same. Distraction, irritability, rash . . ."

Penelope pushed at his chest with both hands. But she didn't push very hard. "I suppose I should be grateful that you're not comparing me to bubonic plague!"

"Are you planning to prove fatal?"

Penelope looked at him levelly. "I have done. I did do. For Freddy."

"I'm not Freddy," he said.

"No," agreed Penelope. "You're not."

She meant it as a compliment. Or, at least, as much of a compliment as she was capable of paying.

Alex's eyelids flickered, and his gaze shifted away from her. Grimly, he said, "I know I have less to offer you than he did. I have no title. I have no prospects other than those I earn for myself."

Penelope looked at him in surprise. "Did you think I would scorn you for that?"

"Not scorn. No." For once, the oh-so-competent Captain Reid appeared to be at a loss. He looked at her wordlessly for a moment, weighing his words. Haltingly, he said, "But it's not what you're used to."

"I didn't like what I was used to," said Penelope bluntly. "I was hopeless in London. Etiquette irritates me, cards bore me, and being told what to do makes me want to go out and do exactly the opposite."

"I had rather noticed that," Alex said, with such tenderness that Penelope found it necessary to look away. "I seem to have made that mistake myself once or twice."

"At least you learned," said Penelope huskily. "Some people never do."

"Not enough," he said, watching her in a way that made her stomach do a curious little flip. "A lifetime would hardly be long enough to learn everything I want to know about you."

"A lifetime," managed Penelope, wondering if she had just heard correctly, "is an awfully long time."

Alex's eyes were very warm. "I don't think I would be bored. Do you?"

Penelope tried to swallow, and found that her throat didn't seem to want to cooperate.

That had sounded remarkably like a proposal. Not that she had terribly much to measure it against. Wryly, Penelope recalled the circumstances of her last proposal. After an hour closeted with the Dowager Duchess of Dovedale, Freddy had staggered out of the Duchess's lair, looking rather more ruffled than when he had entered, shrugged, and said, "Looks like we're to make a match of it."

To which Penelope had replied, in tones of deepest sarcasm, "Oh, goody."

Then Freddy had taken a long, restorative swig from the flask in his waistcoat pocket.

Penelope remembered resenting that he hadn't offered to share.

There was no need for any extraneous inebriate in this circumstance; the way Alex was looking at her was dizzying enough. It was dizzying to think that someone—not just someone, but Alex—could want her for real, for always, even knowing all the things he knew. He had seen her hasty, judgmental, imperious, and even dripping with river water. There wasn't much of each other they hadn't seen. A month-long journey tended to create interesting conditions of proximity. It might be possible to hide one's true nature in a drawing room courtship, but never in a roadside camp's, riding together day in and day out, through rain and mud and ludicrous heat. He had seen everything that Freddy deplored in her, and he wanted her anyway.

It was too good to be true. Therefore, it couldn't be true.

Could it?

"If you feel that way," Penelope said carefully, "why have you been hiding all week? I may not be an expert on the topic, but avoidance and undying devotion seldom go hand in hand."

A slight tinge of color rose under Alex's tan. "How could I possibly say anything to you as matters stood then? Between Fiske and Jack, I was skirting the edge of outlawry. Even once the charges were dropped, what did I have to offer? But then, when the word about the District Commission came through this morning . . ."

He trailed off as Penelope lifted a hand to gently touch his cheek.

"Idiot," said Penelope lovingly. "I would have gone with you without. I rather fancied life as an outlaw."

"Not if you'd tried it you wouldn't," said Alex, but there was a smile fighting to push its way through. "Two weeks and you'd be longing for a proper bed."

"As I recall," said Penelope, letting her eyes drop languidly to his lips, "we did very well without a proper bed once before. I didn't feel the lack of it. Did you?"

Memory sizzled between them, as tangible as touch. It didn't take terribly much to remember just what that touch had felt like, nearly a week's worth of touches, without a single bed in sight. The way he looked at her made her clothes feel several sizes too tight.

There might not be a bed in the room, but there was a very roomy settee. . . .

Blinking, Penelope looked away first.

"I'm not as good a liar as that," said Alex, with a wry grin that encompassed a whole host of very memorable memories. "But this wouldn't be a week. This would be—"

"A lifetime?"

Alex tilted his head in acknowledgment of the point. "At least a few years."

Penelope trailed her fingers along his shirtfront. Now that she knew where they stood, she felt considerably more like herself. Enough like herself to take great pleasure in tormenting him. "So much for forever," she said sadly.

"A few years in that particular district," Alex clarified, catching her hand. He ruined it entirely, however, by twining his fingers through hers, a gesture that entirely belied the substance of what he was trying to say. "Those few years could start to feel like a very long time. The station will be out in the middle of nowhere. There won't be any other ladies there—"

"Good!" said Penelope heartily, startling a laugh out of Alex.

Sobering, he cautioned, "It will be difficult."

Penelope looked him in the eye. "So am I."

With a lopsided grin, Alex lifted his free hand to smooth back the hair from her brow. "Not to me," he said. But then he spoiled it by adding, "But I can't lie to you. It will be isolated. And lonely."

Penelope raised both eyebrows. "Keep this up and I'll begin to doubt that you really want me there."

"I do," said Alex. "More than I can say. I would go down on one knee if I thought it would make any difference. But I wouldn't want to lure you away with me under false pretenses."

"Isolation, outlawry, and lack of prospects." Penelope ticked each off on her fingers. "If this is your version of luring, you're sadly out of practice."

"I haven't much experience at it," he admitted.

Penelope grinned a rogue's grin. "Fortunately," she said dulcetly, "I have."

Linking her arms around his neck, she proceeded to provide a stunning sample of her usual luring technique, although after the first few minutes, it became entirely unclear who was luring whom.

"Does that mean you're coming with me?" he asked breathlessly.

Penelope considered it. "Lure me again," she demanded.

And he did.

Chapter Thirty-Three

R eading through Mrs. Selwick-Alderly's notebooks, I had shaken my head over the complexities of Alex Reid's family relationships. They were nothing compared to Colin's. A cousin turned stepfather trumped a rogue half brother any day.

It couldn't be true. That man couldn't be Mrs. Selwick-Alderly's grandson, Colin's... second cousin? First cousin once removed? Second cousin once removed? Whatever it was, to have your cousin run off with your mother on your father's deathbed represented a pretty major betrayal.

I must have been mistaken. The resemblance was probably only an illusory one, a matter of chance. I was awful at remembering faces at the best of times. It was another classic case of my imagination getting the better of me.

At least, I hoped it was. The alternative was too mind-boggling.

I tugged on Colin's sleeve. "That man—that man talking with Serena—is your stepfather?" I asked, very slowly and very carefully.

"My mother's husband, yes."

I didn't miss the subtle distinction there.

"But—" How could I put this delicately? I couldn't. "Isn't that your cousin?" I blurted out.

"That, too," said Colin, with determined lightness. "Very economical, isn't it? Saves on the Christmas presents."

"Sensible, that," agreed Budgy, his mouth full of tuna tartare. "Bloody pain in the arse, Christmas shopping."

I smiled brightly at Budgy. I had to get rid of him. I had to get rid of him so I could grill Colin.

This all just got weirder and weirder. Colin's stepfather was his *cousin*? This wasn't even P. G. Wodehouse anymore; I had stumbled across the line into Evelyn Waugh. Brideshead Regurgitated didn't even begin to describe it.

What did Colin mean not telling me that his mother was married to Mrs. Selwick-Alderly's grandson?

To be fair, I could see that it was the sort of thing one might not want to trot out on the first date or two, but we had been dating for more than two months now. He had spare socks and a razor in my flat. Enough said.

"Should we—do you want to—" I scrambled for words, entirely at a loss. I would be willing to wager that Emily Post never came up with a formula for dealing with this. "Do you want to, er, go over and say hi?"

I had never felt more gauchely American.

"Not particularly," said Colin, with a tight smile. "But I suppose we're going to have to."

"Bloody relatives," agreed Budgy amiably, around a mouthful of tuna tartare. If one were to consider one's silver linings, Budgy was pure sterling. He seemed to be an extremely restful sort of person to have around in a crisis.

Across the room, Serena's face was hidden by the long curve of her salon-shiny hair, but her posture had tensed into a question mark, shoulders curved forward, head bowed. Her body language screamed discomfort.

I wasn't the only one who had noticed.

"Will you excuse us?" said Colin wearily to Budgy, and I felt all my indignation abruptly evaporate.

As my mother has pointed out to me in the past, men are people, too. When you prick them, they bleed. If we're insecure, they're insecure. If I thought this was awkward, it had to be about ten times worse for Colin.

As we crossed the room, I slid my arm through his in a gesture of girlfriendly solidarity. I don't know if Colin noticed, but it made me feel better.

"What is your, er, mother's husband doing here?" I whispered.

"He's a dealer—an art dealer," Colin specified. "Pretty ridiculous, isn't it?"

I wasn't quite sure where the ridiculous came into it, but it wasn't the sort of thing you could very well ask.

"He got Serena her first job," Colin added.

"Before . . . ?"

A shadow of a smile appeared around Colin's lips at my deliberate obliqueness. "Yes. Before."

A few yards ahead, Serena and her cousin/stepfather were unconsciously mimicking the poses of the couple in the art poster hanging behind them. In the poster, a young lady turned her face away as the beribboned gallant beside her leaned forward, seeking her attention. Like Serena's, the face of the girl in the painting was unreadable, shadowed by her towering hair.

A horrible suspicion blossomed. Forget *Brideshead*, we were talking *90210*, the English edition. Or that Andrew Lloyd Webber musical where everyone sleeps with everyone.

"Your cousin and Serena," I said. "They weren't—"

"No!" The honest horror on Colin's face put that suspicion to rest, at least. "They were rather close at one point, but not like that. Jeremy was—is"—he amended wryly—"considerably older."

I wish I had paid more attention to the dates on those photos. Mentally, I translated "considerably" to "about a decade." He looked to be in his mid or late thirties, which would make him roughly ten or more years older than Serena and I, a little closer in age than that to Colin. Not too old for a teenage girl, or even a girl just out of college, to have a massive crush, especially if he was someone already established in the field she was looking to join.

Remembering Serena's relationship with the archivist in the Vaughn collection, another one of these good-looking thirty-somethings, it wouldn't have surprised me in the slightest if that was what Colin was leaving out, not a matter of fact, but of feelings. Serena's feelings.

No wonder Serena had issues with her mother.

"Your mother is an artist, too, isn't she?" I said.

Colin nodded, and there was a grim twist to his smile as he said, "Jeremy represents her. It's a charming little incestuous tangle, isn't it?"

"Well . . . ," I began, and faltered.

Colin gave me a knowing look.

What else was there to say? It *was* an incestuous tangle.

But I couldn't just leave it at that, not with Colin looking all sardonic and knowing. To agree now would only make him feel worse. And it was Valentine's Day, damn it.

In an attempt at a quick save, I babbled, "It's not that surprising, is it, when families all gravitate to certain professions? Especially something like the art world, where if you don't have an inside connection, it's very hard to know where to go or how to get involved. So I can see how that would happen," I finished all in a rush.

Colin didn't say anything, but one of his arms snaked around my shoulders and gave me a quick squeeze before releasing me again.

I felt my throat tighten up for no apparent reason. Maybe it was because it was Valentine's Day. Maybe it was because I had already had two glasses of pink champagne.

Whatever it was, for no reason in particular, I blurted out, "I like you." And, then, because it felt too stupid to be all emotional over nothing, I added, "Even if your family *is* mad."

Colin choked on a laugh that came out sounding like a snort. "You ain't seen nothing yet," he said, in a truly atrocious American accent. In his normal voice, he added, "Come on. We might as well get it over with."

Words to live by.

I had to scurry to keep up as he picked up the pace. The floor was slick and shiny, hell on heels. I felt like a water-skier being tugged along behind a supercharged boat on uneasy waters. We skidded to a stop in front of Colin's assorted and tangled relations.

"Eloise!" Serena's greeting was pure relief. She launched into a hug before I could even unfold my arms into the proper landing position.

Once we got untangled, I hugged her back, marveling, as always, at the fragility of the bones beneath the expensive cashmere. I didn't think I'd ever seen Serena in anything but cashmere. It was as though, lacking proper padding of her own, she needed the extra insulation.

Next to us, stepfather/cousin and stepson/cousin marked their dual relationship with the briefest of all possible handshakes.

Colin's mother's husband treated us all to a broad, open smile. The sort you see on televangelists and traveling salesmen. I could hear the slap of flesh on flesh as his palm met Colin's. "Colin."

Colin's answering smile was decidedly anemic. "Jeremy," he said, without enthusiasm.

"Hi," I said, sticking out a hand. "I'm Eloise Kelly."

I was tempted to add "Colin's girlfriend," but I wasn't quite sure if we were at the public declaration stage yet.

"Colin's girlfriend!" chimed in Serena.

Well, there was that, then.

Did it count as meeting the parents when it was a stepfather? A stepfather who was also a cousin? I decided not.

Jeremy favored us with an isn't-that-sweet look. "Your first Valentine's Day together?" he said in a knowing way that made Colin stiffen like a shrinky dink in a hot oven.

"Well, you know, it's Presidents' Day that really counts, but you have to make do with what you have," I said flippantly, just to say something, before Colin turned entirely to stone like the children in the wicked witch's garden.

I just hoped he wouldn't ask me what or when Presidents' Day was. Ivy League universities tend not to break for national holidays, so I'd lost all sense of when most of them were. And I'd been pretending to be English for so long, I'd lost track of my own history. I had a vague idea that Presidents' Day was in January or February and was something to do with Lincoln's birthday, but I wouldn't have been prepared to swear to that. If he wanted to know the regnal dates of any British monarch, on the other hand, I was his girl.

"Where are you from, Eloise?" Jeremy asked.

I noted the deliberate use of my name. Very smooth. Not smooth in a sketchy way, but smooth in the way of Ivy League administrators, politicians, and nonprofit fundraisers, peoples used to shmoozing and being shmoozed, where their charm, not their faces, are the deciding factor in their fortune's.

"I should have thought that Presidents' Day reference would have given me away," I said. "America. New York."

"Where in New York?"

Oh, we were playing that game, were we? Fortunately, it was a game I knew how to play and played well. You don't grow up in New York without learning how to play the pecking order game.

"Manhattan," I said sweetly. "Upper East Side."

Colin's stepfather nodded, as though I had given the correct answer in an oral exam. I could see myself being moved from one mental category to another. "Do you know—," he said, and began listing names.

I didn't. But I let him go on anyway, while I made my own mental categorizations. Mrs. Selwick-Alderly's prodigal grandson was definitely what Pammy would call a "smootharse." Too smooth. He was all polish with no contrast, all gloss with no texture. His clothes were perfectly chosen and perfectly maintained, not a stray thread or old stain showing anywhere. His hair was as glossy as Serena's and what lines there were on his face looked like they'd been mapped out by a designer, the modern male equivalent of the beauty patches once worn by eighteenth-century lovelies to draw attention to their charms. Even his speech had been perfected down to the last little nuance. Not too posh, since that would be a social solecism of its own, but just posh enough. Posh enough to sound like he was deliberately trying not to be posh, which is its own sort of bizarre status symbol.

Wishing I had paid more attention, I remembered Colin's father as I had seen him in those pictures in Mrs. Selwick-Alderly's album. For all that they were cousins, you really couldn't get more of a contrast. Colin's father had had a craggy sort of face. Not craggy in terms of irregularity of feature, but craggy as in lived-in. Broken in. Comfortable. Like an old Barbour jacket.

"Sorry," I said, shaking my head as he named a famous gallery about ten blocks from my parents' apartment. "I've walked past it, but I've never been inside. My family aren't really art collectors."

"Next time you're in New York, let me know, and I can arrange a private viewing for you," Jeremy offered magnanimously.

The "we aren't art collectors" clearly hadn't registered. I suppose, in a field like art sales, you had to be impervious to rejection. If you battered away long enough, odds were that you could talk someone into buying.

But it wasn't just that. He struck me as the sort who likes to make a splash, who likes to be in a position to offer favors—even if, in my case, the recipient had no interest in the favor whatsoever. Jeremy still got to make a point of showing that he could. It was another one of those pecking-order games.

Despite the fact that I had been roped into the game as his straight man, Mutt to his Jeff, Elvis to his Costello, I didn't think the performance was aimed at me. Nor was it being staged on Serena's behalf. For all that Jeremy oozed charm in her direction, there was something offhanded about it, more habit than design. Serena wasn't the target either. Colin was.

And Colin wasn't playing.

Having exhausted my limited knowledge of New York galleries, Jeremy transferred his attention to Serena. "Will I see you in March?" he asked.

Visibly uncomfortable, Serena shrugged her shoulders slightly in lieu of an answer. I could see the sharp bones of her clavicle through the soft fabric of her dress.

"March is a busy season for us," she offered, in what was clearly the first stage of a long and elaborate attempt at evasion. A simple no would have been far more effective.

"I'll have a word with Adam," said Jeremy kindly. "I'm sure we can get it sorted."

I presumed Adam must be Serena's boss. It also seemed very obvious that she didn't want whatever it was sorted, but she managed a sickly smile. "Thank you."

"Of course. Your mother would be very sorry not to see you."

Oh, boy. More family drama. I couldn't blame Serena for looking slightly green. I would be green, too, if someone nearer in age to me than my mother presumed to speak to me on her behalf.

Jeremy turned back to me. "Will we see you, too, Eloise?"

He was probably trying to be nice. But that "we" pissed me off on Colin's behalf. It wasn't his place to be inviting me to whatever this March thing was if Colin hadn't. And Colin hadn't. I chose not to dwell on that bit. It was far simpler and easier to be irked at his stepfather instead.

I twinkled sweetly up at Colin's mother's husband. "Will you speak to my boss, too?"

That had not been in the script. Jeremy mustered an uncomfortable laugh. "I'll have to leave that to Colin," he said a little too heartily, before adding, with an admonitory nod to Colin, "Make sure he tells you all the details."

"Don't worry, Jeremy," said Colin dryly. "I will."

Showing more gumption than I had given her credit for, Serena seized her moment. "Will you excuse me?" she said. There were two bright spots of color high on her cheeks. "I have to coordinate with the caterers."

"I have to be off, too," said her stepfather. I had a feeling that if she had said that she had an emergency operation, he would have had a bigger one. "I promised Adam I'd give him my assessment of those new bronzes."

"Don't let us keep you, then," said Colin pleasantly.

"Colin." In reverse of their greeting, like a tape unwinding backwards, Mrs. Selwick-Alderly's grandson nodded to his stepson before sending a practiced smile my way. "A pleasure, Eloise."

"Likewise!" I chimed.

As he turned away, his smiled seemed to hover behind him, like the Cheshire cat's. His teeth were very, very white. That, I have learned, is not normally the case across the Pond. He must have gotten them capped. I wondered if Mrs. Selwick-Alderly had paid for it.

As I watched, Jeremy hailed Serena's boss. At least, I assumed that was who the other man must be. Unlike Jeremy's perfect dental apparatus, he was bucktoothed, and his jacket was tweed over a black turtleneck, rather than an Italian tailored suit, but there was a certain similarity of expression, nonetheless. They were happily smarming away for all they were worth. That should keep him occupied for a while. Serena had gone to ground, not with the caterers, but with Nick and Pammy. I was pleased to see that Nick had slung an arm around Serena's shoulders. Not a particularly demonstrative arm, but an arm nonetheless. Of course, he had been squeezing Pammy's waist earlier in the evening, so it was hard to read too much into it. The main point was that she had a buffer zone.

We hadn't said hi to either Nick or Pammy yet, or to Joan Plowden-Plugge, who was still roaming about like a wicked witch in search of a flying monkey. But I had had enough. I wanted to go home. I had a million questions to ask, none of which could effectively be dealt with in a room full of people. Especially when some of those people were the very people I wanted to talk about.

"So what's this March thing?" I asked in a falsely casual tone.

"My mother's birthday." Colin traded his empty glass for a full one. He offered it to me first. I shook my head. I felt befuddled enough without muddling myself further with a third glass of bubbly. "She's invited us to Paris for a long weekend. Jeremy wants us all to play one big happy family."

"Oh," I said. It was my word of the night. And then, because I couldn't help myself, "How did—?"

I didn't have to finish the sentence. "My mother wind up with him?" he finished for me.

I nodded. "Pretty much."

Colin let out a gusty exhalation, that was probably meant to convey something to me, but didn't. He stared for a very long time at the bronze on its own square stand in front of us. If one didn't know better, the concerned squint could have been taken as the concentration of a serious connoisseur. I had a feeling it wasn't the bronze he was seeing, though.

After a prolonged scrutiny, he finally said, "I suppose it was natural. My father was ill. My mother was much younger. Jeremy was there."

That wasn't exactly what I would call natural, but if it made Colin feel better, I wasn't going to argue.

"Your parents married pretty young, didn't they?" I said by means of encouragement. What I really wanted to know was how *he* felt about all this. But as stupid as I can be about boys, I did know one thing; direct questions about emotions are the fastest way to the end of a conversation.

"My mother was young," Colin corrected.

"How big an age difference was there between them?" I asked, reassuring myself that, yes, Colin and I were only three years apart and that couldn't really be accounted much of anything as far as age differences go.

He had to pause for a minute to do the mental math. "Fifteen—no. Sixteen years."

"Eeeek," I said before adding, inconsequentially, "My parents are six months apart. They went to college together."

"My father had already been through university and the army when he met my mother," said Colin. "She was sixteen."

I couldn't think of anything to say other than another eek, so I didn't say anything at all.

Colin rubbed a tired hand over his forehead. Fortunately, it wasn't the hand holding the champagne, or that could have gotten very messy. I've done that sort of thing before. "I think she thought he was . . . oh, a sort of James Bond. When all he really wanted to do was settle down and be a farmer. So it was something of a disaster."

I felt a slight chill go through me at that James Bond bit, in spite of the heat generated by the press of too many bodies in too small a space. Not so very long ago, I had gotten myself in trouble with my suspicions about Colin's own . . . well, shall we call them extracurricular activities? He claimed to be writing spy novels, but I still had my suspicions.

But I would have dated him anyway, I told myself. It wasn't just the James Bond thing.

Okay, maybe it had been, just a little bit, in the beginning. It had been his ancestors, his Englishness, all those external aspects that had initially attracted my interest. Well, and a certain amount of very evident physical chemistry. But it had been long enough now that those weren't the reasons I stayed. If it were just the accent, or just the titillation of dating a descendant of one of my favorite spies, it would have been easy to call it quits. When it came down to it, I just plain liked him. I couldn't even quite say why.

Why do we ever like anyone? Why does one couple click and another not? It's never neatly reducible to a checklist of quantifiable items, no matter how hard we try to parse it out for the benefit of interested friends and parents. Or even for ourselves. I just knew that I enjoyed being with him. I knew that it made me happier when I saw his number pop up on my cell phone screen. I liked the smell of his aftershave. I liked the way he grinned when I said something that amused him. The idea of Colin as James Bond had been titillating, but I'd be just as happy to take him as a gentleman farmer—so long as he didn't expect me to have anything to do with the livestock.

Fortunately, Colin was too busy dealing with his parents to notice my momentary spasm of guilt-induced soul-searching.

Sixteen. Wow. It boggled the brain. Even if they hadn't gotten married till she was eighteen . . . that was still an eighteen-year-old married to a thirty-four-year-old. No wonder the marriage had failed. From what Mrs. Selwick-Alderly had said, she didn't think much of Colin's mother. But you had to wonder what Colin's father had been thinking, too. At thirty-four, shouldn't he have known better?

"So your father got ill. And then Jeremy came along," I said carefully.

"Yes." With an obvious effort at fairness, Colin said, "He and my mother are much better suited than she and my father ever were."

"And just think—you keep it all in the family!" I said cheerfully.

A ragged laugh ripped out of Colin's throat. "Are you sorry you got yourself involved in all this?"

Leaning against his side, I looked up at him, as though there were only us in that whole, overcrowded space. "I didn't get myself involved in all this. I got myself involved in you. And, no, I'm not sorry."

His hand closed convulsively over mine. "Let's go home," he said.

"What about Serena?"

Colin's eyes pressed briefly shut. When he opened them, he said resolutely, "She'll be fine. It is her party, after all. Unless you want to stay?"

I shook my head. "No."

I knew exactly what I wanted to do with the remains of my Valentine's Day, and it didn't have anything to do with pink champagne or papier-mâché Cupids. I leaned my head against Colin's shoulder, the lacy sleeves of my dress whispering against his jacket.

"Let's go get some grilled cheese," I said.

Historical Note

The Napoleonic Wars had a seminal impact on the creation of British India, that is, British India as depicted in M. M. Kaye novels and BBC miniseries. At the turn of the nineteenth century, British influence in India was still a patchwork sort of affair, acquired by accident and administered ad hoc. The East India Company had acquired some areas by conquest and others by grant from the Moghul Emperors, but large chunks of territory were still outside their jurisdiction. British influence was concentrated around the presidency towns of Madras, Calcutta, and Bombay. Some areas were entirely free from British influence, while others were technically independent, but had signed treaties ceding territory or other concessions in exchange for British military protection.

As if it weren't complicated enough already, Parliament stuck its finger into the pie, subjecting the governance of the East India Company's Indian territories to the oversight of a London-based Board of Control, headed by the Chancellor of the Exchequer. In practice, great power was wielded by the Governor General, appointed by the East India Company, but subject to removal by the Crown. The man on the spot, the Governor General had the power to implement legislation, wage war, and make treaties. In 1804, that man was Lord Wellesley, older brother of the future Duke of Wellington, and prime mover behind the series of conflicts that consolidated British influence in India.

If Lord Wellesley saw Frenchmen under the bed, he did have some reason for it. Not only was Bonaparte's invasion of Egypt in 1798 seen as a threat, but French generals throughout India planted liberty trees, led troops into battle under the *tricolore*, and cooked up elaborate schemes to unite the French forces in India against the British so that the French influence might reign supreme in the East. In 1802, General Perron, in the nominal employ of the Mahratta chieftain, Scindia, went so far as to write Bonaparte for French troops to deploy against the British. He got them, too, a whole boatload of them, although they were sent packing before they reached their destination. General Perron, by the way, is not to be confused with yet another contemporary Frenchman, Jean-Pierre Piron, who was General Raymond's successor as commander of the French force in Hyderabad in the period just prior to this book. Both Perron and Piron were rabid French nationalists and both get a mention in this book but, I promise, they really were two different people, not just a typo. You can chalk the similarity in their names down to yet another dastardly French plot to sow confusion (or just an accident of birth and geography).

Lord Wellesley used the French threat as part of his rationale for incursions against local rulers, radically expanding the scope of British oversight in India, a policy of which the East Company directors back in London did not approve. For more on Wellesley, Wellington, and the Mahratta Wars, I recommend Jac Weller's *Wellington in India*, which lays out the day-to-day military situation, including the fighting in the north alluded to during Penelope's stay in Calcutta, as well as the tantalizing tale of the treasure of Berar, rumored lost during the siege of Gawilighur and never found.

In addition to the political landscape, the cultural landscape in 1804 was also quite different from that of the Raj to come. Many of the conventions we associate with British India hadn't come into being yet. For example, the term *memsahib*, that standard of Victorian literature, only came into use later in the century; *sahiba* was the correct term in 1804. Fortunately, plenty of travelers' accounts exist from this transitional period, giving us a contemporary view of what an English lady would have seen, experienced, eaten, and worn. The large traveling camp needed to convey Freddy and Penelope from Masulipatam to Hyderabad was borrowed from the journal of Maria Graham, who traveled across India in 1809, as were details of food, scenery, and culture. A more intimate view is provided by Mrs. Meer Hassan Ali, an Englishwoman who married a gentleman of Oudh and wrote about her experiences in a tome lengthily entitled, *Observations on the Mussulmauns of India: Descriptive of Their Manners, Customs, Habits, and Religious Opinions.*

Like other British ladies, such as Elizabeth Plowden, who, along with her husband, became close friends with the Nawab of Oudh (Plowden was, in fact, granted her own title by the Nawab), Graham attended nautch dances and other entertainments at the homes of local dignitaries, just as Penelope does in this novel. Unlike the later days of British India, there was a good deal of socialization between Brits and Indians in the eighteenth and very early nineteenth century. During the time of this story, that earlier, easier correspondence was just beginning to break down. For the complicated tale of British interactions with local culture in late-eighteenth and early-nineteenth-century India, I recommend Maya Jasanoff's *Edge of Empire: Lives, Culture and Conquest in the East, 1750–1850* and William Dalrymple's *White Mughals: Love and Betrayal in Eighteenth-Century India.*

It wasn't just relations between British and Indians that were complicated; the British had their own internal frictions due to the odd dual-governing structure of Company and Crown. Among other things, there were functionally two British armies operating in India in 1804: the East India Company's own army and King's regiments, sent out from England. The King's regiments looked down on the East India officers, and the East India Company officers resented the King's regiments, which explains Freddy's attitude towards Alex, who owes his rank to an East India Company regiment rather than the more prestigious royal army.

As for Freddy and his friends, the Hellfire Club to which Fiske, Freddy, and their cronies belonged was based off a club got up by some of the British residents in Poona in 1813, which combined a little pseudomasonic ritual with a lot of sexual experimentation. There were, however, consequences to amorous dalliance. According to contemporary statistics, as many as one-third of the British garrison were infected with syphilis each year. Treatments were slow, unpleasant, and generally ineffective, the most common of which was applying mercury ointment to sores on the afflicted organ. If unchecked, the disease caused the sufferer to run mad. Throughout the eighteenth century, intercourse with a virgin was commonly believed to provide a quick and easy cure for the disease, one which unscrupulous men, like those in Fiske's Hellfire Club, did not scruple to apply. For the pastimes and prejudices of British army officers in India, I relied heavily on Lawrence James's *Raj: The Making and Unmaking of British India.*

While Sir Leamington Fiske, Daniel Cleave, and the rest of the gang are fictional, the narrative is dotted with genuine historical figures who have been dragooned into service for the purpose of my story. Begum Johnson and Begum Sumroo were both formidable figures of their day, one as grand old dame of Calcutta, the other as ruler of her own principality. In Hyderabad, the Resident (James Kirkpatrick), his marriage to a Hyderabadi lady of quality, his self-satisfied assistant Henry Russell, the courtesan Mah Laqa Bai, the Nizam's female guards, the leprous Prime Minister Mir Alam, and the mad Nizam Sikunder Jah were all taken from the historical record, as were the French commanders Raymond and Piron. The missing guns and the tension between the Residency and the Subsidiary Force were also fact, although, in the real version, the problem was embezzlement rather than spies. For all details regarding the characters, culture, politics, and anything else relating to Hyderabad, I am entirely indebted to William Dalrymple's brilliant monograph, *White Moghals*, which chronicles the career of James Kirkpatrick and his controversial marriage to Khair-un-Nissa.

In some cases, rather than directly employing historical figures, I borrowed their characteristics for my fictional folks. Inspiration for Alex's father, "the Laughing Colonel," was taken from James Kirkpatrick's father, a charming philanderer known as "the Handsome Colonel." Alex's troubled brother Jack is loosely based off another real character, James Skinner, the product of an English father and a Rajput mother who committed suicide. Barred from service in the English forces by virtue of his birth, Skinner entered the army of Scindia, a Mahratta leader, under the command of Benoit de Boigne and then Pierre Perron (yes, *that* Perron). In Skinner's case, his talent was recognized by Lord Lake, who managed to bend some rules and take him on, in a rather roundabout way, as commander of an irregular cavalry regiment known as "Skinner's Horse" or "the Yellow Boys," but Skinner was the exception rather than the norm. In researching Jack's predicament, I relied on Skinner's memoirs, *The Recollections of Skinner of Skinner's Horse*, as well as the sprightly biography by Philip Mason, *Skinner's Horse*, both of which provide a vivid picture of the ambivalent position of Anglo-Indian offspring at the turn of the nineteenth century.

The term Anglo-Indian is often a confusing one, since it is used to describe those Englishmen who spent their lives in India as well as those of mixed English and Indian descent. For those in the latter category, a series of laws passed under the Governor-Generalship of Lord Cornwallis drastically curtailed any chances for advancement. In 1791, anyone without two European parents was banned from civil, military, or naval service in the East India Company. By 1795, they were further barred from serving even as drummers, pipers, or farriers. Those wealthy enough to do so sent their children back to England, where there were no such legal barriers to advancement. Those without the funds were forced to do as Colonel Reid did; to send their sons into the service of local rulers, where the Company's rules did not apply. The irregular situation created more than a few conflicting loyalties in those affected by Cornwallis's sanctions. Although Jack Reid is my own invention, I wouldn't be surprised if there were others in his situation who found the rallying cry of *liberté*, *égalité*, and *fraternité* a seductive one.

About the Author

The author of five previous Pink Carnation novels, Lauren Willig received a degree in English history from the Harvard history department and a J.D. from Harvard Law, where she graduated magna cum laude. She lives in New York City.